Entwined

Entwined

HEATHER DIXON

GREENWILLOW BOOKS
An Imprint of HarperCollinsPublishers

Entwined
Copyright © 2011 by Heather Dixon

All rights reserved. No part of this book may be used or reproduced in any manner whatsoever without written permission except in the case of brief quotations embodied in critical articles and reviews. Printed in the United States of America. For information address HarperCollins Children's Books, a division of HarperCollins Publishers, 10 East 53rd Street, New York, NY 10022.
www.harperteen.com

The text of this book is set in Sabon.
Book design by Becky Terhune

Library of Congress Cataloging-in-Publication Data
Dixon, Heather, (date).
Entwined / by Heather Dixon.
p. cm.
"Greenwillow Books."
Summary: Confined to their dreary castle while mourning their mother's death, Princess Azalea and her eleven sisters join the Keeper, who is trapped in a magic passageway, in a nightly dance that soon becomes nightmarish.
ISBN 978-0-06-200103-0 (trade bdg.)
[1. Princesses—Fiction. 2. Dancing—Fiction. 3. Magic—Fiction. 4. Kings, queens, rulers, etc.—Fiction. 5. Fathers and daughters—Fiction. 6. Death—Fiction. 7. Fantasy.] I. Title.
PZ7.D64433Ent 2011   [Fic]—dc22   2010011686

12 13 14 15 LP/RRDH 11
First Edition

Greenwillow Books

FOR LISA HALE

LADIES' DANCE POCKETBOOK: ENTWINE

The Entwine, also known as the Gentleman's Catch, is an amusing and challenging redowa suitable for accomplished partners. Of Eathesburian origin, it dates to circa 1635, when Chevalier De Eathe (also known as the High King D'Eathe) reigned. As magic was common in this time period, the High King would catch and "entwine" people's souls after they had died, and subject them to the darkest of magics.

Over the years, the Entwine has evolved to a simple charade of this concept. Similar to a *trois-temps* waltz, it is danced in open position with a long sash. The lady and gentleman each take ends of the sash, which their hands must not leave. In a series of quick steps (see below) the gentleman either twists the sash around the lady's wrists, pinning them (also known as the Catch), or the lady eludes capture within three minutes' time.

STEPS. Twist (35), Needle's Eye (35), Dip and Turn (36), Lady's Feint (36), Bridge Arc (36), Under-Arm Swoop (37), Thread (37), Beading the Sash (38), the Catch (38).

CHAPTER 1

An hour before Azalea's first ball began, she paced the ballroom floor, tracing her toes in a waltz. She had the opening dance with the King . . . who danced like a brick.

But that was all right. She could add flourishes and turns that would mask the King's stiff, flat steps. If there was anything she was good at, it was dancing. And this year, she was in charge of the ball, as Mother was too ill to host. Azalea was determined it would be perfect.

Unlike the year before, when the Yuletide had ended in a fracas. Too young to attend the annual—and only—ball the royal family hosted, Azalea and her ten younger sisters gathered all the blankets and cloaks and shawls from the palace and hid outside the ballroom windows. Azalea remembered the frigid air, how the rosebushes scratched, and how they had to huddle together for warmth. The ballroom radiated gold through the frozen panes. The girls pressed their noses

1

on the glass and oohed at the dancers, especially Mother, who danced like an angel.

They had fallen asleep right there in the rosebushes, burrowing together like mice. When the girls were discovered missing, Mother had stopped the ball and made *everyone*—including the musicians—search for them. Prime Minister Fairweller had found them. Azalea had awoken in shivers to see him holding a lamp over them and frowning.

The girls had pelted him with snowballs.

They had lost two weeks of dance lessons over that Great Rosebush and Snowball Scandal. It had been worth it, they all agreed. Even so, Azalea hoped this year the Yuletide would end gracefully. Her toes curled in her dance slippers and her hands shook as she fluttered about the dessert table in the ballroom, rearranging the platters and directing the hired help as they brought in trays of lemon custards and cinnamon candies.

Mr. Pudding found her just as snow started to swirl outside the tall arched windows and the musicians had arrived, tuning their violins in the ballroom corner. Azalea knelt on the marble floor in a poof of silks and crinolines, picking up strewn pine needles. Mr. Pudding was their Royal Steward. He was also the Royal Stableman, the Royal Boot-Blacker, and the Royal Things-on-the-High-Shelf-Getter. With difficulty, he knelt to the floor.

"It's all right, Mr. Pudding," said Azalea. "I've got it."

"Right you are, miss, so you do," he said, collecting the needles with gnarled hands. "It's only . . . your mother wants to see you, miss."

Azalea paused, the needles pricking her palms.

"She does?" she said. "The King is all right with it?"

"'Course he would be, miss," said Mr. Pudding, helping her up. "He couldn't be averse if your mum wants it!"

Mother hadn't been taken with a quick, hard illness that swept a person up overnight. Her illness had come slowly and had lasted for years, robbing a bit of her each day. Some weeks she felt better, better enough to take tea in the gardens with Azalea and her sisters and give them dance lessons, and some weeks—more weeks, lately—the light in her eyes flickered with pain. Still, she always said she felt better, and she always gave a room-brightening smile. That was Mother.

With the baby near due now, the King refused to allow Azalea or her sisters to spend tea up in Mother's room, or even to visit longer than several minutes a day. Even so, when Azalea arrived at Mother's room two staircases later, breathless and beaming, it had the mark of her sisters all over it. Mend-up cards with scrawled pictures graced the dresser, and vases of dried roses and pussywillows made the room smell of flowers. A warm fire glowed in the grate, casting yellows over the flowered furniture.

Mother sat in the upright sofa, her auburn hair tussled as always. She wore her favorite blue dress, mended but clean, and rested a hand on her stomach.

She was asleep. Azalea's smile faded.

Secretly hoping the rustle of her skirts would rouse Mother, Azalea arranged the mend-up cards on the dresser, then chastised herself for hoping such a thing. Sleep was the only peace Mother had of late. From the table next to the sofa, the old magic tea set clinked and clattered faintly, pouring a cup of tea in its pushy way.

Azalea did not care for that old silver-mottled tea set. Several hundred years ago, before Eathesbury had streetlamps and paved roads, the palace had been magic. The reigning king, the High King D'Eathe, had gone mad with it. He magicked the drapery to twine around servants' necks, made the lamps flicker to life as one passed, and trapped unfortunate guests in his mirrors, never to release them. Azalea's ninth-great-grandfather, Harold the First, had overthrown him, but still pockets of magic remained in the palace. The old tea set was one of these. It even had a pair of sugar tongs that snapped at the girls' fingers if they wanted more than one cube. The girls called them the sugar teeth, and Azalea guessed they were quite as evil as their creator had been.

"If you wake her," Azalea threatened in a low voice,

picking up the full teacup and setting it on its platter, "I will have you melted down into napkin rings, I swear it."

The teacup hopped back onto the sofa arm and nudged and prodded at Mother's hand. Azalea grabbed it and pinned it between the dented sugar bowl and teapot. The sugar teeth hopped out of the bowl and bit her fingers.

"Ow!" Azalea snapped. "Why, you little—"

Mother stirred.

"Oh, goosey," she said. She opened her eyes and pushed a smile. "Don't be cross. They're only trying to help, you know."

"They're bullying you," said Azalea, whose spirits rose in spite of seeing the pain in Mother's eyes. Mother had a plucky way of smiling that deepened her dimples and brightened the room. "I'll take them to the kitchen. How are you feeling?"

"Mmm. Better. Where are the girls? I wanted to see them, too."

"Out and about. In the gardens, I think." In the hustle and come-and-go of preparations, Azalea had lost track of them. They hadn't even come to see her in her ballgown. Mrs. Graybe and one of the maids had had to help her dress in the kitchen, tightening her stays while she traced her toes on the wood floor, impatient.

"Oh," said Mother. "Well. If they are having a jolly

Christmas Eve, then . . . I'm glad for it. Ah, but look at you! Princess Royale! You look a picture print! The green makes your eyes pop. I knew it would."

Azalea caught her reflection in the glowering tea set. Auburn ringlets framed her face, and her tightly strung corset flushed her cheeks. From shoulder to waist she wore a silver sash. She looked regal, and nothing like herself.

"Everyone says I look like you," said Azalea shyly.

"You lucky thing! Do a Schleswig curtsy."

Azalea's feet took over and she dipped into a curtsy before her mind fully realized it. It flowed from the balls of her feet to her fingertips in one rippled movement and a rustle of skirts. She disappeared into a poof of crinolines.

"Masterful!" Mother laughed. "You're better than me! Up, up, up. Very good! Ladies' cloaks, in the library, gentlemen's hats—"

"In the entrance hall. Yes, I remember." Azalea stood and smoothed her skirts.

"Brilliant. The gentlemen will be mad for you. Dance with every single one and find which one you like best. We can't let parliament do all the choosing."

Azalea's toes curled in her dance slippers.

She hated the sick, milk-turning feeling that came when she thought of her future gentleman. She pictured it as a sort of ball, one that lasted a lifetime, in which parliament chose her dance partner. And she didn't know if he would be a considerate dancer, one who led her through tight turns with ease, or if he would lurch through the steps. Or worse, if he was the sort of partner who would force her through the movements and scoff at her when she stumbled at his hand. Azalea tried to swallow the feeling away.

"I wish you could come," she said.

"Your father will be there."

"*That's* not the same." Azalea leaned down and kissed Mother, inhaling the sweet smell of white cake and baby ointment. "I'll miss you."

"Azalea," said Mother, reaching out to place her hand on Azalea's shoulder. "Before you go. Kneel down."

Azalea did, a little surprised. Her skirts poofed about her. *Poof.*

From the end-table drawer, Mother produced her handkerchief, a folded square of silver. Silver was the color of the royal family. The embroidered letters K.E.W. glimmered in the soft light. Mother took Azalea's hands and pressed them over it.

Azalea gasped. Mother's hands were ice.

"It's your sisters," said Mother. "You've done so well to watch out for them, these months I've been ill. You'll always take care of them, won't you?"

"Is something wrong?"

"Promise me."

"Of . . . course," said Azalea. "You know I will."

The moment the words escaped her lips, a wave of cold prickles washed over her. They tingled down her back, through her veins to her fingertips and toes, flooding her with a cold rain shower of goose prickles. The unfamiliar sensation made Azalea draw a sharp breath.

"Mother—"

"I want you to keep the handkerchief," said Mother. "It's yours now. A lady always needs a handkerchief."

Azalea kept Mother's cold hands between her own, trying to warm them. Mother laughed, a tired, worn laugh that bubbled nonetheless, and she leaned forward and kissed Azalea's fingers.

Her lips, white from pressing against Azalea, slowly turned to red again.

"Good luck," she said.

The King did not look up from his paperwork when Azalea rushed into the library. Two flights of stairs in massive silk skirts had left her breathless, and she swallowed the air in tiny gasps.

"Miss Azalea," he said, dipping his pen into the inkwell. "We have rules in this household, do we not?"

"Yes, sir, I know—"

"Rule number eight, section one, Miss Azalea."

"Sir—"

The King looked up. He had a way of frowning that froze the air and made it crack like ice.

Azalea clenched her fists and bit back a sharp retort. Two years! Nearly two years she had run the household while Mother was ill, and he *still* made her knock! She strode out of the library, slid the door shut with a snap, counted to two, and knocked smartly.

"Yes, you may come in," came the King's voice.

Azalea gritted her teeth.

The King was already dressed for the ball, fine in formal reds and silvers. His military uniform had meticulously straight rows of buttons and medals, and he wore a silver sash across his chest to his waist, like Azalea. As he sorted through papers, Azalea caught words like "treaty" and "regiments" and "skirmish." As Captain General, he would be leaving, along with the cavalry regiments, to help a neighboring country's war in just a few short weeks. Azalea did not like to think about it.

"That is well enough," he said when Azalea stood before his desk. "One cannot run the country without laws; one cannot manage a household without rules. It is so."

"Sir," said Azalea. "It's Mother."

The King set his papers down at this.

"I think we need to send for Sir John," said Azalea. "I know he was here this morning, but . . . something's not right."

The image of Mother's lips, white, then slowly, slowly turning to red, passed through Azalea's mind, and she rubbed her fingers. The King stood.

"Very well," he said. "I will fetch him myself straightaway." He took his hat and overcoat from the stand near the fireplace. "Tend to the guests. They will be arriving soon. And—" The King's brow furrowed. "Take care that your sisters remain in their room. I've made them promise to stay inside, but—it is them."

"You made them promise to stay inside?" said Azalea, indignant. "Even Bramble?"

"*Especially* Bramble."

"But it's tradition to peek at the Yuletide! Even Mother—"

"Tradition be hanged, Miss Azalea. I will not allow it, not after the complete debacle last year."

Azalea pursed her lips. She didn't want the ball to end like it had last year, naturally, but caging them up in the room was unfair.

"That will do, Miss Azalea," said the King. "I've sent goodies to your room, and a dissected picture for them to piece together. They shan't be desolate."

The King turned to go, and Azalea spoke after him.

"You'll be back within the hour?" she said. "For the opening dance?"

"Really, Azalea," said the King, putting on his stiff hat. "Is everything about dancing to you?"

It was, actually, but Azalea decided now wasn't the best time to point that out.

"You will be back in time?" she said.

The King waved his hand in dismissal. "As you say," he said, and he left.

CHAPTER 2

*N*early an hour later, when the tower chimed eight and guests filled the ballroom like brightly colored bouquets, and perfumes and nutmeg and pine scented the air, and the Christmas trees in the corner glimmered and sparkled with glass ornaments, Azalea found herself clasped on the arm of Prime Minister Fairweller.

"He truly can't come?" said Azalea, worried, as Fairweller led her to the center of the ballroom floor. "Is everything all right? Or is he just trying to get out of dancing?"

"He sends his regrets," said Fairweller, "and admonishes you to tend to the guests. He wishes to remain with your mother. Your doctor did not seem concerned."

Azalea pushed the image of white lips out of her mind. Instead, she glowered at Fairweller's black-gloved hand on her arm, escorting her. Why did the King have to ask Fairweller to take his place? Fairweller wasn't bad looking, and he was young—especially for a Prime Minister. But, heavens! Azalea remembered their former Prime Minister, a Lord Bradford. Though the same age as the King himself, he had died when she was little. He was an agreeable gentleman who smelled of soap and coffee and always had a hint of a smile and a light in his eyes.

Fairweller, by contrast, was a thundercloud. He never smiled. The only color he wore was black, even his waistcoat and cufflinks, giving the impression of a sleek, overlarge spider. With the added disadvantage that you couldn't squash him.

"Is Mother having the baby?" said Azalea. "It's a bit early for the baby, isn't it?"

"I hardly know," said Fairweller.

Azalea gave him a dangerously sweet smile.

"I hope you're good at dancing," she said through her teeth. "Or this ball will be completely ruined."

Fairweller brought her into perfect dance position.

The musicians began, the chattering hushed, and Azalea stepped off in waltz time with Fairweller. To her surprise, he was a masterful dancer. He swept her along the dance floor, guiding her about the corners and between skirts, flowing perfectly with the music. In fact, the only thing wrong with dancing with Fairweller was . . . well, dancing with Fairweller.

The waltz ended, the Prime Minister escorted her to the edge of the ballroom, and Azalea was flocked with gentlemen all asking for a dance.

The lively music, the decorations, the snow whorling past the windows and reflected in the mirrors on the other side, and the dancing transformed the ballroom into something almost magical. Azalea nearly forgot, as she danced the jigs, promenades, and waltzes, that the ballroom was old and drafty and the windows leaked when it rained.

She grinned inside every time a gentleman took her into dance position and his eyebrows rose, and rose even farther as he would lead her about the ballroom. They swept past ladies in chiffon and lace, their hoopskirts swaying with her breeze. She danced lightly, followed at even the slightest of touches, had a firm frame and strong form, and never forgot a step. By the time the gentlemen escorted her to a velvet chair at the ballroom's side, they beamed and complimented her on her grace. Azalea returned the compliment with a sleek, deep curtsy that made her green skirts swath the floor in a silky puddle, and giggled inside when their mouths dropped. One day, she was determined, she would be quite as graceful as Mother. Mother didn't walk. She *glided*.

Peals rumbled the floor as the tower chimed ten, and the guests began a bouncy polka. Azalea, who did not like the hard, breathless dance, slipped past the blur of dancers to the corner where the glimmering Christmas trees stood, hoping to spend a few moments out of sight. The ball had gone perfectly so far. If only Mother and her sisters were here, it would complete everything.

Azalea considered nipping upstairs to check on them. She imagined the girls, caged up in their room, music drifting through the floor. They would be sitting at the round table, staring at the picture pieces with glazed eyes. Azalea sighed. She poked one of the ornaments on the ribbon-and-silver decked tree.

The ornaments clinked. A hand shot out from the boughs, a handkerchief between its fingers. Azalea leaped back.

"Dry your tears," said the tree, "young peep."

"Great scott!" said Azalea, taking the handkerchief from the disembodied hand, which slipped back into the tree with a rustle. The handkerchief had sloppily embroidered letters in the corner. B.E.W.

"Only, you looked a nudge away from bursting into tears," said the tree.

"Bramble!"

Behind branches dripping with silver-and-glass ornaments, a pair of yellow-green eyes winked at Azalea. Azalea bit back a delighted cry.

"Hulloa, Az!"

The trees, arranged around the corner of the ballroom, had left an empty pie-bit sort of space, now filled with sisters. All ten of them crowded about together on the floor, hidden, pressed between the trees and the wall.

"Looks . . . comfortable," said Azalea.

"It's not so bad now that we can't feel our legs." Bramble grinned, her thin lips turning up into a wry smile. "It's a bit squashy, but it's worth it."

Azalea peered through the branches. Clover cradled both Jessamine and Kale, who slept soundly. Eve pressed next to her, clutching a book. A pine branch was in her face.

"All right there, Eve?" said Azalea.

Eve turned a page of her book. "The light is bad," she said.

Azalea cast a glance back at the blur of guests, still engrossed in their dance. "The King's going to be dreadfully cross," she said. "Didn't he make you promise to stay inside?"

"We *are* inside!" said Bramble. "Da-dum! Next time the King will have to rethink his wording. Are *you* glad we're here?"

Delight bubbled through Azalea, and she couldn't help but laugh. "Beyond words!"

The girls burst into a chatter.

"The ball is absolutely *marvelous* this year!"

"I can't *wait* until I'm of age!"

"The food looks corking!"

"All the gentlemen are mad after you!"

"Just remember, don't get attached to any of them," said Delphinium, who thought herself an expert in matters of love, now she was twelve. "They're not dancing with you because you're you. They're only dancing with you because if they marry *you*, they get to be King."

Azalea's smile faded. She took a step away from the Christmas trees, feeling as though a hand wrung her stomach.

"Oh . . . stuff it, Delphinium," said Bramble.

"I just think she shouldn't fall in love, that's all," said Delphinium. "Since parliament will choose the next king, she—"

"Yes, *thank* you." Bramble pushed Delphinium back, which made the entire mass of pine trees rustle. Ornaments tinkled. Bramble turned back to Azalea, and her wry grin reappeared.

"I hope you're grateful," she said. "Our Great Christmas Tree Scandal took a lot of time. We told the King we'd be in our room all day—sulking, you know— and then slipped behind here after tea."

"You've been here since tea?" said Azalea. "You must be hungry!"

"Hungry?" said Bramble. "We're *starving*!"

"Oh, yes!" piped the other girls. "We haven't had a crumb to eat, not a crumb crumb crumb!"

The mass of trees shook.

Azalea pulled back, laughing.

"I can fix that!" she said, and she swept to the dessert table.

She filled her plate with every sort of sweet—candied raspberries, rosemary tarts, iced walnuts, sticky sweet rolls—things they had only once a year, since parliament funded the Yuletide ball and could afford it. Their own rather poor household lived on porridge and potatoes. Back at the trees, as the polka wound to an end and a mazurka began, Azalea leaned down, as though to inspect her worn slippers, and shoved the plate beneath the branches. Several pairs of eager hands pulled it in, and the trees burst into delighted squeals.

Every fifth dance or so, careful to fill the plate during quick, breath-stealing jigs so as not to be noticed, Azalea delivered goodies to the girls. They cheered in tiny voices each time. While couples danced the varsovienne, Azalea stacked her platter with ten dainty glass bowls of pudding, a special request from the girls. The spoons and crystal clinked against the plate, piled like a castle. Azalea picked her way carefully to the trees—

—and nearly ran into a gentleman.

Azalea overbalanced with the puddings, and the

top little bowl slid off the rest. The gentleman caught it with surprising speed between his thumb and forefinger, pulling back as Azalea's skirts settled. His eyes took her in, her auburn ringlets and silk dress, and stopped on the plate stacked with puddings. Each one had a wallop of cream on the top.

Azalea, face hot, lifted her chin at him and coldly stared him down, *daring* him to say anything.

He opened his mouth, then shut it. Then slowly, as though afraid she would strike, he cautiously set the pudding bowl back on the top with a crystal *clink*, and backed away.

"Oh!" said Azalea. "You're bleeding!"

And now she saw why he was hiding between the trees and the drapery. He was terribly disheveled! A strand of his mussed hair, the indiscriminate color between dark blond and brown, hung in his eyes. A streak of mud smeared his cheekbone and his fine black suit, and blood and dirt colored the handkerchief he now returned to pressing against his hand.

"It's . . . nothing, really," he stammered.

But Azalea had already set the plate to the marble with a clunk and a clatter of spoons, and produced Bramble's clean handkerchief from her sleeve.

"Hush," she said, taking his hand and dabbing at the cut on his knuckle. "It isn't bad. We'll clean it right up. What were you thinking, using such a soiled handkerchief?"

The cut wasn't deep, and the gentleman held still while Azalea tended to it. His large hand dwarfed her own, and she only just managed to wrap the handkerchief about it.

"My horse slipped on the way here," he explained. His voice reminded Azalea of rich, thick cream, the sort one could add to any recipe to make it taste better. "The Courtroad bridge. I only just arrived."

Azalea nodded, thinking of how the King avoided that icy bridge every winter. Expertly, she tied the ends of the handkerchief in a tight, dainty knot. The gentleman touched it.

"Thank you," he said.

"You probably shouldn't stay much longer," said Azalea. "You need a proper bandage on it, or it will get infected and throb every time you turn a lady into the next step. You wouldn't want that."

"Assuredly not." A hint of a smile graced his lips.

Azalea looked up at him again, this time past the mud and rumpled cravat and hair. Something about him was strikingly familiar. The way he stood; his solemn, gentle temperament. He had a long nose, but it was his eyes, warm and brown, that marked his features. Everyone in her family had blue or green eyes. The brown caught her off guard and fascinated her.

"Azalea, where's our food?" the tree behind her whispered.

"We're sta-aa-arving!"

Azalea kicked back into the boughs behind her, silencing the susurrus with a *clink* of ornaments.

"Did you—" said the gentleman.

"No," said Azalea. "Have we met before?"

The gentleman smiled again and touched the corner of his bandage handkerchief across the embroidered letters B.E.W. "Ages ago," he said. "When we were both younger. You . . . don't remember me?"

Azalea shook her head.

"Sorry," she said. "What's your name?"

He inclined his head. "Lord Bradford."

"Bradford!" said Azalea. "Like the former prime minister?"

"Very much like," he said. And Azalea caught the spark of light in his eyes, twinkling through his solemn expression. It made her smile. No wonder he looked so familiar! She considered him and wondered if he knew that all of Eathesbury expected him to run for P.M., like his father. With his tousled hair and mussed suit, he didn't quite look the picture.

"You're not . . . engaged for this next dance, are you?" he said. "That is, if you—"

He stopped abruptly, clamping his mouth shut. His eyes stared straight ahead. Ornaments tinkled behind them, and Azalea looked down to see a pudgy little hand reaching out from beneath the tree, grabbing at his trouser ankle. Azalea cringed.

"Not there, Ivy, you great idiot," came a whispered voice from among the boughs. "Left—left—no, left is *this* way—"

The hands peeking from between the tree skirts felt around, grabbed the ends of the platter, and slowly, with clinks and clatters, dragged the plate in. Lord Bradford's eyebrows rose as the castle of puddings inched away and disappeared beneath the boughs. Squeals echoed from the trees.

Azalea buried her face in her hands.

"Ah—" said Lord Bradford.

"Don't," said Azalea. "Just . . . don't."

"There you are! Oh, dear. Am I interrupting something?"

Azalea and Lord Bradford quickly stepped apart to see Lady Caversham a pace away, her eyes wide with innocence. Lady Caversham reminded Azalea of one of the dolls in the shops on Silver Street: pale and perfect and expensive. Azalea forced a smile.

"Definitely not," she said. "He's mended up now."

Lord Bradford's eyes turned back to the trees behind

them, his eyebrows high on his head, and Azalea looked up at him with the most pleading expression she could muster, begging him to not make a scene.

"Oh!" Lady Caversham gave a sharp cry. "What was that?"

"What was what?" said Azalea and Lord Bradford at the same time.

"The tree! Something moved behind it!"

The color drained from Azalea's face.

"I didn't . . . see anything," she stammered.

Lady Caversham strode forward, the wispy flounces of her skirts fluttering behind her, trying to peer through the branches. "There was something—oh! There it was again!"

"Lady Caversham," said Lord Bradford, stepping in front of her. He offered his hand and bowed. "If I may have the honor of this next dance?"

Lady Caversham tore her eyes away from the tree and narrowed them at Lord Bradford's offered hand. She cast a glance at Azalea, and a slight smile crossed her perfect face.

"Well, if you *insist*," she said. With a look at Azalea that said *I win*, she grasped Lord Bradford's outstretched hand right over the handkerchief bandage—both he and Azalea winced—and part escorted, part dragged Lord Bradford to the dance floor.

He cast a glance back at Azalea. She fought the urge to pull him back and smooth his hair down.

Azalea didn't catch sight of him for the rest of the night. The ball wound down like a music box, the guests leaving as the hours grew late. Near midnight, when Azalea delivered yet another plate of goodies to the girls, she rolled a Christmas apple underneath the trees, and it rolled back out. They had fallen asleep.

The last dance, the Entwine, was Azalea's favorite. She had hoped to be asked it by Lord Bradford, but he had left, and instead she stood in dance position with a young, rather moist gentleman named Mr. Penbrook, who looked as though he couldn't believe his luck. The rest of the guests moved in a ring to watch as she and Mr. Penbrook took the ends of a long sash.

The musicians began, and—

Slam.

The ballroom doors ricocheted open, startling the guests and silencing the music.

Fairweller.

"The ball is over!" he said, striding to the first window.

Polite protestations came from the guests.

"Minister?" said Azalea, stepping out of dance position. "What are you doing?"

Fairweller did not answer. He took a poker from the

fireplace stand and used it to unlatch the high cords that held the drapery up in arches. The fabric rippled to the floor, masking the frosted windows.

"Oh, ho," said an older parliament gentleman. "It's the little princesses again, is it? Ho, ho! Have you looked in the chandeliers?"

Some of the guests chuckled at this. Azalea flushed.

"Do you need us to find them?" said one of the ladies. "They nearly froze to death last year."

"I need you all to go *home*." Fairweller strode to the next window and unlatched the cords there as well. "If you please."

The guests turned to Azalea, whose cheeks burned.

"Minister," she said.

Across the ballroom, Fairweller's iron gray eyes met Azalea's. Something hardened in them—something Azalea could not read—and it staggered her. She dropped the end of the sash.

"Oh," she said. Then, to the guests, "Th-thank you all for coming. Next year we'll . . . be certain to have a ball that ends normally."

This brought chuckles and a smattering of applause. While Fairweller continued to drape the windows along the wall, Azalea saw each guest to the door, helped the musicians pack up their instruments, and wished everyone a good holiday as they left.

When they were all gone, the ballroom felt hollow.

"You didn't have to end it like that," said Azalea. "It was almost over."

Fairweller finished draping the last window.

"Your sisters, Miss Azalea."

Azalea sighed. Another debacle. The King would be cross again this year, which meant meals in their bedroom and no dance lessons for at least a week. Worn out, Azalea led Fairweller to the trees. He pushed a tree aside, the stand scraping the marble, and revealed the girls.

They slept, snuggled together like a nest of swans, empty pudding bowls and spoons strewn about them. They used tree skirts as blankets, and looked angelic. Nothing like they normally did.

Fairweller stared down at them, unmoving. He opened his mouth, then closed it. He closed his eyes, then opened them. He turned sharply around—and strode across the dance floor. He cast aside the fire poker. It clanged across the marble. He left, slamming the ballroom doors behind him.

The chandelier lamps flickered.

"That," said Azalea, blinking at the ballroom doors, "was odd."

She turned to the mass of sleeping girls, a jumble of brightly colored cottons and shawls among the silk tree skirts, and smiled, suddenly feeling very, very drowsy.

❦

"Wake up! Wake up! Wakeupwakeupwakeupwake*up*!"

Azalea groaned as ten pairs of hands poked her awake. She had been so tired last night, she hadn't even bothered going to bed. Instead she fell asleep right there with her sisters, using a tree skirt as a pillow.

"Stop, stop, *stop*," she moaned. "The buttons of this dress dig into the spine, you have no idea."

"Poor ickle Azalea," said Bramble, deep red hair tangled to her knees. "Poor wee ickle wee tiny baby."

"It's Christmas, Lea," said Flora. "Christmas!"

"We're to have oranges!"

"And sausages!"

"And, and, and a book from the King, even!"

"Christmas, Christmas, Christmas!"

"I know!" said Azalea as the girls pulled her to her feet. She clawed at an ornament snagged in her hair. Her ballgown made her drag. "Slow down!" she said, stumbling over her crinolines. "I can hardly walk!"

Screaming with unholy delight, the girls ran with neck-breaking speed to the nook, where all their oranges and presents would be set up in piles on the table. Azalea stumbled after them, down the hall and through the folding glass doors, only to see them crowded around the table, gawking at it with wide eyes.

There was nothing on it.

Fairweller stood at the end of the nook, his back to them, staring at the drapes covering the glass walls.

"Our oranges," said Ivy, gaping at the table.

"Our books," said Eve.

"Oh, hang," said Bramble. "Our scandal."

The girls began to cry. Azalea, now fully awake, crossed her arms.

"Where is the King?" she said, her voice a hard Princess Royale tone. "Minister?"

"He's out," said Fairweller. "Riding."

"On Christmas morning?"

Fairweller said nothing.

Azalea smiled and turned to the girls. "I'll bet Mother has them up with her. You know how much she loves Christmas."

The girls sniffed and rubbed their eyes. Fairweller muttered something.

"I'm sorry, Minister?" said Azalea.

Fairweller turned away from the curtain.

"I said, your mother is dead." He looked back to the drapes. "She died last night."

CHAPTER 3

*A*zalea smacked Fairweller. So hard her hand stung. She ran from the nook, her hand throbbing, through the old kitchen door and out into the snowy gardens, the ice cold of dawn stinging her cheeks.

How *dare* he! How dare Fairweller say such a thing! When he *knew* how ill Mother was! Azalea had to find the King. Through the garden paths, snow-topped hedges, and frozen topiaries, out of the screeching iron gate, through the meadow, into the frozen wood, Azalea stumbled, following Dickens's hoofprints of upturned dirt and snow. The King would set things right. He would tell her it wasn't true, and—

But you didn't go to Mother's room, a tiny voice whispered through Azalea's angry, burning thoughts. You didn't dare. . . .

"Sir!" Azalea yelled, tripping through the overgrown

woodland path, the cold seeping through her worn dance slippers. "Sir!"

The wood replied with frozen silence.

The trees towered above her, deep blue in the morning light, and Azalea swallowed and coughed as the air stung her throat. Her gloves were streaked with mud, and her heavy ballgown had torn on the snagging, leafless bushes. She leaned against a frozen tree and shivered uncontrollably.

Her lips had been white—

"*Sir!*" Azalea screamed.

The hot, tangled ball of anger inside of her turned inside out. Azalea fell to her knees and began to sob. Hacking sobs, so hard it hurt to breathe. She buried her face in her hands and couldn't stop. Every time she tried to say *Mother*, the word broke in her throat. Mother, incomparable Mother!

The sun rose, casting golden light through the shadows of the trees, glistening through the mist and snow. Azalea came halfway to her senses, through shuddering cries. She pulled her handkerchief from her sleeve, and the silver caught the morning light.

Mother's handkerchief. Azalea vaguely remembered tucking it into her sleeve after she had left Mother's room, telling herself it was too nice to use. Azalea turned the silver piece of fabric in her hands, numb. When Mother had given it to her, she had said—

Take care of your sisters.

The girls! Azalea had left them there, alone in the nook. Had they tried to follow after her? Were they all right? And what—Azalea closed her eyes against the icy morning—what about Mother's baby? She had been selfish.

Take care—

The odd, tingling feeling, only an echo of what it had been the night before, washed through her, to her fingers and throat. Inexplicably, almost magically, it filled a bit of the hollowness inside her. Clutching the silver handkerchief, Azalea stumbled to her feet.

An hour later, still frozen from the wood and streaked with mud, Azalea found the girls in the palace nursery. The nursery was a small, cramped room on the second floor, swathed with lacy white furniture and masses of frills. A nursemaid left as Azalea arrived at the pitiful scene: girls sitting on the floor, among the rocking chairs and the broken dollhouse. They each clutched an orange to their chest with both hands. They were crying. They looked as miserable as she felt.

"You're f-f-frozen," said Clover, who was fourteen. Instantly she was at Azalea's side, pressing her own warm hands over Azalea's stiff ones. Red rimmed her eyes, and her golden hair was tangled and mussed. Like all the girls, she still wore her clothes from yesterday.

"I'm so sorry," said Azalea. "I shouldn't have left you all."

Bramble snapped to attention. She leaped to her feet and threw her orange at Azalea. It hit Azalea's shoulder and bounced to the floor.

"You shouldn't have!" she said. She snatched Flora's orange from her hands and threw it. Azalea didn't move, and it hit her on the side of the head and bounced onto the frilly rug.

"How *dare* you desert us like that!" Bramble threw Goldenrod's orange, and it hit Azalea on the shoulder again. Bramble began to cry anew.

"At least try to dodge them!" she said.

In two strides Azalea was at Bramble's side, pulling her to her shoulder. Bramble sobbed. The girls flocked to Azalea, the younger ones clutching her skirts, all of them a wrinkled mess.

"You're all wet," said Bramble, between hiccups.

"I know," said Azalea. Her hair dripped.

"L-Lea," said Clover. She always had difficulty speaking, as though every word took her entire effort. She pushed a smile. "We . . . have something . . . to show— show you. L-look."

A frilly bassinet stood in the middle of the room, and Clover pulled Azalea to it. A tiny bundle of lacy blanket and dark curls lay inside.

The baby was the tiniest Azalea had ever seen—and she had seen quite a few, now the eldest of twelve. It could fit inside her cupped hands. And a girl, too, judging by the tiny, frilly bonnet. Azalea pulled off her soggy, wet gloves and touched the baby's curled fingers.

"That would be L, then," said Azalea. All her sisters had been named alphabetically, as the King liked everything very much in order. He was particular that way. He even had the jam jars in the pantry indexed.

"Mother n-named her," said Clover. "It's Lily."

"Lily," Azalea breathed.

Graceful, delicate. The baby reminded her of the white garden lilies that bloomed through the snow. Mother always knew what was just right.

"M-Minister said that Mother . . . h-held Lily," said Clover. "Before she—"

Clover didn't finish, because she began to weep anew. Everyone began crying again, sobbing and wet hiccupping. Azalea felt lost, as though she had leaped into the air, a jeté, and kept falling and falling, her stomach turning and waiting to hit the ground that wasn't there. She pulled the handkerchief from her sleeve, and the silver flashed.

Promise me . . .

The tingling prickled to her fingers.

Azalea took a deep breath and moved her feet into fourth position, then traced her toe behind her and dipped into a kneel. Dancing always steadied her. She wiped Jessamine's and Kale's tiny faces, which were streaked and wet. She cleaned their noses, too.

"Do you know," she said, moving to Ivy, "what we haven't done?"

Ivy shook her blond curls.

"We haven't introduced ourselves to Lily." Azalea pushed a smile. "It's her first day here, and all we've done is cry at her. It won't do."

Bramble grimaced. "Oh, really, Az—"

"Come along," said Azalea. She stood and held out her hands. "Join hands, trace the left foot back into a curtsy position number two."

No one moved.

Azalea didn't give up. The girls looked a mix of surprised, shocked, and disgusted as she dipped into a fifth-position curtsy, lowering to her right knee and pointing her left foot in front of her, so it peeked out from her muddy hem. When she straightened, their expressions had softened.

"Your dip was unsteady," said Bramble. "When you switched the balance to your other foot."

"Introduction to royalty curtsy," said Azalea, holding out her hand to Bramble. "No one balances as well as you."

Bramble pursed her lips into a thin red line, but she

took Azalea's hand and stood. In a sweep of long red hair, she lowered into a deep curtsy in a lithe, supple movement. She extended her arm out to the bassinet.

"Too late to back out now, young chit," said Bramble. "Welcome to the royal family."

Azalea took Ivy's five-year-old hand and bowed to her. Ivy twirled underneath Azalea's arm, and curtsied to Lily. Jessamine took Azalea's other hand, and curtsied with her, and then all the girls, eyes red, joined hands. The dance flowed through them, and they moved as one in a reel. Blood flowed to Azalea's cheeks, warming them in a wash. Ankles together, step back, brush forward, touch, bow, in graceful, practiced movements. Their skirts brushed together.

They raised their heads and broke apart, looking shyly at one another, as though not quite sure what had gotten into them.

It was . . . magic. But not the sort like the tea set. Last winter, when Azalea had fully realized parliament's role in her future marriage, Mother had brushed Azalea's hair, dried her face, and brought her to the ballroom. There she taught Azalea a midair mazurka.

"Do you feel that?" Mother said, when Azalea had mastered the dizzy, brilliant step. "That warm, flickery bit inside of you? That's magic. The deepest sort. So deep it doesn't have a name. But it is magic, just the same."

And now, though their eyes were red and puffy, Azalea's sisters weren't crying anymore. It was the warm, flickery bit that did it. They even managed weak smiles.

"Come now, Flora," said Azalea, taking Flora's dainty hand. "A secondhand curt—"

A fuss from downstairs interrupted her. The entrance hall door slammed; a commotion of servants, the bark of the King's voice. The girls' eyes lit.

"The King," said Flora.

"He's back!"

"Steady on." Azalea pulled the younger girls back and smoothed their skirts and hair. Then, with shaking hands, she wrapped Lily in a blanket and herded the girls down the hall. The King. Finally! He would know what to do. He was the most steady gentleman Azalea knew. And he hadn't seen Lily yet—surely he hadn't.

The corridor on the second floor opened to a mezzanine, which overlooked the entrance hall. The King stood at the bottom, speaking in low tones to Mr. Pudding, who kneaded his cap.

Like all of them, the King wore his clothes from yesterday. His uniform was muddy and wet, and several of his medals had been torn off. A streak of blood smeared across his face into his closely trimmed beard. Even so, he stood stiff and formal, regal and proper as always.

". . . in the library. I have business to tend to. I will not be disturbed, Mr. Pudding."

"Aye, sir, but th' princesses, they've been eager to see you, sir—"

"I cannot abide them," the King snapped, in a loud-enough whisper that it echoed in the hall. "I cannot! Keep them away from me, Mr. Pudding!"

Azalea looked quickly from the King below to the bedraggled, wide-eyed girls next to her. Clover held her hands over her mouth.

Azalea blinked away the shock, pursed her lips together, tucked Lily's blanket about her tiny neck, and descended the stairs to the entrance hall in a glide.

"Er—no—miss, I wouldn't do that," said Mr. Pudding as she strode past him to the library door.

Azalea knocked but didn't wait for an answer. She slid the door open. The King stood over his desk, sorting through the top drawer. He pulled out a key.

"Sir!" said Azalea. "We've been waiting for you!"

The King walked toward the door. Azalea ran forward to meet him.

"Look," she said. She pulled the blanket away from Lily's face and showed him the tiny, bonneted bundle.

He didn't stop to look.

"Mother named her," said Azalea. "It's Lily. We thought you'd—"

The King clamped his hands firmly on Azalea's shoulders, turned her about, and guided her almost roughly to the library door. Azalea tried to shake off his iron hands.

"Sir—you don't—sir—"

The King pushed her into the hall.

Azalea twisted around to see the heavy wood-paneled library door slide shut. A faint *click-click* signaled the door locking.

Azalea opened her mouth, but no sound came out. It caught in her throat.

The girls peered down from the mezzanine above, wordless.

"It's just a guess," said Bramble after a moment, "but I don't think he's in the mood to see us."

Not until Azalea had tucked in the weepy, sniffling girls in their tiny third-floor room, combing their hair and telling them stories, and made sure that Lily was settled in the nursery with the nursemaid, did she slip away to Mother's room. Eathesbury tradition required the steward of the family to sit up the first night to watch over the deceased, but Azalea could hear Mr. Pudding's hacking sobs from across the palace, and she joined him in Mother's room, pouring cups of tea to soothe him.

Azalea cried, seeing the holly, pine, and dried flowers

strewn about the room. She bit her lip so hard it numbed, to keep herself from glancing at the bed, but in the end she had to. And it surprised her. Mother lay on the bed, dressed in white, with flowers in her auburn hair.

She looked peaceful. For the past months, when Azalea had seen her, she had lines on her face and pain in her eyes. Now, she rested. The old magic tea set, still sitting on the end table, didn't have the spark of feistiness to it anymore. It slumped on its tray.

Azalea sat on Mother's stiff flowered sofa, picked up the silver teacup, and turned it over in her hands. The silver cooled her fingertips. Engraved on the bottom of the cup was a tiny half-moon with three marks through it. DE. The D'Eathe mark.

Azalea considered the picture of the High King D'Eathe, which she had once found while cleaning the north attic. An ancient, pockmarked fellow with no hair and dark eyes, scowling from the canvas. Even just the memory of his portrait made Azalea shudder. He captured and tortured people foolish enough to wander onto the thorn-shrouded palace grounds. Stories of the High King tearing a person apart, starting with the thumbs, then to the ears and toes, tugging them to pieces like a cricket, to see how long they would stay alive, haunted Azalea in her worst nightmares.

And then, the worst story of all: After they had died,

he kept their *souls*. Their bodies would be found, strewn across the city, but at night, when the palace windows glowed through the thorn vines, the very same person would be seen, silhouetted against the candlelight, walking the halls.

Thinking of it terrified Azalea. Even so, for the first time in her life, she was glad of it. Because if the High King did capture souls, it meant that a person had one. It meant that there was something to the warm, flickery bit inside of you. It meant that Mother wasn't hurting anymore. Azalea clung to that hope, desperately. If that were true, Azalea would believe in anything.

CHAPTER 4

*A*zalea dreamed that night of drowning in torrents of hair, and woke up with hair on her face. She vaguely remembered allowing Jessamine and Kale and Ivy onto her bed when they cried the night before, but she couldn't remember Hollyhock, Flora, Goldenrod, Eve, Delphinium, and even Clover and Bramble coming for comfort. Yet they were all piled together, and those who hadn't fit on the bed slept on the rug next to it, or propped on the mattress.

The girls slowly awoke for the day, washing their faces, brushing their hair, more out of habit than anything. They shared a crowded third-floor room on the north side of the palace, square, with six beds and window seats about the sides, and a massive fireplace at the end. It smelled of powder, flowers, and old wood. A lot of maneuvering and tripping took place when they readied.

Today, however, when they opened their trunks to dress, they were surprised. The trunks were empty.

"Perhaps they're being washed," said Flora as Azalea swept down the hall in her nightgown, the girls padding after. "It could be laundry day."

"Oh, yes, the maids are washing them," said Goldenrod, Flora's twin. The nine-year-old twins reminded Azalea of a pair of dainty sparrows, both timid and eager at the same time.

"They don't wash all our dresses at once," said Azalea. "Something's afoot. Mrs. Graybe!"

Azalea rounded the corner to the mezzanine and made to go downstairs, when she spotted Fairweller in the entrance hall below.

"Oh!" said Azalea. Fairweller's eyes caught her, and he turned his head away to the door. Azalea ducked back into the safety of the hall, blushing furiously.

"Minister," she called out. "Have you seen Mrs. Graybe?"

"Forget Mrs. Graybe!" said Delphinium, running to the banister railing. Being only twelve, she did not care if Fairweller saw her in her nightgown or not. "Where are our dresses? We haven't a stitch to wear!"

"They are in the kitchen. Drying, I believe," said Fairweller.

Azalea inched her way so she could see a sliver of

the entrance hall below. Fairweller kept his head down, focusing on pulling on his black gloves. He had a rosy bruise on his face.

"We were right, then!" said Flora. "They were being washed."

"They were being dyed," said Fairweller. "For mourning. Good day."

Fairweller left before the girls could ask him any more questions. Instead, after the door had slammed, the girls turned to Azalea, their faces puzzled.

"Morning?" said Flora.

"Oh," said Azalea. She had forgotten about this part of a person's death: the isolation, the clocks, the clothes, the rules, the entire year of it—and the silence. Now, it came back, a heavy weight. She exhaled slowly. "Mourning."

Delphinium screamed when they found their dresses, hanging from lines in the kitchen like black shadows. Every stitch of cloth they owned had been dyed unrecognizable.

"It's just a color," said Azalea soothingly as Delphinium cried over her favorite rose-colored dress, now black. "It's all right." She helped unpin the dry dresses and laid them neatly on the servants' table, a pile for each girl. Some were still in the large washtub, billowing night in black dye.

Azalea had the girls dress right there in the kitchen, over bowls of hot porridge. And while they dressed, Azalea told them everything she knew about mourning.

She told them about how balls and promenades and courting weren't allowed, and how they were to keep inside, not even allowed out to the gardens. She told them that the windows would be draped for a year and that they would have to get used to wearing black for a year, too. And she told them about the clocks, how they would be stopped at the time of the person's death, and that music wasn't allowed, either.

It took a while. When she had finished, the girls all looked like miserable, drooping black blossoms.

"Is d-dancing allowed?" Clover stammered.

Azalea bit her lip and turned her head away.

"Oooh!" Delphinium lifted a dainty hand to her forehead, closed her eyes, and fell back onto the wood floor. *Thum-thump thump.*

She lay on the floor, unmoving.

"Oh, get up, Delphi," said Bramble. "When people really faint, they bang their heads up on the floor. It's very unromantic."

"A year!" Delphinium cried. "We're not allowed to dance for a *year*! I'll *die* without dancing!"

"M-Mother would let us dance," Ivy peeped.

At the mention of Mother, the girls' composure,

frayed already, fell apart, and Azalea found herself in the midst of sobbing girls.

Azalea wanted to sob, too. She hated this feeling, one of dancing a step she did not know, confused, bumbling over her dance slippers to get it right. It happened so rarely—she knew *every* dance—that fumbling through the movement frightened her.

This was a thousand times worse. The palace, known for its tall, mullioned windows that dappled light through the halls, would be muffled with drapery, turning day into pitch-black. They would be kept inside, trapped in a cage like those peeping birds at the wire-and-bottle shop on Hampton Street, and only allowed out on Royal Business . . . which would not be often. If Mother were here—

Azalea's throat grew tight, and her chin trembled. She hated herself for it. Mother would have known what to do. Biting her lip to keep from crying, Azalea pulled out Mother's handkerchief. Silver shone in the light, followed by that peculiar tingling sensation. Azalea's throat untightened, and she was able, almost, to smile. There was something to that handkerchief. Azalea did not know what.

But Azalea did know one thing: She was a fast learner. When she fumbled through a dance step, it was only a moment before she caught the rhythm and glided back into the motions. If Mother could smooth things over, then she could, too.

Azalea helped Delphinium up from the floor, and lifted five-year-old Ivy to the table, spooning her a bit of extra porridge from the pot. Ivy had an insatiable appetite. Azalea gently wiped faces and soothed their cries.

"Hush," said Azalea. "It's only for a year. I'll watch out for you all. I promise."

The next evening, the girls set the table in the dining room, their moods as dark as the drapery. The dining room was a fine old space, with a long table, cabinets, and arched doorways flanked with curtains. The hearth in the great fireplace cast a light over their sullen faces, not really making up for the muffled window light. They heard the tower chime seven, the silverware clinking against the plates.

"They can't stop *that* clock," said Delphinium, raising her pointed chin. "You'd need an actual clocksmith for that."

Azalea loved the huge clock and bells at the top of the palace, creaking through the hours and chiming in off-tune peals. It made the palace feel alive, something she desperately needed now that everything had been stifled.

"The King wouldn't allow it to be stopped," said

Azalea, helping Kale onto her chair. "Mother loved it too much."

At the mention of the King, the girls grew quiet. Flora raised a dainty finger, as though she were in lessons.

"Lea," she said. "Do you—do you think he meant it? When he said—"

"Of course not," said Azalea, giving her and her twin, Goldenrod, an encouraging smile. "He's just aggrieved. Like in one of Eve's storybooks."

"I don't know." Eve stared at her plate. "In storybooks the children call their father *Papa*." She removed her spectacles and rubbed her eyes.

Azalea paused. They had never been exactly close to the King, but he had always come to breakfast and dinner, at least. It was a rule they had, to eat dinner as a family. Now, these past several days, he had remained in the library, tending to Royal Business and ignoring them all.

"He's missed every meal since Christmas Eve," said Delphinium. "And he's not coming now. I feel like an orphan."

As if on cue, the King's voice echoed down the hall, stiff, firm words that were indiscernible but most definitely out of the library. The girls lunged for the doors, but Azalea held them back.

"Brush down your skirts, everyone, hands in your lap.

Clover, make them presentable. Bramble and I will fetch him. Behave." Azalea cast a lofty look at Delphinium. "*Orphans*, for heaven's sake."

Through the dark halls of faded wallpaper and mismatched portraits to the entrance hall, Azalea grasped Bramble's hand. Bramble squeezed back equally hard. Azalea hadn't thought she missed the King, his hard adherence to rules and his formalities, but the giddiness in her chest proved otherwise.

Arriving at the entrance hall, they found the King outside the library in discussion with a young gentleman. The gentleman looked up when Azalea and Bramble brushed in. Even though the entrance hall was dimly lit, black linen over the windows, light still caught in the gentleman's warm brown eyes. Lord Bradford!

The King looked up, too, and a frown etched his face. His beard was well trimmed and his suit crisp, but he looked half starved. Azalea felt grateful they would have fish pies for dinner. They filled a person up.

"You're finally out!" said Bramble. "It's about time!"

"We're waiting for you, in the dining room," said Azalea. "We won't start without you."

"Rule number eighteen," Bramble reminded.

The frown lines in the King's face deepened.

"I have business to tend to," he said. Cold, formal,

stiff. "This young gentleman is going to stop the tower for mourning."

"Stop the tower!" Bramble flushed. "What? Sir, you *can't*! Mother loved it! She even had a bucky little dance for it—you remember!" She grasped the King's hand, a plea in her face.

Bramble! thought Azalea. The King's ice blue eyes grew even harder and colder at the word "Mother."

"It's all right," said Azalea quickly, hoping to smooth things. "I'll escort him to the tower. You can go to dinner."

"Very well. You may escort him. And you, young lady"—the King tugged his hand from Bramble's grasp—"will tend to your sisters, at once."

Azalea's chest trilled with hope, right up until the King strode *past* her to the entrance hall doors, taking his coat from the stand and yanking the door open. Hope sputtered into indignation. He was—he was leaving! Azalea stopped the door with her boot before he shut it, biting back the pain.

"You can't leave," she whispered fiercely. "And you can't stay in the library, either. This is more important than R.B. We need you!"

The King released the carved doorknob and left. In a fit of temper, Azalea slammed it after him.

Why was the King being like this? He had never been

the way Mother was, but he had never been like this. Everything was tense and tangled, but Azalea felt she could still manage it all if the King was there. Now she felt abandoned.

Bramble's chin tightened at the door. She swallowed, then snapped to Lord Bradford.

"*You!*" she snarled, her yellow-green eyes flaring. "*You!*"

She dashed down the hall in a rustle of black skirts and deep red hair. Her footfalls echoed.

Only now Azalea realized she had been clenching her fists, hard. She slowly unclenched them, and in the dim light saw the crescent-moon marks her nails had dug into her palms. A bit of skin curled up around each mark, as though Azalea had dug into a bar of soap instead of her hand.

A polite cough sounded, and Azalea flushed, remembering Lord Bradford. She turned.

"I didn't mean—" he said, in his rich voice. He kneaded his hat rim.

"Of course not," said Azalea. "Things are a bit unstrung here. How is your hand?"

"Better," he said solemnly. "Thank you."

True to her word, though feeling wrung inside, Azalea led him up the main stairs of the palace. She didn't say much. He spoke, filling the silence in a mellow baritone way, of how he owned the clock shop on Silver Street, and the King had sent for the clocksmith, but Mr. Grunnings was out, and that he himself knew quite a bit about clock mechanisms, so he came instead.

"I know it isn't allowed to visit, in mourning," he said haltingly. "But I thought if it was Royal Business . . ." He paused. "I wanted to tell you how sorry I was. About your mother. She had the nicest laugh, I think, of anyone I ever knew."

Azalea wanted to burst into tears and throw her arms around his neck. Instead she turned, several stairs above him, feeling the polished banister beneath her hand. She considered his rumpled blond-brown hair and, in a quick movement, reached out and smoothed it down. She had wanted to do that since the Yuletide.

Bemusement passed over Lord Bradford's face, and Azalea, face hot, led him up the rickety stairs to the tower attic.

The tower stood above the entrance hall, square and symmetrical and old. It smelled of sweet must, with a tang of metal. She had to shield her eyes when they reached the main platform. Sunlight streamed through the glass clockface, casting shadowed numbers across the floor. The gears and pulleys clanged and creaked.

Lord Bradford examined it all with fascination, touching each large carriage-wheel-sized gear, his eyes lighting with excitement.

"This is magic," he said, pointing up to the main gear that turned the rod and hands. "I was wondering how the counterweights could propel themselves without any steam or force. Look."

Azalea peered at the gear. Near the center, marked like a smithy's brand, was a DE, identical to the tea set's. The D'Eathe mark.

"It must be," she said. "There are still pockets of magic about, from when the High King lived here."

It should have frightened her, thinking of the palace as once evil and magicked, with the candelabras and ceiling murals alive, but it didn't. It was hard to be frightened of a building that smelled of old toast. Once, Azalea guessed, it had been intimidating and grand, with magic walls you could walk through and flues that didn't have birds nesting in them. When the High King was killed— first poisoned, several times, then shot with pistols, then his head cut off, then burned in the great palace fire . . . no one really liked to talk about it—Harold the First had somehow unmagicked the palace, rebuilt it, and made it a decent home to live in.

Only bits of magic remained. Like the tea set, and the tower.

"My father used to speak of the magic in the palace," said Lord Bradford, walking to the tiny fireplace on the side of the platform. Azalea could feel the floorboards beneath her feet move with each of his steps. "He said when they were boys, he and your father used to play together in the magic passages."

Azalea's eyebrows rose.

How odd to think of the King playing. Or even as a boy. But as Lord Bradford took a small shovel from the hearth stand and walked back to her, the floorboards creaking again, Azalea said, "Magic passages? Here? In our palace?"

Lord Bradford smiled a small, crooked smile, and leaned to her conspiratorially, underneath the slow-turning rod. Azalea drew closer, and caught the scent of linen and a touch of pine.

"That mark, the D'Eathe mark, when it's on brick, marks a hidden passage. Did you know that? You can open it by rubbing silver on it."

"Really!" said Azalea.

"If I recall, though, he said they were only used as storage rooms now." Lord Bradford shrugged apologetically. "Unexciting, I'm afraid."

Azalea nodded but shelved this piece of information in the back of her mind.

With the task at hand and still holding the shovel, Lord Bradford slipped up a small set of ladder stairs to the bells-and-gears platform, just above her. The mass of machinery and creaking gears hid him, and Azalea bit her lip and curled her toes in her boots. Far too soon, a gritty, rusty squeaking seized the air. And then silence fell. The ticking halted. Azalea reached up and touched the clock-hand rod, feeling her stomach turn as the rod did not.

Lord Bradford emerged from the gears without the shovel, his face sober again. Azalea, eager to leave, led him down the stairs.

He seemed to sense she was not in the mood for conversation and kept a solemn silence between them.

Azalea stopped when a thump sounded and Lord Bradford gave a soft "Oo."

"Are you all right?" said Azalea.

"Um, yes," he said after a pause.

"Attack!"

The battle cry echoed throughout the tower, making the bells reverberate. Bramble's voice! At once potatoes flew through the air. *Thump! Thump! Thump-thump!* In the dim light at the bottom of the stairs were all the girls, their skirts pulled up like baskets as they threw. Potatoes rained, hitting brick walls, the spindly railing, thumping against the wood floor, and hitting Lord Bradford. He blocked them dexterously with his arm.

"Have you all run mad?" cried Azalea. "Stop at once—ow!"

A potato boffed her on the side of her head. Delphinium

lobbed another one, which Lord Bradford caught in his tall hat before it hit her.

"What are you doing?" said Azalea, running down the remaining steps. "Eve! Flora and Goldenrod! And Clover—not *you*!"

Clover, who had not thrown anything at all, stepped back, blushing to tears.

"And *you*," said Azalea, turning on Bramble. "What are you, *three*?"

Bramble at least had the decency to look ashamed. For about two seconds. Then she raised her chin, coloring angrily.

"We can't just do nothing," she said. "If he doesn't start the tower again, we'll never be on time for anything, and if we're never on time—"

"The King will be even crosser than he was before!" said Delphinium.

"He's leaving for war soon and we may never even see him again." Goldenrod's voice broke.

Once again, Azalea stood in the midst of girls, the familiar chin wobbles and wet cheeks overcoming them. Jessamine curled up on the floor, her lacy pantelettes poking up in black ruffles, and began to wail in a tiny crystalline voice.

"I have a watch."

Azalea started, remembering Lord Bradford. He

stepped to the bottom of the stairs and offered his hand
to Azalea. On it lay a gold watch, chain, and fob.

"Please take it," he said. "You can keep it in your
pocket, hidden away for mourning, and you can still keep
time."

Azalea could tell it was an heirloom. The gold between
the ornamental swirls had been worn down to black.

"We can't take that," said Azalea.

Bramble snatched the pocket watch from his hand
and drew back, holding it against her chest.

"You—!" Azalea made to fetch it back, but Bramble
pulled far out of her grasp.

"We're keeping it for ransom," said Bramble. "You
can have it back when you set the tower."

Lord Bradford bowed. "As you say," he said.

"It's ours until then."

"Just so."

"You can't get it back until then."

"As you say."

"And—and—well—all right, then," said Bramble.

Sick with embarrassment, Azalea picked up the
potatoes while the younger girls crowded about Bramble,
who showed them how a pocket watch wound and
clicked open and shut. Not until everything had been
tidied did Azalea realize Lord Bradford was no longer
in the room.

Azalea flew out the tower door, through the hall to the entrance hall mezzanine. He was just leaving. Azalea, breathless, stopped at the top of the stairs and leaned against the banister.

"Sir," she called out. "Lord Bradford."

He turned. His eyes lit up, seeing Azalea.

"Thank you," said Azalea.

Lord Bradford bowed deeply, removing his hat, which re-rumpled his hair. When he straightened, he was smiling, as crooked as his cravat, and Azalea couldn't help but smile back.

CHAPTER 5

The funeral was the next day. The princesses huddled together beside the grave, as far away from the stone as they could without being disrespectful. The graveyard was filled to the brim with mourners, overflowing to the street, all in black suits, black veils and bonnets. Horses for the procession had been brushed with black dye; streetlamps swathed with black fabric. Everything, black.

Snow fell, stark pieces of white against the scene.

The King stood across the grave from them, with members of parliament. He kept his hands firmly to his sides and sucked in his cheeks, which he did when he was displeased. He did not look at the grave. He did not look at them. He looked at . . . nothing.

Prayers said, pine boughs, holly, and mistletoe placed on the grave, and the masses of people sifted out the rickety gate. A luncheon for family and parliament members would be held afterward, at a coffeehouse. The King left with the mourners, without a word. He hadn't even cried. Azalea tried to keep her nails from digging into her palms. They still stung from yesterday.

The girls remained behind until the graveyard became empty and desolate. They stared at the weeping angel statue. Snow landed on their hair, bits of white against their heads of red, gold, and brown, melting to droplets in the silence.

"They'll miss us," said Azalea, after a while. "And we'll eat with the King. He has to, if there are guests. That's the rule."

The girls kept silent, clutching their cloaks and shawls tightly around their shoulders, shivering.

"Miss Azalea."

Azalea turned to see Fairweller, looking graver than usual. He motioned to a small path through the gravestones and trees, hat in hand.

"If you will walk with me?"

Azalea walked through the frozen twigs and frosted leaves with him, feeling the girls' curious eyes follow her. She winced a little, thinking of all the endless teasing this would produce. Fairweller, handsome, young, disagreeable as hornets. He smelled like peppermints.

"The Delchastrian prime minister was here," said

Fairweller at length. The snow crunched beneath his feet. "At the funeral. Did you see him?"

Azalea recalled the bearded man with a monocle, and nodded.

"You know that Delchastire has, for some time, been pushing us to fulfill our alliance in their current skirmish, and that your father—and I, and the regiments—will be leaving for war soon?"

Azalea stopped abruptly. Her skirts upset the snow at the side of the path.

"He's not leaving now?" she said.

Fairweller nodded, grave. "They gave him leave enough for your mother, but now he must tend to duty. The regiments may leave as soon as tomorrow, before the next storm sets in. I thought you should know before the papers do."

Azalea was speechless. Mother had always been the one to tell her such things before, and smooth everything over. Hearing it from Fairweller added iciness to the wind. Azalea pulled her shawl closer.

"That's so soon," she said. "Surely he doesn't have to leave yet? What about mourning?'

Fairweller gave a slight shake of his head. "Politics is notoriously unfeeling," he said.

"But he's the king! He doesn't even have to go! The Delchastrian king won't, surely!"

Fairweller reached above him and snapped an icy twig from its branch. He considered it in his gloved hands before speaking.

"There is an old magic," he said slowly. "A deep one, made of promises. It hearkens back to the High King D'Eathe, and the first Captain General. Your father swore such an oath to Delchastire when we made this alliance. We all did. It cannot be taken lightly."

"He swore an oath," said Azalea, in an empty, hollow voice.

"As such, we must go. If it is any comfort, my lady, I do not believe it will be a long war. Less than a year, surely."

Azalea leaned against the trunk of a frozen tree, trying for the umpteenth time not to cry. Fairweller's gray eyes, colorless like the rest of him, considered her, and after a long moment, he bowed. He left through the iron gate a length away.

The bushes behind her rustled, not from the wind. Azalea stared at the snow-packed ground, and sighed.

"You can come out now," she said.

Sisters emerged with hardly a sound from behind the tombstones and naked trees where they'd been hiding. They looked at Azalea with wide and frightened eyes. Clover clutched Lily to her chest. They remained quiet, all except eleven-year-old Eve, who scooped up snow, fashioned it into a snowball, and pelted Mother's weeping angel statue. *Piff.*

"I hate that statue!" she said. "It doesn't look like an angel at all!" *Piff.* "She looks like she's choking on a spoon!" *Piff.*

"Eve," said Azalea. Eve hiccupped, took off her spectacles, and rubbed her eyes with a red hand.

They all stood, miserable and still, their hair whipping about in the wind, now gusting. Azalea took a breath.

"Flora," she said. "Goldenrod, can you do a mazurka step? Do it right here."

Flora sniffed and shook her head.

"It's not so hard," said Azalea. "Just try it. It's all right, you can do it here. No one will see you."

Flora tried halfheartedly. She stepped back, quarter turned, but stepped on the wrong foot over and lost the step. Her chin wobbled.

"I can't do anything in these boots," she said. "They're too stiff."

"That was good!" Azalea lined the twins up next to her. "You had it halfway. Break it apart. Come along, Goldy. Left foot first, step back. Turn, good, hop right, slide-turn together. Good!"

"We did it!" cried Flora. She did the step again, her light brown braid bouncing with each hop. Goldrenrod echoed her steps.

"It's easy!" said Goldenrod.

"You both learn so quickly," said Azalea, smiling. "Let's all try it, in a reel. Join hands. Holli, Ivy, you younger ones, just do the basic step. All right?"

None of the girls objected, not even Eve, who almost smiled and said, "We must be breaking at least fifty rules." They joined hands, Clover stooping to link her free hand with Kale. In the snow, trying to ignore the tombstones about them, they began. Step, slide, together, forward. They touched hands together in the center, then broke apart, gave a clap.

The rhythm caught quickly. Azalea found herself forgetting about the wind and the cold, and dancing in a graveyard or even in mourning, about how wearing stiff boots hurt when she danced, and instead felt the familiar thrill flutter through her chest. The warm flickery bit. All the girls smiled now.

Just as Azalea began the next quarter turn, the girls broke apart. They crowded behind Azalea, ruining the dance, then folded their hands and looked to the ground.

"What's wrong?" said Azalea. "You were lovely." Frowning, she turned around—to see none other than the King over her.

The dance was knocked from her. Azalea stumbled back.

"Sir!" she said.

The King opened his mouth, then shut it. Then opened it again.

"What are you doing?" he said.

"Oh," Azalea stammered. "Just . . . dancing, actually."

"Yes, I can see that," said the King.

The girls shuffled their feet in the snow.

"We were quiet about it," chirped Hollyhock. "Quieter than crickets!"

The King scratched his head distractedly. Up close he looked so tired and worn, the little lines around his eyes deeper than Azalea remembered, as was the wrinkle between his eyebrows.

"Don't be cross," said Azalea. "It's all right, truly— no one saw us."

"Just because no one sees or hears, that does not mean it is all *right*," said the King. He took Azalea by the shoulders, firmly enough that it made Azalea cringe.

"Mourning," said the King, "is meant to show the grief inside us. Dancing dishonors your mother's memory. It is badly done, Azalea! As the future queen, you should know better! *Badly* done!"

The reprimand stung. Azalea suddenly felt how cold the wind was, and how it bit her face. She turned her head.

"Go home," said the King, releasing her and rubbing his hand across his face. "All of you. At once, before it storms."

That evening, Azalea argued with her sisters. Very rarely did they argue, but tempers were high, and they had been made to eat dinner in their room, a cramped and stifling punishment. Rain pattered against the windows, and dripped into a bowl on the table from the leaky roof. The girls huddled around the massive fireplace, faces pinched as they sipped mushroom soup. At least the soup was hot.

"I just think we should all apologize," said Azalea. She buttered another leftover-from-the-luncheon roll for Ivy, who grasped it eagerly. "Even if we don't agree with him. We can't leave it like this."

"I just think it's rum," said Bramble, rubbing her hands against her steaming bowl. "The first time he speaks to us in days, and he yells at us."

"He'll speak to us before he leaves," said Azalea. "He has to. It's rule number twenty-one. You remember? Giving a formal good-bye. We always line up in the entrance hall before he leaves on extended R.B."

Bramble smiled a thin, grim smile.

"Eating with a family was also a rule," she said.

Delphinium's lips, throughout the exchange, became

tighter and more pursed. She kept casting glances at Eve, who had been drawn and silent all evening. Eve sat on the edge of her bed and let out the strangled noise of crying while trying not to cry.

"Eve?" said Azalea.

Eve toyed with her spectacles in her lap.

"All right," said Azalea. "Delphinium?"

Delphinium raised her pointed chin, casting a stubborn, defiant look. Eve swallowed and spoke.

"He won't say good-bye," she said. Her dark blue eyes remained focused on her spectacles. "He'll leave without even coming to see us."

Everyone looked at each other, then at Azalea. Azalea's brows creased.

"Now, Eve—"

"She's right," said Delphinium, tossing her wadded-up napkin to the ground. "Oh, crabskins. I can't believe you all haven't figured it out yet. Eve and I figured it out two days ago!"

"What are you talking about?"

"The King," said Eve. "He doesn't—" She tugged on the ends of her thick dark hair. Delphinium stepped in.

"He doesn't love us," said Delphinium. "And he doesn't want us."

She was so pale, Azalea wondered if she actually would faint, instead of just feigning it. Hollyhock, Ivy, and the twins looked from Azalea to Delphinium, their eyes wide. Azalea crossed her arms.

"What? Of course he loves us," she said. "Of course he does. Delphinium, really."

"He—he would eat meals with us," said Flora bravely. "And—and he let us have dance slippers, for lessons."

"He ate meals and gave us dance slippers," said Delphinium, "because Mother was here and she wanted him to. Can't you *see*? The only time he *ever* paid any attention to us was if Mother wanted him to. Now that Mother's gone, why would he care? He's probably glad he's leaving."

"Delphinium—"

"Lea?" said Flora.

Azalea stacked the empty bowls together so hard they knocked together. She told herself she didn't have favorite sisters, but if she did, Delphinium would not be one of them.

"It's nonsense," said Azalea. "Bramble doesn't believe it, either."

"Well, Az." Bramble tapped her spoon against the rim of her bowl. "He hasn't made a great show of loving us."

Azalea set the bowls down on the table with a clatter. "You too? How could you all think such a terrible thing? He—he wanted to open the ball with me, remember?"

"Because Mother told him to," Delphinium whispered.

"And he left you with Fairweller."

Azalea threw a spoon at Delphinium—it missed and hit the drapes of the window seat behind her—and she turned hard, her skirts swishing behind her. She strode to the door.

"I'll go fetch him, and bring him up now," she said, her hand grasping the latch so tightly her hand throbbed. "You'll see. It's not true! You'll see!"

The door was open when Azalea reached the library. She knocked on the wainscot next to the doorframe, and peeked in.

A figure hunkered over the King's desk. Azalea, disappointed, saw it was not the King, but Mr. Pudding. He was wrapping books in cloth, in his slow, elderly sort of way, and smiled when Azalea came in.

"Miss!" he said. "It's dropping chill, miss."

"Where is the King?" said Azalea.

Mr. Pudding's smile faded, and he couldn't seem to meet her eyes.

"He's left, miss. Off to th' port."

Azalea's nails dug into her palms; something hard tangled in her throat.

"He didn't!" she said.

"He said he didn't want to disturb, what with the bustle and upset of business and such, miss. Er . . . miss . . ."

Azalea swept from the library, her knuckles ghost white.

Azalea knew, in her subconscious mind, that what she was doing was quite stupid. She disliked horses, yet managed to saddle Thackeray with a side saddle by herself, and now jostled upon him to the port. Azalea hated riding. Dancing was easier, and it couldn't buck you off. It also didn't smell so . . . horsey.

In her fervor, Azalea had forgotten a cloak. The freezing sleet soaked her thoroughly. She hardly noticed it. Hot, burning blood flooded through her, and it kept out the chill.

The port wasn't far. All the ships docked and managed their trade at the Rosings River, which ran through the city. Pinpricks of streetlamp lights grew larger as Azalea neared the dock. By this time she had lost the reins, which dangled and whipped about, and she grasped for dear life to Thackeray's mane. Sleet cut in drifts as Thackeray's hoofs clattered onto the wooden planks.

In spite of the weather, the port hustled with activity. Dozens of men led soaked horses up a ship's plank, and loading cranes lowered nets of crates onto other ships. Azalea caught the smell of wet, old wood and saw Fairweller in the distance, before she heard the King shouting orders. She wove through the mass of cavalrymen and horses.

"Sir!" Azalea yelled. She pushed her horse into a graceless canter to the King, some lengths away, but lost her balance on the saddle and fell as Thackeray pulled up next to Dickens. She grabbed at the satchel hanging over Dickens's back and discovered, as it clanged to the ground, that it was the silver sword.

The sword was a dull, dented, mottled thing with a swirled cage handle, and it usually lay in a case in the portrait gallery. The King brought it to speeches and parades, because it had been owned by Harold the First, and had Historical Importance. Azalea realized he would be taking it with him to the war, too.

"Azalea!" Two sturdy hands helped Azalea from the wet wood to her feet. The hands turned her around, and Azalea found herself face-to-face with the King, worry lining his brow. "For heaven's sake! You haven't even a cloak."

"I didn't think of it," said Azalea, realizing that she shook. Her black dress clung to her, wet through.

The King unbuttoned his thick-weave coat, pulled it off, and slung it over Azalea's shoulders. It encased her so heavily she nearly buckled underneath it. He then lifted the sword from the planks and inspected it, frowning.

"You've put a crack in it," said the King, showing her a tiny hairline mark before slipping it back into its satchel sheath. "This is governmental property, Azalea. What are you doing here?"

"You're leaving," said Azalea between shivers. "You didn't even say good-bye! The girls—"

Shouting interrupted her, men yelling to the King about load lines, splitting regiments, supplies. The smell of wet horse, the words the King shouted back, the creaking of the poles and hooves on the planks—all felt foreign to her. Azalea grasped the King's coat about her neck, tightly, and the boiling hotness escaped to her tongue.

"You can't leave yet!" she said. "Rule number twenty-one! We have rules!"

The King turned to her, his fine red uniform now black from the rain. Lightning flashed, casting harsh shadows across his face. "I cannot leave the men here, Azalea! They need their general."

"If you don't come," said Azalea, "the girls will think that you . . . that you don't—*please*, sir, you've got to come and say good-bye!"

"Minister Fairweller," the King called out. "Minister, escort Azalea back to the palace. And for heaven's sake, don't let her fall off!"

In a moment, the King had lifted Azalea back onto Thackeray and handed the reins to Fairweller, who had pulled astride on his pure white horse, LadyFair.

A teakettle screamed inside Azalea, burning her fingers, making her throat tight and her head dizzy. Fairweller led her off the dock, LadyFair's tail twitching and bobbing in front of her. Fairweller, thankfully, remained silent.

The anger that burned in Azalea was so acute, so searing, that her hands acted of their own accord. Azalea leaned forward, and before Fairweller had fully escorted her onto the cobblestone street, she yanked the reins from his hand.

"My lady!" said Fairweller. She left him behind at a gallop.

"So!" cried Azalea through the pounding sleet as hoofs clattered back over the wood. "So!" She pulled up to the King, so hard that Thackeray skidded.

The King looked up from the reins in his hand. His eyebrows rose at her, then furrowed.

"Azalea—" he said. Azalea cut him off.

"You *knew* how much we thought of you! You could have at least—at least *acted* like you cared!"

She pulled his overcoat from her shoulders, and wadded it into a heavy, wet ball.

"Shame on us for giving our affections to someone so undeserving. If you don't want us, then—fine! We don't want *you*!"

She threw the coat with all her might at the King. It fell only a foot from her in a soggy pile on the platform.

"Good-*bye*!" she said.

She jerked Thackeray around and pushed him into a hard gallop, away from the port, through the slick streets, back to the palace. A marvelous, euphoric feeling fired her to her fingertips and cheeks, and she almost laughed with a sheer, angry giddiness.

By the time Thackeray had reached the palace gate, though, the blaze had faded to a dull throb, the giddiness to hurt. She turned the horse about and stared down at the sliver of river, lit by the pinpricks of port lamps. The sleet melted on her face and weighed her down to exhaustion.

"Good-bye," she said.

CHAPTER 6

"*M*asterful!" Mother laughed. "You're better than me! Up, up, up. Very good! Ladies' cloaks, in the library, gentleman's hats—"

"In the entrance hall. Yes, I remember." Azalea stood and smoothed her skirts.

"Brilliant. The gentleman will be mad for you."

"I wish you could come," said Azalea.

"Your father will be there."

"Actually, no," said Azalea. "He'll be up here with you. I'll end up dancing with ghastly Fairweller."

"I beg your pardon?" said Mother.

"Great scott," said Azalea. "I'm dreaming it. Again!" And she awoke.

For a while she lay staring at the bedcurtains draped above her, her hair in auburn tendrils over the pillow.

That dream! She thought she'd gotten rid of it. She'd

not had it for at least three weeks. That was better than at first, when it came nearly twice a week, three months in a row. It was always so *real*. She could smell Mother's white-cake, medicine, and baby-ointment scent, and feel the warmth of the fire next to Mother's chair. Azalea wished she could dream about the picnics and trips to the market. Not Mother's last minutes, when she was in such pain. Azalea hated thinking of Mother in pain.

And yet Azalea wished she could have made the dream last longer.

Fumbling for Lord Bradford's watch in her nightgown pocket, Azalea clicked it open, feeling grateful for it all over again. With the windows hidden behind black drapery, even daytime in the palace felt like night.

Still early. Azalea tucked the blanket around Kale, her bedmate, and made certain Lily slept in her bassinet, then slipped from the room.

Although it was June, the ballroom's marble floor was cool against Azalea's bare feet. The lamp she held made the chandeliers glimmer and reflected back from the mirrors. She set the lamp down and curtsied deeply to her reflection, pointing her back toe, lifting her arm out. She loved the stretch and pull of her legs when she danced. She lifted herself onto her toes and released into a spin, feeling her nightgown breeze around her, fixing her view on the far wall through each turn, her feet turning, her head turning faster, stopping at each rotation as her body swirled beneath her.

"Y-you look beautiful."

Azalea eased out of the spin into a curtsy, then straightened to see Clover at the doors, holding Kale in her arms. The outlines of sleepy girls in nightgowns appeared behind them.

"Good morning," said Azalea, smiling. "Early morning. Did Kale wake you?"

"Good guess," said Bramble. She ran a hand through her tangled knee-length hair.

Azalea smiled and shook her head. Though only two, Kale had a screaming voice to shame a prima donna. In fact, once she started screaming, she only stopped if she got what she wanted, or if she threw up. Azalea lifted her from Clover's arms, and Kale latched her hands around Azalea's neck. Azalea shifted, keeping Kale's mouth from her shoulder. Kale was also a biter.

"You—you had—the dream again, didn't you?" said Clover as they all sat down around the lamp. Her golden hair reflected the lamplight. "That's—why you came down here?"

Azalea shrugged.

"M-maybe you should—should write the King about it," said Clover. "He might—know what to do."

"Have you run mad?" said Bramble. "What would he care?"

Clover gave a half shrug and lowered her eyes to her hands.

"Come now, everyone," said Azalea, straightening up. "We made an agreement. No talking about the King."

The girls clasped their hands and kept their eyes down. It reminded Azalea of when she had returned to the palace that late December night, shivering, so soaked she dripped puddles on the rug. She didn't tell the girls then. They could read it in her face. They had helped her into dry clothes and brushed and braided her wet hair, all without a sound.

Azalea didn't say anything after that, either, because the words would fester and burn, searing anyone who heard them. So they blistered and raged inside her, curling into tightness in her throat. She hid it well in front of the girls. Tiny crescent scars marked her palms.

"What were you dancing?" said Goldenrod.

"Oh, just this and that. I thought a zingarella"— Azalea smiled and said to the ceiling—"if only I could find enough people to dance it with me."

With a cry of delight, the girls jumped to their feet and Azalea lined them up, showing them how to point their toes and turn on the balls of their feet, and how to jump lightly with just a flick of their foot. A rosy pink touched their pale cheeks, and the mirrors along the wall caught their smiles as they turned, all seeming to feel the warm bit of flicker inside them. Azalea loved dancing for that glow.

"But the zingarella is a closed dance," said Delphinium, after she had executed a perfect spring-and-land in third position. "All the good dances are. I wish we were old enough to dance with gentlemen."

"Gentlemen, shmentlemen," said Azalea. "Don't you remember lessons with Mother? We danced reels and quadrilles and all sorts of things without a partner."

"But it's different, with a gentleman."

Azalea considered, thinking of the Yuletide ball and the dizzy thrill of being led in perfect form. Stepping as one with a gentleman, sweeping past the other dancers in a billow of skirts. Dancing *was* different with a gentleman.

A lamp appeared at the ballroom doors, giving highlights to the mirrors and chandeliers. Mr. Pudding, white hair mussed, held the lamp in one hand and rubbed his face with the other. Azalea realized, with all the laughing and dancing, that they had made quite a racket.

"Dancing again, misses?" he said.

Azalea gathered the girls, now yawning and dragging their feet, and herded them out the ballroom to the grand staircase.

"Now, miss, I don't think it will do, not at all," said

Mr. Pudding as Azalea nudged them up the stairs. He stood at the bottom of the staircase, holding the lamp and frowning. Mr. Pudding's frowns were nothing like the King's. Mr. Pudding's frowns were actually more *perplexes*. He cleared his throat and took a deep breath, signaling an almost-lecture-but-not-quite-because-he-was-just-the-royal-steward-and-not-the-King. "I can understand cutting about a time or two, it's not so much dancing I'm worried about, misses, even I myself would turn the other cheek when you trip about, misses, but it's against the rules and I've taken charge of ye all, y' see, and I can't let you break the rules of mourning, not even for dancing, which I know your mother loved. I'll have to lock the ballroom, misses, and I'm afraid that if I catch y' at it again, I'll feel it my duty to write your father."

The girls inhaled sharply at this last bit, the word "father." They leaned into Azalea's nightgown as Mr. Pudding, fumbling with his great ring of keys, locked the ballroom door with a *click-click*. Seeing the younger girls start to tear up, he gave them his lamp and promised to send biscuits and tea to their room, nearly crying himself. But he did not unlock the ballroom.

"I think really he means it, this time," said Delphinium as they trudged up the creaking staircase, dragging sleepy younger sisters. "He actually locked the door. And he's never threatened to write the King before."

"That lock's nearly impossible to pick," said Eve, tugging on the ends of her pretty dark hair, which she did when she was worried. "That could be a problem."

"*Our* problem is that we've been getting caught," said Azalea. She carried both Jessamine and Kale, one on each arm, and rested on the landing. She leaned against the wallpaper, underneath the dusty portraits of Great-Aunts Mugwort and Buttercup, and exhaled. Every morning these past months, when Mr. Pudding arrived with the *Harold Herald*, the girls took it from his hands and pored over it, eating their porridge and sorting through every article, hoping for news of the war. Their loyalty ended there. The King could manage himself. Clover once suggested writing him, a thought they quickly squashed. Azalea was sure her pen would snap in two if she tried.

"No more dancing," said Azalea. "We can't get caught again. This is our secret."

"He'll write the King—"

"Oh, the *King*," Azalea spat. The words burned, singeing the air. "What right has *he* to know? The King is *not* a part of this family!"

Clover cradled Lily's curly head to her chest, biting her lip. Flora and Goldenrod clasped their dainty hands in each other's. Azalea tried to soften her words, but words from a tight throat could only come out taut.

"He's not," she said. "No need to let him know."

Tap. Tap. Clinkety tap-tap.

It had been two weeks since they had last danced, and Azalea lay in bed, awake again. A dream hadn't roused her this time, but rather an odd tinny noise that had been clinking across the wooden floor of their room, under their beds and butting against the wainscot with a *clinkety tap-tap.* It sounded like . . . well, quite honestly, it sounded like a spider dragging a spoon.

Azalea knew it couldn't possibly be that (or, rather, she hoped it wasn't), but even so, she heaved herself from the bed and grasped one of Hollyhock's boots, strewn across the floor. The tapping now clinked from the fireplace, and Azalea caught a glint of silver among the soot. Raising the boot, she tiptoed to the unlit hearth.

The fireplace in their room was massive—so large that Azalea could stand up in it and her skirts wouldn't brush the sides. The silver hopped. Azalea dove.

In a puff of soot, Azalea found herself sitting in the hearth, and the silver bit skittering away like mad. Azalea grabbed at it and was rewarded with a very sharp, very *familiar* bite.

"You!" Azalea seethed, leaping up. Now she recognized the half-hopping half-skitter motion. The sugar teeth! Azalea sprang and laid a heavy foot on the teeth. They struggled beneath her bare foot like a mouse in a trap.

Still in the hearth, soot streaking her nightgown, Azalea grasped the sugar teeth tightly, so they wouldn't nip her, and examined them. They had been dented and were now black with soot. Azalea wondered what they were doing about, wandering the palace on their own. Normally they wouldn't leave sight of the rest of the magic tea set in the kitchen, clanking against the cream bowl and flicking sugar cubes at anyone who happened to pass by. Come to think of it, Azalea hadn't seen that tea set for several months, at least. She leaned against the fireplace brick wall, wondering where it had gone.

And then she pulled away from the fireplace wall, because the brick her shoulder had leaned against was curiously uneven. Forgetting the sugar teeth—which hopped out of her hand and skittered away—she traced her fingers over the etching. It was hardly visible in the dim light, and covered in soot. In fact, because of the shape of the mantel, unless one actually stood in the fireplace, one wouldn't see it.

Azalea's heart pounded against her nightgown. She brushed the soot away from the brick. Her fingers shook. The form of the etching grew discernible—a half-moon D, with three lines slashed through the middle.

A *magic passage*!

CHAPTER 7

*A*zalea stared at the wall. Her heart beat in her ears.

A magic passage! In their *room*! She tried to remember everything Lord Bradford had said about passages, those months ago. The King used them as storage rooms now, yes, but, well, magic was magic! Azalea wondered how large this room was. If it didn't have too many trunks or boxes about the sides, could it possibly be large enough to—

Azalea curled her toes in the soot, aching to leap in the air.

How had Lord Bradford said to open it? Rubbing silver on it. Well, that was fortunate! Azalea cast her eyes about for the silver teeth and found them sitting at the edge of the rug.

"Come along," she said, in her nicest whisper. "I won't hurt you."

The sugar teeth skittered away.

"You rotten little—" Azalea started to go after them, pulling Mother's handkerchief from her pocket to protect herself from the bite—and then stopped.

The silver glimmer of the handkerchief always caught her off guard. A light tingling sensation washed over her, and Azalea held up the piece of silver fabric, smiling. The King had given this to Mother years ago, embroidered with her initials and the color of the royal family. Though the fibers were soft and pliable, like linen, it was made of actual silver thread.

Stepping back into the hearth, Azalea touched the handkerchief to the DE mark. She paused, wholly unsure of what it would do. Even so, excitement tickled her fingers. She rubbed the handkerchief against the brick.

At first, nothing happened. Azalea's arm grew tired. Half a minute of rubbing, and just as she was about to give up, the mark grew warm. Then hot, then it burned through the handkerchief to her fingers. Azalea pulled away sharply.

The DE symbol glowed silver. Azalea gasped. The mortar around the bricks began to shine, spreading the molten silver light to the other bricks, so bright that Azalea shielded her eyes. The silver seeped across the wall to form a tall arch edged with glowing swirls and leaves.

The light burst.

It took several moments for Azalea to be able to see again. When she could, her breath was stolen. The fireplace wall had transformed to an arched doorway, edges glowing with ivied curls and leaves. A thin curtain of silver sheen billowed gently in the archway, gossamer drapery in a slight breeze.

A *tink tink tappety* startled Azalea, and she found the soot-covered sugar teeth at her feet. They leaped up and tugged on the hem of her skirt.

"Shh, go away," Azalea whispered, casting a glance at her sisters' beds.

The teeth dropped to the ground, the metal squeaking. It almost sounded like a whimper.

"Oh, *now* you want to come?" said Azalea.

The teeth hopped around madly.

"Oh . . . very well. But you have to *behave*." Azalea scooped them up into her pocket, and hesitated. She knew that all she would find was, perhaps, old furniture and books, but . . . still. Casting a glance back at the beds, and seeing the bedsheets stirring, Azalea threw hesitations aside, took a deep breath, and stepped into the glowing, glimmering silver.

It felt as though she had stepped into a silver waterfall, ice cold, washing over her head and shoulders. An inside-of-a-teapot smell suffocated her. Another step, and Azalea inhaled a breath of fresh air. Shivering, she shook away the tendrils of twinkling light and rubbed her arms.

She stood on a small wooden landing, about the size of the fireplace. In front of her, stairs curved downward. Azalea swallowed, pressed her hand against the brick wall, and began to descend. The rickety wood creaked underneath her bare feet, and darkness enveloped her. Her hands shook as she felt her way about. She wished she had brought the lamp.

A hard, scuffing sound shattered the silence. Azalea cried out.

"Stop, stop, *stop*," came a voice from above her. "Really, Az, you're as bad as Kale!"

Light filled the passage, and relief flooded through Azalea as Bramble emerged around the corner, holding Lily and grinning a wry, delighted grin.

With more thumphing and scuffing down the creaky stairs, all eleven of Azalea's sisters appeared around the bend, sleep in their feet, but mouths open and faces alight. Clover was the only one with enough sense to bring the lamp.

"The room burst with light," said Bramble. "It was like waking to a sunrise—and we haven't seen that in months. Az . . . the fireplace wall—"

"I know," said Azalea. "Can you believe it?"

The girls huddled closer to Azalea, and as they crowded about the lamp, she told them what Lord Bradford had said about magic passages. She told them about the sugar teeth, escaped from the kitchen cabinet and caught in their room, and using the silver handkerchief to open the wall. The girls' eyes, already wide, grew wider with fascination.

"I should have woken you all," said Azalea when she finished. "I was too eager to wait, I suppose. But I'm glad the passage stayed open for you. Is it still?"

"No," said Eve. "It's solid now."

"The mark is on this side, too," said Bramble. "I suppose we'll give it a rub when we need to get out." She shivered, looking at the brick around her. "I wouldn't want to be trapped in this place."

"Where does it lead?" said Flora.

"I don't know." Azalea peered into the darkness, into the curve of more stairs. "Probably it's just a storage room, but it might have bits of magic left to it, like the tower. Want to find out?"

"*Yes!*"

Clover handed Azalea the lamp, and Azalea led them down the stairs, holding it high. The staircase descended much farther than she expected, and only after several lengthy minutes did the passage lighten. They turned the next curve, revealing an archway below. A soft, silver light emanated from it. Azalea's brows furrowed. Bright moonlight? Indoors?

The girls stayed back as Azalea descended to the doorway. Hands quavering, she leaned against the edge and looked.

She stepped back, dumbfounded.

The scene washed over Azalea like a crystal symphony. A *forest*.

But nothing like the wood behind the palace! Every bough, branch, leaf, and ivied tendril looked as though it had been frosted in silver. It shimmered in the soft, misty light.

Azalea inhaled, catching the muted scent of a morning fog, with a touch of pine, and stepped through the doorway into the bright forest. Everything sparkled in bits, catching highlights in glisters as she moved. Even the path beneath her feet. She turned to a glass-spun tree on her left. Silver ornaments glowed among the delicate silver leaves—glimmering glass plums. Azalea touched one. Its edging glittered as it swayed. Next to the ornament, strings of pearls swathed each branch in swooping arcs.

"It's so beautiful," whispered Flora. The girls had followed Azalea through the doorway, their voices hushed.

"Like winter, when the snow's just fallen," Goldenrod whispered.

"Or . . . the Yuletide trees," said Clover.

Azalea thought it looked a mix of all of them—the

gardens, the palace, and the Yuletide—all mixed into one and dipped in silver.

"Az, what is this place?" Bramble looked up, gaping. The tallest of the silver trees disappeared into a mist.

"I think it's the palace," Azalea managed to say.

Bramble arched a thin red eyebrow, grinning. "Not *our* boot-blackened palace! No wonder we were never told about this passage—we'd never come back up!"

Bramble was right. Azalea touched a swath of ribbon and pearls, feeling the knobbly string between her fingers. She hadn't expected to find so much magic, and all beneath their room!

The girls slowly walked down the path; everything was quiet, muffled, as though in a snowfall. Every so often, Azalea reached out to touch a silver-white branch or a teardrop ornament, just to remind herself she wasn't dreaming.

Ahead, the silver branches of a large willow tree curtained the end of the path. Nearing it, they heard the tinkling of a music box playing faintly in the air. Quiet as it was, all the girls looked about them, eyebrows raised. When they drew closer, the timbre of the music changed. It became fuller, fleshing to a soft three-quarter-time orchestral melody. Azalea's feet itched to twirl.

"It's coming from beyond the willow," Delphinium whispered.

Azalea stepped to the glistening silver leaves. She slipped her hand between the branches and parted them.

The girls gasped.

The path did not end. It rose into a dainty arched bridge, leading to the center of a silver-lilac pond. The water cast dancing white reflections all about the bridge.

And, at the end of the bridge, silver vines curling over white latticework and reaching to the top of its domed roof, stood a pavilion. Filled with *dancers*!

Ladies, dressed in bright silks and chiffons billowing with each step. They spun and twirled, their colorfully dressed partners taking their hands and sweeping them into the dance.

Azalea pulled away from the willow branches, and they fell back into place. Suddenly she was frightened. This was too much magic, magic Mother surely hadn't known about.

"Let's get out of here," said Azalea. "We shouldn't be here."

"What?" cried the girls.

"I beg your pardon," said Bramble. "*We* shouldn't be here? What about *them*? Cutting about in *our* palace? Why weren't we jolly well invited?"

"Who are they?" Clover stammered.

"I don't know," said Azalea. "But it doesn't feel right." She suddenly wished they hadn't come.

"*I* want to get a closer look!" said Delphinium, and she pushed past Azalea, through the willow leaves before Azalea could even start to grab her back.

"Me, too!" cried Hollyhock.

Azalea grasped her arm, but Hollyhock writhed free and ran after Delphinium. In a rush, all the girls ran past Azalea, disappearing through the willow leaves. Panicked, Azalea dove through the silver after them, over the arched bridge.

To her relief, however, the girls didn't leap up the pure white stairs to the dance floor, but instead scampered into the bushes about the outside, making them rustle with a faint clinking sound. Azalea only had a moment of shock before Bramble burst from the silver leaves, grabbed Azalea about the waist, and yanked her in. In a whirl of silver Azalea found herself on her back in a patch of silver-spun rose bushes. A branch dug into her spine. The girls grinned down at her.

"Just like old times," said Bramble, grinning and pulling Azalea partly up. "We'll call this one the Great Leftover D'Eathe Magic Scandal."

"How about the Great We're Going To Get Caught Scandal?" Azalea whispered crossly.

"Oh, *do* stop whining," said Delphinium as they nudged her to the edge of the pavilion among the foliage, abloom with silver roses and pearls. "Have you ever seen such dancing in all your life?"

Kneeling up and peeking through the lattice, Azalea's temper dissolved. She inhaled the scene like a sugar dessert. The ladies wore dresses she only dreamed of, brocade and gold trim, with towering white plumed wigs. The gentlemen wore frilled cravats about their necks and brightly colored waistcoats. Nothing like the conservative, boring black suits of Eathesburian gentlemen.

"Are they real?" Eve whispered. "It feels almost . . . hollow."

The girls ducked as a couple swished near the ledge. The lady's massive skirts should have caused a breeze, but Azalea felt nothing.

"Magic," she whispered.

"Magic or not," Delphinium whispered, "we really should have been invited to this. It's *our* palace, after all."

Azalea felt a tug on her nightgown sleeve and found Ivy pointing with insistence to the dessert table at the far side of the pavilion. It had been set with iced buns, treacle tarts, candied plums, chocolate-dipped strawberries, linen napkins with lace at the edges. A dark-gloved hand plucked one of the napkins from the pile, and Azalea's heart stopped.

A gentleman stood there, by the table. He was dressed all in black. Not boring black, but *dashing* black. One so smooth that stars would have gotten lost in it. He wore a costume of a long waistcoat and a sweeping cloak that brushed the edge of the marble.

It complemented his face, a specter of high cheekbones with hints of long dimples. His midnight hair had been pulled back into a ponytail, and his eyes—even across the distance—blazed pure black. Azalea had never seen anyone so . . . beautiful.

While Azalea stared, the gentleman took the lacy napkin in his long fingers and ripped it in half. With ease, as though it was made of paper. He doubled up the pieces, halved them again, then again, until they were just tiny bits. Then he raised his hands to his lips, and blew.

The pieces fluttered, transforming into sparkling bits of snow, swirling over the dancers. The girls sighed in awe.

"Who is he?" whispered Flora and Goldenrod at the same time.

"No idea," Azalea whispered. "But he's *real*."

The gentleman's eyes swept over the scene and, in a fleeting moment, stopped on the lattice the girls peeked through. On *Azalea*.

Azalea's heart jumped in her throat, and she ducked into the bushes, pressing up against the side of the pavilion. She waited for her heartbeat to slow down enough that she could distinguish the beats from one another, then dared another peek through the lattice.

This time, her eyes met black boots. She bit back a gasp and craned her neck.

The gentleman was leaning on the railing, looking into the distance. He hadn't seen them! Azalea covered Lily's tiny mouth as they all stared up at him, frozen.

The gentleman released a sigh. A long, sad sigh, as though torn from the depths of his soul. Then, abruptly, he walked away. The girls exhaled.

"That," whispered Bramble, "was close."

"Let's get out of here."

This time no one argued. They crawled to the bridge and were nearly to the steps, when Azalea glanced up at the dancers one last time—

And saw Ivy among them.

She stood just next to the dessert table and had helped herself to a plate, a napkin, and every goody she could reach. She beamed as she piled cream bun after chocolate roll on her already-stacked plate. No one had noticed her, either, not even the gentleman, who stood at the other side of the pavilion, taking a dancer's hand. Her small white-nightgowned form blended in with the tablecloth.

"Oh, no," whispered Delphinium. "No no *no!*"

"Blast it, Ivy, do you always have to *eat*?" seethed Bramble.

Azalea stood as high as she dared and tried to catch

Ivy's eye. It seemed to take hours. Ivy hummed and licked her lips and picked up a dough ball that had rolled off her plate.

When Ivy *did* finally look over at the entrance, Azalea motioned desperately. Ivy blinked, nodded at Azalea, set her plate on the floor, took the hem of her nightgown, and brought it up so it made a basket. Her chubby little legs skipped to the table, where she proceeded to gather enough food in her nightgown to share with all of them.

"No, Ivy, *no*," Azalea moaned. "That was a *come here* motion!"

And then Ivy, her skirt heavy and swinging with foodstuffs, walked *straight across the dance floor.*

"They might not see her," whispered Delphinium. "They might not. She's small enough—"

The dancers screamed.

Skirts rustled, heels clattered against the marble, masking the entrance. The music-box orchestra clicked and ground to a stop, as though something had caught in the gears. In all the frenzy and billow of skirts, Azalea heard Ivy's tiny five-year-old voice cry:

"Lea!"

Azalea sprung.

"Over the bridge!" she yelled. The girls untangled themselves from the bushes, tripping over one another as they fled. Azalea leaped up the pavilion stairs and shoved her way through the dancers, who screamed again. Ivy stood in the middle of the floor, clutching her nightgown hem to her chest, her chin quivering.

Azalea skidded to Ivy and grabbed her around the middle, scattering tarts everywhere. Ivy let out a cry. Azalea *ran*. Her soot-streaked nightgown flapped against her legs and her hair streamed out behind her as she dashed to the entrance. The dancers backed away—

—and *disappeared*.

"My lady! Wait!"

Azalea rushed down the stairs and stumbled to the bridge.

"Please, my lady!"

She careened into the girls at the arch of the bridge, and they scrambled to find their footing.

"If you don't stop, I'll make you stop."

Azalea dared a glance back at the gentleman. Kneeling on the stairs, he dipped a gloved hand into the water.

A rushing, gushing pouring rumbled through the mist.

The girls shrieked as water streamed and frothed over the lower ends of the bridge. They fled back to the middle arc, water surging past the willow branches and lapping at their heels. In just seconds, the lake rose to the top of the pavilion stair, enveloping the silver rosebushes and locking the girls on the bridge's arched center.

The water settled. The willow branches floated. The girls huddled to Azalea.

"I said *please*." The gentleman stood. He was breathless, pale, as though he had exerted himself to sickness. He leaned against the doorway lattice, panting. "Aren't you supposed to do what I say, when I say *please*?" He removed his wet glove, finger by finger, then wrung it out. Drops plinked into the lake.

"This is my only pair," he said. "I do hope you're happy."

Azalea opened her mouth to stammer out an apology, or a cry, or anything, but the words caught in her throat. The younger girls clung to her nightgown skirt. The gentleman, still breathless, eased into a smile, and then into the most graceful bow Azalea had ever seen. His arm swooped behind him.

He laughed as he straightened.

"My ladies," he said. "Do forgive me. Did I frighten you? Oh, dear, I must have. Look at you, all huddled together like that."

The girls kept their mouths clamped shut.

"You're pale as pearls," said the gentleman. His voice was smooth as chocolate. "You must forgive me. Only it is the first time I have seen *real* people since the High King D'Eathe."

CHAPTER 8

*T*he reflections of the rippling water danced over them, casting highlights onto the lavender mist.

"D'Eathe," Clover stammered.

"You're *old*!" said Hollyhock.

"No one can live for over two hundred years," said Eve, tugging on the ends of her dark hair. "It's impossible."

The gentleman laughed, though it had an edge to it.

"I *am* old," he said. "The inside of me is cracked and faded with dust. But I am not dead. And—I am not living, either. I am . . . undead."

The girls cast one another confused glances. Azalea remembered the stories she'd heard about the High King. He could capture the deads' souls. . . .

"It is difficult to explain," said the gentleman. "But I owe you this much. Please."

In a sleek, silky movement, the gentleman produced dainty teacups on saucers by cupping his hands together and unfolding them. Each teacup filled to the brim with tea; he slipped them into the water and blew, sending them drifting and bobbing to the girls like candles on tiny boats.

The girls scooped up the saucers from the water, all exclamations, and Ivy had slurped the last drop from her teacup before Azalea could stop her, smacking her lips with delight. Sighing, Azalea cautiously took a sip of tea. The flavor of butter and berries melted over her tongue, leaving nothing to swallow. Magic tea.

"I am a highborn gentleman," he said as they pressed the teacups between their hands. "A lord. When the High King D'Eathe reigned, I was a member of his court."

The girls inhaled a tight, hard breath, all at the same time. The gentleman smiled, tight-lipped.

"Ah, yes," he said. "I was his *friend*, even. Ah, do take heart. I am not so villainous. I was only a boy."

And then he spun a story with his smooth chocolate voice, so enthralling the girls forgot the teacups clasped in their hands and hung on every word.

Azalea imagined their small country when the gentleman had been young, with the city's streets dirt and not paved, with the wood wild and the palace new.

"I was young," he said quietly. "And a fool. The

High King had made an apprentice of me, teaching me charms and bits of magic. But he went mad, surely you know of this. When I heard of what he did to souls—" The gentleman touched a finger to a vine at the arched doorframe, tracing it, thoughtful. "Well—I joined the rebellion, naturally."

The pieces congealed in Azalea's mind. The same rebellion headed by her ninth great-grandfather, Harold the First. Azalea listened, rapt.

"It was a betrayal the High King refused to suffer." The gentleman's long fingers closed over a silver leaf and snapped it from the vine. "I was found, naturally. I was no contest for his magic. And it wasn't good enough for him to simply kill me. Instead, within his fine magic palace, he magicked me here. I was made the keeper of this pavilion. Because, more than anything, the High King loved to *dance*."

Eve choked on her tea.

Bramble said, "You're making that up!"

Flora said, "Was dancing even invented back then?"

The gentleman laughed.

"You like dancing, do you?" he said. "You would have been impressed with the High King. Every night he brought his court to dance in this pavilion. And I, a part of it, tending to it, the servant and fool of the High King. Humiliating.

"And then, after countless nights of dancing, the High King and his court vanished. In some trick of magic, I, too, faded into the walls and foundations of this building, a helpless piece of thought among the bricks and granite. Only recently have I been released enough to become keeper again, though still nothing more than a piece of magic, like this pavilion, and still unable to go beyond these steps. So it is."

The gentleman finished, smiling sadly. Azalea grasped her teacup in her hand, feeling the porcelain beneath her fingers. Trapped . . . the gentleman had been confined to the palace—just like them.

"You poor thing," said Flora.

"Are—are you hungry?" said Clover. "Do you need food—or—anything?"

The gentleman laughed. "Why, you charming little thing," he said. "No. I am quite all right."

Azalea said, "What is your name?"

The gentleman's black eyes turned to Azalea. They took in her shabby, soot-streaked nightgown and her auburn hair, unpinned to her waist. A hint of a smile graced his lips as Azalea, flushing pink, pulled Lily closer to hide herself.

"Keeper," he said. "That is what I was called by the High King. I have no other name anymore."

Keeper. An unusual name, for a most unusual

story, and a most mysterious gentleman.

"Pray forgive me," said Mr. Keeper. His long dimples appeared as he smiled. "I will lower the water presently and let you free. But please, may I have the honor of asking who *you* all are?"

Azalea flushed, remembering her manners. She curtsied and introduced them all, from herself—"Azalea Kathryn Wentworth, Princess Royale"—to Bramble, Clover, Delphinium, Evening Primrose, Flora, Goldenrod, Hollyhock, Ivy, Jessamine, Kale, and tiny Lily, now asleep on Clover's shoulder. Each girl bobbed a curtsy at her name, and Eve gave the "But I'm just Eve, really, not the Primrose part," which she said at every introduction. The gentleman gave them each a bow, so graceful he rippled.

"Wentworth," he said. He smiled.

The pavilion shimmered in the silver mist, and the magic lulled them. Jessamine yawned and leaned against Clover's leg, and Kale curled up in a little ball at Azalea's feet. Azalea knew they had to leave but wished they didn't. Her eyes met the Keeper's, across the lilac-silver pond, and he still kept the smile on his lips.

"Princess Azalea Kathryn Wentworth," he said. "Look in your pocket."

Azalea touched her nightgown pocket, feeling a flat, stiff piece of paper. Puzzled, she pulled out an envelope embossed with silver swirls. The girls leaned in and gave *oohs* as she broke the seal and unfolded it.

The Princesses of Eathesbury
are
formally invited to attend
a ball
tomorrow night
courtesy of
the Pavilion Keeper

"Was it a dream?" said Flora, the next morning, snuggling into her pillow. All the girls had slept late and awakened with excitement shining in their eyes.

"No dream," said Bramble, grinning a sleepy, wry grin. She scuffed the floor near the fireplace. "Dreams don't leave sooty footprints."

A fizz of delight sparked in the air. A great tingle of excitement they hadn't felt since the Yuletide. Azalea felt for the invitation in her nightgown pocket—and found nothing. Magic, again.

The girls chattered sleepily over a breakfast in the nook, stirring their porridge but too thrilled to eat it. Azalea insisted they at least try to eat, before lessons began.

"It's so . . . unusual," said Clover, turning her spoon in her mush, her pretty face almost aglow. "That gentleman . . ."

"Mmm!" said Delphinium. "That gentleman!"

Warmth rushed to Azalea's ears as she thought about the gentleman; the way he glided across the floor, the way he blew on the bits of napkin in his hand and how they had swirled into snowflakes, how his dark eyes had taken her in.

"He's a rogue," said Azalea firmly. She coaxed a spoonful of porridge into Kale's little mouth. "I have a mind not to return."

The girls yelped, horrified.

"Oh, *no*!" cried the twins.

"You *can't*!" said Eve.

"We *have* to go back," said Delphinium. "I need to dance so much, my feet hurt."

"Az," said Bramble, pulling her chair closer, so they saw eye-to-eye over the cream pitcher and threadbare tablecloth. "Don't you see how *perfect* this is? *Finally* we have a place to dance, one where no one could possibly discover us!"

"Of *course* I've realized it!" said Azalea. Her toes curled in her stiff boots, aching to spring into a dance. "It's just so—extraordinary!"

It twisted her thoughts, thinking of the Pavilion

Keeper living in the walls of their palace, unknown to the royal family. The King knew about that passage—surely he did; hadn't Lord Bradford said as much? But the Keeper and the magic he couldn't possibly know of. To him the passage was a storage room, possibly for old trunks and broken furniture. He couldn't know of the Keeper, with his dark, rakish eyes and sleek ponytail.

No, the King *definitely* did not know of Mr. Keeper.

What had happened, Azalea wondered, to free the Keeper enough from the walls of the palace—enough to magic a storage room into a fairyland—but not enough to free himself?

"Even if we wanted to dance," said Eve, who looked crestfallen, "we couldn't. We don't have any dance slippers."

This put a damper on everyone's excitement. They couldn't dance barefoot, not with a gentleman there, and they couldn't dance in their old, heavy boots—their feet would get twisted. As if it could hear them, rain began pattering against the draped windows.

"Actually," said Azalea, slowly folding her porridge with her spoon. "I think we might."

She brought them all upstairs to the east attic, and among the dusty broken toys, the dripping roof, and ramshackle furniture, she unlatched a trunk. Before mourning, they had practiced dancing every day, so much that they had worn out the seams of their slippers. They even had a shoemaker who would bring the repaired slippers to the palace each morning. It was a luxury that Mother insisted on and the King reluctantly allowed.

Since mourning, they hadn't been allowed to dance, but they had the slippers they hadn't used on Christmas. Azalea pulled out a bundle and unwrapped it, revealing eleven brightly colored pairs of slippers. The girls ooohed.

They tried them on, right there in the dusty attic, and everyone was delighted to find that the slippers still fit. A little tight, but slippers never hurt the feet like boots did. Delphinium turned a graceful spin, sending puffs of dust about them.

"I feel like a princess," she said.

That night they readied in a flurry of delight. Hair brushed, pinned, and braided; dresses buttoned, tied, poofed, and smoothed. Azalea produced dried flowers from a box underneath her bed, and the younger girls beamed as the older girls pinned the delicate crinkly blossoms in their hair and tied their slippers.

With the handkerchief and another burst of silver, the girls shivered as they passed through the billowing magic waterfall. Tonight the silver forest dripped here and there, though instead of raindrops, it dripped pearls. They reflected the light of the lamp as they fell. Azalea caught one in her hand, and it wetted her glove as a normal raindrop would, but left a pearly white spot.

Just before the bridge, Azalea set down the lamp and pulled the willow branches aside, revealing the glimmering white pavilion. The girls clasped hands and walked forward. Pearls rained into the water with soft *ploop*s.

The Keeper stood at the entrance, cutting a sharp, smooth outline against the white silver. He dipped into a bow, so deep he fell to one knee.

"You came," he said.

"Of course," said Azalea, forgetting that she ever had doubts.

"Welcome," he breathed. "My ladies."

He extended his arm to the dance floor. With a squeal of delight, the girls bounded up the steps and onto the marble. Azalea smiled and followed after, her slippers so soft she could almost feel the marble veins. They looked about them, taking in the velvet, backless sofas on the sides for resting, the dessert table piled with chocolates and buns, the domed ceiling above them.

Azalea turned to see the Keeper at the entrance, folding his arms, his black eyes on her. She turned her head, feeling a blush rise to the tips of her ears.

"I do hope my ladies will enjoy their night of dancing." The Keeper backed out of the entrance, onto the first stair. Delphinium gave a cry of protest.

"You're leaving?" she said.

Mr. Keeper smiled. Even his smiles were sleek.

"I do not dance," he said. "I am only the Keeper. I leave dancing to those who are more gifted than I."

The white rain gusted in thick patters above them, and pearls dripped in sheets over the sides. A curtain of white masked the Keeper from the entrance. When the drops subsided and the bridge and rosebushes were revealed once more, he was not there.

"Wow," said Hollyhock. "Wow!"

The blush still heated Azalea's face. She turned to the girls, smiling as the invisible orchestra tuned and sprang into a lively melody.

"A schottische!" said Azalea. "Do you remember this? Mother taught it to us hardly a year ago—you'll remember! Come along."

They joined hands, and Azalea taught them the dance. *Step-hop, hop, touch, hop.* She taught them to turn their feet just so, and the girls learned it quickly. Even two-year-old Kale stepped on the right beats in the next dance, a spinner's reel.

Quadrilles, gorlitzas, a redowa waltz, and more reels. The hours passed, the girls laughing as Azalea turned them in the steps.

She loved this. The feeling of stretching herself tight,

releasing, spinning, falling breathless and feeling the air across her face. Seeing her sisters so happy, their pale cheeks pink with delight. It was magic.

Lord Bradford's watch read well past one when the girls finally sat down together in the middle of the dance floor, exhausted, happy, their dresses like black blossoms over the milky dance floor. The youngest girls had fallen asleep, curled up on the red velvet sofas, and Lily, who had been passed from sister to sister and squealed with glee every time she was spun, slept soundly on a chair cushion. Her skirts poofed in the air, revealing ruffly little pantelettes.

"My slippers are worn out," said Delphinium. She untucked her feet and showed everyone her pink toes, peeking through the seams.

"Mine, too," said Hollyhock. She sat with her feet forward, her small green shoes torn. All the girls adjusted positions then, showing their ragged slippers. They laughed and wiggled their toes.

"That means a job well done," said Azalea. "When you wear out your slippers like that. That's what . . . what Mother used to say."

The girls grew quiet. Flora clasped her hands in her lap. Azalea blinked at the ceiling, strings of pearls swooping in arcs above her.

"I miss her," Flora whispered.

Goldenrod nodded. Bramble pursed her lips and stared at the floor. Clover traced a vein in the marble, just barely touching it with her fingertip.

"When—when I dance," she said quietly. "When I dance, I—I forget all the—the bad things."

Eve toyed with her spectacles. "Like Mother not being here," she said.

"Like mourning," said Delphinium.

"And the King," said Bramble quietly.

"I—I only remember the good things. That is the b-best thing about d-dancing."

"Then come back."

The low, smooth voice startled them.

"Mr. Keeper," said Azalea, standing quickly. The girls stood as well, smoothing down their black skirts. Mr. Keeper stood at the entrance, his face a touch sober, his voice steady.

"You cannot dance up there," he said, quietly. "I can see you are in mourning. But you are welcome to dance here, among the magic. Please. Come and mend your broken hearts here. Come back, every night."

Azalea felt like laughing and crying at the same time.

CHAPTER 9

$\mathcal{T}$he next day, the girls brought the worn slippers to lessons in a basket, and after Latin Azalea taught them how to mend the torn seams. It took a stronger needle and thimbles, and Azalea only managed a mediocre job of repairing the dainty things. Even the twins, who had clever hands, took several hours before they had stitched the slippers properly. Everyone became frustrated at the task, and Hollyhock, brash and unthinking at eight years old, threw her thimble across the table.

Azalea understood their impatience, though it disheartened her. They couldn't request the services of their shoemaker, even in secret. Mr. Pudding was in charge of the accounts while the King was gone, and they couldn't stir up any suspicion. Azalea tried to be cheerful.

"I think we may be able to make them last two or three weeks," she said, bundling the last pair of slippers into the basket. "If we back them with a sturdier fabric, and are careful. That's plenty of dancing."

"Oh, only two weeks?" said Flora.

"What if we danced barefoot?" said Hollyhock.

"Why, Hollyhock," said Azalea raising her eyebrows and turning to the red-headed, freckled girl.

"Where *were* you born?" Bramble and Clover chimed with Azalea, their fingers at their collars in a gesture of shock.

Everyone giggled. That was one of Mother's phrases. Hollyhock ducked her head, beaming sheepishly.

"I know," she said. "I forgot."

"I wouldn't want—want Mr. Keeper especially to—to see our ankles again," said Clover, who busied herself retying the slippers' ribbons into dainty bows. "His eyes seem to catch everything."

Azalea had to agree with that. It made her chest tickle.

Though they had agonized over the mending, that evening the girls hopped with excitement as Azalea helped them tie on the repaired slippers. Even Lily liked them, grabbing at the bows around the girls' ankles and stuffing them in her mouth. The girls slipped through the passage and into the silver magic, their slippers peeking in bright, colorful glimpses from beneath their black skirt hems.

The pavilion was dark when they arrived, but Mr.

Keeper was there. He smiled when they climbed the steps and bowed deeply, with a "My ladies." The girls passed by him onto the dance floor, but Azalea stayed back and gave Mr. Keeper a graceful curtsy.

"Thank you," she said, before joining the girls on the dance floor. When she glanced at the entrance again, Mr. Keeper had vanished.

"Off-putting, how he does that," said Bramble.

In the middle of the dance floor sat twelve teacups in a ring. In each one stood a candle, flickering merrily.

"The candle dance!" said Azalea. She picked up one of the teacups. The candle sputtered but did not go out. She smiled and placed a teacup on each of the girls' heads.

"We haven't danced this for years," she said. "Not since Mother took ill. Don't let the teacup fall off. Grace—balance, that's what this dance is about."

Azalea showed them how to move on their feet without letting the top part of them bounce. The invisible orchestra accommodated them, only playing slow songs, and by the end of the night, even Ivy and Jessamine stepped without losing their candles.

"And two, feet together, and dip. Very good! Sweep a curtsy to your gentleman."

The girls dipped a curtsy. Their teacups fell off their heads and clattered to the ground. Azalea, laughing, picked them back up, and the candles inside flitted back to life.

"Curtsies next time," she said.

"Azalea," said Flora as they set the teacups on the dessert table. "Could you show us the Soul's Curtsy?"

The chattering hushed. Azalea hesitated.

"Go on," said Bramble, grinning. "They're old enough now."

Azalea smiled, inhaled, and touched her right foot in front of her. She traced it in a circle behind her, then slowly sank to the left knee. With strained balance, she folded herself up as she disappeared into the poof of her skirts. Her legs twisted like pretzels beneath her. She bowed her head, nearly kissing the floor, and extended her right arm above her, her left tucked behind her back. The girls applauded.

"How beautiful," said Flora.

"Now *that's* a curtsy," said Bramble, helping Azalea up.

"But it's not just for anyone," said Azalea. "It has to be for your husband, or royalty. Like a king."

Flora giggled. "For you that will be the same thing!"

Azalea smiled again, but this time it was strained, and as Bramble teased the girls into learning the dip, Azalea escaped to the edge of the pavilion. She leaned on the railing and looked miserably over the misty lake.

She hated feeling helpless. It writhed in her stomach, choking her with thoughts of dancing the rest of her life in the arms of a gentleman who pushed her about and laughed when she stumbled or, worse, didn't even look at her at all. She wondered if she would be able to give the Soul's Curtsy, with all her heart and soul, to anyone, and the thought made her ill.

Around her, the leaves of the rosebush ivies rustled, then curled and entwined through the lattice. Their buds bloomed into fat, silver blossoms, revealing pearls for middles.

"They're . . . lovely," said Azalea, after the initial surprise. "Mr. Keeper."

She turned and there he was, behind her, soundless as midnight. Azalea's heart beat a pace faster.

"You're upset," he said, in a low, gentle voice. Azalea felt the warmth of a blush creep up her neck.

"No," said Azalea. "Not."

"Ah," he said quietly. "But I can guess what you're thinking. You are thinking, if you were born after one of your sisters, perhaps things would be different for you. Are you not?"

The warmth of the blush dropped, replaced with cold shock.

"Not—quite—I—" Azalea stammered.

Keeper held up his gloved hand.

"I should think," he said, taking a step closer to her, so close Azalea should have felt his warmth, but did not. "If you were born after your sisters, it would be one of them faced with such a duty. And, from what I have seen of you, Princess Azalea, you would do anything to keep them from unhappiness. Look."

Azalea looked over at the dance floor, where Bramble had made the younger girls sit on the floor, while she, Delphinium, and Eve leaped over them. The younger girls squealed uproariously whenever the skirt hems brushed their faces. Bramble was saying, "Don't jump up, Ivy, you great idiot, do you want your head to get knocked off?" Azalea stifled a laugh, and the terrible, helpless feeling eased. A little.

"One day, my lady," said Mr. Keeper, stepping aside and allowing her to join them, "I should hope I would be fortunate enough to see such a graceful, unearthly curtsy from you again."

The girls were late to breakfast the next morning, and to lessons. When they arrived at the nook, their now-cold porridge sat on the table, and their teacher, Tutor Rhamsden, was there as well. He sat in his usual seat and was, in fact, asleep, leaning on his cane, upright but snoring.

He slept quite a lot. No one ever had the heart to wake him.

"Why is breakfast so early?" Bramble moaned, laying her head on the tablecloth. "Why are lessons so early?"

No one answered, for they all nodded in a doze. Four-year-old Jessamine curled up on her chair and buried her head in Azalea's lap.

That night, however, after a long afternoon of mending the slippers, the girls were wide awake with excitement, passing through the silver forest. Mr. Keeper greeted them at the entrance, bowing them in and disappearing with a faint smile. Azalea was glad—she suddenly felt shy and nervous around him.

The girls discovered twelve delicate lace-and-satin fans waiting for them, and they gasped with how fine they were. Clover, who was good with fans, taught them how to snap it open with a flick of the wrist, how to throw it in the air and catch it, and how to flutter it just above the nose, shyly, demurely. The girls cheered for her.

"I'm only good . . . because—because I'm shy," she said, blushing.

They returned through the fireplace to their room with visions of fan tatting rippling through their minds. The next night, they learned new waltz steps, how to flow up and down on the beats. The next night, jigs. And the night after, a morris dance, with silver-and-white satin sticks that had bells attached with ribbons.

No words could describe those warm summer nights, dancing at the pavilion. Euphoric, delightful, brilliant, all would fit. It was what Azalea felt when she saw the girls, beaming from learning a new step, or how to balance on just their toes, or when Azalea tucked them into bed, their cheeks flushed and smiling.

"Sometimes I wake up," Flora said one morning, "and I wonder if it's even real."

"It feels like a dream," Goldenrod agreed, sleepily.

Mornings came much too early, and after the girls had groggily dressed, they stumbled to breakfast late. They mended slippers over their porridge, or in the afternoons in the cool cellar. The slippers became more tattered each day, and Azalea had to back them with extra fabric from old tablecloths, because the satin frayed so. They couldn't last much longer, Azalea knew, but she would sew her fingers raw to make them do. She had to immerse herself in the silver forest, in the dancing, if only for one more night.

And though she wouldn't dare admit it to anyone, she wanted to see Mr. Keeper again.

He hardly ever spoke to her or any of them, other than to welcome, bow them in, and wish them a good night when they left, but the essence of him lingered. When Azalea spun, spotting her head as her skirts billowed around her, she could *swear* she glimpsed his midnight eyes watching through the lattice, or at the entrance, but when she turned about again, she saw only rosebuds. His sleek movements mesmerized her, and she wondered how he danced. She wished desperately to see it.

"Poor Mr. Pudding," said Eve, one night in early August, at the pavilion. They had danced until their slippers had been worn to pieces, and now sat in a circle on the floor, exhausted. When they had come to the pavilion that night, streamers lay on the floor, and they spent the next several hours dancing among ribbons.

"He nearly started crying this morning," Eve continued, "when we came late and wouldn't eat breakfast, because it was cold."

"Poo on Mr. Pudding!" said Delphinium, who was often cranky when she was tired. Azalea, on the other hand, helped the girls to their feet, nudging the younger ones awake and scooping a sleeping Lily into her arms.

"We *have* been staying out too late," she said. "We'll have to be more attentive." She slipped her hand into her skirt pocket for Lord Bradford's watch, to see the hour. Azalea kept the watch in her pocket every night, checking it from time to time, always taking the girls back before it grew too late. It was easy, however, to forget about the time when the pavilion spun around them. Azalea dug into her skirt pocket a littler harder, and found nothing but a thimble.

"Bramble, have you seen the watch?"

"Me? No." Bramble yawned.

"Has anyone seen the watch?"

The girls only answered with blinky, sleepy eyes. Anxiety seizing her throat, Azalea paced the dance floor, searching the marble, wondering if it had fallen from her pocket during the ribboned mazurka. She couldn't just lose the watch like that—it wasn't hers!

Azalea turned again, and this time the weighty, dark form of Mr. Keeper stood in the entrance, a silhouette of roguish ease. His hands cupped around an object, holding it close to his nose. Eyes closed, he inhaled deeply, as though breathing it in. Azalea caught a glimpse of gold between his long black fingers.

"Mr. Keeper!" said Azalea, relief washing over her. She strode to the entrance. "You found it!"

Mr. Keeper's eyes snapped open, sharply black. Sighting Azalea, the sharpness diminished, and a flicker of a smile appeared. He lowered his hands. The watch, fob, and chain nestled in his gloved palms.

"Yes," he said smoothly. "It had clattered to the edge here. Forgive me."

Azalea made to pluck it from his hands, but his fingers closed on the watch, and he pulled back.

"Mr. Keeper," said Azalea.

"Such a fine clock," he said softly. "It belongs to your gentleman?"

Azalea's breath caught from her throat to her chest,

and her heart thumped in her corset. At the lattice beside them, the leaves rustled in the unfeeling breeze.

"Not . . . mine," Azalea stammered. "Please, Mr. Keeper, if I could have it back—"

Mr. Keeper reached out and brought her hand to his. Azalea gasped; the press of his fingers seemed to touch her core. He felt so *solid*. It both thrilled and frightened her. Turning her palm upward, he placed the watch and chain in her shaking hand and curled her fingers over it. His hands lingered upon hers.

Then, in a silky movement, he released her hand and bowed them out, so quickly Azalea couldn't recall even going over the bridge. She clasped the watch in her hand so hard the gold ornament curls imprinted her hand through her glove.

Several hours later, when her heartbeat had slowed to its normal pace, and Azalea didn't blush every time she thought of Mr. Keeper's hands on hers, she turned up the lamp on the round table in their room, retrieved a bit of newspaper from under her bed, and sat on a pouf, studying both the watch and the paper.

The Delchastrian war had had two battles in the past month, which worried them all. Between lessons and meals, and now slipper mending and sleep, Azalea read the *Herald* aloud to the girls. Worry etched in their faces. Afterward Azalea would have them tear and roll old tablecloth fabric for bandages.

This past week, however, the girls had squealed with delight over the paper. Azalea's name was mentioned in Lady Aubrey's gossip column. Lady Aubrey wrote the "Height of Society" news, which, in Eathesbury, usually involved a discussion on why Lady Caversham and Minister Fairweller would be such a fine match. Mother had never approved of Lady Aubrey's column, and Azalea did not either—in theory. She couldn't help but be interested this past week, when she was the subject.

"It looks like Lady Aubrey's given up on Fairweller," said Bramble, teasing and holding the paper just out of Azalea's reach. "Look who she's slated to be your fine gentleman."

Azalea managed to grab the paper from Bramble's hands, and the girls read over her shoulder. Lady Aubrey wrote of a Delchastrian gentleman, one dripping with lands and railways, who had the most unfortunate surname: Haftenravenscher. She spoke of what a marvelous match it would be economically, and had even interviewed him:

Lord Haftenravenscher states, "I think it would be corking to meet the princesses! I say, did you hear their palace was magic? It must be corking to live there. Our mums were great friends, ages ago! Like sisters! I say—it was a rum blow to hear the news. What a piece of you that takes. I say."

The rest of the article followed more or less the same, with a lot of "I say"s.

Delphinium giggled at the paper. "Imagine having that surname! Azalea Haften-rafen-what?"

Bramble rolled her eyes and slipped the paper from Azalea's hands.

"Don't be stupid," she said, rolling it up and tapping Delphinium on the head with it. "Someone as rich as him would never bother with us. Read the article. We're just sport to him."

Azalea ran her fingers through her long auburn hair, feeling a touch unwell. Bramble was right, of course. In fact, if there would be an arrangement between her and Lord Haftenravenscher, he would probably resent her for being penniless. It all felt like an ill-timed dance of accidents.

Still, Lady Aubrey's column was not the reason she had kept the paper. On page three, where the captains and conditions of each regiment had been listed, Azalea found Lord Bradford's name—*Captain* Bradford's name—and although there hadn't been any more information than that, she had pored over the type, worrying the paper until her fingertips were black. Now she considered the watch, tracing the gold ornamental swirls.

Your gentleman. Why would Mr. Keeper have guessed such a thing? If anyone had seen the watch, they would have guessed was it the King's. How Mr. Keeper knew it belonged to a gentleman, not *her* gentleman, naturally, but a gentleman. . . . That was . . . unsettling. The glint in his eyes, just before they met hers . . .

Azalea gripped the pocket watch, suddenly feeling protective. They had kept it too long as it was. When Lord Bradford came back from the war, she promised herself, she would give it back.

CHAPTER 10

*T*he end of summer brought warm rains that pattered against the draped windows and scents of lilac wafting from the gardens. The girls by now knew everything from a ladies' chain, to an Eathesburian quadrille, to dance positions one through four, and every galop ever invented.

One hot day near the end of August, when the girls were enjoying tea in the cellar among the crates of potatoes, Eve burst through the door, flushed and breathless and waving the paper about in the air.

"Look," she managed to say between breaths. "Look!"

They looked.

"The war!" cried Azalea.

"It's over!" said Bramble, gaping and smiling at the same time.

"Over!" the girls echoed.

"A victory!"

"Huzzah!"

The younger girls hopped around in a quasi-reel, crying, "Huzzah! Huzzah!" in squeaky, excited voices, and kicking up dirt.

Azalea pored over the headlines and articles, heart fluttering so quickly she thought it would burst. It had ended with a battle; Azalea raked the front page, and then the ones after, searching for any familiar names among the wounded.

"Anyone we know?" said Bramble. "Anyone...at all?"

"No," said Azalea, relief sweeping over her. "No."

Everyone exhaled.

"Not that we cared, naturally," said Bramble.

"Naturally," said Delphinium.

"I mean, I certainly don't."

"Neither do I."

"It's *over*!"

The paper changed so many hands that day that it became wrinkled and curled. Mrs. Graybe made cinnamon bread, a treat they could only afford on holidays, and Mr. Pudding walked about the palace, singing "Huzzah" in wheezing, out-of-tune tones. The *Harold Herald*, alive with news of the war, even printed an extra edition the next day, and among the news of the front page, the girls discovered that Minister Fairweller had been wounded. Clover, so tenderhearted, cried.

"Oh, he's probably all right," said Bramble. "It would take a lot to kill him. Like garlic and a stake through the heart."

Clover still cried. That was Clover for you.

All of Eathesbury seemed to spring with life now the war was over. Gentlemen came and left the palace on Royal Business, speaking with Mr. Pudding about regiments and ships returning to port. Minister Fairweller was the first of these to arrive, striding into the palace on a sunny Tuesday morning.

He did not extend any greeting to them, in typical Fairweller fashion, but instead went straightaway to the library to sort through paperwork. To the horror and utter fascination of them all, he had a red, raw wound that extended from beneath his collar up the side of his neck, reaching his ear. It was bandaged, but a rust red mark had soaked through. He winced whenever he turned his head.

Clover, flaring pink with indignation, stormed into the library with a steaming kettle of ginger tea and a teacup, and set them both hard on the King's desk.

"You," she said. "You—you—you—you drink this! At *once*!"

Clover was so very rarely angry that this was both

amusing and frightening. Fairweller paused in his paperwork and blinked at her, which made Clover even angrier.

"Three cups," she said, pouring the tea and thrusting it into his hands. "Three cups, at least! Have you seen the doctor? Well? Drink it!"

Fairweller drank.

He was not used to being ordered about, Azalea supposed. He lived alone in his austere manor. Clover folded her arms and watched him with pursed lips as he meekly sipped the tea. He almost looked like a frightened schoolboy. The girls watched from the doorway of the library.

"Will the King be home soon, Minister?" said Flora, the first to dare a question. She raised a finger, as though she were in lessons.

"He should arrive within three weeks," said Fairweller, smelling the tea and cringing. "He remained behind to see to the regiments. If you had written him, you would have known this already."

The girls flared up with indignation.

"We haven't written *him*?" said Bramble, her ears red. "He hasn't written *us*!"

"Yes." Fairweller took a sip of the strong-smelling tea. "Your family is very interesting."

Entwined

Fairweller wasn't the only gentleman to arrive. Several days later, among the exciting come-and-go of Royal Business, Azalea followed humming noises, and discovered a tall, thin young gentleman in the portrait gallery. He had his hands shoved in his pockets, and he bobbed on the balls of his feet.

The portrait gallery was a long hall, with windows along one side and oil paintings along the other. It was a hall reserved for visitors and guests, with sofas so fine that if one sneezed ten paces away, they would stain. The girls weren't allowed to touch them. Velvet ropes blocked glass cases of government documents, standing on pedestals in the middle of the room. The gentleman, next to one of them, caught sight of Azalea, and he brightened.

"Oh, hulloa!" he said, in a strong Delchastrian accent. "I say! Hulloa!"

"Hu—I mean, hello," said Azalea. He reminded her of a long, stretchy piece of taffy wearing a checkered waistcoat. She stared at his offensively green bow tie.

"I say! Are you the princesses?" He beamed as Clover, Delphinium, and all the younger girls arrived behind Azalea. "I've heard stories! Spiffing to meet you, just *spiffing*!" He strode to Azalea, grasped her hand, and shook it vigorously, as though she was a gentleman.

The younger girls giggled and whispered to one another behind their hands. Azalea pushed a smile and tugged her hand away, feeling slightly defeminized.

Bramble arrived at the gallery door, pink cheeked, her thin lips turned in a grin. Several pins had fallen out of her deep red hair, giving it a slightly tumbled appearance. She worked to pin a strand back.

The gentleman's eyes caught her, and his smile faded.

"I say," he said.

Bramble's grin disappeared when she spotted the gangly fellow.

"Who the devil are you?" she said.

"Um, Lord Teddie," he said, scrunching his hat rim between his fingers. "Um, our mothers were chums. They did watercolor together. Ages ago. They were like sisters. So, that, you know, makes us, um, cousins. Um. Except, actually, we're not."

Bramble's eyes narrowed.

"Oh, so *you're* Lord Haftenravenscher," she said.

Lord Teddie beamed. "Oh, well done," he said. "You said it right. Except everyone calls me Lord Teddie, Haftenravenscher is such a mouthful, I know it is. So you can call me Lord Teddie. Rolls off the tongue. Teddie Teddie! Haha."

"We're not allowed visitors in mourning," said Bramble. "Especially those who think they're on holiday."

Her tone was so cold, it made the smile slide from

Lord Teddie's face. Instantly, however, it was back, and accompanied with a bounciness to his feet.

"Oh, I'm not visiting!" he said. "Strictly R.B., that's me! Ha! Rhyme. I say, is this one your mother?"

He waved his hat to the small picture of Mother hanging on the wall. The Wentworth family only owned one portrait of her, painted when Azalea was little. They hadn't had the money to commission a conservatory painter, and so had gotten something that *sort of* looked like Mother, if you squinted and turned your head. Azalea was surprised the King hadn't locked it away. Every other stitch of dress, jewelry, and hair comb had been locked in trunks, then locked again in Mother's room.

Lord Teddie peered at the portrait through squinted eyes.

"It *sort of* looks like her," he said. "But it hasn't got zing. The light. In her eyes."

Azalea tilted her head, nonplussed. The girls cast one another glances.

"You knew her?" said Eve.

"Oh, great muffins," he said, bouncing up and down again. "*Everyone* knew your mother. I knew her before she boffed off to Eathesbury! Met her at one of Mother's balls. She taught me a bit of the Entwine, you know. I was five."

"You were *five*?" cried Hollyhock, tugging at his hand.

"You weren't of age and they let you go to a ball?"

"Crumbs, yes! Best way to learn how to dance, I say!"

The younger girls crowded about Lord Teddie, hopping with eagerness. Azalea groaned inwardly, thinking of the headache she would have explaining to the girls that they still wouldn't be allowed at balls until they were fifteen.

Lord Teddie took the attention, the tugs on the suitcoat, and the pestering questions with a great bashful grin.

"Well," he said, ducking his head a bit shyly before plucking the picture from the wall. "I suppose I ought to go, then. Before the cab leaves without me, anyway. Unless, you know, you wanted to . . . invite me to dinner, or something."

"Oh, stay for dinner!" the younger ones peeped.

"What are you doing with Mother's portrait?" said Bramble.

Lord Teddie's face turned a bright shade of red, looking at the portrait tucked beneath his arm, then to Bramble, then back to the portrait.

"Um," he said. "Nothing."

"You're taking it!" Bramble's eyes flared a bright yellow. Azalea knew that look. She grabbed at Bramble's hand, hoping to pull her back before Bramble's mouth whipped like a viper.

"No—no—no—" Lord Teddie backed away, using

the portrait as a shield. "I mean—well, yes, I am, but—well, look, I have permission!"

Still holding up the portrait, he fished in his suitcoat and brought out a folded note. Bramble snatched it from his hand and read it. Her thin red eyebrows arched above her forehead.

"No," she said. "He wouldn't—"

Azalea took the crumpled note from her and read the King's stiff, formal penmanship. It was addressed to Mr. Pudding. Short, concise. It dictated that the gentleman would be taking Mother's portrait.

That was all.

It occurred to Azalea, through the mist of shock and disappointment, that she should have expected this. With everything else of Mother's out of sight, it was only a matter of time before the portrait was gone, too. Perhaps they were even lucky, in that someone rich was willing to buy it.

"You're really going to take it!" Bramble's eyes blazed. She clenched her fists and bore in on the gentleman. "Everything else of Mother's is locked away; we don't have anything left! How could you come in here—and—and *do* such a thing? You have no *soul!*"

Lord Teddie cowered.

"Toodle pip," he said, and bounded off.

Bramble charged after him in a flurry of black skirts and crinolines. The girls followed at a bound, hoping to catch up. Lord Teddie's long legs sent him flying out the entrance hall door before they even reached the mezzanine. He barreled into the waiting cab's door, losing his hat, and the carriage was off in a spatter of gravel.

His head peeked above the back window in time to see Bramble throw his silk hat to the ground, and grind it into the gravel with the heel of her boot.

That night at the pavilion the girls didn't dance. Instead they sat in a circle and spoke in low voices. It didn't hurt so much, somehow, when they whispered. Above them, the invisible orchestra played soft, soothing gavottes.

"I *know* it didn't look like her," said Bramble, in a hollow voice. Her venom had dwindled to weariness. "I can't believe he would just *take* it. I can't believe the King would let anyone take it."

"*I* can," said Delphinium, tucking a torn ribbon into her patched slipper. "Honestly, nothing the King does surprises me anymore."

"What will happen?" said Eve. "With the King?"

There was a pause, so quiet the mist could almost be heard outside.

"Nothing," said Azalea. "He'll go back to the library. Things will be the same."

"Like when Mother was here?" Flora and Goldenrod looked at Azalea with bright eyes.

"No," said Azalea, feeling a tight, hot sensation rising in her throat. "Look, we promised not to talk about the King."

"We can't . . . just pretend—like—like he's dead," said Clover.

"Why not?" said Bramble. "I mean, things would have been different, wouldn't they? If it was him instead of Mother who—"

She abruptly stopped, her face flaming.

"I didn't mean that," she said. "I didn't."

"It's true, though," said Delphinium. "Don't you remember, how much it *hurt*, when he never came to dinner? How much it hurt, when he said—"

"Stop!" said Azalea, on her feet. "Stop, stop, *stop*! We don't talk about this!"

Azalea paced, her fists clenched so tightly they shook. Her nails bit into her hands, in spite of the gloves she wore, and she clenched them harder, wishing it would sting harder. When her hands stung, the inside of her didn't so much.

The girls kept their lips pinched, their eyes wide on Azalea. Normally Azalea kept her temper hidden, but now it burned to her eyes, and her skirts swished hard about her.

"He's going to find out about this, you know," said Delphinium, from the floor. "The pavilion. Us dancing."

"No, he's not," Azalea spat. "He *won't*. He has no part of this. It's the only thing we have now, and I *won't let him take it away*!"

The words seared, whipping the mood into a smoldering head.

"Hollyhock will blather it about," said Delphinium quietly. "You know she will."

"I will not!"

"We could promise to keep it a secret," said Flora timidly, huddling close to Goldenrod as Azalea paced in front of her. "Goldy and I shake hands when we have a secret."

"It has to be *more* than that," said Azalea. "It has to be something we'd never break, something we would *never* give away!"

She turned sharply, and stopped at Jessamine's frightened bright blue eyes, and Ivy's pudgy hand clasping Clover's. The pavilion felt muffled, silent, but Azalea was suddenly aware of how her words rang. She swallowed, trying to calm herself down.

"Sorry," said Azalea. "I just—"

Realizing her face was wet, she pulled the handkerchief from her pocket. It flashed and glimmered in the pavilion light. Always taken aback by the slight tingling sensation when she saw it, a new idea occurred to Azalea. She folded the handkerchief in her hands, considering.

Entwined

Would it work?

"I once made a promise," said Azalea. "I haven't broken it yet."

She told them, with difficulty, what had happened that holiday night, in Mother's room. Not about how cold Mother's hands were, or how white Mother's lips had been—but she told them about the promise.

"There's something to it," said Azalea. "I'm always reminded of it, whenever I look at the handkerchief."

The girls' mouths were slightly open. Bramble raised her chin.

"All right," she said. "If Mother did it, then—we'll give it a go, too."

The handkerchief was large enough that everyone could touch a piece of it—just. Azalea spoke the promise. She had them promise not to tell anyone, or show anyone, and never let anyone know about the passage or the pavilion or the Keeper. Especially not the King.

The moment the girls echoed the last word, Azalea felt the odd tingling sensation spread from her middle and shiver through her whole self, leaving remnants of goose prickles across her arms.

The girls let the handkerchief go, at once. Eve brushed off her hands, as though they had something on them, and Clover just looked from her fingers, to the handkerchief, and back to her fingers.

"What," said Bramble, "was that?"

Azalea shivered as the tingling dissipated.

"I don't know," she said.

"I think," said Clover. "That . . . is a promise we had b-better keep."

CHAPTER 11

*A*zalea had an odd dream, not many days later.
Not the one with Mother. Instead, it was just the
assortment of scenes Azalea often had when she realized
she was dreaming, but too tired to wake up from it. She
and her sisters danced in the snow, leaping, turning, while
Bramble talked about pickled apricots.

The setting faded from the gardens to their room as a
door creaked, followed by heavy footsteps. Bramble was
suddenly wearing boots. They laughed as she stomped to
Jessamine and Clover's bed, next to the door, stopped,
and walked to the next bed.

"Should we wake them then, sir?"

Mr. Pudding's voice sounded at the doorway, and
suddenly he was in the dream, too.

"Certainly not. Let them sleep."

Immediately, it was the King who wore the boots, not

Bramble. And her sisters were not dancing, but asleep in their beds. Azalea stirred.

In her dream, the King walked to each bed and pushed the bedcurtains aside, looking down at Azalea's sisters. He reached Azalea's bed, and Azalea felt the brightness of a lamp being held over her. The King made a noise in his throat.

"Sir?" said Mr. Pudding.

"It is nothing. They have . . . grown so, that is all."

"Aye, they do that."

More footfalls, this time stopping at Lily's bassinet near the door.

"Lily," said the King.

Everything was silent for such a long time that fairies started to hop around the room. They disappeared as the footfalls started again, and the door closed with a creak. For a moment, Azalea lost herself in dreams of dancing at the pavilion. Her upper consciousness tugged at her.

The King, the King, he was here, he was here . . . his voice . . . it had sounded so *real*. It occurred to Azalea, in a dreamlike way, that it *had* been real. This hadn't been a dream . . . wait, this *hadn't* been a *dream*!

"Gah!" she cried, leaping from her bedsheets.

It was morning. The girls were crowded about the window over the front court, kneeling on the pillowed windowseat and peeking through the edges of the drapery.

Azalea rubbed her sore shoulder and joined them. They gazed through the crack of the window down below, and Azalea's throat tightened, seeing the King.

The girls said nothing, and the silence was heavy. They stared down through the window. The King turned Dickens about, and Azalea saw his left hand had been bandaged.

"He's been wounded!" she whispered. "That wasn't in the papers!"

"Aye." Bramble was pale. "Probably he didn't want a fuss made over it. He can't manage the reins with it. It must hurt."

"He fwightens me," whispered Jessamine. Although four, she hardly ever spoke. Hearing her glass-spun voice was a rare occasion.

"Me, too," said Azalea. She pulled the drapes closed.

Brushed, washed, braided, and scrubbed, everyone except Flora and Goldenrod went down to breakfast. Goldenrod often had trouble waking after a late night, and Flora always stayed with her to coax her down to breakfast. Azalea promised they would save a bit of porridge for them.

When they arrived at the folding nook doors, however, everyone gave a cry of delight. On the table lay a spread of deep brown cinnamon bread and jugs of cream. There were even three bowls of jam and sugar.

They stifled the cry when they saw the King standing at the head of the table, looking at the bay windows as though there were no drapes. Azalea felt the girls instinctively draw near her skirts. Even Lily, in Azalea's arms, clutched at her collar.

"You're late," said the King, and he turned to face them.

Azalea felt a jolt.

Months had passed since she had seen him, face-to-face. His light hair and close-trimmed beard had streaks of white, and the lines in his face seemed deeper. Even so, he stood tall, sturdy, so much like the kings she read about in history books. None of the girls moved.

"Go on, sit down," said the King. "It won't do, half past eight! It is out of order. The bread is nearly cold."

Still the girls did not move. Bramble's lips were pursed so tightly they became a thin, razor-sharp line. Azalea held Lily so hard she whined. Azalea's arms shook, too. Partly from nervousness, but more from the searing boiling sensation that flamed within her.

"We apologize for being late." Azalea's voice came out smooth and cool. She gained courage from this. "Your ship arrived last night?"

"Just so," said the King. He sat down at the head of the table, and motioned for the girls to sit. "I didn't think mush would suit today. Come along." He took a cinnamon-swirled loaf from the table, and began to break it into pieces in a bowl. He did this with some difficulty, because of his bandaged hand.

"It l-looks like it hurts," Clover whispered, leaning in to Azalea.

Bramble leaned in on her other side. "What do you think happened?" she whispered.

"I don't know," Azalea whispered back.

"M-maybe we should—should ask—"

"No," Delphinium whispered from behind. "If he won't tell us, then we don't want to know."

"But—"

The King frowned at them, gathered about the glass doors, the *psss pssss psss* of their whispered conversation making the frown more stern. He set the loaf down.

"If you are inclined to speak," he said, "you may speak aloud. We have rules in this household—"

"What happened to your hand, sir?" said Azalea.

The whispering hushed. The King's two unbandaged fingers tapped against the loaf. He hesitated, then spoke.

"It was cut on the side of a bayonet."

The girls gasped. Azalea gripped Lily.

"Oh," she said, flustered. The girls drew together, *pss psss pssss*, while Hollyhock whispered fervently, "What is a bayonet? Someone tell me what a bayonet is!"

"Has Sir John seen to it?" said Azalea.

"It is *fine*," said the King. "Come in and sit down, at once. I won't have you standing about."

The girls looked to Azalea, and she gave a short nod. Normally they seized upon the chairs like starving orphans. Now, however, they seated themselves quietly at the end of the table.

The King frowned at this arrangement. None of the seats next to him had been taken.

"Where are the twins?" he said.

"A little behind," said Azalea, handing Lily to Clover. "They'll be here in a moment."

The King sucked in his cheeks. Azalea could see it was taking him great effort to keep from a lengthy lecture.

"Very well," he said at last. "We shall wait for them before we begin. But as of tomorrow, this tardiness will not be acceptable. Mr. Pudding informs me that you have been arriving to breakfast and lessons at half past nine! Half past nine, Miss Azalea! He tells me you retire at the proper time in the evening, and yet— What is to be said for it?"

Azalea clenched her hands beneath the table, her nails digging into her palms.

"Time is a bit hard to keep without the tower," she said in a calm voice.

"Then you may ask the hour of me, any time you like. I have a watch."

"Oh, marvelous," Bramble muttered. "Just what I want to do, boff off to the King every time I need the minute."

Azalea gave her a warning look. The King sucked in his cheeks, paused . . . and changed the subject.

"Miss Ivy," he said. "What do you have in your hands?"

Ivy, who sat next to Azalea, looked up from her lap to the King, to Azalea, to the King, then back to the object in her pudgy hands. It was a partially devoured loaf of bread. She didn't say anything because her mouth was stuffed full. Her eyes filled with tears.

"Oh, let her eat it," said Azalea, putting her arm around Ivy before the King had a chance to say anything. "It's her favorite food."

"There are rules in this household," said the King, though not unkindly. "We have meals as a family."

And here, just as the King said it, the temper that Azalea had skillfully pushed and smothered flared into a horrible, hot beast. Even her eyes grew hot.

"Of course," said Azalea. "You would know a lot about that rule, naturally." She adjusted the spoon next to her bowl. It clattered against the table. "If it is just the same to you, sir, I should like very much to have this meal in our room."

Everything stopped then; Eve's feet scuffing against

the floor, Hollyhock tugging on the tablecloth, Clover smoothing Lily's dark curls—all froze. They stared at Azalea with wide eyes.

The King's expression darkened. Frowning, his eyes fell over the holiday spread, then to the girls. He did not seem to like the turn this breakfast was taking.

"Very well," he said. "As you wish. You might as well take tea and dinner in your room as well, as you seem so inclined to it."

"Excellent," said Azalea crisply. An angry, absolutely euphoric sensation burned through her. "I would rather like to spend the entire next week with meals in our room."

"Oh, but why stop there?" said the King. "If you are so devoted to eating meals away from the table, then you may have them in your room for the rest of your lives."

"Excellent," said Azalea.

"Excellent," said the King.

It wasn't exactly a glare that Azalea and the King locked on each other, but their eyes met with such intensity that it smoldered. Azalea finally broke, unclenching her fingers from her stinging palms. She stood and made to gather the loaves and stack the bowls.

From down the hall, the echo of light feet and cheery, tiny voices reverberated into the nook.

". . . but I really don't know if we can make them last

another day," Flora's voice was saying. "I mean, look at this hole!"

Blood drained from Azalea's face as Flora and Goldenrod appeared at the glass doors, beaming . . .

. . . and holding the basket of slippers. Flora was holding up Hollyhock's small green slipper.

They froze at the scene before them.

"Oh!" cried Goldenrod.

The King's eyes fell on the twins, then on the basket, a jumbled mess of dance slippers. His eyebrows rose.

"Run," said Bramble.

The girls scattered.

In a flurry of overturned chairs and crinolines, girls fled down the hall. Azalea ran after, trying to catch up to them. Hollyhock had flown to the kitchen, Delphinium down the side hall, Eve up the servants' staircase in a flicker of black skirts. Clover, pale as death and near tears, clutched Lily, unmoving. Azalea caught up to the twins, fleeing to the entrance hall, Bramble taking the slippers from them at a run.

"Never fear, young chicks!" said Bramble, pulling the basket into the crook of her arm. "Hide in the gallery for now, beneath the north exhibit. I'll come and fetch you in a minute. If I don't come back—don't slow me down!"

This last part she directed at Azalea, who had grabbed her arm.

"What are you, *mad*?" said Azalea. "Now he'll *really* know we've been up to something!"

"Who *cares*?" said Bramble, yanking her arm away from Azalea. "I can't stand him!"

A firm, solid hand grasped Azalea's wrist.

"Into the conservatory, young ladies," said the King. "*Now.*"

Bramble broke free, gripping the basket with both hands. She bounded in an arc about the newel post and leaped up the stairs.

"Miss Bramble!" said the King.

"Down with tyranny!" Bramble cried. "Aristocracy! Autocracy! Monocracy! Other ocracy things! You are outnumbered, sir! *Surrender!*"

Sucking in his cheeks, the King did not chase after Bramble, but instead militarily escorted Azalea and the chin-wobbling twins to the conservatory, which was what the King called the nook. Clover, Lily, and all the rest except Bramble stood in a line against the rosebush ledge, cheeks flushed, hands clasped, eyes down.

The King disappeared; several minutes later, a loud crash came from the kitchen, followed by the clatter of spoons scattering across the floor, then a falling lid, ending the chaos with a *wah-wah-wa-wa-wawawawawathunk*.

In a moment the King returned, firm hand clenched on Bramble's shoulders, guiding her into the nook, the other holding the basket. He had a spoon-sized welt across his cheek. Bramble's lips were so thin Azalea couldn't see them.

The King closed the folding glass doors and set the basket on the table. The twins hiccupped as the King examined the mess; tattered, jumbled, patched beyond recognition. He lifted a used-to-be-red slipper, and the ribbon fell off.

"Well," he said, after a long, long moment. "Well."

He set the slipper down, sucked in his cheeks, clasped his hands behind his back. He took in air to say something, then exhaled. He picked up a slipper from the basket, and put it back.

"I am *heartily* disappointed in you all," he said quietly. "Heartily disappointed."

None of the girls could even raise their eyes to meet his. Eve plucked a leaf from the wilting rosebushes in the ledge, shredding it into minuscule bits, and Ivy didn't even eat a bit of the cinnamon bread she had snuck from the table.

"Please don't be cross with them," said Azalea. "It was my fault in the first place."

The King sighed.

"And I expect you wear every pair out each night, Miss Azalea? Nonsense." He folded his arms. "So this is why you are behind your time every day. Dancing at night, in mourning, when it is *strictly* forbidden. You all know it is not allowed!"

"No one hears us," said Hollyhock, twining the end of her apron string around her eight-year-old hand. "They can't hear a peep."

"No, I expect they probably can't," said the King. "If there was enough floor to dance in your room, which there is not, it would most certainly make a grand racket, would it not? So. If you cannot be heard from your room, then, where *could* you be dancing? Hmm? There are no secrets and underhanded dealings in *this* household, young ladies. If you are harboring a secret, then I will be told at once."

A strange sensation of cold, tingly prickles passed through Azalea. She cringed, feeling the wash and needles of it to her fingertips, and looked at the other girls. Eve was shaking her hand, as though trying to shake off the feeling. Hollyhock wiped her hands on her skirts. Bramble cast a glance at Azalea, one thin eyebrow arched. They had obviously felt it, too.

"We . . . can't tell you," said Flora, to the floor.

"We promised we wouldn't." Goldenrod shrank against the rosebush ledge, looking very much like she wanted to disappear.

"With 'Zalea's silver handkerchief," said Hollyhock.

The King's entire countenance changed, from

maligned to staggered. He turned to Hollyhock, his eyebrows furrowed, his eyes searching.

"You made an oath?" he said. "On silver?"

Hollyhock flushed so much it hid her freckles.

"We promised t' not tell the King," she mumbled.

The King stepped back, pressing his hands against the table ledge behind him. If it hurt his bandaged hand, he did not show it. Instead he fixed Azalea with an icy blue stare. Azalea could not read it.

"What you have done," he said, "is called Swearing on Silver. It is a very *serious* oath. Where did you learn such a thing?"

Azalea clutched the handkerchief in her palm, so tightly it dug Mother's initials into her hand.

Swearing on Silver.

So Mother had made her Swear on Silver. Azalea didn't know what it meant, but it couldn't be bad, not if Mother had done it. Azalea bit her lip, closing her eyes against the frigid gaze. She could never tell the King about Mother, how cold her hands were and how she had made her promise.

"Very well," said the King, when Azalea kept her eyes closed. "Very well." He took the basket of slippers from the table.

"These will be flung into the stove—"

"Oh!" cried Delphinium, followed by a *thump-thumphf.*

"—and you are all to spend the rest of the day in your room, considering the implications of mourning," said the King, stepping over Delphinium on the floor. "At once. You may *not* take the bread with you."

CHAPTER 12

That night, the girls put a chair up against the door and slipped through the billowing silver passage, down the stairs, through the forest, and to the pavilion in their stiff, hard boots. Their heels made a *clickety click click* the entire way. Mr. Keeper met them at the entrance, bowing as usual. His eyebrow twitched at their shoes, and his dark eyes met Azalea's. They took in her set jaw, her blazing eyes, her starkly straight posture, and he backed away, bowing again before leaving.

The dance began with an esperaldo, and Azalea, cheering up a mite, taught the girls the hard *stomp-click-stomps* of the rhythm, showing them how to scuff their soles with the beat, and how to make the sound of their shoes match the accents of the music.

After a while, with the continued chafing, and the rough twists and turns of the boots, the girls started to sit out dances. By the end of the night, they limped. They limped back through the silver forest, up the winding staircase, through the passage to their room. Azalea poured a steaming kettle of water into basins for the girls, and they soaked their red, chafed feet, yawning.

"We did it," said Delphinium, raising her chin. "The King thought he could stop us from dancing, but he didn't."

"Oh, aye," said Bramble. She looked at everyone's red feet, and winced. "We showed *him*."

The next morning, the younger girls complained as they put on their boots, and the older girls clenched their jaws and bit their tongues. Azalea, who had danced harder than anyone else out of sheer stubbornness, felt her right foot throb with each step. Fortunately they did not see the King all day, for he was out on R.B., dismissing the regiments, and therefore was not there to reprimand them on their self-inflicted injuries.

That night, after fish stew and biscuits in their room, the girls *click-click*ed down to the pavilion, slower this time. No one felt like dancing, but they did anyway. Their movements were ungainly and unbalanced. By the third dance, the younger girls whined and sat on the sofas, eating cream buns. Azalea tried to coax them into a simple reel, but they wouldn't budge.

So she danced by herself. The hard soles gave her

speed when she spun, and the girls cheered for her. It ended badly; she overbalanced and twisted her ankle. The girls flocked to her side in an instant, helping her up while Azalea insisted she was fine. Standing with careful balance, her cheeks warmed as she turned to the entrance and realized Mr. Keeper had seen her fall. His dark eyes drank her in, but he pulled back, as she was flanked with so many sisters. Azalea felt the strange thrill of fear and delight course through her.

"Perhaps my ladies ought to retire for the night," he said in his chocolate-smooth voice, as the girls tagged after Azalea, who, with Bramble's help, limped past the entrance.

"Thank you, Mr. Keeper," said Azalea, sure her face was crimson. She could feel the sticky slickness of blood between her toes. "I don't know how we'll ever repay you for letting us dance here."

The faintest of smiles traced Mr. Keeper's lips.

"I'm sure I can think of something," he said.

Everyone put up a fuss the next morning about wearing boots. Azalea coaxed and teased and eventually they all laced up, making faces. Hollyhock made the most noise, and Azalea realized why after removing a spool of thread, a spoon, a penny, and three green buttons from her shoes. Since their boots were passed from sister to sister, the younger ones were expected to stuff the toes if they didn't fit.

"Oh, Holli." Azalea sighed, stuffing Hollyhock's boots with her own stockings. "These things won't help your feet. What about the old samplers from last week?"

"I los' them at the pavil'n," Hollyhock mumbled. Her face was radish red, almost matching her hair. "I took off m' boots and no one saw me but I forgot t' put them back on."

Azalea sighed again. Hollyhock was always losing things.

"I hate being poor," said Delphinium, serving herself some porridge from a pot on the round table. "If we weren't, we could afford shoes that actually fit and weren't worn by a hundred older sisters."

"You know, speaking of losing things, I can't find my embroidery needle anywhere." Flora pursed her lips as she finished dressing Lily in a frilly black outfit. "I was nearly finished with the sampler, too."

"That's rum," said Bramble as she buttoned up her blouse, ignoring her bowl of porridge. "Last week I lost my pair of lace gloves."

"Really, you all," said Azalea. "Perhaps we should index everything like the King does, just so we know where things are."

Lessons began late that morning; Tutor was already

asleep at the table. Books and grammarians were passed around, slates and chalks, and Azalea began the lessons in a whisper. Hardly two minutes later, the King arrived at the folding doors, a bowl of stir-about in his bandaged hand and a stack of post in the other. He appeared preoccupied, but when he saw them all, he drew up.

His eyes took in Tutor Rhamsden, dozing over his cane, and Azalea, standing at the head of the table, SPONDEE, SPONDERE, SPONSUM written on her slate.

"Young ladies," he said.

"Good . . . m-morning," Clover managed to stammer. The rest of the girls sunk in their chairs, keeping their eyes on their chalk-smudged hands. The King frowned but did not comment. Instead he set his bowl on the table and handed Azalea the stack of letters he held.

"Miss Azalea," he said. "These are addressed to you."

The room burst with a ruffle of whispers, skirts, and the scraping of chair legs, as the girls flocked to Azalea, looking over her shoulder with *oohs* and *aahs*. These were *nice* letters, embossed with swirled words and sealed with ribbons.

"Invitations!" said Delphinium.

"For balls and things!"

"Oh, Lea, you're *so* lucky you're of age!"

"Just remember, they're not inviting you because

you're you, they're inviting you because whoever marries you gets—"

"Oh, shove it, Delphi!"

"*Open* them!"

"Why would they send invitations?" said Eve, always so logical. "We're in mourning."

"It's impolite not to," said Azalea. "When Mother was ill, we still received invitations, though they knew she couldn't go. I'll show you how to write a letter of declination this afternoon."

One by one, Azalea broke the wax seals. She recognized names from the Yuletide guests and several of Mother's friends, all inviting her to upcoming balls and promenades and drawing-room dances. Pleased, Azalea saw that several also instructed her to bring "Miss Bramble," and one even included Clover in the invitation, though she wasn't of age quite yet. Bramble grinned, almost *shyly*, and Clover lowered her pretty blue eyes to the tablecloth, beaming. Azalea passed the invitations around, giving the girls a chance to touch the embossing and smell the perfumed stationery.

"It's *so* awful we're in mourning!" said Hollyhock, rubbing her fingers over an invitation's knobbly seal.

"It doesn't matter anyway." Delphinium passed around the flower-scented invitation. "Azalea's going to marry Fairweller."

Time halted.

"Eve and I figured it out," said Delphinium, barreling on. "No one would want a foreigner for king. Fairweller is Eathesburian *and* he's the Prime Minister *and* he's rich."

The blood drained from Azalea's face. Her mind revolted, and she imagined colorless Fairweller, his spiderlike arms clasped around her waist and his breath in her ear. She gagged.

"Oh, indeed," said the King, giving the girls a start. He rubbed his bandaged hand by the rosebush ledge, frowning. "None of you shall be met with someone you are not fond of. That is the rule."

The sick heaving in her stomach faded enough for Azalea to stammer out a "thank you" to her slate.

The next statement the King made was more to himself than to the girls:

"The question is, how to become acquainted with gentlemen while in mourning. Hmm."

Azalea gathered the letters into a neat stack. Ivy limped to Azalea with the last invitation, her steps ungainly. The King looked up.

"Ivy," he said. "What is wrong? Have you a sore foot?"

Ivy paled. She cast a desperate look at Azalea.

"I—I—I don't know," she squeaked.

"Come here. Let me see."

"It's all right," said Azalea. "Sit down, Ivy."

The King's frown became pronounced as his eyes caught Azalea's feet, nearly hidden by the chair legs. Azalea realized she was lifting her sore foot. She set it down, and winced.

"Hmm," said the King. He strode to Ivy, took her under the arms, and lifted her onto the table. Ivy, who was only five, after all, began to whimper as he unlaced her boots and gently tugged them off.

The stockings came next, and the King frowned at her feet, blisters on her toes and ankles chafed red.

"It's just, you know, boots," said Delphinium.

"Off with your shoes," said the King. "All of you. At once."

Cries of protest followed; the King did not relent. While Tutor snored, the King lifted Jessamine to the table and pulled off her shoes, revealing tiny red feet. An examination of Kale produced the same.

Under the threat of sending for Sir John, the older girls slowly removed their boots, unlacing them and tenderly tugging. Delphinium's feet had blisters at the toes and ankles, and Eve's right foot was swollen. Bramble's foot had bled into her stocking, but Azalea was surprised to see her own feet were the worst. Her toes had started to bleed again, giving her stockings a brownish red stain. Her left ankle was swollen.

"Oh, indeed!" said the King, examining their feet. "Indeed! You have all been dancing! Dancing, after I expressly forbade it! Even so!"

The girls' faces blushed crimson, but they said nothing. A stubbornly quiet nothing. The King sucked in his cheeks, then exhaled.

"You know what mourning is," he said. "You know what mourning means. I will have no more of this dancing. How could you treat your mother's memory in such an *appalling* way?"

Azalea pressed her palm against the slate lying on the table, and pulled her thumbnail across it, trying to distract the hot, boiling words from reaching her mouth. It was Clover, however, who spoke for all of them, uncharacteristically brave.

"We can't stop . . . dancing," she said, in a voice as sweet as honey. "It . . . reminds us of—of Mother."

The girls nodded eagerly. The King cringed, as though Clover's words had burned.

"It won't help anything," he said brusquely. "It won't do anything. Nothing will come from dancing."

"But it does help," said Clover. She kept her eyes down, lashes brushing her cheeks, but she pulled the courage to step forward. "Mother would—would dance at night, too. In the ballroom—and—and you were there, and you danced the Entwine, and—you caught her, and she kissed you. On the nose." Clover blushed deeply. "I think it was the sweetest thing I've ever seen."

She said it with fewer pauses than usual, as though she had recited it a hundredfold. Azalea pulled her hand away from the slate, thinking of Mother and the Entwine, the tricky dance with the sash. If Mother had gotten caught, it was only because she had let the King catch her.

The King backed up, taut, against the rosebush ledge, the dry thorny branches pressing into his back. His face had become severe.

"It helps to remember," said Clover.

"We will not speak of your mother," said the King. His voice was even, but harder and colder than frozen steel. "You are finished with your lessons. Go to your room."

The words lashed. Clover cowered, swallowed, then pushed her way out of the nook, clutching her boots and limping. They could hear her choked weeping echoing down the hall.

"Oh, Clover!" cried Flora. Hands linked, she and Goldenrod bounded after.

"Oh, look what you've done!" said Delphinium, crying angrily. She swept Lily into her arms and took off unevenly after them. Kale, Eve, Jessamine, Hollyhock, and Ivy ran out, followed by Bramble, who shot the King a flaring look as she left.

Tutor Rhamsden snorted, reciting Latin in a doze. *"Tero, terere, trivi,"* he wheezed.

"Azalea—" said the King.

Azalea stacked the slates, her nails digging so hard into them that her fingers hurt. She stopped at the folding doors before leaving.

"Perhaps they remembered," she said quietly, "you couldn't abide us."

Sir John came that evening. The girls sat on the edges of their beds, and he knelt in front of each of them, asking questions in his quiet, doctorly way. Ointments, bandages, and candy sticks were given. The King stood in the doorway, his arms crossed and face lined.

The poking and prodding made Azalea nervous, and she hugged a pillow while Sir John bandaged her ankle, frowning at her feet. He spoke in low tones to the King as they left the room.

That night, when Mrs. Graybe and one of the maids came to deliver a dinner of potato soup, they left another basket on the table. The girls seized upon it, and when Azalea unfolded the cloth from the top, she gasped.

Nestled inside, in a bundle of colors and ribbons, lay twelve pairs of dancing slippers.

Azalea was so relieved she laughed aloud. The girls squealed with delight and overturned the basket, sending a waterfall of satin onto the rug. They found their slippers and tied them on. There was even a tiny blue pair for Lily.

"Lovely!" said Delphinium. "*Real* slippers! It's like walking on air! Even with the bandages on!"

"Oh, joy, rapture, joy, all that," said Bramble. Her yellow-green eyes sparkled at Azalea. "Sir John must have convinced the King."

A card had been tucked inside the basket, and Azalea unfolded it to read:

I expect you to be on time to all your lessons.
I will not hear a word of your mother, or dancing.

It was the King's hand. Azalea blinked at the note.

"Is—is something wrong?" said Clover.

"No," said Azalea, feeling lost. "We win."

CHAPTER 13

$\mathcal{D}$ ancing in slippers after two nights of boots was heaven; stepping on clouds. Although none of them could dance for very long, they laughed as merrily as though the Great Boot Bungling had never happened. They felt especially cheered in learning the next morning that the shoe arrangement would be the same as before, when Mother had taught them dancing. The shoemaker would mend their slippers every day, bringing the mended set to the palace and taking the basket of the torn ones away. When the twins realized this, they nearly cried with relief. They had pricked their fingers raw trying to stitch the soles.

The next day was Sunday, the girls' favorite day. Before mourning it had been the scourge of the week. Now, on their only day allowed out, they sat obediently through Mass, even more subdued than usual because the

King stiffly sat with them. Then, when the bells rang, they slipped out to the graveyard behind the cathedral.

It wasn't much of an outing, nothing like the flowered hedges and mossy fountains of the gardens, but the sun fell over everything in dappled yellows, and the air smelled like leaves, and the girls delighted in their time outside the palace.

After some time, the King arrived at the iron gate, tugging his glove over his bandaged hand, to see them draping posy strings over the weeping angel. He frowned.

"The carriage is waiting," he said when Azalea came to him, Lily in her arms. "Azalea—"

"Don't be cross," she said, trying to stand up to his towering sturdiness. "Let them have a little more time. It's our only chance outside. It counts as Royal Business, doesn't it?"

The King remained frowning, taking in Lily's pale face, then Azalea's, framed with black bonnet and veil. He turned his attention to the girls timidly playing in the sunlight, faces white, and his frown became more lined.

"I expect it does," he said. "Don't be long."

The King made to leave for the street. Azalea struggled inside herself.

"Wait," she said.

The King turned, and Azalea tried to stammer out something.

"Thank you," she said. "For the slippers."

The King sucked in his cheeks, leaving indents on either side of his face. His fingers tapped the rim of the hat he held.

"I am not condoning this," he said.

"No, sir," said Azalea quickly.

"We are a house of mourning. You will be on time to all your lessons, and your meals, and there will be absolutely no talk of dancing. Is that clear?"

"Yes, sir."

"And I most certainly *do not* approve of you all keeping secrets. You know I know where you go, and I know you know *I* know of it."

"Um," said Azalea. She tried to untangle the sentence, and gave up. She wondered how much of the magic in the passage he knew about. Did he know about the forest? She doubted it. Without Mr. Keeper, it was probably just an old storage room.

"There will be no secrets in this household." The King set his hat on his head. "I will walk home. Mr. Pudding will wait with the carriage. And, Miss Azalea, take care your sisters don't muss themselves. We are having guests for dinner tonight."

The girls' room that evening was a chatter of disagreement, the younger girls alternately jumping on their beds and peeking through the windows, keeping the lookout for arriving horses. They hadn't had guests to dinner in months.

"No," said Delphinium, stubbornly sitting on her bed. "We can't. We swore to have meals in our room forever. We can't stand eating with the King, remember?"

"She has a point, Az." Bramble brushed through her sleek red hair. "I'd rather just stay up here. He can't really expect us. Besides, I get too . . . chokey around him."

"It *is* the rules," said Flora.

"Seventeen, section two." Eve rubbed her spectacles on her pillowcase hem.

Clover, who could never think unkindly of anyone, said, "He did—let us have our slippers."

The girls pursed their lips and looked from Azalea to Delphinium to Clover to Bramble to Eve. Azalea clicked Lord Bradford's watch open, shut, open, shut. She imagined the dinner table, the King and the guests sitting in awkward silence, staring at their soup. And after, the coffee in the library. The King was terrible at conversation—it was always up to Mother to glide between topics and steer the discussion. Azalea looked at her palms, still marked from her nails, then looked at the basket of slippers, tied together and ready for the night. She clicked the pocket watch closed.

"Rule number seventeen," she said. "Everyone wash up."

Washed and combed, the girls arrived at the dining room arches only a few minutes late. The King stood quickly when they arrived, and stared at them for several moments. His expression was unreadable.

Fairweller, Azalea was chagrined to see, was a guest. He sat to the right of the King and looked mildly annoyed, as always. His neck looked better.

The third guest had a gentle, solemn air to him. Azalea hesitated at the entries, her hand automatically touching the watch tucked in her pocket.

It was Lord Bradford. He bowed his head at her.

Azalea had to remind herself to breathe. He was back! And all right, too. She knew he'd been all right, of course, the papers never reported him as wounded, but it was an entirely different matter seeing him *here*, those soft brown eyes twinkling at her. . . .

"It's that rotten shilling-punter nuffermonk who stopped the tower!" Bramble whispered. "I hope he chokes!"

"He is a *lord*," said Azalea. "And if you do anything to him, I'll break your neck."

Mrs. Graybe came from the kitchen door with a dozen

plates, as though she had expected the girls to arrive at any moment, and Azalea helped her set the table while the gentlemen helped the girls with their chairs. Above the noise and clatter of dishes, the King leaned in to Azalea.

"It is high time you all decided to eat dinner as a family again," he said in a low voice.

"It's just for tonight." Delphinium, seated next to Azalea, spoke without moving her eyes from the plate.

"Rule number seventeen," said Eve reluctantly, from the other side.

The King straightened. His face held an odd expression. For a moment, he simply stood. Then his expression lapsed into unreadable, and he turned away.

The dinner of basted chicken, potatoes, and cake progressed well. Bramble seized the salt cellar, and Ivy spooned gobs of jam onto her chicken, but overall they behaved properly. At the end of the table, Fairweller and Lord Bradford discussed politics, and the King remained pensive.

"Parliamentary elections begin this next year," Fairweller was saying. "The House could use a fine young head. . . . His Majesty and I thought you might be persuaded."

Next to Azalea, Bramble had borrowed one of Delphinium's drawing pencils and was writing on her napkin.

"To run?" said Lord Bradford.

His way of speaking fascinated Azalea. He was frugal with words. It was a stark contrast to her life with a dozen girls and thousands of easy words.

Kale, next to Lord Bradford, had eaten one piece of potato and seemed no longer hungry. She stood on her chair and reached for Lord Bradford's wine. When he moved it out of reach, she pouted and sat down hard on her chair. Then she snuggled up to him, rubbed her cheek against his arm, and *bit* him.

Lord Bradford inhaled sharply.

"I'd rather not," he said to Fairweller, gently untangling Kale from his arm. "I haven't a head for politics."

"In my experience," said Fairweller, "the best men for the country are those who do not. Your father was a very fine member of government. It has always been expected that you would run as well."

Azalea caught a glimpse of what Bramble was writing on her napkin, faint in Delphinium's violet pencil:

We still have your watch. You can have it back tonight. All you need to do is sneak up after dinner, set the tower, and flee the country. Agreed?

Azalea burned with embarrassment as Bramble folded the napkin around the pencil and passed it to

Lord Bradford with the rolls. Lord Bradford took it and unfolded it in his lap. His dark eyebrows rose a fraction of an inch. Then he folded the napkin and placed it under his plate. Bramble's yellow-green eyes narrowed.

"I'm flattered," said Lord Bradford in his rich cream voice. Azalea hung on to the timbre of it, wondering if he had ever sung a glee or a catch. It was a voice that would mellow out the choir and give it a fuller sound. Lord Bradford continued. "I would rather not run for parliament."

Bramble had taken another pencil from Delphinium, and Azalea's napkin, and wrote something new.

You're afraid of the King. Admit it.

Azalea grimaced at her untouched food, burning in humiliation as Lord Bradford took the napkin and read it. This time, he looked to be discreetly writing something back beneath the table.

"It's not a matter of wanting to or not," said Fairweller, who appeared more annoyed by the minute. "Or even what party you will run for. It is more a matter of duty. I find it odd you are shying away from this. He would be a fine member of the House, would he not, Your Highness?"

"What? Hmm? Oh. Yes. He would."

Fairweller blinked at the King for a moment, in which Lord Bradford handed Bramble her napkin. She opened it and turned a rosy pink.

My lady, it read, *who isn't?*

Bramble pursed her lips and kicked Lord Bradford beneath the table—hard. His face twitched before regaining its solemn expression. Azalea buried her face in her hands.

"All we ask is for you to consider it. That is all," said Fairweller.

"Oh." Lord Bradford's voice was slightly strangled. "Yes. Thank you."

Bramble threw the pencil-smudged napkin onto her plate. "I'm done," she said. "May we go to our room now?"

For the first time since the beginning of dinner, the King snapped to awareness.

"Oh, no," he said. "Certainly not. To the library, young ladies." He stood and cast a significant look at them all. "Those are the rules."

Already horrified by her sisters' treatment of Lord Bradford, Azalea spent the evening in the library sitting on the sofa across from him, dying a thousand tiny deaths. Delphinium "accidentally" spilled coffee on him, Lily crawled to his shoe and began gnawing on his laces, and Ivy and Hollyhock crowded him on both sides, stitching samplers and asking him every two minutes what he thought of them. He replied he thought them very fine.

In fact, he almost seemed to be enjoying himself. Inexplicably, so did the King.

Intent on saving some aspect of the evening, Azalea herded the girls upstairs, then slipped to the front court, where Mr. Pudding tended to Lord Bradford's horse. Azalea explained why she was out, and he gave her the reins, patted her on the head, and went inside.

Azalea waited patiently, twisting the reins around her hands. Lord Bradford's horse pawed the gravel, but was well trained enough that it did not try to nose her hair, a horse trait Azalea hated. Presently Lord Bradford appeared at the door with a stack of books, probably political, as the King and Fairweller bid him good night. Azalea ducked behind the horse, grateful that black blended in with so many things.

When the door closed, Azalea stepped out from behind the horse.

"Lord Bradford—"

"Gaah!"

He fell back against the banister, tripping over the stairs.

"Sorry! Sorry!" said Azalea. "I didn't frighten you?"

"No, no, quite all right," he said. He peeled himself

from the banister and set to picking up the scattered books. "Naturally—"

"Naturally—" said Azalea, relieved. She picked his hat from the gravel and helped him with the books. "Sorry. I just had to apologize. About tonight. Honestly, we don't kick or bite or throw potatoes at all our guests."

A crooked smile touched Lord Bradford's lips.

"Your family has spirit," he said, taking his hat from Azalea. "I enjoyed the evening."

"Well, yes, you've just come from a war," said Azalea.

Lord Bradford laughed. It was a nice laugh. Quiet, unpracticed, sincere. Azalea liked it.

"I'm so sorry we've kept this for such a long time," she said, pulling the watch from her skirt pocket. She unfolded Mother's handkerchief from around it, and offered it to Lord Bradford cradled in her hands. "We shouldn't have taken it in the first place."

Lord Bradford's eyebrows rose at the offering, and he opened his mouth, then closed it. He lowered his eyes to the books in his hands, then back to Azalea, and he managed a smile.

"When we first met," he said, "ages ago, you gave me a candy stick. Just like you did now, with your hands like that. Do you remember?"

Azalea raised an eyebrow.

"It happened when my father had just died," he said, quietly. "You came to the graveyard, licking a candy stick. You saw me. You put the stick in my hands, folded my fingers over it, and kissed my fingertips."

"That must have been sticky," said Azalea.

Lord Bradford laughed. A warm, tickling sensation rippled through Azalea, and a memory flickered through her mind; one of wandering off from Mother on market day. The air smelled of cider. And then, peeking through the iron slats of the graveyard gate and seeing a forlorn boy on a stone bench. The memory, so distant, felt like a faded dream.

"You know," he said, "all these years I thought you were your sister."

Azalea gave a nod-shrug. "A lot of people make that mistake. It's because we're so close in age—less than a year apart each. In fact, of all of us, Clover looks the oldest, we think."

"I still have your handkerchief, from the Yuletide."

"Raspberries, do you really?"

He produced a crumpled, clean handkerchief, and gave it to Azalea. She tried to hand him the watch, but he wouldn't take it.

"It's still for ransom, is it not?" he said. "I'll collect it when I set the tower again."

Azalea smiled, warmth rising to her cheeks. "Well, it

has been awfully useful. Thank you, Lord Bradford."

He mounted with ease, even with the books, and smiled a crooked smile.

"Mr. Bradford," he said sheepishly.

"Mr. Bradford," said Azalea. And now, her cheeks burned. It wasn't unpleasant.

"Thank you," he said, tipping his hat. "For the pleasant evening. Sleep well, Princess Bramble."

"*What?*" said Azalea.

But he was already off at a canter, spattering gravel. Azalea gaped after him, then turned to the handkerchief in her hands. The sloppily embroidered B.E.W. in the corner made all the warmth drain from Azalea's face.

"Bramble!" she said. Ever since the Yuletide, he had thought her Bramble!

Azalea looked up to see him pull up at the gate. His eyes caught her, still at the steps, and he smiled and saluted. Then he was gone.

Azalea hugged herself, thinking that she would have to set things straight when she saw him again. If she saw him again.

"Good night," she said.

CHAPTER 14

That week, Azalea taught her sisters the Entwine. It was a tricky waltzlike dance, and a competitive one, where the lady and the gentleman each held an end of a long sash and weren't allowed to let go. The gentleman would try to "catch" the lady—bringing the sash about her wrists by pulling her into under-arm turns and stepping about her, while the lady would turn and unspin and twist out of his arms, trying to keep the sash from tangling. Two years before, Mother had brought a skilled dance master to lessons to dance the Entwine with Azalea. Azalea had deftly ducked and slipped from his quick, skilled movements, and by the end of the three minutes, both of them exhausted, the dance master smiled and gave her a bow of admiration and respect. Ever since then, whenever she danced the Entwine, Azalea felt a high-trilling piccolo in her chest and her feet felt like springs.

Bramble tied a handkerchief around her arm and played the gentleman, speaking in gruff tones and making such a spectacle that the girls laughed madly.

"My laaaaaadeee," said Bramble, bowing deeply to Azalea. The girls giggled uproariously, and Azalea sighed. Teaching closed dances without a gentleman was the most difficult thing so far.

"My lady," came another voice, and all the girls turned to see Mr. Keeper at the entrance, watching them with dark eyes. He smiled, and the two long dimples on each side of his mouth deepened.

Azalea stepped back. The piccolo trill in her chest glissandoed like mad. She swallowed, discreetly trying to wipe her hands on her dress. His eyes seem to see right *into* her.

"Do forgive me," he said, stepping onto the dance floor. His feet made no sound. "I could not help but notice. Perhaps *I* could have the honor of this dance?"

A hush fell over the girls. Azalea imagined herself in Mr. Keeper's arms, and the piccolo trill in her chest squeaked into tones only tiny birds could hear. If he danced like he moved—in smooth ripples—he was a very good dancer indeed.

"I thought you said you couldn't," said Eve.

"My lady, I said I do not dance. That does not mean I cannot."

"Do you even know the Entwine?" said Flora.

Mr. Keeper strode to Azalea, his dark eyes drinking her in. His cloak billowed behind him.

"My lady," he said, without turning his eyes from Azalea, "I invented it."

In a satinlike movement, Mr. Keeper had wrapped Azalea's arm about his and had escorted her to the middle of the dance floor. So silky and gentle. Azalea blinked and realized that he had turned her around into an open dance position. She swallowed. It was hard.

"We've only been practicing with this," said Azalea, producing Mother's handkerchief. "It's a bit short, I'm afraid."

It flashed silver in the pale light. Mr. Keeper flinched.

"That won't do," he said. "But, ah! Here is one."

Mr. Keeper flicked his hand, and a long sash appeared from nowhere. He shook it out with a snap. The bright red color flared against the pale whites and silvers. It was Azalea's turn to flinch.

Bramble took charge of Mr. Bradford's pocket watch, setting it on the dessert table to mark the time. The Entwine was exactly three minutes long. The girls watched, giddy with anticipation, as the invisible orchestra began a slow waltz.

Azalea shook, nervous, as Mr. Keeper stepped in time, turning the sash about her as she stepped out.

He *did* dance like he walked and spoke, with polished movements. Unhumanly graceful.

"My lady glides like a swan," he said. He pulled the sash up and brought her under his arm. "You are the best I have ever danced with. And I, my lady, have danced with many."

He pulled the sash even closer, and Azalea caught a look in his eye—the same hungry glint she had seen when he had Mr. Bradford's watch.

Convulsively, Azalea dropped the end of her sash.

That was immediate disqualification. The orchestra stopped.

"Only forty-five seconds," said Eve, looking at the watch, disappointed.

"You know, Mr. Keeper," said Azalea. "We've never really been properly introduced. Mother always said—"

"Ah, your mother," said Mr. Keeper. His black eyes were completely emotionless. "I expect your mother always had sweet little things to say. Such as, 'You're only a princess if you act like one,' and other such nonsense."

"Well," said Azalea, coloring. "What's wrong with that?"

Mr. Keeper gave her a thin, cold smile.

"Nothing at all," he said.

"You know, Az has a sharp point," said Bramble as she and Clover gathered the sleepy younger ones together.

"We hardly know a guinea's peep about you. Where did you learn how to dance like that?"

Mr. Keeper's thin, cold smile became even colder.

"I once knew a lady," he said, "who could dance the Entwine nearly as well as your sister."

Delphinium, lifting Ivy to her feet, perked up. Of all of them, she read the most romantic stories and drew the fluffiest of ball gowns on her stationery, and Azalea knew she wouldn't leave until she had turned Mr. Keeper's heart inside out, begging for details of romance.

"Were you in love?" she said. "Oh, *do* tell us about it. We only hear ghastly things about that time, with the revolution and everything. I want to hear something romantic."

"Delphinium," said Azalea.

Mr. Keeper held up his hand, silencing her.

"It is all right," he said. He turned to Delphinium, his cloak brushing the marble. "I will tell you about the lady I loved."

The girls settled together on the entrance steps, not even breathing, for fear it would rustle the rosebushes about them and mask Mr. Keeper's words. Mr. Keeper stood unmoving on the dance floor.

"Once upon a time," he said. His voice dripped in silk strands. "There was a High King, who wanted more than anything to kill the Captain General who incited a rebellion against him. It consumed him. The desire to kill the Captain General filled him to his core, and he spent *every* breath, every step, thinking of ways to murder the Captain General.

"But he was old, and time passed, as it always does."

Mr. Keeper paused. Bramble cast a slightly bemused glance at Azalea, her eyebrow arched.

"So," Mr. Keeper continued, "he took an oath. He filled a wine flute to the brim with blood. And he swore, on that blood, to kill the Wentworth General, and that he *would not die until he did.*

"And then, he drank it.

"The end."

There was a very ugly, naked silence after that. The girls' mouths gaped in perfect Os.

"Sorry?" said Delphinium. "I missed the part about the lady?"

"Ah," said Mr. Keeper. "The blood. It was hers."

The girls pushed one another through the fireplace wall, stumbling over skirts and tripping over untied slippers in a frenzy. They swarmed to the lamps on the table and by the door, turning up the oil as high as it could go.

"For the last time," said Azalea as the girls flocked about the lamps, the younger ones gripping Azalea's skirts, "it's not true! Settle down!"

"Aaaah! Oh, ha ha, Ivy, it's just you, ha ha ha." Delphinium shakily sat on the edge of her bed, her hands fumbling with her slippers as she pulled them off.

"It really sounded true!" Hollyhock squeaked. "It really did!"

Azalea hesitated.

Unlike the rest of them, she had heard this story before. Only in snippets, sometimes in hushed tones when the maids walked by, or reading in Tutor's *Eathesbury Historian* when he had dozed off. No one ever spoke it aloud.

Those hundreds of years ago, the High King had captured Harold the First's daughter, in the gardens. Back then the gardens had been made of thornbushes that grasped at persons' hands and necks of their own accord, pulling them into their prickly branches. He took her into the palace, and several days later, a box appeared at Harold the First's manor. Among the tissue papers lay a hand. It belonged to her.

The story then echoed Keeper's, with the High King drinking her blood, swearing to kill her father. Her body was found later, in pieces in the thorny garden. Azalea shuddered. She hated thinking of the next part of the story.

At night, the palace windows lit with a weird, bright yellow light, Harold the First's daughter could be seen wandering the halls, feeling her way about with *both* of her hands. The High King had somehow kept her soul. And she felt about with both hands—because . . . because . . . Azalea couldn't bring herself to think of it in a complete sentence, but it involved a needle, a thread, and the soul's eyelids.

Azalea nearly dropped the lamp she held, her hands shook so. She managed a smile, set it on the round table, and began to help the younger girls undress.

"It's only *partly* true," she said firmly. "Yes, he drank blood, but it didn't do anything. You know the picture of Harold the First, in the gallery? He died of *old age*. He killed the High King. The blood oath didn't work. Drinking blood can't do anything more than if you've pricked your finger and sucked on it. It's all tosh."

"He made it sound so vivid," said Flora, huddled with Goldenrod under their bedcovers. They hadn't bothered to undress.

"The High King did a lot of awful things," said Eve as Azalea pulled the twins gently from their bed and helped them into their nightgowns. "He trapped people in mirrors. They died there."

"That's—not—as bad as—capturing souls, I should—should think," said Clover, stammering more than usual.

"What a great load of rot," said Bramble. She threw her slipper at the wall. It hit the wainscot next to the door and fell into the basket. "And what a rot of Keeper, telling a story like that. Didn't he realize it would scare the tonsils out of the younger ones?"

Azalea rubbed her skirts, still feeling Keeper's hands against hers.

No one slept well that night. Azalea brought up two steaming kettles of tea for everyone, cooing and soothing them when they awoke with a cry. The younger girls crawled into her bed, burying their noses into her sides, patting her cheeks each time they stirred.

When Azalea awoke, it was late and she was cranky. She became doubly so when she discovered that Mr. Bradford's pocket watch had been left at the pavilion.

"I didn't mean to leave it," said Bramble, in the same beastly mood. "It wasn't my fault—we were in such a hurry to leave, after that ghastly story!"

"Mr. Bradford trusted us," said Azalea, angry with herself. "He trusted *me*."

Bramble looked at Azalea up and down, an odd light in her lemon-green eyes.

"Go to it, then," she said, herding the girls out the door. "I'll start the wee chicks on their lessons."

Several minutes later, toes curling in her boots, Azalea rubbed her handkerchief against the mark until it burned and the light burst. She had never been to the pavilion in the day. Descending alone into the silver brilliance felt different. Everything was muffled, and Azalea's boot clacks left no echo.

When she reached the pavilion, it stood dark, shadowed in the silver mist. Keeper was not there. Azalea knocked, lightly, on the arched doorframe.

"Sorry, hello?" she said.

Knocking made her feel less intrusive. She slipped onto the dance floor, and nearly jumped out of her boots when the orchestra burst into a lively jig.

"Shh!" she seethed. "Quiet! Hush!"

The orchestra cut off, except for a violin that screeched a happy solo. When it realized the rest of the orchestra had quit, it slowed with an embarrassing rosined whine.

Azalea searched the pavilion for a sign of the watch, and as she turned, felt the prickly, uncanny sensation of someone's eyes on her. She looked up, and let out a cry.

There, on the *ceiling* like a big, black spider, was Keeper.

Azalea's heart nearly leaped out of her corset. She stumbled back.

Keeper pushed off from the ceiling and flipped to the ground in a swoop. He landed, catlike, on his feet, and straightened. His cloak settled around him.

Azalea darted for the entrance. Keeper was there in an instant, blocking her way. He smiled a long-dimpled smile.

"My, you startle easily," he said.

"You—it—on—ceiling . . ." Azalea choked.

"Oh, do calm down, Miss Azalea." In a silky movement he brought Azalea's shaking hand around his arm, smoothing her quaking fingers over his black suit-coat sleeve. "Living in such a small pavilion for so many years makes one, ah, creative. And you, Miss Azalea, I am pleased to see you here. Even if you are here for another gentleman's watch, and not for me."

Azalea tried to pull her arm away, but Keeper only smiled, pressed his long fingers over hers, and escorted her to a sofa next to the dessert table.

"Do sit down. You are trembling. It is my fault; I know it. That story last night. I hope you can forgive me for it."

He produced a cup of streaming tea from nowhere, it seemed, and offered it to her, but Azalea waved it away.

"Where is the watch?' she said.

"Ah, so quickly to the point. That is bad manners, you know."

He set the teacup on the table, and next to it, lifted the lid from a small platter. Instead of housing a tiny cake, the plate held the pocket watch. Azalea reached for it.

Keeper closed the lid with a clink.

"Mr. Keeper," said Azalea.

Keeper had no hint of a smile as he set the covered plate aside and lifted the lid off a larger tureen.

Azalea gasped. On the platter lay an assortment of

odds and ends. A pair of lace gloves, a needle with a scarlet thread, one of Jessamine's stockings, Ivy's spoon, Eve's pen, all among other things of the girls'. Azalea was aghast.

"Those are ours!" she said.

"I know," said Keeper. "I like to keep things."

"That's stealing!" said Azalea.

"You must forgive me," he said. "But I am desperate. I need a favor from you, and your sisters. A great favor indeed, and I don't believe any of you would help me unless I did something, ah, unconventional. I want to be freed, Miss Azalea."

Azalea frowned. Keeper was—well, *Keeper*. Magical and beautiful and part of the ethereal pavilion. She shifted on the velvet sofa, feeling both consternation and guilt.

"I . . . hadn't thought of it," said Azalea.

"I know," said Keeper. He smiled, but not bitterly. "Perhaps you will now?"

"Oh, honestly," said Azalea. She stood up and strode to the entrance with a *click click click*. The familiar hotness had begun to run through her, and she felt she needed a breath of real air. "I can't believe you would just—just *steal*!"

"Step out of that entrance," Keeper called, "and you and your sisters will never be welcome here again."

Azalea stopped so abruptly her skirts swished the threshold. She glanced back at Keeper to see if he was in earnest. A touch of a smile graced his lips, but his face was deadly serious.

Azalea's toes curled in her boots. She suddenly hated Keeper.

"Don't—" she stammered. She couldn't manage to meet his eyes. "It's . . . just . . . We've got to keep dancing here, Keeper. It's all we have. Don't take it away. Please."

"Then you will help free me?"

Azalea gripped the side of the arched entrance, wishing to feel some sort of silvery texture beneath her palms. Instead she felt a strange glassy smoothness, and it frustrated her.

"Fine," she said, her nails clicking against the post. "For the dancing. And the watch. What do we have to do?"

Though she couldn't hear Keeper's footfalls behind her, she felt his presence draw near to her, until she could almost sense his sleekness, and his eyes on her back.

"The High King magicked many things," he said, in his smooth voice. "Your palace. This pavilion. And I. He was fascinated with magic. It was, to him, a science, dealing with force and matter and auras. There are different sorts of magic, too. Some are much stronger than others.

"Miss Azalea, there is an object in your palace that has been magicked so strongly, it keeps me weak. Confined."

Azalea recalled Keeper raising the gushing, foaming water to the top of the bridge. He had been panting when he stood. Breathless and drawn, taxed almost to illness. Azalea scuffed her boot on the marble.

"A magic object?" she said. "Here, in our palace?"

"Yes."

"What is it?"

"I do not know. But here is a thought: Until earlier this year, I was hardly more than brick and mortar. Something happened to the magic object—it was partially broken. Broken enough that I have my magic back, at least in part."

Azalea's eyebrows knit. They hadn't anything magic, unless it was the tower, and that wasn't broken, only stopped. They had the old, dented magic tea set, one of the few remnants of the High King. Although—Azalea's brows knit further—she hadn't seen that tea set for quite some time.

"I need you to find the magic object, and destroy it," said Keeper. "Your period of mourning ends in but three months. Surely that is enough time?"

Azalea tapped her toe against the ground, the misty air stifling her.

"We . . . don't have much magic left in the palace," she managed to say. "We could probably find it, if I had all the girls search—"

Keeper took Azalea's hand from the silver doorframe into both of his, and pressed his lips against it.

"He did *what*?" Bramble cried.

"I know, I know," said Azalea. She sliced bread with a vengeance.

It was afternoon, and Azalea had just finished telling them the entire story at tea in the kitchen. The girls' eyebrows had risen and furrowed with each part of the telling, and at the end, their eyes were circles. Their muffins and tea had been forgotten as they stared at Azalea across the scrubbed servants' table.

"What a rotten shilling punter!" said Bramble, tearing her bread to bits. "I can't believe he stole our things! *Especially* the watch! We stole that watch first, fair and square!"

"Something magic?" said Eve, passing out the sliced cheese. "But what's left? I suppose there was the harpsichord—although that broke before the King was even born."

"Well," said Azalea, "there's the wraith cloak—"

"The what?"

"The cloak that would make you invisible. The High King would use it to slip into the city unseen. That wasn't unmagicked, but it was given away. No one knows where it is now, but surely it's fallen to pieces. So, that just leaves—"

"The tea set," said everyone in unison.

Azalea sighed and dipped a piece of her bread in her raspberry tea. "Right. But I haven't seen that for ages. Even the sugar teeth—they disappeared after that first night. Does anyone know what happened to it?"

No one had.

Clover, who had been feeding Lily sips of tea with a shaking teacup, remained flushed and silent through the entire exchange, her rose red lips pursed. Now, all of a sudden, she burst into sobs.

"It was my fault!" she cried. "I did it!"

Everyone exchanged glances before turning back to Clover, who sobbed into her napkin as though she had unbottled her heart. She even looked pretty with a dribbling wet face.

"Um, sorry?" said Azalea.

"*I* broke it!" said Clover. "I broke the tea set!" Hiccupping, she raised her chin, defiant. "With a *fire poker*!"

The story spilled from her between stutters and shuddering breaths. It seemed as though she had been aching to confess.

Several months ago, when she had been ill, Mrs. Graybe set the magic tea set to tend to her. It kept pushing at Clover and nipping at her to taste the nasty-smelling tea, and finally, when she couldn't take it any longer, she took the fire poker and *bashed* the tea set in. And not just once—repeatedly. There were still dents in the wall.

The girls gasped at this part.

The story became even more scandalous. Clover gathered up the pieces of the tea set in Lily's baby blanket and, late at night, slipped out and dumped the tea set into the garden stream.

"And the pieces—the pieces—they were still *wriggling*, and—oh! It was like I had drowned them alive!" Clover hiccupped. "But I am *not* sorry! I hated that horrid tea set!"

By this time, all the girls were laughing so hard they could hardly breathe. Bramble laughed so hard tea almost came out of her nose. Azalea laughed, more in shock that honey-sweet Clover could do something so violent.

"The teeth must have escaped while you murdered the rest of it," said Bramble, cough-laughing into her napkin. "Ha ha ha! You know, sometimes I think Clover is harboring some deep, dark shocking secret. Fire poker! Ba-hahahahaaa!"

The girls laughed all over again. Even Clover managed a small, wobbly smile. Azalea rubbed her thumb, remembering how the sugar teeth had nipped her fingers.

"I suppose that settles it," she said. "We've got to find the sugar teeth."

That night, in their newly mended slippers from the shoemaker's, Azalea had the girls search for the sugar teeth where she last remembered having them—in the silver forest. They had never properly explored the silver bushes and prickly pines off the path, and the girls searched back and forth, setting ornaments swaying and upsetting the bushes with a rustling fabric sound. Flora and Goldenrod even brought sugar cubes, in case they found them.

Thoroughly late for dance practice, the girls emerged from the sparkling foliage displeased, black dresses coated in silver dust.

"It's like looking for a needle in a stack of hay," said Delphinium as they made their way to the bridge. "*Silver hay.*"

"The sugar teeth aren't down here, let's face it," said Bramble. "They would have attacked one of us by now. They've probably run away. I'd bet a harold they've thrown themselves off the garden bridge to join their beastly comrades. Anyway, who cares if we set Keeper free or not? He's creepy."

"*I* certainly don't," said Azalea. "And if you don't either, maybe we should forget dancing and go back to the room."

"Steady on," said Bramble, two spots of pink on her cheeks. "I didn't mean it like *that*. Probably every gentleman was creepy back then. I mean, let's not be hasty or anything. Anyway, where else are we going to dance?"

"It's more—than just—dancing," said Clover. "We're—doing exactly what the—the High King did to p-poor Mr. Keeper. Dancing and just—just leaving him there. It's so unkind of us."

A guilty solemness fell over them all as they realized Clover was right.

"Well," said Bramble. "At least we have until Christmas." She pulled aside the willow branches.

Keeper stood framed by the entrance of the pavilion, his face lined. Behind him, in the middle of the dance floor, stood a pure white maypole, twisted like a marshmallow candy stick. Twelve colored ribbons dangled from it, bright and sleek. It could have been Azalea's imagination, but Keeper looked paler, and a touch older than he had that morning.

"Not a word to Mr. Keeper," said Azalea quietly. "We know how it feels to be trapped."

The girls gave the palace a full combing for the sugar teeth the next day. Rain pattered against the draped windows as they searched in the silver cabinet, turning up mismatched forks and spoons and an old shriveled potato. They sorted through the cabinets and even picked the lock to Mother's room. All her powder boxes, dresses, and jewelry had been locked tightly away, her nightgown lay on her bed, and everything felt strange and muffled.

The girls left the room, trying to swallow the choking emotion without smelling the white-cake and baby-ointment scent.

They searched through the portrait gallery, among the spindly sofas and tables, while the younger ones sat on the long red rug and ate bread and jam.

"What about this?" said Eve, at the end of the hall. She peered through a glass case on a pedestal, which held Harold the First's silver sword. The same one the King had taken with him to war. He took it to parliament meetings as well, and when the occasion called for it, speeches. It was ceremonial.

Azalea, for the first time, looked at it closely through the glass. More of a rapier than a real sword, the sort gentlemen two hundred years ago would duel with, it was old, dented, unpolished, and the mottled dark gray masked curly carved ornamentation along the side. Azalea peered closer and saw the thin crack up the side. Her brow creased, thinking of the sickening clang it had made when she'd fallen against it at the port.

"It can't be that," said Bramble. "That's not magic."

"Wait," said Azalea. "It was broken earlier this year. And it's old enough. We might as well see."

With Bramble's help, Azalea lifted the case and set it gently on the ground. She pushed her sleeve back.

"Don't touch it," said Eve when Azalea reached for

it. "Only the King can use the sword. It's . . . legend, or something. I read it."

"Lighten up, Primmy," said Bramble.

The girls held their breath. Azalea slowly grasped the handle beneath the swirls.

She screamed.

The girls panicked and screamed, air-curdling screams.

"Ha—ha ha." Azalea laughed and pulled her hand away. "Just kidding."

The girls glared at her. Azalea thought that rather unfair. If Bramble had done the same thing, they all would have thought it a riot. She sighed.

"It's just an old sword," she said, replacing the glass. "Even if it was magic, we couldn't get rid of it. It's governmental property."

The girls continued their search of the palace, progressing slower and slower as the day wore on, until they ended with a halfhearted search in the leather-and-wood-smelling library. The King was gone on R.B., and the younger girls played with the ladders underneath the iron mezzanine, rolling along the bookcase walls and hitting the end with a thump.

A commotion of cries and gasps brought Azalea to the King's carved wood desk, the other girls following after. Eve gaped over the morning's edition of the *Herald*, which Delphinium gripped tightly in her hands. Their eyes were wide.

"Is it Lady Aubrey's column again?" said Azalea, a hint of a smile crossing her lips.

"Just *look* at this!" Delphinium cried. She had a shrill, cutting voice, and it rang across the walls of books. Azalea's smile faded. She took the paper from Delphinium, open to the announcements section, and skimmed over the engagements and births and weddings. There, between two engagement posts, lay a large advertisement with an ink tick next to it. Azalea read.

ROYAL BUSINESS; STRICTLY
FOR THE YOUNG GENTLEMAN WHO MEETS THE CRITERIA—
A RIDDLE TO SOLVE:
WHERE THE TWELVE PRINCESSES OF EATHESBURY
DANCE AT NIGHT
AS WELL AS LIMITED ACQUAINTANCE
WITH THE PRINCESS ROYALE
THREE DAYS' STAY IN THE ROYAL PALACE
WILL BE GRANTED.
THE FOOD AND BOARD WILL BE FREE.

INQUIRIES TO BE SENT TO HIS ROYAL HIGHNESS
HAROLD WENTWORTH THE ELEVENTH OF EATHESBURY

"*What?*" Azalea cried.

Bramble took the paper from Azalea's hands and

read it herself. Confusion, then anger, passed over her. The younger girls whined to see what the fuss was.

"Oh, we shall see about *this*!" said Bramble, brandishing the paper. She marched out of the library, the girls running after. As if on cue, the entrance hall door opened, and the King stepped through. He was dripping wet from the rain. He hardly had his umbrella closed before the girls flanked him.

"What," said Bramble, brandishing the paper in his face, "what, sir, is *this*?"

The King frowned, looking mildly surprised and chagrined.

"Oh," he said. "So you have found it."

"Of course we found it!" said Delphinium. They followed him, a swarm of bees, as he methodically removed his soaking overcoat and hat. "A 'riddle to solve'? Balderdash!"

"How *could* you?"

"Now the whole country knows we dance at night!"

"If you are willing to tell me where you go," said the King crisply, "I will be happy to rescind the advertisement. As such, however, perhaps you will think twice before you make an oath like that again."

"But sir," said Eve. "Don't you already know where we go? Why turn it into R.B.?"

The King sighed and set his soaking umbrella against the hound umbrella stand.

"Because, Miss Evening Primrose," said the King, "even I will admit we must get certain things accomplished in mourning."

. . . acquaintance with the Princess Royale . . .

Azalea leaned against the heavy library door, hand on her stomach, trying to swallow a sick feeling. A Yuletide parlor game came to mind, one in which the gentlemen would step on slips of paper. They danced the gorlitza with whichever lady's name was written upon it. This was worse, though; this was marriage arranging, not just a game.

Other memories came, too; the King handing Azalea the invitation and saying, *The question is, how to become acquainted with gentlemen while in mourning.* Years ago, when Azalea had discovered that the crown princess of Delchastire was betrothed to a prince nearly forty years her senior, Azalea had fussed with the article so much it had turned her fingers black with ink.

Mother brushed through Azalea's hair that night, and Azalea didn't have to say anything; Mother knew.

"Oh, goosey," she had said. "Don't worry so. The King would never set you with someone you weren't fond of."

"You're on a king hunt!" said Bramble, bringing

Azalea back to the present. The girls cornered the King against the umbrella stand, where he firmly stood his ground.

"No, no, no," said the King, looking annoyed. "That isn't it at all. There is method in it. You will see."

"Mother wouldn't have done this!" said Bramble.

"*She* wouldn't have used Azalea as bait!" said Delphinium.

"Enough, *enough*!" said the King. "That is enough. You shall have to come to the reckoning that it is I who you have, and not your mother, and so it is. Nothing can help that. Despise me for it, as I know you all do, but when the guests arrive, we shall *all* be agreeable, and we shall *all* eat dinner together as though we are a very, very happy family! Which we are! Is that clear?"

The King's voice ended short of a yell, silencing them.

"Excellent," he said. He rubbed his bandaged hand over his forehead. "I look forward to having meals with you all again."

CHAPTER 15

*T*hree days later, just as lessons finished up and the girls stacked books and brushed off slates in the nook, the King arrived at the glass folding doors. A gentleman was with him, meticulously dressed in a deep blue suit with an extremely ruffled cravat.

"Ladies," said the King, in his stiff, formal way. "This is Mr. Hyette. He's a distant relative of ours. And our first guest."

The girls broke into hushed whispers. Mr. Hyette's eyes took in the chalk-smudged tablecloth, the wilted rosebushes, and dozing Tutor Rhamsden. His eyes grimaced, if his face did not. He eased into a smile and a bow.

"Why, these are the little princesses I've heard so much about," he said, straightening. "And—ah, this is the future queen." He stepped forward and took Clover's hand.

Azalea flushed. The younger girls giggled. Clover blushed furiously and tried to slip her hand from his.

"N-n-no—no—not I—"

The King stepped between the gentleman and Clover, frowning and breaking their hands apart. "Mr. Hyette, indeed! This is the third eldest. She is not even of age yet!"

The younger girls giggled madly. Eve and Delphinium snorted into their grammarians. Mr. Hyette flashed a very white, straight smile.

"Forgive me," he said. "There are so many. Will you introduce me?"

Introductions were made, sans Lily, who napped in the nursery. When the King finished the introduction with Azalea, Mr. Hyette's eyes caught her, and his face fell.

Azalea decided that these next few days were going to be very lonely ones for Mr. Hyette.

"You are all to entertain Mr. Hyette this afternoon," said the King. "In the gardens."

Slates clattered onto the floor.

Five minutes later, the girls stood at the open kitchen door, blinking in the brilliant overcast light. The smell of lilacs, roses, sweet peas, and honeysuckle mixed with the scent of crisp late summer leaves. None of them had been in the gardens for nine months, and the bright saturated greens, reds, and violets overwhelmed them. It reminded Azalea of Mother, beautiful and bright, thick with scents and excitement. And the King—he was like the palace behind them, all straights and grays, stiff and symmetrical and orderly.

"It's really allowed?" said Flora, her eyes alight at the colors.

"Allowed allowed?" said Goldenrod.

"For the last time," said the King, pushing them gently out the kitchen door and onto the path. "It is *Royal Business*! Go on. Get some color in your cheeks."

The younger girls screeched and ran off into the bushes. Bramble, Clover, and the other girls rushed after and gathered them back, reminding them of Section Five—Rules in the Gardens. Vast and sprawling, the gardens were so big it took nearly an hour to walk all the way around them, and young ones could get lost if they wandered off the brick paths. Azalea made to follow after them, through the trellised walkway, but a strong hand took her and held her back. Mr. Hyette.

"I say," he said, smiling his very white smile and pulling her a touch closer. "You don't look half bad in the sunlight. It brings out a perky red in your hair."

"Oh, honestly," said Azalea, trying to tug her hand away gently. "Mr. Hyette, please."

"You don't find me handsome?"

"No."

Mr. Hyette's smile faded.

"Now see here," he said. "You certainly have no right to be picky. Everyone knows the point of this silly riddle is to find the future King."

"Well—so what?" said Azalea. She tried pulling her hand free again.

"So your father had to *advertise* for suitors. And after meeting your rambunctious family, I can see why. Your pretty sister is the only one worth my time. However, if you are *nice* to me these next few days, perhaps I'll—"

"Mr. Hyette."

Mr. Hyette released Azalea as though he had been shot. The King still stood in the kitchen doorway, giving Mr. Hyette a cold, icy look. Azalea gratefully ran to him.

"Mr. Hyette, go away," said the King. "Azalea—a word."

Mr. Hyette, petulant, stormed down the path. The King made to say something, and for the first time in Azalea's life, he looked uncomfortable. He looked as though his insides had curled into an overspun thread, twisting on itself.

"Azalea," he said finally, "as this charade progresses, you will tell me if you are . . . fond . . . of any of the gentlemen?"

Azalea stared at him, a hot blush rising to her cheeks.

"Nat—naturally," she stammered.

The King's internal thread visibly untwisted.

"Just so," he said.

Azalea ran through the gardens, her black skirts billowing in the breeze of honeysuckle and lilac. She had forgotten how fresh and alive the gardens felt, with bright flowers bursting all over it like fireworks. Though a bit unkempt, with ivy growing over the path and moss clinging to the marble statues, it towered above her in a fine display of overgrown topiaries, thick trees, and flowered vines curling about the trellises. Shadows dappled her as she ran.

This riddle was an enigma, Azalea decided. And so was the King. She had thought, these past few days, that this R.B. was only a way to attract possible future kings. Like a ball, but allowed in mourning. Now, Azalea wondered, had the King contrived the game for *her*? Why would he be anxious if she was fond of a gentleman, before parliament decided?

And the gardens. Azalea hadn't expected that to come from this riddle. Had he known how much they missed it? And eating dinner with him. That was decidedly odd. He never seemed to care about it before.

Azalea found the girls in the fountained section of the gardens, crowded with white statues and ponds rimmed with marble. Water burbled and gushed, and a small breeze blew a curtain of mist about, making bits of rainbows. The younger girls had taken off their boots and stockings—strictly not allowed, as the gardens were public—and dipped their toes in the mossy pools.

Sitting on the edge of a marble fountain, Azalea told them about what the King had said. A thoughtful silence followed, only the burbling water breaking it.

"You know," said Eve, trying to pin a freshly picked flower into her dark hair, "I sometimes wonder if the King is, you know, clever. Not like us, of course. But clever in a quieter sort of way."

Bramble dipped her fingers into a standing pool, sending ripples and bobbing the lilies. She looked more serious than Azalea had ever seen her.

"If it's true," she said slowly, "then we all have more of a hand in our future gentlemen than I thought."

"It's me that has the arranged marriage, remember?" Azalea folded her arms. "The rest of you get your choice."

Bramble looked up from the pool and smiled, but it hadn't any wryness to it.

"No, Az," she said. "I don't think we do."

She stood, dried her hand on her skirts, and kept the unhappy smile still on her face. She dipped a deep, graceful Schleswig curtsy to Clover.

"Clover," she said, "is so beautiful. She is the prettiest of all. You saw how Mr. Hyette was with her. He would have been delighted to marry her."

Clover fumbled with the flower she pinned in Kale's hair.

"Horrors," she said, trying to smile.

"Once she comes of age in December," said Bramble, "she'll be snatched right up by the first gentleman who sees her. Like a golden nightingale. And she's so blasted *sweet*. She's far too sweet to object. She would just go along with it."

Clover blushed furiously. "N-no," she stammered. "It won't—be like—like that."

"And me," said Bramble, and even her pushed smile faded. "Well . . . me. I've got too little dowry and too much mouth. And no gentleman likes that. The King will be grateful to have anyone take me."

The fountains burbled, the trickling masking the girls' silence. Azalea touched her stomach, thinking of the terrible sick feeling that overwhelmed her every time she thought of her future gentleman. Now, she realized, Clover and Bramble had it, too. They looked miserable.

Azalea stood.

"There's a dance Mother once taught us," she said, walking to the standing pool. Among the lily pads stood twelve octagonal stepping stones, in a circle. The water lapped just above them. "Here, on the stones. Let's try it."

Though not a soul was about, the older girls were slightly worried that someone might wander by and see their ankles. Still, with a little coaxing, everyone's shoes and stockings lay in a jumbled pile, and Azalea walked about the rim of the pool, helping everyone to their granite stones. They nudged the lily pads off with their toes.

Azalea took her stone, slimy and skiffed with water, and the girls giggled as the water lapped at their toes. The point of this dance was balance: jumping from stone to stone without falling into the water.

"You always manage it," said Bramble, curling her toes on the slick stone. "Turning things right."

"That's what sisters do," said Azalea. "We watch out for each other. Don't we? The King would never arrange your marriage—and I would never let him. I promise."

Bramble's thin lips curved in a smile to the water at her feet.

Azalea counted off; two emphasis beats in six, everyone made ready to step off—when the hydrangea bushes a length away rustled and bobbed. The girls nearly slipped off their stones.

"Someone's there," whispered Jessamine as they all caught themselves.

Azalea followed her bright blue eyes into the bushes.

"Ah-ha!"

The girls shrieked. Azalea fought for balance on her stone, her hem dipping into the pond. A splash sounded behind her, followed by another splash, and Azalea twisted around, finding Kale and Eve sitting in the water, coughing and sputtering and soaking wet. Eve's spectacles were askew. Kale had a lily pad on her head.

Laughter sounded from the bushes. Mr. Hyette emerged, a walking stick tucked underneath his arm, laughing heartily. He clapped his hands.

"Well done, my ladies," he said. "Well done. Caught you dancing in public, and in mourning. Oh, dear, won't the King be pleased I've put a stop to it."

Kale inhaled a deep, sputtering breath and let out an ear-ripping scream.

"You terrible man!" cried Eve above Kale's screams, leaping to her stockings. "How dare you!"

Mr. Hyette laughed even more heartily. "You have very dainty ankles," he said.

Azalea snatched up her boots and stockings from the jumbled pile and marched straight to the palace, crossing over the grass and through the bushes. The girls ran after, leaving a trail of water. Mr. Hyette laughed and strolled after them.

"Your Majesty!" Azalea shrieked when they reached the kitchen. "Your Ma-jes-ty!" Combined with Kale's screams and the girls' angry voices, the entire racket echoed throughout the palace.

The King emerged from the library, paperwork in hand, eyebrows furrowed.

"Well, what is it, what is it?" he said crossly. "Can you not let me work for five minutes at a time?"

The girls burst into angry cries. Kale let out another piercing shriek.

"Him—him—him—" said Delphinium, pointing a shaking finger at Mr. Hyette, who laughed still. "He—he—him!"

"He—he—he was spying on us!"

"And we weren't even wearing our boots!"

"Or even our stockings!"

Thumpfwhap. The King threw Mr. Hyette up against the paneling. Mr. Hyette's head slammed against the wainscot.

Kale stopped midscream, hiccupped, and giggled.

"Mr. Hyette!" said the King.

Mr. Hyette struggled against the King's steel grip.

"Ow," he said. "I say, ow!"

The King yanked Mr. Hyette from the wall and grabbed him by the scruff of his fluffy cravat. He handled Mr. Hyette out the entrance hall doors, slamming them behind him. Outside, gravel scuffled.

"I say," said Bramble, in an impeccable impersonation of Mr. Hyette. "I say, I say! I say—this Royal Business could actually be quite a lot of *fun!*"

CHAPTER 16

*M*r. Hyette set sail that evening, with his limbs still intact. Azalea was glad the King didn't challenge him to a duel. The King was old-fashioned like that, and Azalea sincerely didn't think Mr. Hyette deserved a bullet in his arm.

It did mean, however, that the girls had to stay inside the next two days. They stubbornly ate meals in their room, and between lessons Azalea had them help her search through the attics for the sugar teeth. "Searching" consisted of Azalea bossing the girls into rifling through the old trunks and dusty hatboxes, which they did with loud complaints. Whenever Azalea turned away, they ran off.

Instead, in preparation for the next gentleman, they made a List of Kingly Qualities. It included things such as "Nice to sisters" and "Gives sisters presents." The list was four pages long by the time the second gentleman, a Mr. Oswald from the Delchastrian university, came.

He arrived with stacks of books, inkwells, and a general good-natured air that did not mind if the girls flocked to him and teased him about his bushy muttonchops.

"He is writing a book," said the King, following them out into the sunny, crisp gardens. "About the gardens here. We have two of his books already. Library, north side, O. What say you, Miss Azalea? Does he pass that list of your sisters'?"

Azalea cocked her head. Was the King actually teasing her?

"He'll have to shave," she said, deciding to take his lead.

"And what," said the King, stroking his own close-trimmed beard, "is wrong with whiskers?"

Azalea laughed, surprised at the King's uncharacteristic funning.

Dinner was different, too, with the girls bringing in flowers for the centerpiece, teasing Mr. Oswald, and chattering on about the gardens over fish stew. The King asked them how their day went, and they answered shyly that it had been very fine. Azalea asked him how his hand was, and he sucked in his cheeks, raised his bandaged hand, and wiggled his fingers in response. Dinner didn't progress so differently than it did when they had eaten with him before, but it was . . . nice. Something twisted inside Azalea. She had missed eating as a family.

In his three days' stay, Mr. Oswald toured the gardens and scribbled in his notebook while the younger girls plucked snapdragons and pansies to show him. He was fascinated with the lilac labyrinth, the fountains, and the midnight flower clock, ringed about with stepping stones. The King remained in the gardens, too. He brought all of his work, inkwells, papers, blotters, and set them on a stone bench, stubbornly keeping sight of them all. He worked over papers while the girls took tea underneath canopies of ivy and honeysuckle, the fresh breeze ruffling their hair and dresses.

At night, Azalea pinned the soft blooming flowers into the younger girls' hair, and they crowded in front of the vanity, trying to catch a glimpse of their reflections in the small mirror.

The next gentleman came as Azalea sorted underneath the beds in their room, searching for the sugar teeth and only turning up dust, buttons, and several dead spiders. She abandoned her search to tend to the gentleman, reluctantly.

It was Mr. Penbrook, from the Yuletide. Still moist, too. A thin sheen of sweat glazed his face. While they took tea that afternoon in the gardens, he talked, and talked, and talked about parliament, passing bills, and how much his estates brought in. Bramble stood behind him and pretended to pour tea on his head.

Eventually the girls scarpered off with the cheese, and Bramble made to follow them into the blossoming foliage.

"Wait," said Azalea, nearly overturning her wicker chair. She grabbed Bramble's hand. "We haven't finished searching the room."

"Oh, really, Az," said Bramble, pulling her hand away. "We have plenty of time. If we find them now, that's the less time we have to dance in mourning."

"But what if we don't find them before Christmas?"

"Oh, they'll turn up," said Bramble, smiling brightly. "Ready to massacre the next person. Maybe we'll get lucky and it will be him."

From his wicker chair, Mr. Penbrook smiled at both of them. A vague, clueless smile.

"Don't leave me," said Azalea. "Please."

Bramble dipped into a flowing gracious-to-leave-you curtsy, her thin strand of balance infuriatingly perfect. Then she took off into the bushes.

"Miss Azalea!" said Mr. Penbrook. He grasped her hand. "We are finally alone! It is fate!"

"Mr. Penbrook!" said Azalea, trying to twist her gloved hand from his grip. "Really!"

"I am quite taken with you, Miss Azalea!" he said.

"Oh, honestly," said Azalea. "I can't feel my fingers anymore. Please let go."

Mr. Penbrook released her hand, but he remained smiling his wet smile. Azalea peered past his face and even past the King, who stared at Mr. Penbrook with narrowed eyes, and saw the purple-flowered hedges in the distance.

"Mr. Penbrook," said Azalea, standing. "Do take a turn through the gardens with me."

Mr. Penbrook bounded to his feet. Azalea ran against the breeze to the lilac labyrinth. The thick smell of lilac dizzied her, and she had to duck beneath the hanging branches as she ran.

"Hurry now, Mr. Penbrook," said Azalea, turning through the twisted, leafy tunnels. "You've got to keep up!"

"Ah, I see! Ha ha! This is perfect, my lady! Ah . . . princess . . . you are going a bit fast—"

"Come along, Mr. Penbrook!"

"Princess? Princess Azalea? Hello?"

Guilt reamed through Azalea as she finished searching the bedroom by herself. She knew she shouldn't have done it. Unfortunately Mr. Penbrook was the sort of gentleman Mother had told her about. You could poison their horses, steal their pins, set their manors on fire, chop off their fingers, and they would still think you the sweetest little thing.

After dark fell, Azalea sent Mr. Pudding to fetch him. Mr. Penbrook arrived at the dining room, dazed, twigs in his hair, and smiled broadly at Azalea. Azalea groaned inwardly.

The next morning Mr. Penbrook did not show up to breakfast. Azalea discovered that the King had sent him to write a forty-two-page report on the bridge conditions in Hannover. Both relieved and shy at this, Azalea helped Mrs. Graybe make basted chicken for dinner—the King's favorite dish—and decided that having meals with him these next few weeks wouldn't be so bad after all.

"So far we've been through *eight* gentlemen," said Eve, one night several weeks later, at the pavilion. They retied their dance slippers, now coming apart at the seams, and sat on the floor in a ring. It was early morning, and the youngest ones had fallen asleep, little lumps on the side sofas, and everyone was yawning, signaling to Azalea that it was time to gather up the flock and go to bed.

"Eight gentlemen," Eve continued, "and something's been not quite right with every single one of them."

"Oh, they've been all right," said Azalea, wiggling her toes. She could see a bit of pink through the torn seam. These past few weeks had been a flurry of activity, with dukes and counts and even a viceroy arriving in very fine carriages. Viscount Scantlebury had even helped her look—unsuccessfully—for the sugar teeth in the cellar, and Sir Dietrich had actually been interesting to talk to. Azalea thought they were all nice—though not in a heart-twisting, breath-catching way. "They've all been awfully polite," she said, as though to make up for not fancying them.

"You're only saying that," said Bramble, "because you're too nice. We've found *plenty* of problems with them. Eve?"

Eve brought out a folded piece of stationery with the gentlemen's names on it, and scrawled ink comments next to each one.

"Duke Orlington."

"Had a wince. Next."

"Baron Rosenthal."

"Ha! He ate more than Ivy!"

"Oh, really," said Azalea. "That's not a good reason to discount—"

"Marquis DeLange," Eve continued.

"Ugh, he was shorter than *all* of us!"

"That's not—" said Azalea, but then changed her mind. It, actually, was.

"Anyway, the point is," said Bramble, waving Eve's piece of stationery away and smoothing her skirts primly over the marble. "None of them have been good enough for you."

"Azalea," said Delphinium. She sat on the marble across from Azalea, and leaned in to whisper, resting her elbows on the floor. "What about . . . you know . . ."

Azalea immediately colored, thinking of a gentleman with soft brown eyes.

"Keeper," Delphinium finished. She bit her lip and looked around, her light blue eyes flickering with fear, as though afraid Keeper might have heard, then turned back to Azalea with a devilish sort of grin.

"Keeper?" said Azalea. "No, thank you!"

But the girls all now had wicked little grins across their faces, and Azalea cringed. She recognized those looks, and they said "merciless teasing." Azalea had put up with quite a bit of that for the past several weeks, as the gardens turned from greens and purples to golds and reds and yellows. While the younger girls fought for seats next to the gentlemen at the dinner table, Delphinium drew pictures of what Azalea's children would look like if she married them, and Bramble kicked her under the table to make her squeak.

"Keeper," Bramble said in a syrupy voice, grinning. "Have you met anyone so blasted *handsome*?"

"Hush," said Azalea through her teeth. "He can probably hear you!"

"And so dashing," said Bramble, though her tone was a touch lower.

"And so perfect."

"I've never seen anyone with such . . . fingers," said Goldenrod.

Everyone paused.

"Well, yes, his fingers, too," said Bramble. She stood with a flourish and made the other girls get up, forming a ring around Azalea. Azalea groaned. This was a parlor-game dance, one where the person in the middle was the ball, and the girls "threw" her to each other, each with something to say.

"So suppose Azalea finds the sugar teeth after all," said Bramble, taking Azalea by the shoulders and spinning her. Azalea rolled her eyes but obliged, and let her feet turn beneath her. A slight push, and Azalea spun to Delphinium.

"She breaks them," said Delphinium, catching Azalea and pushing her to Hollyhock in a spin, a ball with skirts.

"Snap!" said Hollyhock.

Azalea flinched. Hollyhock fumbled to spin her to Bramble again.

"And in a burst of fireworks, he emerges from the passage! *Burst*!"

She pushed Azalea to Eve. Eve stopped Azalea from spinning, and paused.

"What then, though?" she said. "Keeper can't have anywhere to go."

"Well," said Bramble, her grin fading. "I suppose he'll try to court and marry Az. He likes her best."

Azalea paused, wondering how it would feel to be pressed up against Keeper, his long fingers cradling her head, his lips touching hers. If he kissed as well as he danced . . .

Her face burned like mad. She cast a fervid glance at the entrance, praying Keeper couldn't see her.

"He arrives at the palace doors, on a fine black horse," Delphinium prompted, picking up Bramble's lost thread, and Eve spun her again, "silver flowers in his hand—"

"And the King opens the door—" squeaked Flora, who caught Azalea.

And then, everyone stopped. Azalea's skirts twisted, then settled. It occurred to all of them what would happen next.

"And boxes Keeper straight in the face," Azalea finished.

Everyone managed to giggle, though it was true. Azalea shook her head, smiling.

"Well," said Eve as they gathered the sleeping girls up from their cushions. "It would be odd if you married him anyway."

"Aye," said Bramble. "Your children would be disappearing all over the place."

As they left, Keeper appeared at the arched entrance,

bowing them out. When Azalea thanked him, his long fingers twitched. Azalea wondered if he had heard the whole thing. In a fleeting moment, she almost wished the King *did* know about Keeper. He had eyes that seemed to see everything.

Still, it wasn't just Keeper the King would certainly dislike. The King surveyed *all* the gentlemen who came to the palace with that freezing-ice look he was known for. When December dawned, crisp and cold, curling the garden leaves with frost, the King used a look just as frigid on Viscount Duquette. Viscount Duquette had only been invited because he was a university fellow, which the King seemed to prefer. But Viscount Duquette, handsome, well educated, graying at the sides, had come for one reason only: Clover.

"Your beauty has reached somewhat legendary status, where I am from," he said over a dinner of hot soup and rolls. He raised his wine glass to Clover, who blushed to shame. "I am pleased to see the rumors were no exaggeration. To fine beauty, my lady, to romance, and to stories of golden hair."

The King threw Viscount Duquette out.

Doomed to be stuck inside for the next two days, the girls bickered and snapped at one another, and Clover looked close to tears. She cast longing glances through the curtains to the gardens, then would turn away quickly.

Lately she had been helping Old Tom clip and bundle the plants before the snow came, but Azalea hadn't thought she enjoyed it that much.

"It's all my fault," she said, when they prepared tea in the scrubbed kitchen. "If I hadn't—"

"What, been born pretty?" said Bramble. She swished the water in the kettle. "*This* is why we need to watch out for each other. Az knows."

"We can use the extra time inside to look for the sugar teeth," said Azalea.

The girls groaned.

Bread and cheese had been sliced and the servants' table had been set when the King arrived. The girls stood not just from protocol, but from surprise. Next to him, dressed in a fine black suit, with a gold-tipped walking stick, stood Fairweller.

"Ladies," said the King. "This is our guest for the next two days."

Spoons clattered.

"You're joking," said Bramble.

"That will do." The King's voice was crisp. "Minister Fairweller has been very generous to volunteer so you could all be allowed out."

"But you said Azalea wouldn't—" said Flora.

"For heaven's sake!" said the King. "Just tolerate him for the next two days, will you?"

They made Fairweller carry the basket. And the blanket. And the steaming kettle. He did so without a word. Half an hour later, they huddled under the tea tree, a great cozy pine in the wall-and-stairs part of the garden that blocked out the wind. Blanket spread, food unbundled, tea poured in steaming puffs, all without a word from Fairweller. There'd been no room on the blanket, so he knelt on the sappy needles that coated the ground.

Azalea busied herself with blowing on the younger girls' tea, cooling it, trying to avoid eye contact. Eve gave a cough.

"You know, Minister," said Delphinium, looking him up and down with her blue eyes. "You really aren't bad looking. A red-colored waistcoat would do wonders for you. You should wear one to your next speech. All the ladies would tease their husbands into voting for you."

Fairweller's lips grew thin.

"I would rather not talk about politics at this moment," he said.

The girls exchanged glances.

"*Can* you talk about other things?" said Bramble.

"I can be agreeable," said Fairweller. "If the other party is."

"Oh, well," said Bramble. "There goes that, then."

"Minister, why are you doing this?" said Azalea, setting her teacup on its saucer. "I mean, it's nice of you to offer so we can be in the gardens, but surely you would rather be in your own manor? We know you don't like us very much."

Something flickered in Fairweller's face as his colorless gray eyes took in all of them.

"I am doing it," he said, "because it is clear to me you have found one of the palace's magic passages in your room."

Teacups rattled. Flora grasped Azalea's hand.

"And if you expect me to stand idly by," said Fairweller, "and let you become trapped or worse with magic—"

"Trapped?" said Clover.

"It's not dangerous!" said Flora.

"Magic, shmagic," said Bramble, setting her teacup down with a clink. "We can see right through you! You're only here because you wanted to become acquainted with us. Admit it."

Fairweller's lips narrowed to razor-thin.

"It is not . . . the only reason," he said.

Azalea nearly spit her mouthful of tea. Bramble gaped, horrified. Clover's face was so pink even her ears blushed. Flora broke the silence first.

"But you're a Whig," she said.

"This has nothing to do with politics," said Fairweller.

"We're very picky about our husbands," said Bramble, picking apart her bread. "*And* our brothers-in-law."

Fairweller stood, nearly hitting his head on the pine branch.

"You make yourselves perfectly clear," he said. "But then, you always have."

He left. He didn't thank them, or even bow. He just stepped over Lily, who played with the blanket hem, fought his way out of the needles, and was gone.

"Well, that went well," said Bramble.

Azalea sliced more bread, tucked shawls tighter around the girls' shoulders, trying to smooth things over. Everyone was cranky as they realized they had to go inside now. Azalea tried not to think of Fairweller, his thin mustache and piercing gray eyes.

Minutes later, as they bundled things up into the basket, another voice sounded, carrying through the cold air. This one, if possible, was worse than Fairweller.

"My lady," the voice called in a singsong tone. "My lady—I know you are out here—"

"Great waistcoats," said Bramble as the color drained from everyone's faces. "It's Viscount Duquette! He's back!"

Clover, pale as death, only had a moment to slip out

the back of the pine tree and flee before a pair of shiny boots appeared at the branch-flanked entrance. This was followed by a handsome, smiling face and then all of Viscount Duquette, brushing off pine needles and smiling wolfishly.

"Ah, here you are," he said. "Bundled up in a little cocoon. Where is the butterfly?"

"Oh, brother," said Bramble.

"What are you doing here?" said Azalea, grasping in the basket behind her for the butter knife. Her hand found a teaspoon. It was better than nothing.

"I've come to make a proposal," he said, his eyes raking over them. "Before anyone else does. As soon as she is of age, gentlemen from everywhere will be flocking here, and I plan to snatch her up—"

"*Your Majesty!*" Azalea screeched. "*Your Majesty!*"

She knew the King couldn't hear her. He was inside, tending to papers. Still, Azalea clung to the hope that yelling would be enough to scare the Viscount away.

"Ah, perhaps she slipped out the back, then," said the Viscount. "She can't be far away."

Another pair of shiny black boots appeared at the entrance.

Azalea almost cried with relief. Almost, except that these boots did not belong to the King. This figure didn't even bother to bend down into the entrance, but instead pushed his way through the upper branches. Pine needles showered over them.

Minister Fairweller.

He surveyed the scene, Azalea backed up against the tree trunk, grasping a spoon, and the girls huddled behind her, clutching their teacups, cowering away from Viscount Duquette.

After a long, awkward moment of silence, Fairweller turned to the Viscount.

"Who are you?" he said, in his cold, flat voice.

The Viscount, half a head shorter than Fairweller, sized up his fine dress and walking stick, and gave Fairweller a short bow, clicking his heels.

"Viscount of Anatolia, sirrah, knight of the fourth order and—"

"You are Viscount Duquette."

Something in Fairweller's tone made the Viscount twitch.

"He wants to mawy Cwover," whispered Jessamine in a tiny, crystalline voice.

"So I have heard," said Fairweller, unmoved. "Also, from what I have heard, Miss Clover does not care for the match."

"Ah, never mind that," said the Viscount with a wry smile. "We are men of the world, are we not? Ladies like *her* are easily bullied."

Fairweller's finger twitched against his walking stick.

"Minister, Clover's gone, isn't she?" Azalea bit her lip and pleaded to him with her eyes. Fairweller stared back at her, his iron eyes unreadable. Azalea's heart fell. He wasn't going to take her lead.

"Miss Clover," said Minister Fairweller to the Viscount after a long moment, "is not here. She has gone to a speech with her father, in Werttemberg. I could set you up with a carriage, if you'd like."

The girls' mouths dropped open. Viscount Duquette did not see.

"Well!" he said, clicking his heels together. "It is nice to see that *someone* behaves like a gentleman around here!"

The girls found Clover about an hour later, hiding among the untrimmed unicorn and lion topiaries, weeping on a stone bench. They flocked to her, wrapped an extra shawl around her shoulders, and told her the story.

"Werttemberg, though," said Eve. "That's two countries away!"

Clover wept and laughed at the same time.

CHAPTER 17

"*C*an I not trust you for five minutes with a gentleman without scaring him away?" said the King, displeased when he found them later, playing spillikins in the entrance hall and decidedly Fairweller-less.

The girls smiled sheepishly and did not tell him about Viscount Duquette. That would render him murderous, and he had been in such an agreeable humor of late. He still lectured, naturally, when he caught the twins sliding down the banister, or when Kale spilled an inkwell on the dining room rug, or Hollyhock embroidered the curtains together. But he paid attention to them at dinner, too, and asked them how their day had passed. None of them supposed they had grown fond of this (they always felt so nervous around him), until one night the King was gone on R.B., and the girls had to have dinner without him.

It felt . . . empty.

"He saw us shivering, in the kitchen," said Flora as they tied up slippers one early December night. "And he had Mr. Pudding build up the fire in the kitchen stove *and* the fire in the nook and put two extra scuttles by each!"

"And he always wants them to be well built!" said Goldenrod.

"And he says, when it is Christmas, we shan't have any gentlemen come!"

"It will be a holiday! A real holiday!"

The girls beamed. A glimmer of excitement had sprung to life within them when the gardens had frosted, curling the leaves and coating the flower bushes, statues, and pathways white. They waited anxiously for snow and, with hopeful eyes, for something else: the end of mourning.

"It's less than a month now," said Eve as Azalea braided Hollyhock's bright red hair. Her cheeks were rosy with excitement. She was becoming prettier every day, even with spectacles. "It's hardly even three weeks," she said.

"I can hardly, hardly wait!" said Hollyhock.

"We won't need a gentleman to go out into the gardens!"

"We can just . . . go!"

"And we can wear color again!"

"And we can *dance*!"

"We already dance," said Azalea, but she smiled as they hopped from one foot to another, bumping into their poufs and the round table and their beds, throwing pillows with excitement. That night, in keeping with the season, she taught them a Christmas jig. In this step, the lady put her hand to the gentleman's, raised it to eye level, and they turned about each other. Clover played Azalea's obliging partner, catching the gentleman's steps perfectly.

"Break apart, turn around," said Azalea, her skirts twisting with her. She winked at the girls, crowded in a black mass on the marble floor, turned to face Clover again—

—and found herself facing Keeper.

"Oh!" said Azalea.

"He . . . sort of . . . cut in," said Clover, to the side of her. Her skirts still swished from Keeper spinning her out. She blinked, her pretty face alight with surprise.

Keeper took Azalea's hands in his, sending a shiver up Azalea's spine, before she could pull away. He lifted them just above their lips, keeping his eyes on hers the entire time.

"Ah, the holiday window," he said, turning her about with ease. His cloak hem brushed the marble. "It didn't seem right for you to dance it without a gentleman."

Azalea's eyes narrowed. A hot flick of temper sprung in her chest, coursing to her hands. She didn't like being pushed. Instinctively, she tugged her hands away.

"Clover was doing fine—" she said.

Lightning fast, Keeper snatched her hands back. He gripped them so tightly, Azalea inhaled sharply. Her fingers throbbed in his grasp.

"You haven't been looking for it," he said. His voice was soft and low. His eyes bore into her, and she avoided them by looking at his neck, eye level for her. A muscle clenched in his neck, just above his cravat. "You haven't even been trying."

"We have," whispered Azalea, hot blood searing her cheeks. Her fingers throbbed in Keeper's squeezing grip. "Let me go."

Keeper smiled, gently. "Perhaps you could try just a *touch* harder?"

Azalea writhed her hands from his grip. They slipped from their gloves, which remained hanging in his long fingers.

"We have until Christmas," she said.

Keeper, his eyes never leaving her, tucked the empty gloves into his waistcoat. For the first time, Azalea realized how dead and cold his eyes were. Unlike Mr. Bradford's, they had no light in them.

"So you do," he said.

The next day, Azalea's fingers were bruised and swollen. It hurt to hold a pen and button her blouse, and she was annoyed and angry.

"Honestly, if no one is going to help me find the sugar teeth," said Azalea as they bundled up for the gardens, "then we shouldn't even be dancing there."

An uproar of protestations and foot stomps met this, as well as a thundercloud over the girls' temper. Azalea clenched her fists, which only hurt her fingers more.

"What about the stream?" said Bramble. "Have you looked there? The sugar teeth are probably nosing about for the rest of the tea set."

Taking Bramble's advice to heart, Azalea strode to the furthermost part of the gardens that morning. This part of the gardens hadn't been tended to for years; tree roots broke up the pathway into stumbling bricks, and the dried fall leaves of the trees blocked out the sun, branches right at eye level. It smelled of rotting wood and wet weeds. Ivy, moss, and tree roots grew over everything, and it was coated in a blanket of crispy fall leaves.

Lord Howley, the newest gentleman of the game, followed after Azalea. He was a Delchastrian MP, had thick sideburns and a mustache, and was so arrogant he wouldn't even speak to the younger girls. He had badgered and badgered Azalea, asking her where she was going, until she finally told him.

"Magic tea set?" he said, tripping over a tree root. "I thought the Eathesburian royal family had sold that old thing. I saw it advertised."

"We didn't," said Azalea. She didn't go into details. The year before, when Mother had gotten terribly ill, the King had sent for a Delchastrian doctor. Silent and brooding, he prescribed medicines so expensive they had to dismiss one of their maids. The King even threatened to dispose of their dance slippers, but did not, at Mother's insistence. Instead, Azalea and the girls spent hours baking muffins and breads to sell. The King had advertised the old magic tea set, but for some reason, no one wanted sugar teeth that could gouge their eyes out.

Still, it had turned out all right. Mother had gotten better—a little.

"You know, you wouldn't need to sell your things if the King raised the taxes on your imports and exports," said Lord Howley as they picked their way over the uneven brick, bringing Azalea back to the present. "Tax and two-point-five variable percentage rate—"

"The King hasn't raised the taxes in over two hundred years," Azalea retorted. She pushed a branch out of her face, and it snapped back, hitting Lord Howley's. Lord Howley sputtered but pressed on.

"If I were king," he said, "I could change that." He

pushed a sly smile. It made his mustache bristle.

Azalea turned about on the corner of a brick, balancing with impeccable grace. She smiled broadly at him, the sort of smile where she knew her dimples showed deeply.

"Lord Howley," she said. "Why don't you tell the King about that *marvelous* three-party system you were explaining earlier? He'd love to hear it."

Lord Howley pushed a branch out of his face. "I don't think he likes me very much," he said.

"He's that way to everyone. Besides—" Azalea clasped her hands together, still beaming. "It would *impress* him!"

"Do you think so?" Lord Howley brightened.

"Oh, yes. He loves it when people tell him how to run the country."

Lord Howley strode off to find the King, who tended to paperwork in a nearby section of the gardens, and Azalea exhaled in relief. Several minutes later, she stood at the edge of the garden stream, a picturesque thing with a stone bridge arched over it.

After looking into the rushing current, Azalea lost hope. The stream was too deep and choppy to see the bottom. She balanced on a rock, leaning over to spot any glints of silver, and when she couldn't, daintily leaped to another rock in the middle.

Something out of the corner of her eyes caught her attention. A dark figure—not black, but dark brown, broad shoulders, holding a tall hat and a stack of books. Azalea had a moment to take in the rumpled hair—

—before she lost her balance and crashed into the stream.

Ice water enveloped her. The shock slapped air from her and she flailed, the current pulling her crinolines and skirts. The world muffled into freezing, garbling underwater sounds of heartbeats in her ears. Azalea panicked.

A warm arm grasped her about the waist and pulled her to the surface. Gasping for air, Azalea found herself looking into an even warmer pair of soft brown eyes. Mr. Bradford!

Azalea coughed and sputtered, flushing because the water was only waist deep. And then she flushed deeper, because Mr. Bradford had his arm around her waist, keeping the current from taking her.

"Are you all right?" he said. Water dripped down his face and long nose.

He's talking to you! her mind yelled. He's talking to you! Say something clever! Say something clever!

Azalea said, "Mffloscoflphus?"

"The water is rather cold," he said. He pulled her to the bank. Azalea chattered and shivered and coughed, and he continued asking her if she was all right. She wasn't.

She was morbidly embarrassed, that's what she was.

"Thank you," said Azalea, through chatters. She managed a shivering smile as he helped her to the broken path. "What are you doing here?"

"I've come to return the books I borrowed," he said. Even dripping wet, his hair still stuck up in tufts. "I've been looking for the King."

Azalea guessed he had gotten lost—she still could get lost in this part of the gardens. She insisted on taking him to the King, who wasn't far. She also insisted on helping Mr. Bradford gather his books and hat, which he'd thrown down pell-mell and which lay in a jumble over tree roots and fallen leaves.

To his credit, Mr. Bradford did not ask what Azalea had been doing in the stream. Together they walked over the uneven path, ducking tree branches, leaving a trail of water on the old brick.

"What would you do," said Azalea, to keep from chattering as they hurried on. Their boots *oosh eesh oosh eesh*ed with every footfall. "I mean, if you did win a seat in the House?"

The light in Mr. Bradford's eyes brightened.

"I don't know," he said.

"Gutters for the Courtroad bridge, so it doesn't get icy?" Azalea teased. Mr. Bradford grinned bashfully, and absently smoothed down his wet hair.

"I've been thinking about transportation and things," he admitted. "Railways."

"A railway!" said Azalea. "In Eathesbury?"

"I went to the Delchastrian Exposition last year," he said as they progressed into the tamer part of the gardens, where the trees actually stood in rows and the trellis above them didn't have too many vines hanging in their faces. He had a spring to his steps and was more animated than Azalea had ever seen him. "Such technology, it is beyond me! They've a new engine; the pistons utilize the steam differently so it harbors more energy. It's a wonder. I could only think, if Eathesbury had that! All our imports and exports are through ship and cart—"

He spoke on, of roads and checkpoints and imports, surplus and expenses, and in his excitement, Azalea could only think, Egads. Fairweller was right. You *would* be a good M.P.

". . . I suppose it's a bit boring," he admitted, when he had finished after several minutes. "But I could talk all day about it."

"Not boring at all," said Azalea, smiling. "Mr. Bradford, why don't you run for parliament? You would be quite as good as your father."

Mr. Bradford's cheerful demeanor went out like a snuffed candle. He fell quiet, his eyes solemn and serious.

After a long moment, he said, "Government wore my father down." His rich-cream voice was low. "After my mother died. It etched in every line of his face and pushed him to breaking."

Azalea reached out a soggy glove and touched his arm. Softly, just at his elbow. She wanted to give him toast. The sort that had melted butter and a bit of honey spread on top. It was a stupid thought, but there was something comforting about toast.

Mr. Bradford turned, and though his eyes were sad, they were hopeful, too. He placed his own soggy gloved hand over Azalea's. Azalea's heart nearly exploded.

"Princess—*aaack!*"

They broke apart, stepped away from each other, and turned to see Lord Howley at the end of the trellis path, shaking out a handkerchief to hold to his face. In the distance, on a stone bench, was the King. He looked irritated. "Lord . . . Howley," Azalea stammered.

"What the devil *happened* to you?" he said. "You smell like—like—wet fabric! And who the devil are *you?*"

Mr. Bradford turned to stone. Even his brown eyes hardened. The only movements to him were the bits of water that dripped off his face and suitcoat. He looked at Lord Howley, his expression completely unreadable, then to Azalea, then back to Lord Howley.

"This is Lord Howley," said Azalea, hoping to smooth over the awkwardness with Princess Royale grace. "He's a guest here. On . . . Royal Business."

"Oh. Yes." Mr. Bradford remained stony. "Royal Business. I have heard of it."

Who hasn't? Azalea thought. To Mr. Bradford, she suppressed a smile. "If Lord Howley becomes King," she said, "he says he'll raise the taxes."

"Oh, *does* he?"

For a moment, the gentlemen glowered politely at each other.

"Well," said Azalea, breaking the tension. "I'm an icicle. I've got to get changed. There is the King, Mr. Bradford. Thank you—again."

Mr. Bradford visibly softened, no longer stone when he looked at her. He bowed smartly, clicking his heels together in regimental fashion.

"Princess," he said.

Azalea ran to the palace. She dripped the entire way there, determined that the next time she saw him, she would have his watch in her hand. Her icy skirts and blouse clung to her, but she didn't feel it, for how much a pair of soft brown eyes could warm her.

CHAPTER 18

*S*now came a week before Christmas, turning the gardens into a fairyland. Everything shimmered with white ice, each twig and stubborn leaf coated. All the statues had cakes of snow on their heads, and it topped the hedges and pergolas dripping with icy vines. The air had a new, fresh smell and the cold whipped the girls' faces, leaving them rosy cheeked.

They spent the day playing snow games, sliding on the pond ice, and throwing snowballs at the latest gentleman, Baron Hubermann. He was a decent sort, but he stormed away the third time they knocked his hat off, and the girls gathered at the end of the gardens to watch the King, riding in the meadow.

"He's a very fine rider, is he not?" said Delphinium as they peeked through the iron gate, watching the King canter on Dickens. He nodded at them as he galloped past. Each hoof fall left a great chunk of snow upturned.

"I think we should go in now," said Azalea. "If you all help me set the table for dinner, we can look in the silver cabinet again for the sugar teeth."

The girls let out a collective groan.

"I can't believe you still care about that," said Bramble.

Azalea was rankled. "He has Mr. Bradford's watch!"

"So what?" said Bramble. "Mr. Bradford is rich. He can buy another one."

Azalea kicked snow onto Bramble's boot.

"Anyway," said Bramble, good-naturedly scuffing the snow off. "I've been thinking. We only have a few more days to dance in the pavilion, before we can dance anywhere we like. So, what if, on our last night there, we just said, 'Hulloa, Keeper, this has been ripping, thanks for the dances, we'll keep our eyes open for the magic thing and the moment we find it we'll nip on back. We know where to find you!' I mean, that wouldn't be bad, would it? I just don't like the thought of him toddling about outside of the pavilion."

"Exactly," said Eve, bundled up so only her pink cheeks and spectacles showed. "If we did set him free, what would Keeper do? He can't have any lands or manor anymore."

"Keeper?" said Bramble. "Who cares about Keeper? What about *us*? If the King found out we'd been off dancing around someone like Keeper, he'd murder us. As far as we know, the King hasn't been through that passage since he was a wee chit—if he ever was a wee chit, which I doubt—and I'd like it to stay that way."

The King pulled up short at the gate, scattering snow. Dickens snorted and shook his mane.

"Come into the meadows, ladies," he said. "You're all crowded about so. It's not against the rules; it's royal property. Come along."

The gate screeched with cold and rust as they opened it and moved into the bright blues and purples of dusky snow.

"Would any of you like a ride?" said the King.

The girls backed away.

"No, thank you!" squeaked Ivy.

"Definitely not!"

"I don't think so."

The King frowned at them, the younger girls clutching Azalea's skirts and only just peeking out at Dickens, who pawed and sent great puffs into the air. The King sucked in his cheeks, gave a short nod, and urged Dickens into a gallop.

Moments later, as the girls breathed sighs of relief, the King turned Dickens about and streaked toward them.

They cried out and backed against the stone wall. Leaning down from the saddle, the King reached out his arm, and whisked Hollyhock up as he galloped past. Hollyhock let out a brilliant scream.

Azalea gaped as the King pulled Hollyhock onto the saddle in front of him, keeping his arm tightly about her waist. Her screams turned to laughter. The King cantered around the meadow three times and pulled to a halt in front of the girls. Hollyhock slid from the horse, dizzy, but with a huge, delighted grin on her freckled face.

"We went so fast!" she said.

In a bustle of black skirts and scarves, the girls begged for a turn. The King obliged. He scooped each girl onto his saddle and galloped about the meadow. Eve, Delphinium, Ivy, and the twins each had a chance, clutching to Dickens's mane as Dickens cantered beneath them. Jessamine clutched the King's neck and buried her head in his waistcoat, only peeking out with one bright blue eye. Clover and Bramble even had a ride, but only, they insisted, because they held Kale and Lily, and the little ones should have a turn. Bramble grinned, albeit bashfully, as she slid off the horse, Kale in her arms.

"Miss Azalea," said the King, holding his hand down to her.

"No, thank you," said Azalea.

The King frowned, but pushed Dickens into a snow-churning gallop. Two seconds later, Dickens streaked toward her and the King leaned down, his arm out. Azalea hardly had a moment to realize what he was doing when she felt a *thumpf!*, and blues and whites whorled around her as her throat tried to jump out of her mouth, and the King hoisted her onto the saddle.

When the world stopped twisting around her, Azalea tried to slip out of the King's grip and back onto solid ground.

"I don't like riding!" she said.

"If you didn't squirm so, you would like it better," said the King. "Don't dismount now! You'll break your head!"

He galloped Dickens to the side, into the long blue shadows of the trees, pulled back, and dismounted. Azalea was left alone on the saddle, clutching Dickens's mane.

"Try it alone now," he said. "I taught you when you were six. You were a fine little rider then. Do you remember?"

"No!" said Azalea.

"You remembered how to ride last winter," said the King quietly. He had his arms crossed. "You rode very well, one night last winter, if I remember."

The horse beneath Azalea shifted, and she clutched to keep her balance.

"That was nearly a year ago," she stammered.

"Some things are burned into one's memory."

The King helped her down gently onto solid ground, and didn't say another word. Later, in the straw-smelling stables, the King made all the girls help feed and brush the horses. The girls took turns with the brushes, and Flora and Goldenrod even found some sugar cubes in their apron pockets. They squealed with laughter when Dickens nosed their cupped hands.

"Where did you learn that, sir?" said Azalea, as the King tended to the other horses. "To snatch us up like that, while you were galloping?"

"Ah." The King threw the blanket over Thackeray. "Regiment practice. It is an old tradition, from the revolution. They say the rebellion—the cavalry—burst through the windows, thorns, and vines, and scooped up the prisoners from the magicked palace. Romanticized, of course. It is tradition, however, so we practice it. On sacks of wheat and potatoes."

Azalea smiled. "I hadn't heard that, sir."

The King smoothed the blanket on Thackeray's back. He opened his mouth, and shut it. Then he opened it again, and after a moment, said, "You used to call me Papa, do you remember that?"

The question took Azalea back.

"No," she said.

The King frowned. Azalea hastily revised.

"I mean," she said. "Papa . . . well . . . it doesn't really suit you. I've never felt it does. The girls, too. I only remember calling you sir. As such."

The King sucked in his cheeks and tugged on the ends of the blanket, straightening it. He did not say anything. The smell of horse suddenly felt overwhelming.

A cry of delight broke the tension, and Azalea gratefully ducked into the main aisle. Hollyhock, who had been digging through old saddle satchels hanging from pegs, had found something hidden in an aside saddle. The girls flocked about her, oohing.

She clutched a jet brooch in her freckled hand. A tiny bit of worn silver rimmed it, and the glass caught the golden lamp highlights of the stables. Azalea bit back a gasp.

"That's Mother's!" she said, delighted. "All her things aren't locked up!"

"She must have put it in the satchel," said Eve. "Maybe she was afraid to lose it."

"She . . . used to wear it all the—the time," said Clover. "Just . . . here." She touched the top button of her collar.

"It's beautiful," Flora breathed.

The King finished hanging the brushes on the pegs, in order, coarse to soft, and turned to see what the fuss was about. His expression turned to ice when he saw

Hollyhock's freckled hand curled around the brooch. He held out his hand.

"Give it here," he said. "It is not yours."

Hollyhock clutched the brooch to her chest.

"I founnit in Mum's satchel. Can we keep it? 'S black. I'll share. I really will."

"It belongs with your Mother's things. Not with you, Miss Hollyhock."

Azalea maneuvered so she was in front of Hollyhock. "Sir," she said. "Why not? We'll share it among ourselves; it won't be breaking mourning."

"That isn't the point, Miss Azalea."

"What if we just borrowed it? For the next six days? Just until mourning is over?"

"We'll be careful with it," said Eve.

"Oh, please, sir! *Please!*"

The younger girls jumped up and down, hands clasped in begging, and Ivy even dared to tug on the King's suitcoat.

"Enough!" said the King, cutting them short with a brusque wave of his hand. "Enough. Six days, that is all. *Six.* Is that understood? I am doing this against my better judgment. Not a scratch, young ladies!"

"Bramble," said Azalea that night, as they danced a quadrille. They danced in lines opposite each other, crossed and turned and traded places, the music a lively jaunt. She crossed diagonal, bending down to join hands with Jessamine, and stopped across from Bramble. "Bramble, do you remember calling the King Papa?"

Bramble crossed behind Azalea and backed up to her place.

"What?" she said.

"The King. He said we used to call him Papa." Azalea walked with Flora up the line. "He seemed sure of it. And—" Azalea paused. "And I think—I think he *wants* us to call him Papa."

The music ended, but the girls forgot to curtsy.

"He said that?" said Bramble.

"No," said Azalea. "Not as such."

"Puh-*pah*?" said Hollyhock. "Him?"

"It doesn't really fit him," said Eve. "*Papa* is more a storybook thing."

"He is—trying," said Clover.

Delphinium sat on the marble floor, stretching her foot out, her pink toe peeking through the torn seams.

"I don't think he can be a *Papa*," she said. "Not after everything. I *still* get angry."

Azalea pulled off her black glove and considered the red fingernail prints in her palm. She sighed.

A clattering across the dance floor interrupted her

thoughts—the brooch. Hollyhock had been fiddling and fumbling with it all night, unpinning it to polish it on her skirt hem, pinning it again. Now she had spun about with it in her hand, and had accidentally released it.

"Oh, Holli, honestly," said Azalea, striding to pick it up, by the lattice. "If you can't keep it pinned to your—"

A pair of black gloves scooped it up just as Azalea leaned down to take it.

Azalea straightened sharply. "Give it *back*!" she said.

Keeper, only a few inches from her, his dark form taking up her entire vision, rubbed his thumb over the smooth, curved surface of the brooch, and he lazily regarded Azalea, making no other movement.

"Keeper!"

He inhaled slowly, took Azalea's outstretched hand—shudders went through her throat, he felt so *solid*—and pressed the brooch into her marked palm.

"I was only picking it up," he said, quietly. His thumb rubbed a red nail mark on her hand. A smile crossed his lips. "Temper, temper."

Azalea pulled her hand away, her ears hot, and gave the brooch back to Hollyhock. All the way through the silver forest and back up the passage, she wiped her hand on her skirts, trying to get rid of the silky feeling of Keeper's thumb stroking her palm.

The next morning, Azalea awoke to a commotion. A quiet one, with whispering, the rustling of bedsheets and blankets. Hollyhock, Ivy, and the twins mussed their beds, lifting pillows with the blushing look of someone trying very hard not to look like they were blushing. Azalea groaned.

"Oh, Hollyhock," she said. "Please don't tell me you've lost what I think you've lost."

Hollyhock burst into bawls.

"I—I—I didn't mean to!" she cried. "I just lost it!"

All the girls, now awake from the ruckus, set to looking for the brooch. They shook out dresses, rummaged, folded, unfolded, smoothed, searched. Azalea took Hollyhock by the shoulders.

"You brought it back, didn't you?" said Azalea. "After Keeper picked it up, you pinned it to your blouse?"

Hollyhock gulped and hiccupped.

"I don't remember!" she said. "I put it in my pocket, I think!"

"Keeper!"

Azalea spat the word, the loudness deadened by the curtains and bedsheets. Everyone stopped rifling through the linens. Bramble gave a last shake to Hollyhock's boots, and a spoon clattered onto the wood floor.

"We . . . don't know it was him, not for certain," said Clover, wrapping ribbons around the worn slippers.

"Oh, it was him all right!" The familiar boiling-blood sensation began to heat her fingers. She recalled the cold deadness of his eyes when he pressed the brooch into her hand. Azalea snatched the silver handkerchief from her apron pocket.

"Tell Tutor I won't be to lessons," she said. "Invent some sort of disease. I'm going to *get it back*."

Azalea hardly paid attention to the glimmering silver-white forest as she hurried through, hot temper speeding her steps. The stale, stagnant smell of the pavilion suffocated her, so different from the gardens. It felt dead. She shoved the silver willow leaves aside, *click click click*ed over the bridge to the pavilion.

Keeper lay balanced across the railing, between the arched sides of the lattice. His cloak dripped to the floor, a strand of midnight hair over his eyes. He looked like a black, serpentine cobweb clinging to the lattice. Only his long, gloved fingers moved.

They crawled and wound about a scarlet-colored web with uncanny dexterity, a needle dangling as he did so. He was playing spider's crib with Flora's embroidery thread. And while he played, he murmured a nursery rhyme:

"How daintily the butterfly
Flits to the spider's lace

Entranced by glimm'ring silver strings
Entwined with glist'ning grace.

"How craftily the spider speaks
And whispers, 'All is well,'
Caresses it with poison'd feet
And sucks it to a shell."

"Where is it?" Azalea stood in the middle of the dance floor, arms crossed, so tense she could hear the blood rushing in her ears.

Keeper twisted his hands, the string wrapping even more weblike about his fingers.

"Ah, my lady," he said.

"Where is it?"

Keeper gracefully leaped from the railing to the floor.

"Do you know why I am called Keeper?" he said. "Because I *keep*. You have known me thus long."

"Give it back."

"No. It is the first thing I have that is your mother's. I will keep it."

The tight parts of Azalea's dress—her corset, the cuffs of her sleeves, her collar—pulsed.

"Oh, no hard feelings, my lady," said Keeper. "I simply think you are not trying hard enough. Your mother's brooch should give you all . . . encouragement."

The hard, burning heat inside Azalea went *snap*.

"It won't," she spat. "Keep the stupid brooch. Keep the stupid pocket watch. Keep the gloves and sampler and whatever else you've stolen. You can enjoy them on your own. We're not coming down here again. We never should have trusted you in the first place."

She swept around, skirts twisting hard against her, eyes searing, and strode to the entrance. Keeper laughed.

"One last dance, my lady, before I am never to see you again?"

Azalea turned at the entrance, eyes narrowed at Keeper. They burned his image into her mind, his hard, black form cutting against the soft silver, his sleek, rakish ponytail pulled back from his pale face. His dead eyes.

"I hate dancing with you," she said.

She stepped on the threshold.

A grating, cracking-ice explosion seized the air. The silver rose bushes that flanked the sides of the pavilion shot up, black-thorned monstrosities, curling themselves around the lattice. They twisted over the entrance, and Azalea stumbled back before the thorns snagged at her skirts.

Light strangled out of the pavilion as the vines encased it. A new, weird yellow light sputtered to life on the ceiling, and Azalea gasped as hundreds of candles flickered above her, pressed against the casement of the dome, all melted shapeless and creating eerie shadows.

Azalea whipped about sharply.

"Open it up, Keeper," she snarled. "Enough of your stupid games."

"What a shame," said Keeper, still at the side of the ballroom, smiling lazily, "that you don't care to dance. I've planned such a magnificent ball!"

Dancers burst through the pavilion's thorn-shrouded lattice, sweeping tight circles with their partners. A gust of air whirled over Azalea, and the dancers swirled past her in a twist of colors, chiffons and satins brushing her own black, shabby skirts. She bit back a scream.

The dancers were masked with ornate, gilded animal heads. A golden-furred jackal, and his lady, with feathers and a gold beak. Masks with eyeholes rimmed in gems and embroidery clung to the dancers' faces. This was a masked ball, something Azalea had only heard of. In her imagination they had been more innocent; gentlemen dressed as hussars and ladies with white, glittery masks attached to a stick. Not this chaotic meshing of gilded beasts and opulent monsters.

In a garish whorl of colors and ribbons, the dancers settled into two long rows, packed so tightly their skirts bunched at odd angles. At the end of their aisle stood Keeper, straight and at ease. The candlelight seemed to make him darker, no highlights or shading over his black form. A twist of a smile graced his lips.

"Welcome, my lady," he said, "to the D'Eathe court. Do you like it?"

Azalea glanced back at the entrance. She wondered if she could somehow push her way through the vines.

"I ask you again." Keeper's voice was cold. "May I have the honor of this dance?"

"Snap your own head off," said Azalea.

Keeper gave a smart bow.

"I'll assume that is a no, thank you," he said. "Still, I would advise you not to take this dance without a partner to lead you. It could be, ah . . . precarious."

Keeper clapped his hands together, twice, and the masked ladies flicked their fans open in unison. Azalea stepped back.

"Don't haste away, my lady," he said. "There is a guest I have invited whom I am sure you do not want to miss."

The music began. The sweet music-box orchestra had been replaced with a symphony starved on scraps of minor key. A chorus of sickly violins grew to a forte, and the dancers stepped smartly together.

Azalea turned to the entrance, and was blocked. A bear, cat, and wolf stepped in front of her, turning about in the dance. Ladies whipped their fans out, their hands clasped with their gentleman beasts. Azalea stepped out of the way, narrowly missing a collision with a lynx, who pushed just past her. There was no room—the moment one couple moved, the next pair stepped in, ladies' skirts pressed together, squashed.

It's only magic, Azalea thought, trying to reassure herself. Not real. She pushed her way through the lynx and the wolf. The couple turned sharply, and Azalea was thwacked across the face by the gentleman's hand.

She hit the marble floor, face stinging, before she realized what had happened. Cringing, she yanked her hand away before it was chasséd with a buckled shoe. That had felt plenty real. The dancers were not going to stop for her.

Azalea scrambled to her feet, drowning in the skirts, before the couples stepped together and turned, hard, into a promenade. Every lady whipped a fan out, broke apart from her partner, and fluttered the fans against their feathered gold-and-black masked faces.

In a blur, they snapped their arms out. Azalea stumbled backward to avoid a hand gripping an ice pink fan. She overstepped, and her arm brushed against the fan's edge of the next lady. At first she felt nothing, then saw that blood had dripped onto the crush of gold skirts. She grasped her arm and craned her neck. The fan had sliced her sleeve, and a little deeper.

Azalea pressed her hand against the cut and glanced up to see Keeper at the far end of the dance floor, black figure cut against the garish reds and golds. He was smiling at her.

Dancers turned about and crossed arms. In the exchange, Keeper disappeared. Azalea swallowed, her mouth dry, and stepped into position with them, keeping with the ebb and flow. She mouthed the steps, reminding her feet to stay attentive, keeping in time with the quadrille-waltz hybrid, and tried to work her way to the entrance. The heavy metallic taste of fear coated her throat and weighed her down. Her limbs shook, but her fear pushed her onward into the steps.

Azalea turned into the next dance set, and stopped.

A figure wearing a plain dress stood still among the gaudy, glinting sworls of dancers. Azalea caught the pale face, the dimples, the slightly mussed auburn hair, and her knees nearly gave way.

Dashing back around, pushing skirts away from her, Azalea craned to see the figure. A closed fan smacked her across the face, but she didn't even feel it. Through the gaps of moving dancers, Azalea saw the woman again, and her heart leaped into her throat.

Her dress was light blue, worn and mended, but clean. A jet brooch was pinned to her collar. Azalea had to blink, hard.

The dancers turned with their partners, hands pressed against hands, then, all at once, stepped back into two rows. A hesitation step; the longest Azalea had ever witnessed. Feathers bobbed as though underwater, and skirts settled even slower. Azalea was again at the end of the aisle they made, and, at the other end—

Mother.

The words from stories Azalea had heard so long ago echoed through her mind.

Their souls—

The High King could capture souls—

Azalea choked.

The dancers joined hands, circling around them both, and turned in a reel. The music sped to a booming, drunken waltz. Jacquards and brocades spun around in a blur. Azalea stood in a maelstrom of dancers, stunned, staring, emotions twisting within her even harder than the dancers around her.

She stepped forward, taking in Mother's bright eyes and kind face, creased with the familiar look of pain. Her mouth seemed a blurred smile, and Azalea gaped at the scarlet lines about Mother's lips, ringed with purple bruises. Azalea suddenly realized—

Her mouth had been sewn shut.

Azalea cried aloud. In a panic, she *ran* to Mother, fumbling for the scissors she usually kept in her apron pocket. Today, however, she had dressed too quickly and her pockets were empty. Her hands shook violently, and her knees could not carry her any longer.

Mother's arms caught her before she collapsed to the floor. She pulled Azalea into a tight embrace. She felt so *solid*. Real! Nothing like the gossamer spirits of death in storybooks. Azalea couldn't bear to look up as Mother pulled her even tighter, pressing Azalea's cheek against her blouse. Azalea could smell the baby-ointment and white-cake smell as she took shuddering breaths. Mother stroked her hair.

Azalea tried to speak but choked on the words. Mother brought her to arm's length, and with her thumb brushed away a tear on Azalea's face, her own eyes wet. And even with her lips stitched and bruised, Mother still tried to smile. To comfort *her*.

"Mother—!"

The dancers swept between them, breaking Azalea from Mother's cold embrace. The room spun. Azalea fought desperately through the dancers, pushing bunches of silks and chiffons out of the way. Through gaps in the garish colors that filled her vision, Azalea struggled for another glimpse of Mother, but saw nothing. She had vanished.

"Keeper!" Azalea screamed. *"Keeper!"*

Billowing skirts shoved her to the floor. A lady's heel trod on her hand. Azalea scrambled to her feet, hysterical, pushing her way through the dancers. They pushed back tenfold harder.

The music crescendoed as Azalea was shoved against to the ground, this time hitting her head. Colors burst through her vision. The hems of gaudy skirts brushed over her, quiet as snowfall, slow, unfocused. Slower, and slower, and slower.

The music faded.

Azalea was only vaguely aware the dancers were gone. A glow of silver-white cast over her, and the pavilion eased back to its magic self. Azalea lay curled, her cheek against the marble, chest heaving. The marble was wet. Azalea did not know if it was tears or blood.

A black boot appeared in her vision, followed by a knee as Keeper knelt down in front of her. He was panting, his face drawn. Still, his eyes were lit with triumph.

"How dare you," Azalea choked. "How *dare* you! I'll *kill* you!"

Keeper reached out his long fingers and caught her arm, drawing his thumb across her cut. Azalea tried to summon all her strength to lash out, but she could not; as though her limbs had no blood she lay helpless on the marble. She hadn't even the energy to flinch as he drew his fingers to her neck.

"Hush," he murmured. "There now. Hush." He traced his finger along her jaw. "That is a sweet thought," he whispered. "Except, my lady, I cannot die."

"You're him," said Azalea. And it wasn't so much a whisper as a choke.

"Quite."

He touched his fingers to her lips.

"I expect," he whispered, "you are wondering what you could *possibly* do to keep me from hurting your mother further. Is that not so?"

Azalea cringed.

"I will tell you what I want, my lady," he said. "My freedom. It is all I have ever wanted. Find the magic object, and destroy it. You have until Christmas."

He pressed his finger hard against her lips, as though to hush her. They throbbed against his finger.

"This is between you and me," he said. "No one else. It is upon *you*. If you do as I say, no more harm will come to your mother. Is that not a fair trade?"

Azalea trembled.

Keeper stood, his cape rippling straight. He pulled something from the air with a flash of silver, and tossed it. It skittered to the marble with a *clinkety clink clink* in front of Azalea. The sugar teeth shivered.

"And," said Keeper, his eyes cold. "You are never to refuse me another dance again."

CHAPTER 19

*A*zalea did not know how she got back to her bedroom. She only remembered stumbling through the glimmering wall of the fireplace and falling to her knees, scattering soot everywhere.

She lay curled on the floor for a long time, her head pounding.

Eventually she pulled off her dress and mended the cut sleeve, sewing perfect, tiny stitches automatically. After that, she poured water into the basin and washed her cut. In the vanity mirror, her face was drawn and ghastly white. The bruises weren't showing yet; they would.

She touched her lips. The breath choked in her throat, and she had to turn away.

A dull glint of silver struggled through the folds of her rumpled dress on the floor. She had somehow remembered to put the sugar teeth in her pocket before leaving. Now, as she examined them, nicked and dinged with patches of dull, brassy color, she swallowed. Instead of the tiny prongs facing inward, the sugar teeth had been bent entirely backward, so the prongs faced out.

Azalea imagined Keeper lazily toying with the teeth, bending and twisting them as they trembled, in the silence of the pavilion.

"He's had you this whole time, hasn't he?" she whispered.

They shuddered.

In a few minutes, dressed again, she turned up the lamps in the portrait gallery, casting a light over the display of the silver sword. So dull and old . . . it didn't even glimmer in the light.

"It has to be this," said Azalea to no one but the sugar teeth, which she had wrapped up and put in her pocket. She touched the glass over the hairline crack in the sword, and shook her head. "It has to be magic. But I can't figure out how."

Azalea sat on the floor, her dress poofing around her, and pulled her knees to her chest. She buried her head in her skirts.

Keeper was the High King. The portrait of the High King, hidden away in the attic, leered at her from her memory. The ancient, melted-wax skin. The painter had gotten him all wrong, painting him old and hideous. But the dead, black eyes were the same. Azalea pushed her head against her knees, trying to stop the throbbing.

He could capture souls. . . .

Keeper was *mad* if he thought she was going to bring the girls down there again. She would have to keep them from going through the fireplace—without telling them anything. Keeper would *know* if she had told them. He knew everything. Azalea rubbed her lips into the cotton weave of her dress, wincing. *The stitches . . .*

He had promised to leave Mother alone, hadn't he? He wouldn't dare—not when he needed Azalea so much to free him. Azalea pushed a quaking smile and put her hand over the sugar teeth in her pocket, trying to comfort them.

"I have until Christmas to figure something out," she said. "That's five days. That's plenty of time, yes?"

The sugar teeth trembled.

Well after tea now, Azalea wandered through the corridor in search of her sisters. She had descended to the second-floor hall when she heard an odd thumping noise, followed by rummaging and assorted clanks. They came from the bucket closet across from the mezzanine.

"Hello?" said Azalea. And, realizing someone had been locked in, she turned the key still in the knob and clicked it open.

Brooms spilled out. Mops spilled out. A gentleman spilled out. He had a bucket on his head. And wore an offensively green bow tie.

"Lord Teddie!" said Azalea.

Lord Teddie sprang to his feet. "Hulloa, Princess A!" he said, taking the bucket off his head and beaming. His curly hair was mussed. "We all missed you at breakfast! I ate your bowl of mush. I hope that's all right."

"What are you doing here?" said Azalea.

"Oh! Ha! I bet you are wondering that. I'm here on Royal Business. For the riddle! Unless, of course, you mean in the broom closet, which I'm in because we were playing tiddle and seek after breakfast and . . . someone locked me in."

"That would be Bramble," said Azalea. "Usually she locks them in the gallery. She must really not like you."

Lord Teddie's face fell.

"Pudding head," he said. "That's me. And she's quick and smart as a horsewhip."

Azalea marveled as he snapped back into marvelous good humor, an emotional elastic. His hazel eyes brightened.

"Well, that takes pluck anyway, I should say!" he said. "I've never had a girl do that to me before! What a rum girl! Absolute pluck!"

"You didn't bring Mother's portrait?"

The spring in Lord Teddie's spine slumped a tad.

"Ah," he said. "Actually, no."

"Oh!" Completely unbidden, the portrait of Mother flew to Azalea's mind, this time with her mouth stitched shut. It stabbed her in the stomach, and Azalea had to lean against the mezzanine railing, gasping for air, to keep from throwing up. She tried to shake the image from her head.

"I say," Lord Teddie stammered, as she choked for breaths. "I say—are you all right? Your color—I didn't mean—that is—Hulloa? I say, hulloa? Are there any servants about?"

"I'm all . . . right," Azalea managed. "Just . . . I need some air."

Azalea tried to go down the stairs, but the room spun, and she sat on the top stair, leaning her head against the cold iron posts. Lord Teddie did his best to cheer her up. He handed her a candy stick, recited limericks, guessed at all her favorite dances and told her which ones he liked best. Eventually Azalea managed to push the picture out of her mind, and even managed a smile when Lord Teddie tried to juggle the coins from his pocket and they pelted his head.

". . . I don't *know* where Clover is, she's probably off helping Old Tom in the gardens, she's been running off to do that lately—Jess, what?"

Bramble's voice carried down the hall. Lord Teddie, picking up the coins from the rug, straightened, motionless for the first time Azalea had seen him. Bramble appeared around the corner, followed by the mass of girls, running in tiny steps to keep up with her stride. When the girls saw Lord Teddie, a ripple of excitement ran through them.

"Lord Teddie!" cried Ivy as they flocked to him in a mass of black skirts.

"Word Teddie!" cried Kale, who was just learning to talk and parroted everybody.

"What ho!" said Lord Teddie. "What ho! What could you all possibly want?" He bounced on the balls of his feet, beaming. "Hmm? Oh . . . all right!"

He produced from his pocket wrapped ribbon candies, which the girls squealed over and passed among themselves, unwrapping for one another and smelling the mint-and-treacle flavors. Bramble had remained behind, her jaw up and her hands clenched.

"Bramble thaid you ran away to the butterfly forest," said Ivy, who was reaching into Lord Teddie's suitcoat pocket for more candies. She had a lisp ever since she had lost her two front teeth.

"I *was* in the butterfly forest," said Lord Teddie. "I decided to come back for tea."

"Tea was ages ago!" said Eve. "You must be hungry!"

"Oh, I'm all right!" said Lord Teddie. "I don't eat

much! Just a bit of ham and a sweetmeat or two and I'll be right as rain!"

There was a sticky silence. Ivy looked guiltily at the candies in her fist.

"We have bread," said Bramble. Her voice reverberated in the silence of the hall. "And cheese. I'm sorry if that's not good enough for you."

Lord Teddie's eyes caught Bramble's mended, shabby dress. For a sliver of a second, his grin flickered. It was back immediately. The tips of his ears shone pink.

"I *love* bread!" he said. "I love bread and cheese, cheese and bread! I eat them all the time! I'll probably *turn* into a great wheel of cheese, I like it so much!"

Bramble turned her head. Her ears were pink, too. When she lifted her yellow-green eyes, they caught Azalea, sitting at the top stair, hidden by the crinolines and skirts of the others. Bramble pushed past the rest of the girls and ran to Azalea.

"Az," she said, falling to her knees and taking her hand. "You're white! What happened? What did he *do* to you?"

"Nothing, it's nothing," said Azalea. She grabbed at Bramble's arm, pulling her back, for Bramble looked ready to attack Lord Teddie. The yellow in her eyes flared. "Steady on," said Azalea. "He didn't do anything."

Bramble cast one more angry glance at Lord Teddie, but her eyes calmed into their light green as they took in Azalea. She tucked a loose strand of hair behind Azalea's ear.

"Is it the brooch?" she said.

Azalea wrapped a finger around the iron baluster next to her face, squeezing it hard. The corners bit. Bramble made a face.

"Clover thought Keeper wouldn't give it back, the rotten thief," she said. "Wonderful. The King is going to go spare when he finds out we haven't got it."

"Who *cares* about the King anymore?" said Azalea. "I'll be the one to tell him we lost it, if I have to. But— I'll think of something first. I will." She glanced at Lord Teddie, who had pulled a coin from Jessamine's black curls, making the girls squeal with laughter and Jessamine smile bashfully.

"I'll tell you more tonight," Azalea said. "When the gentleman isn't here."

That evening, after coffee in the library, where Lord Teddie taught the younger girls how to play ring-a-hoop with pen and old inkwells, the girls gathered in their bedroom, passing out the mended slippers from the basket and brushing their hair. Delphinium took the vanity chair, dreamily running her fingers through her wavy blond hair and gazing at her reflection.

"I've decided I'm going to marry him," she said. "Lord Teddie, I mean."

"Don't be daft," said Bramble, throwing pillows on the bed behind her. "You only like him because he's rich."

"Well, why not?" Delphinium turned. "I'm pretty enough. If he stops making up stupid rhymes, and learns how to dress, and perhaps stifles that silly laugh he has, then in a few years, we—"

"He'd see right through you." Bramble sat down on one of their threadbare embroidered poufs, crossing her arms. "So don't rally up your hopes, young peep. Gentlemen like him don't marry penniless."

Delphinium's lips tightened, and she tugged the comb through her hair. Azalea, between the hearth and the round table, chose this time to produce the sugar teeth from her pocket and lay them on the table, to the initial fright of the girls, who leaped back.

When the sugar teeth only lay and shuddered with a faint clinking sound, the girls crept to the round table, forgetting that they had been the scourge of the palace before. Horrified that the teeth had been bent inside out, they spoke in hushed tones.

"Who would—do such a thing?" said Clover, stroking them gently.

"Oh, Keeper, of course!" said Azalea. "Of course it was him!"

Bramble took a dried pink rose from the vase in the middle of the table and snapped off the blossom. "Rotter," she said, pulling the leaves from the stem. "When I see him, I'm going to tell him exactly—"

"*Don't!*" Azalea yelped.

The girls stared at Azalea, hands halted about their slipper ribbons, mid-tie. Azalea rubbed her hand against her aching forehead.

"Look, just—let me handle Keeper, all right?" she said. "And the teeth—well."

They stared sadly at the twisted piece of metal. None of them liked to see the sugar teeth as such, so forlorn and helpless, shaking. Glumly, they took Azalea's powder box and shredded bits of dried petals in it, making a little bed for them. Azalea agreed to slip away to the kitchen and fetch some sugar cubes, and maybe a teacup to keep them company. Inside, she clung to the thin hope that if she stayed in the kitchen long enough, the younger girls would have fallen asleep and she could convince them to stay in their room tonight. It hadn't happened before, but Azalea had seen Kale's and Lily's nodding heads, snuggling into the crook of Clover's arm.

Azalea arrived at the creaking kitchen door and pulled back when she saw the King sitting at the scrubbed servants' table, drinking a cup of cold leftover coffee and sorting through a stack of paperwork in the flickering candlelight. His hand was better now—though it moved stiffly as he shuffled the papers. He looked up when Azalea arrived, and Azalea twined her fingers through the weave in her shawl. His intimidating frown always made her feel as though she were balancing on a three-story banister.

"It is decidedly late, Miss Azalea," said the King, setting his teacup down. "You should be in bed."

"Yes, sir," said Azalea. She stared at his paperwork. He was *always* doing paperwork. She wondered for the first time if he disliked it.

"Did you come to eat something? You know the rules."

"No, sir."

"You didn't eat your dinner." The King marked a bit of paper with his pen. "You missed breakfast, and tea, and I saw you give your food to Miss Ivy at the table. Am I to believe you haven't come down here for food?'

"Yes," said Azalea shortly. "If I were hungry, I would have eaten. I'm fetching something for the girls."

The King sucked in his cheeks at her tone. Azalea, her fingers still twined in her shawl, opened the cabinet next to the stove and began to sort for the sugar cubes.

"It is gone, isn't it?" said the King without glancing

from his papers. "None of you wore it today. I knew the moment—the very moment—I let you take it from my sight, it was gone. I gave that brooch to your mother, Miss Azalea, and now it is gone."

Azalea paused, her shaking hand resting on the cold glass of the pear preserves, between the jars of peaches and plums.

Of *course* he knew it was gone. Azalea doubted anything escaped his notice. He knew everything—

Well . . . yes. He *did* know everything. Much more than her, at least, when it came to magic. A glimmer of hope lit inside her. Perhaps finding the sugar teeth would help her solve things after all. Azalea swallowed.

"Sir," she said, closing the cabinet door and pressing her back against it. The knobbly handle pressed into her corset. Her hands still trembled. "Um. Do you remember . . . how the sugar teeth were magic?"

The King looked up.

"Were?" he said.

In their room, the King nudged the sugar teeth. They fell to their side, clinking against the polished tabletop. The girls crowded about them, biting their lips.

"They look poorly," he said. He picked them up and examined them, drawing his thumb across the poking-out teeth. He made to bend them, but stopped when he saw the metal would only snap if he did. He set them down. "What happened to them? Who bent them like this?"

A cold tingling feeling washed over Azalea, prickling and giving her goose bumps. She coughed and tried to shake it away. Everyone must have felt it, for they all shifted on their poufs and beds, rubbing their fingers and cringing. Eve tugged on the ends of her dark hair. The oath . . .

"Come to think of it," said the King, "where is the rest of the magic tea set? I haven't seen it for some time."

The girls cast nervous looks at one another, but Clover spoke up.

"It's all right," she said, sitting on the edge of her bed and stroking Lily's dark curls. Lily lay asleep on her lap. "It's my fault. I'll tell him."

Clover told the story of how, in a foul temper, she had bashed up the set and thrown it into the stream. She told it all with her chin up, her beautiful face pale—but, surprisingly, without a stutter. The King's eyebrows knitted at first, then rose, until he was just staring at her with his mouth slightly open. Azalea guessed that he would have been cross if any of the rest of them had done such a thing. But with honey-sweet Clover, the King just gaped.

"Your mother often thought," he said slowly, when

she had finished, "that one day you would do something truly surprising. I certainly did not expect this."

Bramble flashed a grin at Azalea.

"What now, sir?" said Flora.

"What now?" The King turned his attention to the quaking sugar teeth. "Well. I suppose we ought to unmagic them."

He left the room. Some minutes later, he arrived again and shut the door behind him. In his stiff hand, he held the old, mottled silver sword. He gazed at the sugar teeth, lost in thought.

"Unmagic," said Azalea, turning the odd word in her mouth. "You'll take the magic from it?"

"Just so."

The girls watched, rapt, as he gently and solemnly lowered the sword to the sugar teeth. He touched the silver to silver with a soft *clink*.

As quick and quiet as a snuffed candle, the sugar teeth . . . lost their luster. They looked the same, but . . . Azalea couldn't describe it. No longer shuddering, the teeth somehow seemed at *peace*. Everyone exhaled silently.

"Well," said the King. He picked up the teeth and slipped them into his waistcoat pocket, as delicately as a lifeless sparrow to be buried. He turned to the girls.

"What did your mother do?" he said.

"Sir?"

"When it was time for bed," said the King. "Tell me."

The girls exchanged nervous glances. He was talking about Mother.

"She used to help the girls with their prayers," said Azalea, hesitant. "And—sometimes she would read stories."

The King set the sword on the table, next to the vase.

"Very well," he said as the girls whispered to one another. "I will read you a story."

The whispering stopped.

Jessamine slid from her bed to the ground, the untied purple ribbons of her slippers trailing, and dug a storybook out from Eve's trunk. She held it out to the King in her tiny four-year-old hands, her crystal blue eyes hopeful.

The King sat on the rug and leaned against Delphinium and Eve's bed, and the younger girls shyly sat next to him, peering at the pictures. Clover smiled, her right dimple showing, and hugged Lily to her chest while Bramble, sitting on her pouf, cast a wry, surprised grin at Azalea.

"'In a certain country . . .'" he began, his voice stiff with the words.

He read the stories of "Hans and Gretchen," "The Goats of Hemland Shire," "The Dainty Princess." He wasn't like Mother, who read with all the voices and a bubbled laugh at the words, but . . . he was all right. Everything felt warm and safe, among the linens, the flickering fire, and coziness of their room.

The girls' eyes grew heavy, and their heads drooped. The King himself grew drowsy, his voice reading slower and slower, until finally he shook himself, and with Azalea's direction, put the right girls in the right beds. Then he left with the sword and a good night.

The sword! Azalea's mind whirred. She rolled the dry, crinkly rosebud from hand to hand across the table, sorting things out. Somehow, it was magic after all! How, Azalea did not know, but surely it had unmagicked the palace those hundreds of years ago, at the hand of Harold the First. No wonder Keeper wanted to be rid of it! It could unmagic *him*!

Hope humming through her, Azalea took her shawl from the peg by the door and slipped into the cold hall. She ran down the stairs, quiet in her bare feet, turning the corner into the portrait gallery. Edges of the glass cases and gold ends of the velvet ropes glimmered in the dim light, and Azalea found her way to the sword display. The King never left anything out of place, and for once Azalea was glad of it. She lifted the glass case from it and, ten minutes later, was back in her room.

None of the girls awoke as she turned up the lamp and

smothered the fire in the hearth. She turned everything in her mind, over and over. She would unmagic the passage. They wouldn't get the brooch or the watch back, but that didn't matter anymore. What mattered was that Keeper would be rendered powerless—

Or would he? Azalea hesitated. With the blood oath—and the sword broken now—

"Shut up!" said Azalea to her thoughts. She grasped the rapier's handle with both hands beneath the silver swirl guard cage, stepped into the fireplace, and touched the silver edge to the DE.

Nothing happened.

Nothing had happened before, of course, when the King had unmagicked the sugar teeth, but she had felt something. Something different. Now, as her excitement faded, the logical side of her mind took over.

What was she *thinking*? Unmagicking the passage would do *nothing*—Keeper couldn't die, could he? He would still be there, along with his magic, with the addition that he would be angry. Azalea had the foreboding that he was going to be cross already, since they hadn't come to dance. If she had truly unmagicked it, Keeper would be left with Mother's soul—

In a panic, Azalea snatched the handkerchief from her pocket and rubbed it against the magic mark.

It became hot, so hot it burned. Dizzy with relief,

Azalea pulled her hand back. The mark glowed for a moment, and faded back into the stone. She swallowed, gripped the sword, and strode from the fireplace, leaving a trail of soot.

After discovering the kitchen empty, Azalea arrived at the library, panting. She didn't bother to knock, late as it was, but instead shoved the door open. The darkness surprised her; she turned up the nearest lamp, and discovered the King lying on the sofa near the piano, underneath an old blanket. He stirred as Azalea drew near.

"Sir! Sir, you— Do you sleep here every night?" Azalea frowned at the stiff, hard furniture. "That can't be comfortable."

The King brought his arm over his eyes as Azalea turned up both the stained-glass lamps on his desk.

"Azalea, really!"

"This is important," said Azalea. Sword still in hand, she swept to him. The black sheet over the piano swayed with her breeze. "Sir, this sword. Can it be mended?"

The King roused, not in good humor at seeing Azalea with the sword.

"Great . . . waistcoats, Azalea," he said. "That is governmental property! Take it back to the gallery, at once."

"Sir, *please*," said Azalea, on the verge of tears. "Can

it be mended? Can you fix the magic in it? *How* is it even magic? Sir, please!"

Something in the King softened. Perhaps it was Azalea's desperate eyes. He sighed, rubbed his face, and stood.

"Come along," he said. "It is time you knew."

CHAPTER 20

The gallery was so cold that Azalea could see her breath, even in the dark. She shivered and pulled her shawl tighter around herself; the King stirred up the hearth beneath the wall of portraits and added coal to it.

"Well," he said. He set the sword on the red velvet of the pedestal and lifted the glass case back over it. He looked worn and tired but had enough firmness in him that his shoulders remained straight and solid. He was made of starch, Azalea thought. Starch and steel. "It is something that only the royal family, or the prime ministers have known," he said. "It is not generally spoken of."

"It's magic, though?"

"No," said the King. "And yes."

Azalea took a bite of her bread and cheese, not tasting it. They had taken a detour to the kitchen, where the King took a bit of bread and cheese wrapped in a cloth and gave it to Azalea. Now he sat next to her, on one of the fine sofas by the mantel. The spindly legs creaked.

"Azalea, you know about Swearing on Silver. Do you not?"

A slight tingle rose in Azalea's chest, and she thought of Mother's handkerchief.

"I don't think I do," she said slowly. "Not fully. If . . . you make a promise with silver, it . . . helps you keep your oath? Just like if you . . . swear on blood . . ." Azalea stopped, shuddering. The King considered her.

"Yes," he said. "It is like the blood oath the High King made, before he was overthrown. But it is the full opposite. Just as strong, but with silver as the mediator."

"And it makes the silver . . . a sort of magic?"

"Just so," said the King. "But a much stronger magic than the common sort. Stronger than the magic of the passage or the tea set, because it is sealed with your word. The people under the High King D'Eathe had very little, but what silver they had they kept close. Wedding bands, family heirlooms, and such. They believed silver the purest sort of metal. It was with those things they made the sword and swore to protect their families and their country. We swear on it now, in parliament."

Swearing on Silver. A stronger magic. Everything connected in Azalea's mind, a magic sealed with silver. She set the bread and cheese on her lap and pulled

Mother's handkerchief from her pocket, turning it over in her hands, remembering how Mother had pressed it into her palms.

"It doesn't make sense, though," said Azalea. "If this were true, then Mother's handkerchief would be magic. But it's never unmagicked anything. Or—" Azalea thought of the sword, and how it didn't unmagic the passage at her hands. "Perhaps there is something wrong with *me*."

The King stood and tended the fire with a poker, for it had started to die.

"There is nothing wrong with you," he said. The firelight illuminated his face, deepening the wrinkles by his eyes. "The sword has been sworn on for many years, by kings and ministers. As such, the magic in it runs deep. For those who have sworn on it. To our visitors and guests, and even you, it is only a sword. Even so, your handkerchief is magic—for you and you sisters, weak as it is. You cannot expect one promise—"

"Two," said Azalea quickly. "Mother had me swear on it. Before . . . before she . . . died. It . . . well." She turned her eyes to the bread in her lap, feeling silly. But she couldn't discount the first promise she'd made—it had felt so strong.

The King was quiet for a while. He looked at the handkerchief she turned in her hands, the silver shimmering softly in the lamplight.

"I gave that handkerchief to your mother," he said. "As a wedding gift."

Azalea held it tightly, praying he wouldn't ask for it back.

He did not. Instead he said, "What did you promise? May I ask?"

Azalea traced the embroidered letters with her thumb. She hadn't even told her sisters this.

"That . . . I would take care of the girls," she finally said.

There was a moment of silence, but not awkward silence.

"I'm not doing a very good job of it," Azalea mumbled.

The King's firm, heavy hand rested on Azalea's shoulder. It was such an unexpected gesture of affection that it rendered Azalea speechless. The King removed it, quickly, but his voice was gentle.

"You've done a fine job," he said. "You cannot expect it to be as powerful as the sword. But I should think your handkerchief harbors a deep magic nonetheless. You have made it so."

Azalea focused on her bread and cheese to keep from making a scene. She thought of Mother, hand over Azalea's heart, sitting next to her in the ballroom, and telling her about the deepest sort of magic. The warm, flickery one.

Azalea knew it wasn't the common magic, nor was it the cold, shivery prickles of Swearing on Silver.

"What of the other magic?" said Azalea. "The one Mother used to speak of? The one without a name?"

There was a pause, the longest yet. The King stroked his well-trimmed beard, looking at the drapes across the hall. His eyes were bright, but sad.

"Yes," he said. "They say there is a third sort of magic."

Azalea waited, her food forgotten in her lap. The King shifted, stiffly, and considered the fire poker in his hand.

"It is," he said finally, "the deepest magic of all. So deep, and rare, it doesn't even have a name. It needs no silver. It has to do with the piece of you that is you, inside. Your soul. A promise so deep, it blurs the line between mortal and immortal, souls that have passed on. This unnamed magic has caused many strange things to happen. So it is said."

"Such as?" said Azalea.

"I don't know."

"You . . . haven't seen any evidence of it?"

"No."

"Do you believe in it?"

The King sighed. "I don't know, Azalea. I truly don't. But your Mother did. More than anyone I knew."

Azalea gazed at the glow of the fire flickering in the

hearth next to her, thinking about the warm flickery bit. She hadn't felt it for days, even when she danced. It was easy to believe in things, when Mother was here. Now, thinking of Mother, images of white lips and red thread passed through her mind, and it was as though a bucket of frigid stream water poured through her lungs and stomach. Azalea stood quickly, upsetting her cheese and bread, and hurried to the glass case that held the sword.

"Earlier this year," said Azalea, "I broke this, at least in part. Would the magic be strong again, if it were mended?"

"I expect not. It would have to be sworn on again, many more times after it was fixed," said the King.

"Oh." The gush of ice-cold water coated her inside again, and Azalea shivered so hard her teeth began to chatter. She jumped when the King placed her shawl over her shoulders.

"It is late," said the King. "I'll stoke the fire in your room, if you like."

"Sir," said Azalea as he led her out of the gallery, "the blood oath the High King made—to not die until he killed Harold the First . . . didn't Harold the First die of old age?"

"Not to die until he killed the Captain General, I believe it was. No, he unfortunately lived to be a great old age."

"Unfortunately?" said Azalea.

The King sucked in his cheeks, as though loathe to tell her. In the faint light, he looked like the first king's portrait hanging on the gallery wall behind him; same jaw, light hair, close-trimmed beard.

"He went mad," said the King. "Our first king. It is . . . a bit of a family secret. He overthrew the High King, unmagicked the palace with the sword, but—" The King shifted. "He thought the High King was still here. In the palace."

The blood drained from Azalea's face.

"He believed the High King's essence, or something of the like, still existed, in the foundation or paneling or such. It is silly, of course, to consider it now. Even so, when he passed the title of Captain General to his son, Harold the Second, he fell into madness. He wandered the halls at night, certain the High King would return to murder—"

"The Captain General, the *Captain General*!" Azalea cried. "That would be you!"

"Miss Azalea, it was years ago! Your color—it is only a story!"

"The first king! He was telling the—"

Azalea was *bludgeoned*.

When she was seven, she had been thrown from a horse and had the air knocked from her. It left a hollow space of nothing, and she heaved for air to fill it. This was much the same, but with a great rush of hard prickles. It took her breath away and choked her throat, stole air from her lungs. A great wave of icy tingles flushed to her fingertips and feet, and over her head. She gasped.

"Good heavens, Azalea, are you all right?"

The oath! Azalea fell against the wainscot of the hallway, the painful tingling coursing through her in riptides. In a dizzy whirl, she felt herself plucked up and into the King's arms.

Five minutes later, a ruckus ensued in the room as the King set Azalea onto her bed. Lily awoke with a cry, and Kale, who was never happy when she was tired, began to scream. Candles were lit and lamps turned up, and girls sleepily flocked to Azalea's bed. Azalea gasped for air, feeling the cold pinpricks ream up and down her skin.

"What happened?" said Clover, wetting a cloth in the basin, and dabbing Azalea's face.

"She had a sort of fit," said the King. "I think her underthings may be laced too tightly."

All the girls, including Azalea, blushed brilliantly.

"*Sir,*" said Eve. "You're not supposed to know about the U word!"

"Am I not? Forgive me."

When the color returned to Azalea's cheeks, they pushed the King out of the room, a crease between his eyebrows, and set to unbuttoning her. Azalea hoped the unlacing of the corset would return her breath to her, but it took an hour and two cups of piping hot tea for the strangled feeling to leave. The fear and hopelessness remained, however, and Azalea slept in a choke.

Azalea slept so late she nearly missed dinner the next day. She rushed to the dining room, shaking off the groggy stupor, and found the girls setting the table, their faces stung red from playing outside. They chattered about the day's events. Clover looked especially pretty, with her hair pinned up and her corseted figure ablossom, a lady even though she was just fifteen. Fifteen! Today was Clover's birthday, and Azalea had slept through nearly all of it, including the Great Corseting and the birthday center reel. Feeling sick all over again, she caught Clover's hands and tried to smile.

"Many happy returns!" she said. "I can't believe I slept through so much of it."

"You were ill," said Clover, squeezing Azalea's hands.

"I'll make it up to you. I promise. Do you like the corset?"

Clover tried to keep from smiling, but her face glowed.

"I . . . can feel my heartbeat in my stomach!"

"Aye, that's what it feels like to be a lady!" said Bramble, among the general riffraff and clattering of seat taking and plate getting. "It's corking. I love it."

Azalea only picked at her bowl of potato soup as dinner progressed. Her hand kept twitching to feel the watch in her pocket that wasn't there, anxious for the time. She feared Keeper would become angrier with each passing minute they weren't there.

The King, on the other hand, looked in good spirits, seeing Azalea at the table, and Lord Teddie was in even finer spirits, because that was Lord Teddie. The younger girls fought for seats next to him and clamored for his attention.

"At least Azalea remembered," said Delphinium in a low whisper. Azalea fed Lily, sitting on her lap. "The King hasn't said a thing. Not one thing!"

"He's forgotten. I was afraid he would," said Eve.

"Great scott, Clover." Azalea cast a glance at the head of the table. "You haven't told him?"

"Well . . . we're in mourning." Clover smoothed the napkin in her lap. "And—it would just make him feel bad that he had forgotten."

"If it was important to him," said Delphinium primly, "he would remember."

On the other side of the table, the girls squealed with laughter as Lord Teddie chattered like mad. He ate far too much soup and far too many biscuits to account for his lean, gangly figure, and he read them a book called *The Eathesburian Holiday Guidebook*, which he had brought from Delchastire.

"It has an entire section just on the gardens! The fountains and statues and all things gardeny," he said, as the girls climbed over one another to peek at the etchings inside. "It says if you're lucky, you might even see the rare flowers of Eathesbury!"

The girls giggled so hard, Hollyhock choked on her soup.

"That's *us!*" she cried, after coughing. "We're the flowers of Eathesbury!"

"And all of you, pretty as buttons!" said Lord Teddie, beaming at them. He looked over to Bramble, who wore a bit of holly in her deep red hair, and he smiled.

"Clover," said the King, interrupting the melee. He had been casting distracted glances at Clover all through dinner. Azalea knew why. With her hair up and her eyes alight, Clover looked like a golden version of Mother. She even had the smile that lit the room. "Miss Clover . . . you look . . . very nice," he finished, lamely.

Clover's deep blue eyes brightened.

"Do you think so?" she said.

The King cast another distracted glance at her, then glanced at Azalea. Azalea mouthed the word *birthday*.

The King's face grew more confused. Azalea mouthed it again. The King opened his mouth, then shut it, frowning.

"It's her *birthday*," said Delphinium, who couldn't seem to take it any longer. "It's been her coming-of birthday all day, and she's been waiting for you to remember, and you *haven't*!"

The King froze with his wineglass halfway to his mouth, his expression unreadable.

"Birthday?"

"It's her coming-of," Azalea explained.

"And you forgot," peeped Hollyhock.

The King unfroze and set his glass down. "Oh, indeed," he said. "I—I can hardly remember my own birthday."

"It was my coming-of birthday last January," said Bramble, gripping the handle of her glass, "and you forgot that, too. You weren't even here."

"I turnt eight last spring," said Hollyhock, "'n I didn' even get any present at all!"

All the girls joined in.

"I was thirteen last April and it *rained* on my birthday and I didn't even get to wear anything special—"

"We turned ten—just two months ago—"

"I usually get a book for my birthday—but—this year—"

"You forgot my birthday, too."

"And mine."

The girls looked miserable. The King opened his mouth, then shut it.

"Sir!" whined Lord Teddie. "You forgot *my* birthday, too!"

Bramble gave a surprised laugh, then slapped her hand over her mouth, as though shocked at letting it out. The tension broke. The girls laughed sheepishly, and Lord Teddie beamed. He probably did not have many ladies think him funny. In fact, he probably got slapped by a lot of them.

"That will do," said the King. He looked somewhat relieved.

Eve was sent for some wine, and a touch of ceremony ensued as the King uncorked the bottle. Clover, however, turned her glass upside down.

"I would like to be temperance," she said firmly.

"What, not like Fairweller?" said Bramble.

"Yes," said Clover. "Like Fairweller."

This immediately ushered in a round of teasing, especially on Bramble's part, but the King immediately corked the bottle and sent the wine out.

"It is Clover's birthday," he said. "She can do as she pleases. Is there anything you should like for your coming-of, Miss Clover? Surely there is something you want."

By the King's voice, Azalea supposed Clover could ask for a pony. Clover gave her room-brightening smile.

"May we have a Christmas tree?" she said.

The King's face wiped of emotion. Azalea bit her lip. Mother used to be in charge of the Christmas tree festivities. Even when she was ill, she helped with the trimming, laughing and singing and helping to make berry chains and watercolor decorations.

"Please," said Clover. "We could—all go to the library, and—and make ornaments and thread berries for it? As a family—like we used to."

"What?" said Delphinium. "But what about danc—"

Azalea trod hard on her foot.

"I think it's a marvelous idea," she said. "Oh, sir! Please say yes!"

The King's fingers tapped against the glass, his cheeks sucked in.

"Oh, please! Oh, please!" cried the younger ones.

"*Only* because it is Clover's birthday," he said, finally, to cheers of "Huzzah!" "We shall see about the tree. We are a house of mourning, you will remember that!"

"Oh, *yes*, sir!" the younger girls squeaked, hopping around the table in a pseudo-reel. Clover beamed, so angelic it made the room glow.

CHAPTER 21

*I*n the library, among the warm golds and browns of the book-lined walls, Clover took charge of the decoration making. She set Delphinium, who was good with pencils and colors, to watercolor bits of stationery, and Hollyhock and the younger ones to winding and knotting yarn into balls. Even Lord Teddie set to work, sweating over knotting the ornament strings to perfection. Over mugs of steaming cider, and the King's slightly bemused expression at them as he penned a speech, the library echoed with laughter and warmth, and everyone felt an aura of holiday cheer.

Everyone, except Azalea. The crafting would keep the girls from dancing, and it both pleased and worried her. Shaking, Azalea kept pricking herself on the needle she used to thread the dried berries. Finally, after drawing blood from her thumb, she excused herself and ran upstairs.

It was late now. Fear curled in her stomach as she rubbed her handkerchief against the passage.

Please, she thought to herself as she pushed through the passage. Please . . . please . . . let Mother be all right. . . .

Azalea rushed through the silver forest and arrived at the bridge, shawl wrapped so tightly around her shoulders she felt them pulse. Equally tightly she grasped the handkerchief, her one comfort. It was magic. It, perhaps, kept Keeper from doing anything really terrible. She remembered, once, how he had flinched at it.

In the pavilion, Keeper paced, a flat silhouette against the silvers.

"Ah!" he said, without stopping to bow. "Good evening, Princess. So Her Highness feels inclined to grace me with her presence tonight. Come for a dance?"

Azalea kept her mouth shut and her feet planted on the bridge.

"Where are the rest of you?"

"It's . . . Clover's birthday tonight," she managed to stammer.

"And the night before?"

Azalea dug her fingers into the silver weave.

"Come now," said Keeper. "I am only curious. You have never missed dancing before."

"The . . . King read them a story, and . . . they fell asleep."

"How sweet." Keeper leaned against the arched doorframe. Twined throughout his fingers was the scarlet embroidery thread. Azalea stared at it, the red burning green into her vision. "Especially since you all hate him so much. Oh, don't flinch like that, my lady. You think I haven't seen it in you?" Keeper's long fingers wound around the thread, twisting it and pulling it into weblike shapes. "If it is any comfort, I hate your father as well."

"You don't even know him."

"Do I have to? I hate him because he is the Wentworth General. I've thrived on that hate. Hate, in its own way, is a virtue."

Azalea cast a furtive glance at the willow branches behind her. She scrunched the handkerchief even tighter in her hand. "Mr. Keeper," she said. "Please. About Mother—you won't . . . that is, if you could—could maybe cut—"

"*Perhaps,*" said Keeper, cutting her short. "Go back, and bring your sisters tomorrow. Do not miss another night. And then, we shall see. You have been looking?"

"I hardly have a choice."

"No, you hardly do. *Goosey.*"

The needle, dangling from the end of the thread,

flashed in the pale light. Azalea cowered against the swirled railing of the bridge.

"Go now. Bring them back tomorrow, and dance your little dances. You will *not* miss another night." His voice was dangerously smooth.

Against the pale mist of the pavilion, Keeper held up the thread, a knitted web shape between his hands. In reticulated scarlet string, it read:

3 days.

"Masterful!" Mother was laughing, her bubbled laugh that put everything at ease. Her hair was askew, as always, the mussed look making her even more charming. "You're better than me! Up, up, up. Very good! Ladies' cloaks, in the library, gentlemen's hats—"

"In the entrance hall. Yes, I remember." Azalea smiled, too, and pushed herself to her feet, the crinolines and silks of her ballgown settling about her.

"Brilliant. The gentlemen will be mad for you. Dance with every single one and find out which one you like best."

Even the milk-turning feeling from talking of her future gentleman didn't feel so curdled, not when she was with Mother, who made everything better, like treacle in a pie.

"I wish you could come," said Azalea.

"Your father will be there."

Azalea shook her head sadly.

Perhaps it was because Azalea had broken from the real script of the dream, or that her eyes couldn't quite meet Mother's—even so, as she did, the flower-papered walls of Mother's room faded and seeped away with the sound of freezing ice, to the dark pavilion, packed with masked dancers and black-thorned vines. Mother had tear streaks down her face. She tried to smile, but cringed with pain. Her lips had been sewn shut.

The dancers swept forward, their powdered wigs and dripping lace dresses pushing Azalea backward, throwing her off her feet.

She fell, her stomach twisting—

—and woke with a jolt, panting.

The early morning fire had died, and the room was cold. Shaking, Azalea slipped from her bed and added coal, unsteady from the dream. She tried to smother images of dancers pulling Mother away, her face marred—

"A dream," Azalea echoed. "A dream . . . a dream . . ."

She still remembered the scent, baby ointment and cake.

The night before, she had somehow arrived back at the room through the shimmering curtain, trying to swallow the heaving within her stomach. The girls had come only minutes later, and still delighted with the ornaments they had crafted, they chattered on about embroidered holly and cinnamon-scented pinecones. Azalea pushed a smile as she helped undress them, then curled up in a ball on her bed, still in her clothes, wheezing in silent gasps until she had sunk into a fitful sleep.

Now, the image of Mother fresh in her mind, Azalea's feet overrode her head, and, taking a shawl, she slipped out of the palace into the cold, frozen morning.

The graveyard tasted like icy mist, glowing blue in the dawn. Snow and frost covered every headstone, branch, and iron railing. It was like walking through a winter palace. Azalea pulled the shawl tighter around her shoulders.

The weeping angel over Mother's grave had an icicle hanging from its hands and a hat of snow on its head. Mother would have thought it funny. Azalea did not. She brushed off the snow hat and snapped the icicle with the end of her shawl. She stared at it, forlorn and shivering, and as she more fully awoke, her spirits fell.

What was she even *doing* here? She'd had some vague idea that people visited graveyards to find a connection—or *something*—with the dead. That somehow she would know what to do, if she stood next to Mother's grave, hoping for some sort of answer.

But now, huddled under the naked trees and staring at

the frosted statue, she realized the graveyard was empty. Azalea's throat grew tight.

"Where's that deep magic now, Mother?" she said. Her choked voice echoed through the graveyard. "That warm flickery bit? If any of it were even real, you could make it so I could at least—at least *tell* someone. You said it was more powerful than magic! Than Mr. Keeper—and—and—"

The wash of prickles strangled the words from her as soon as she said *Keeper*, and she fell to her knees on the grave. The snow froze through her dress. She gasped for air, and slowly regained her breath as the tingles subsided.

"I can't even speak it to the dead," she whispered. She laid her head against the skirt of the statue, wishing the frozen stone would burn through her skin. "Stupid oath," she said. "Stupid me."

The iron gate shrieked.

A gentleman entered the graveyard, carrying his hat and a ring of holly. He wore a thick brown coat, had a long nose and terrifically rumpled hair.

Azalea had the fleeting idea to make the weeping angel pose, in hopes of blending in with the statue. Instead she shrank back against the statue, willing herself to fade away. But Mr. Bradford's eyes immediately found her, huddled at the base of the statue. In a horrific thought,

Azalea realized he had probably heard her yell.

"Princess!" he said, removing his hat. "Forgive me. I sometimes come here, early, before morning Mass. I didn't mean to intrude."

"Not at all," said Azalea, as though they chatted over tea instead of shivering in a graveyard. "I was just . . . visiting."

"It helps sometimes," he said.

"No," said Azalea. "It doesn't. It's empty."

Mr. Bradford considered her. He crunched through the snow to Mother's grave, knelt in front of it, and set the holly down in front of the angel, next to Azalea. She could feel the warmth of his arm.

"My lady?" he said. "My shop is hardly a few paces away, and there's always an ember going. Could I make you some tea? It will warm you up. You look frozen."

"It's all right," said Azalea, trying to lurch to her feet. "I have to get back to the palace. I can't let anyone see me out. Mourning, you know. It isn't far."

"The shop is closer," said Mr. Bradford. "And your lips are blue."

"Surely not."

"More of a purplish, then."

Azalea pressed her lips together into a line, both trying to warm and hide them, and glanced up at Mr. Bradford. Part of his collar was twisted up against his face, the other side down, and his dark cravat was turned askew. Azalea twisted her fingers at the knot in her shawl to keep from reaching out and straightening it.

"Please," said Mr. Bradford.

And his eyes—the same color as cinnamon bread, Azalea realized—had such a look of concern that Azalea melted.

"You know," said Azalea as he helped her to her feet with a strong arm, smiling nearly as crooked as his cravat. "One day you'll rescue me, and I'll actually look nice."

"You always look nice," said Mr. Bradford.

Azalea could have kissed him.

Mr. Bradford's shop *wasn't* far. Just in the square outside the cathedral. Fortunate, too, since Azalea's feet had frozen into blocks of ice and she half stumbled and was half carried. Mr. Bradford helped her along as though she weighed nothing. He wrapped her up in his coat, and his warmth seeped into her skin.

The clock shop smelled of wood and oil. Dozens of clocks—cuckoo clocks, bell clocks, clocks with rose-shaped pendulums—lined the walls and sat in a glass case at the front of the shop. It was a fine old building that could afford to have an ember lit in the stove at any hour.

Mr. Bradford set a kettle on the stove and unlocked

an understairs closet, revealing more coats hanging from pegs, while Azalea slowly unthawed on a stool by the stove.

"Are you here often?" said Azalea, raising an eyebrow at his familiarity with the shop.

"Yes," Mr. Bradford admitted. "I often come to help Mr. Grunnings with the clocks."

"Help?"

"I like to take them apart."

Ah, thought Azalea. She remembered once how the King had unshelved the entire library and sorted through the books a different way, because he had said it would work better. Azalea hazarded a guess.

"And you like to put them back together in different ways?" she said.

Mr. Bradford lit up.

"Oh, yes," he said. "Some of those clockwork designs are terribly antiquated. You have to wind them two times a day, at least. Surely there is a better way to harbor energy in such a tiny mass." Still smiling, Mr. Bradford turned to the coats, which were old-fashioned and far out of style. It looked more like a storage closet than anything. A very old, shabby rag cloak hung from one of the pegs. Mr. Bradford glanced at Azalea's feet. "Perhaps another coat, about your feet?"

Azalea smoothed back her skirts to look. She closed

her eyes with embarrassment. She couldn't find her boots in the dark that morning and, frustrated, had grabbed what she thought were her green dancing slippers from the basket. One was. The other was Bramble's red slipper, knotted around her left foot. It looked terrible . . . and festive, in a way.

"I—ah, can be a touch impulsive, I'm afraid," Azalea admitted, cringing. She tucked her mismatched feet back under her skirts.

"It's true, then," he said. "You really do dance at night."

Azalea had opened her mouth when movement outside the shop window caught her eye. A great white horse pawed at the cobblestones. A dark figure came up the stairs.

In a rush of billowing skirts, Azalea ran for the nearest hiding place—the closet.

Which Mr. Bradford was already in. He was shoved against the wall as she leaped into it, pressing her skirts flat and yanking the door shut behind her.

Pitch blackness enveloped them. A broom handle clunked against someone's head, and it wasn't Azalea's. A bell jangled outside the closet, signaling a customer's arrival.

There was an awkward moment of silence.

"Eerck," came Mr. Bradford's voice.

"Sorry," Azalea whispered, realizing she pressed right up against him. He smelled like fresh linen, soap, and pine. She resisted the impulse to bury her nose into his cravat and inhale.

"It is, ah, togetherness," he stammered. "I think—"

"Please," Azalea whispered fervently. "Please. Fairweller is out there. Don't let him see me. Please."

A walking stick rapped against the counter. Mr. Bradford's hand took Azalea's.

"Forbear," he said. Then, with quite a lot of racket and rustling of coats, skirts, and the maligned broom, he was out, carefully closing the door to a crack behind him. Azalea peeked through the sliver of light.

"Minister," said Mr. Bradford. "Good morning. The shop isn't open yet. Mr. Grunnings will be in, but in two hours, I should think."

"I saw a light," came Fairweller's voice, completely emotionless and flat as always. "I thought to come in. I ordered a lady's watch from Delchastire that was to be sent here, and it is already a day late. Do you have it?"

A lady's watch! Azalea leaned forward for a better look, catching a bit of Fairweller's face and the counter.

"A shipment came yesterday afternoon, I believe. What does it look like?"

"It is silver. A ribbon clock. And—" Something flickered over Fairweller's face. Azalea wished she were closer. "And delicate. So delicate and fine that . . . a person would not touch it, for fear of breaking."

Azalea gaped. Fairweller! Fairweller was in *love*! She resisted the impulse to laugh an evil laugh. Oh, the poor lady. She waited while Mr. Bradford arrived from the back room, carrying a small box. The watch must have been expensive, as Fairweller wrote a bank note for it. When he took the box from Mr. Bradford's hands, he handled it with the utmost care, cradling it. Azalea was astounded beyond words.

When the door jangled closed, Azalea burst from the closet.

"Good heavens," said Mr. Bradford. "There's a lady in my coat closet."

"Did you see that?" said Azalea. "Fairweller! In *love*! I'll bet that was an engagement gift. I wonder who it is. Lady Caversham? She must be *mad*."

Mr. Bradford smiled. Azalea chattered on as she helped him prepare the tea from the boiling kettle, taking over the strainer when he fumbled with it. Soon enough they sat on the stepping stools in front of the black stove, Azalea wrapped in two coats and slowly unthawing while they drank tea from the shop's old mugs.

"I hope he loves the lady because she is her," said Azalea, thoughtful as she stirred her steaming tea. "And I don't like Fairweller, but I hope she loves him, too. I hope she's not marrying him for his money. That would be so . . . sad. She should marry him for his mind and soul."

"You're a romantic?" said Mr. Bradford.

"No," said Azalea. "Not. I think that's what everyone wants. I mean, I would want someone like—"

She cut off abruptly, horrified that her mouth had run off before her mind had caught up with it. She had almost said "like you."

And then she realized *she had meant it.*

She was in love!

The tea in her mug shook as she blinked at it. In love! Azalea had always smothered the thought—what was the point? Parliament would choose her husband. And yet here he was in front of her, the perfect king—even the King would admit that—and the perfect gentleman, with his soft, cinnamon bread eyes and his gentle touch, his quiet wit, rumpled hair, crooked, bashful smile. He was so *lovable.*

Blood flushed to Azalea's cheeks as she suddenly became shy.

"Yes," said Mr. Bradford. Even his voice was lovable. "I should think you are right."

"Ha," said Azalea, giddy. "Yes."

"In fact, I feel a bit of pity for your older sister," he said.

The ticking of the wall clocks cracked like whips.

Azalea slowly lowered her mug.

Oh . . .

That. She had forgotten about that! He thought she was Bramble! More unpleasant thoughts bubbled to the surface of her mind. They would probably never get his watch back. And—why the devil did he feel sorry for her?

"You pity her?" said Azalea slowly.

"Because she is the future queen consort. I expect a person can't find genuine attachment in that."

Azalea's fingers tightened on her mug's spoon.

"But . . . what if she . . . found someone who . . . perhaps . . . did love her?" said Azalea.

"Would he be a good king, though?" said Mr. Bradford. "I should think—"

"*You* would be a good king," said Azalea.

Mr. Bradford looked unsettled. He turned his spoon in his mug.

"I think not," he said.

"You would," said Azalea, clutching her mug so tightly it burned her hands. "You're sensible, and kind, and good with politics—"

"Well," he said, coloring. "That is—kingship . . . I—I could never want it on my head."

Azalea's insides sank. Her heart, stomach, all the blood and curly insides that lay in a person's torso fell hard to her feet. She blinked at the dregs in her mug.

"You really wouldn't?" she said.

"It would . . . be ghastly, don't you think?"

"Ghastly," Azalea echoed. Beneath her smile, she wanted to cry.

"Your father does an excellent job," said Mr. Bradford, seeming to sense a conversation gone awry. "He is a fine king—our best. What I mean to say is—"

"No, no," said Azalea in a hollow voice. "You are quite right. Any gentleman with common sense wouldn't want to be king. The Princess Royale shouldn't possibly expect more."

Azalea stood, took her mug to the glass counter, and set it next to the teakettle, placing the spoon beside it. She was finished.

"What I mean to say is," said Mr. Bradford, finishing his thought. "Is—it is—Miss Bramble—" He stood, leaned in, then back, caught between going forward or retreating. In the end he remained by the cheery stove, holding his mug and nervously stirring with a *clinkety clinkety clink*.

"What I mean to say is," he said, "Miss Bramble, I know you are in mourning. But I had a thought. Perhaps . . . to call on you? After mourning is through? If it is agreeable with you, of course. Naturally. And your father. Naturally."

Clinkety clinkety clink clink.

Clinketyclinketyclinkclinkclinkclink—

"I need to go," said Azalea.

Mr. Bradford's entire countenance fell. He was far too bright a gentleman, Azalea knew, to misconstrue that for anything else.

"Naturally," he said.

"They'll miss me at breakfast," said Azalea.

"Nat-naturally," Mr. Bradford stuttered. He somehow regained his solemn composure and helped Azalea with her things. "If you want. I'll call a cab and escort you back. Take this coat—it's freezing out."

"I don't want a cab," said Azalea, near tears. "I'll walk back."

"You will not," said Mr. Bradford, with an edge Azalea had never heard before. "You'll freeze. You will take a cab."

Azalea whipped around to face him—

And Mr. Bradford said, "Please."

She relented. She had to. He was only being kind, and she couldn't blame him for that. Azalea was wrapped in an old-fashioned lady's coat. Mr. Bradford hailed a cab, and moments later they trundled in awkward silence to the palace. Mr. Bradford, sitting across from her, focused on the riding whip in his lap. He twisted the end loop of it around his fingers, around and around, until surely it cut through his glove. Azalea miserably stared at it.

Oh, how could she be so *stupid*? She always knew it would be like this, she had just stupidly hoped that—

Azalea cried. Not the noisy sort, but the sort you could blink away if you were careful and didn't think about how awful you felt. She turned her face to the window.

"You're cross with me," Mr. Bradford finally said. He leaned his head back against the leather seat, untangled his fingers from the riding whip, and fumbled in his suitcoat for a handkerchief, which he handed to her. "I'm—I should have done it properly. I should have asked your father first, or had my aunt invite you to tea—"

"It's not that," said Azalea. "It's nothing to do with you. It's just—circumstances."

Mr. Bradford blinked several times.

"Circumstances," he said. The edge to his voice was still there. "Naturally. Of course it is circumstances. I suppose you could have any fellow you wanted, couldn't you." He twisted the riding-whip loop around his fingers again, hard. "Well, I couldn't let you freeze to death. Tell me, these *circumstances*, Miss Bramble. Do they have to do with a *Mr. Keeper*?"

A stab of fear shot through Azalea. She looked up sharply, blood draining from her face. Now Mr. Bradford turned to the window, avoiding her eyes.

"I heard you outside the graveyard," he said. "Forgive me. I shouldn't have listened. Is he one of the gentlemen from your Royal Business?" Mr. Bradford kept his eyes on the passing town houses and brick shops.

Azalea grimaced. Mr. Bradford took it as a no.

"A gentleman, though?"

Azalea could only dry swallow. Mr. Bradford turned to her. Concern was etched in his face.

"Is it to do . . . with magic?"

Azalea choked. The carriage jolted to a stop just outside the palace gates, and she flung herself to the door without waiting for Mr. Bradford to help her out.

"I'm late," she said. "Thank you for the tea. Good-bye."

Mr. Bradford leaped from the carriage after her. "Wait—Miss Bramble—"

"*Don't* call me that!" said Azalea.

Something, perhaps hurt, flickered through Mr. Bradford's soft eyes.

"Princess Bramble," he said.

"I'm Princess Azalea," said Azalea. "Azalea, for heaven's sake. It was Bramble's handkerchief I gave you at the ball. I . . . meant to tell you. I'm sorry."

Mr. Bradford's dark eyebrows knit, then rose. He opened his mouth, but no words came out.

Azalea did not stay to see any more. She ran through

the gate and through the gardens, skirts billowing and lungs burning. She slammed against the brick of the palace, sobbing, trying to erase the image of Mr. Bradford's hurt expression from her mind.

A long while later, numb both inside and out, she went inside. The warm kitchen air burned her cheeks. She wanted dearly to collapse into bed. Passing the nook glass doors, however, she drew back. Instead of the usual morning sight—the girls yawning into their porridge as the King sorted through the post—all the girls laughed and chattered as Lord Teddie passed around a platter full of flat cakes. The King sat at the head of the table, bemused. Lord Teddie laughed and jabbered so loudly Azalea could hear him through the glass.

"You put berries, or cinnamon, or whatever you like on it and fold the sides around—oh, well done, Hollyhocky! It's ripping! Oh, hulloa, Princess A!"

Azalea made to run, but in an instant Lord Teddie had thrown open the glass doors and pulled her in.

"I don't feel like eating," she said as everyone pushed her to a seat. She was too tired to make a fuss. "What is all this?"

"Ha!" Lord Teddie beamed. A bit of flour smudged his nose. "That's what your father said. I was just explaining to them, I just was explaining, I saw Miss Bramble yesterday at breakfast and I saw how she *hates* porridge and who can blame her, really? So I thought, I say! I'll make a corking present! So Cookie and I went to market yesterday and we were up early this morning and we made a Delchastire breakfast and it's *smashing*! Isn't it, Cookie?"

It was hard to tell what Mrs. Graybe thought of Lord Teddie. She set a jug of cream on the table, said, "Yes, m'lord," and left for the kitchen.

"We eat it with our *fingerth*!" cried Ivy, whose hands dripped with jam.

"Use a knife and fork," said the King. "We are not animals! Silverware, at once."

"Oh, but that would ruin it!" said Lord Teddie. "Breakfast is meant to be splattered everywhere! It wakes a person up!"

The King sucked in his cheeks.

"Young man," he said, a term that did not bode well for Lord Teddie. "Does your ship not leave today?"

Lord Teddie's face fell.

"Oh . . . yes," he said. "It does." He gave a wan smile, and stumbled on. "I—I wish I didn't have to go. These past several days have been ripping. Rippingly ripping. I—I'm awfully chuffed about you all. I . . . sort of feel at home here."

Lord Teddie smiled hopefully at the King over the dripping jam jars and jugs of milk.

"I wish I could stay longer," he said. "If I were to be invited, I would."

The King folded his arms, complete iciness. A pang of sympathy ran through Azalea.

"Perhaps you can visit next year, Lord Haftenravenscher," she said.

Lord Teddie brightened. A little.

"Oh . . . all right," he said. "Or you could all come to my manor! Mother will host a corking ball; we have a horrifically gigantic ballroom, you'll love it!"

And then Lord Teddie turned to Bramble, who Azalea realized had been silent the entire time. She hadn't greeted Azalea, or even looked up. Instead she stared at her lap, fingering the threadbare black lace on her cuff that was coming unstitched. She kept pressing the frayed ends back into the cuff, over and over, almost feverishly. Her lips pursed together so tightly they were white.

"Do you like it, Bramble?" said Lord Teddie. "Better than porridge, I should think!" He hopefully nudged a jam jar toward her. "Er . . . princess?"

Bramble tore her eyes from her lap and fixed a celery green glare on Lord Teddie. It froze the smile on his face.

"Mrs. Graybe," she said. "Mrs. Graybe! Do we have any porridge?"

"What?" said Lord Teddie. "You don't want—"

"I *love* porridge!" Bramble snarled.

"But—"

"I don't *want* your stupid charity!" Bramble cried. "Go back to your stupid manor! Leave us alone!" She threw her cake at him. It missed and landed jam down, on the floor.

"Miss Bramble!" said the King. "Apologize, at once!"

Bramble shoved her chair aside and fled from the nook, her face buried in her hands. Bramble never exactly cried, but she had a sob-whimper that squeaked when she inhaled, and it echoed *sob squeak sob squeak-squeak-squeak* down the hall.

Lord Teddie stared at the glass nook doors, then at the flat cake breakfast, then back at the doors. His mouth tightened. He leaned and shoved his plate away.

"The devil," he said, in a tone that was not jovial or cheerful at all. "My ship leaves soon, doesn't it. I suppose I ought to go catch it, then! Good day!"

Azalea found Bramble, several minutes later, huddled behind the curtains on the window seat. The window light made her deep red hair fiery. Bent over with squeaky sobs, she fumbled with a needle and thread and tried, one-handed, to mend the shabby bit of lace on her cuff.

"I hate him," she sobbed. "And I hate *me*."

Azalea took Bramble's arm and mended the cuff

herself, then unpinned Bramble's hair and combed it until Bramble dipped into a fitful sleep. She could understand, a little, how she felt.

Their sulky moods trickled down to the younger ones, who argued and whined, Christmas spirits low. Perhaps the King had noticed it, for just before tea, a great commotion of stamping boots and calling orders echoed from the entrance hall, and the girls ran to see the hullabaloo. The King, dusted with snow and pine needles, arrived at the palace main doors tugging a great pine tree. The girls squealed with delight.

"Clover's Christmas tree!"

"Huzzah!"

The girls joined hands in a reel and started to sing a nonsense Christmas song.

"It is *not* a Christmas tree!" said the King, so firmly that all the girls stopped jumping about. "This is a house of mourning. It is nothing more than a tree. I thought it would look nice. Inside. That is all."

Puddles formed on the wood as the King began to set it up in the corner beneath the mezzanine, the girls hopping from foot to foot.

"Are we allowed to decorate this tree-that-is-not-a-Christmas-tree-that-is-just-meant-to-be-inside?" said Bramble.

The King took in Bramble's red eyes and hollow-cheeked face and frowned.

"If you will pluck up, young lady," he said. Then, as the twins brought the basket of yarn-stitched ornaments from the library, "Where is Miss Clover?"

Everyone looked about, surprised. Clover wasn't with them.

"She's probably helping Old Tom in the gardens again," said Delphinium. "She's been doing that a lot lately. Running off to the gardens."

"More cider for us," peeped Hollyhock, bringing a steaming mug of rewarmed cider from the kitchen. Azalea took a shawl and was out the door.

"I'll fetch her," she said.

Since it hadn't snowed for several days, the garden paths had been cleared, and Azalea saw no footprints. So she searched for the likeliest places Clover would be: the stone benches in the overgrown topiaries, the stairs by the drained fountains. She kept an eye out for Old Tom's wheelbarrow.

She had nearly given up when another sight gave her pause. In the far back part of the gardens, tethered to the gazebo, was a large white horse with a long, snowy mane. LadyFair, Fairweller's horse!

The old garden gazebo was a sort of Eathesbury lovers' landmark. They had been chided as children to leave it be and let the couples visiting the gardens have their time alone, but Azalea still remembered peeking with her sisters through the lattice, listening to gentlemen read poems or murmur sappy words of love.

It had been funny, then. Now, having some experience of love, Azalea didn't see much humor in it.

Still . . . Fairweller . . .

Curiosity overriding her sensibilities, she pussy-footed over the path and crouched down beneath the bushes, just next to the splintery latticework. She peered up through the holes.

Only feet were visible, the rest blocked by the underside of the bench. Azalea recognized the immaculately shiny boots of Fairweller. The lady's boots were hard and stiff, not unlike Azalea's, which meant she was poor. That ruled out Lady Caversham, then. Azalea listened, patient.

"You trace your toe back," came Fairweller's voice, "touch your toes, step aside. Other foot steps back. Well done."

He was teaching the lady a version of the waltz Azalea did not know. The lady's shoes turned, graceful. She was good, even in boots. So was Fairweller. Azalea remembered how well he had danced at the Yuletide.

The lady said something, so quiet Azalea did not hear it.

"*You* are very good," came Fairweller's voice. "You are incomparable."

The lady's feet turned again, meaning Fairweller had brought her into an under-arm turn, spinning her. Her feet stepped just in front of Fairweller's, and stopped. The lady laughed quietly, a light, pastry-sweet laugh, then—

Silence. Azalea drummed her fingers against the lattice, waiting for something to happen.

"I've spoken to Father Benedict."

Fairweller's voice was low and quiet. The lady's feet stepped back.

"He says he is willing at any hour. We could leave tonight. On my ship. I'll take you to Delchastire. The ballrooms there are so grand, they are fit for you—"

"No."

The lady's voice was firm, and the timbre of it made the hairs on the back of Azalea's neck prickle.

"Oh, my lady. Your father would never approve. I know him too well."

Azalea leaned in. Elopement . . . forbidden love . . . if Fairweller was caught courting a young lady without her father's permission, he would end up in a duel. Azalea cringed.

"It is not the way a wedding ought to be done," said the lady. "Weddings are meant to be with family. I will not allow it unless my sisters are there."

Azalea stopped breathing. The sweet, crystal way the lady had said "my sisters" curdled in her ears.

"If your sisters come to your wedding, my lady, it will only be to murder me."

Azalea slowly stood.

"Well, at least they will be there."

Fairweller laughed, a foreign sound to Azalea, and through the lattice and dead vines, she saw his dark figure pull the lady into his arms. A lady who had golden blond hair, rosy cheeks, and a smile like a chorus of angels.

Clover.

CHAPTER 22

"Oh—*oh*!" Azalea stormed to the entrance of the gazebo. On her way rested Old Tom's snow-capped wheelbarrow, and she snatched up a frozen pair of gardening gloves from it.

Fairweller and Clover broke apart at the sound of her boots stomping up the stairs. Fairweller turned to face Azalea—

And got smacked in the face with a pair of ice gloves.

"How *dare* you!" cried Azalea. "Just because she's beautiful and kind doesn't mean you can—can do *this*!" She whapped him again across his handsome, colorless face. Her temper flared, stinging her eyes. "You know better! The King will never stand for it!"

Fairweller flinched at the word *king*. "I don't—" he began.

Whap!

"I think you ought to go now, Minister," said Clover, grabbing Azalea's hands and pulling her away before Azalea could manage another whap. "It's all right. I'll talk to her."

Fairweller opened his mouth, closed it, opened it, cast a despairing look at Clover, and closed it again. He took his hat from the frozen bench, looked again at Clover, then mounted LadyFair and left.

When the hoofbeats faded, Clover broke her serene calm and laughed. She threw her arms around Azalea, laughing and weeping at the same time.

"I'm *so* glad you know!" she said. "So glad! It's been wholly torture to keep it to myself! I thought I would burst!"

Azalea made an odd strangled noise.

"Yes—I suppose it's a bit of a shock," said Clover.

"A bit!" said Azalea.

Clover pulled Azalea to the rickety gazebo bench and clasped Azalea's hand in her own. "It does make him seem like a—a cad, doesn't it? But it wasn't him at all. I've loved him for *ages*, Lea. For over a year!"

Azalea stared at the dainty ribbon watch pinned to Clover's waist. It was beautiful, held suspended in a sweep of silver swirls. Clover gently touched it.

"You know—since—I'm not very good at—at

speaking, I like to just—*watch* people," said Clover. "Ever since he became the Prime Minister, I've watched Fairweller. Did you know he's a member of our household?"

"Only technically," said Azalea.

"Yes," said Clover. She smoothed a fold on her black skirt. "But he's always acted like it, too. Even—even when we've treated him so horridly. Do you remember when Ivy got lost in the gardens, when—when she was four?"

"Yes," said Azalea slowly. She brought to mind the image of Ivy chasing after a hopping bird with a hatbox, pushing her way through the bushes one fall afternoon. They had laughed over it and returned to clipping flowers for Mother's room. They thought nothing more of it until Ivy hadn't shown for dinner. They all blamed one another for not watching her, then ran to the chill gardens to find her.

"She turned up, though," said Azalea defensively. "She's never far from the dinner table, you know that."

"She turned up," said Clover, "because—because Minister Fairweller searched the wood with his hound. I—I was at the back gate when I saw him leading LadyFair out of the mist into the meadow, Ivy huddled on her back. It—it was like a picture from one of Eve's storybooks—except for the part where Ivy threw up all over him, when he helped her from the horse."

Azalea opened her mouth, then shut it.

"And—and the Delchastrian doctor, the one who came last year—" Clover began.

"Oh, honestly!" said Azalea, grinding a dried leaf into the wood floor with her boot. "You're not going to tell me he had something to do with that, too? We scraped to pay for those medicines!"

"Minister Fairweller," said Clover, standing abruptly, "paid for nearly *all* of them."

"He did not!" said Azalea, coloring.

"I—I heard him speaking to that doctor," said Clover. "Late one night, and—and I had to send letters of inquiry to sort it all together. Minister made it a great secret— of course he had to! The King would *never* allow such help!"

Clover paced the gazebo floor, almost feverishly. Wooden planks creaked, and her skirts swished with her stride. She clenched her fists.

"Last year, Lady Caversham—you remember her? She found me in the gardens, and—and she told me she would give me a penny if I delivered a note to Minister Fairweller."

"A love letter?" said Azalea. "How awful. Well, at least you got a penny out of it."

"I did *not*!" said Clover, her blue eyes blazing. Her skirts snapped as she turned. "Of *course* I didn't take her money. When she left I—I just stared at that horrid perfumed letter and—and I couldn't *bear* to think of Fairweller with her! He was too good and noble and—and—" Clover's fists shook. "And I realized *I* was in love with him! And I would marry him! *Fairweller was mine!*"

"Yes, all right, naturally," Azalea squeaked. She cowered under Clover's tirade, gripping the edge of the bench. A dozen tiny slivers embedded themselves into her palms. She suddenly knew how the tea set felt in its last moments. "What did Fairweller say? When you delivered the note?"

"Oh," said Clover, calming a little. "Well . . . nothing, actually. I sort of . . . accidentally . . . tore it to pieces."

"Accidentally," Azalea echoed.

"And threw it into the fire," said Clover.

"Oh."

Clover tugged the ends of her shawl around her shoulders, and smiled bashfully. "Well," she said. "He was mine, after all. And now he's *finally* noticed me. I thought I would have to smack him across the head with a book or something." She sat down next to Azalea, still beaming. "But he came around."

In Azalea's shock, something surfaced.

"Clover," she said. "You're not—not—"

"Stuttering?" Clover beamed. "I . . . still do. A little.

But Minister has been so easy to talk to, and—well. He says I have a pretty voice," she added shyly.

Azalea had nothing to say to that.

"He wants me to elope."

"I *heard*."

"Oh—but I can't! He's certain the King would never allow our union. If Mother were here, she could talk to the King. But—" Clover fingered the swirls of the watch at her waist, then brightened at Azalea. "Perhaps *you* could!"

"Definitely not me," said Azalea.

"Oh, Lea!" said Clover. "Who else can do it? You're the closest thing to Mother we have!"

Azalea pinched the slivers in her palm with her fingernails, biting her lip. The King would be up in arms over this. Fairweller, courting Clover, not only in mourning, but without the King's approval or knowledge. There would be a duel. Azalea did not like Fairweller, but she did not want him hurt. At least, not a *lot*. All this pulled her down like heavy crinolines, adding to the burden of Keeper's threat. Azalea closed her eyes.

"I'll think about it," she said.

Clover leaped up and threw her arms around Azalea, beaming to tears.

That afternoon, as the girls busied in the kitchen baking gingerbread ornaments for the tree, Azalea nervously slipped into the library. The door was already open.

The King stood when he saw her. Sitting across from his desk was a gentleman, who stood as well. Azalea did not recognize him, staring at his hairy eyebrows and dark under-eye circles. He reminded her of a rainstorm. She made to retreat back into the entrance hall.

"Oh, Azalea. No, it's all right, don't go," said the King. "We were finished. Good day, Mr. Gasperson."

"Good day," said the gentleman, drawing out the word *day*. Azalea gave him a wide berth as he clumped out of the library.

"Who was that?" said Azalea when the door had slid shut. "I thought we wouldn't have guests for Christmas."

"What? Oh, certainly not. He's—official R.B., of sorts. Come in, have a seat. I need to speak with you."

"Good," said Azalea. She sat on the sofa across from the desk. "I need to speak with you."

"Excellent. We'll speak together." The King opened the cabinet behind his desk and pulled out two glasses with a small decanter of brandy. He poured a little into each and handed one to Azalea. "We don't talk much, do we?"

Azalea eyed her glass, wary. What did the King want to talk about? Surely *good* things were not preambled with "We need to speak."

"Tell me, Azalea," said the King. "What did you all think about Lord Haftenravenscher?"

The King did not drink his brandy. He looked intently at Azalea.

"Lord Teddie?"

"Yes."

Azalea smiled, considering Lord Teddie's parlor tricks and boundless good humor.

"He's a decent, happy sort," she said. "The younger girls were mad after him. Even Delphinium liked him. But I think he only had eyes for Bramble."

"Oh, you think so?" said the King.

Azalea's smile faded. She rested her glass in her lap. "Is he hoping to give the riddle another go? Is that what this is about?"

"No, no," said the King. "Nothing like that."

Azalea thought of the jam cake hitting the floor that morning, and sighed. She couldn't forget the spark in Lord Teddie's hazel eyes when he looked at Bramble. Surely he was fond of her, but he had done everything all *wrong*. Azalea almost wondered if he really did only think them a jolly sport.

"That's good, then," she said. "I don't think Bramble could stand to be humiliated again."

"Humiliated?"

"It was just this morning?" said Azalea, exasperated.

"Oh," said the King. "Yes, I remember." He sat down on his stiff, high-backed chair.

Azalea sipped her brandy, a tiny sip, only enough to cover her tongue with the burning taste of wood and sour boots. She thought again of Lord Teddie's hopeful smile when he looked at Bramble, and sympathy sprang inside her.

"Perhaps he could come to our Yuletide ball," she said. "If he truly is fond of Bramble, he should prove he's in earnest. Not this riddle nonsense. Something to show we're not just sport to him."

A frown started to line the King's face.

"Yuletide ball?" he said.

"Oh, yes," said Azalea, straightening in her chair. "That's what I wanted to talk to you about. I think— now that mourning is over, we should have a Yuletide. Not for me, naturally. It's never mattered for me. You know that. But for Bramble and Clover, they're both over fifteen now, and they should meet gentlemen. Real gentlemen and not the riddle nonsense. If they don't, they'll just fall in love with—anyone. I thought perhaps Clover could host it?"

The King's frown, above his neatly sorted paperwork and blotters, was now fully pronounced. Azalea hurried on.

"Everyone's been so excited for mourning to end,"

said Azalea. "It doesn't have to be a large ball, just a small one. Please."

Azalea waited. The King stood, and paced in front of his desk, distracted. When he finally spoke, he did not meet her eyes.

"Azalea," he said. "About mourning."

Azalea lowered her brandy glass.

"You and your sisters have managed all of mourning quite well," said the King. "I'm pleased with you all. But mourning, it is a symbol. A way of being. It . . . I—I don't believe we are ready to lift mourning."

This took a moment to sink into Azalea's mind.

"Oh," she said slowly.

"It's rather not even mourning for you all. You still have dancing, and the slippers," said the King.

"Oh," said Azalea.

"And the gardens, too."

Azalea stared at the brandy glass, shifting it from hand to hand, watching the reddish yellow drink swirl.

"I don't know what I'm going to tell them," she mumbled. "They've been so excited for the windows, and dresses and things."

The King was quiet. "Azalea," he said. "I know mourning means very little to you and your sisters, but it means a great deal to me. A very great deal."

Azalea traced a brocade flower on the arm of the

chair. She should have expected this. Everything else was going wrong; it was too much to hope that this wouldn't. Only three more nights until Christmas. The world felt in a blur. She had to think of some way to ruin Keeper before then. The brandy in her glass shook. What was stronger than a blood oath?

The warm flickery bit. Oh yes, that was right. Ha. Mother had always spoken of it. Azalea wasn't sure if she really ever had felt it. If it truly was stronger than the other sorts of magic, surely it could help *somehow*. Azalea raised her head to the King, who brusquely put the brandy back in the cabinet, and her heart fell. Even his movements were cold.

"I wish you were someone I could talk to," she said quietly. "I could always talk to Mother."

"I am not your mother." The King's tone was brusque as he locked the cabinet.

That was true enough. Azalea set her brandy on the King's desk. She felt slumped, weary, and even her gait lagged. Her gracelessness must have shown, for when she reached the door, the King said, "Azalea." His eyebrows were furrowed. "Is something wrong?"

In the soft lamplight the King looked so deeply concerned that, for a moment, Azalea almost felt that she *could* talk to him. She paused.

"Sir," she said. "When we dance at ni—"

Fwoosh.

A mass of prickles swept over her, hit her so hard it pummeled the breath from her. Azalea gasped. Her blood rushed in waves. It bristled in frigid pinpricks all over and stole her voice.

Dizzy weakness flooded her head. Speckled dots filled her vision and turned to blotches.

"Azalea—" The King's voice sounded distant.

Everything fell black.

When Azalea came to, her head throbbed and she had to blink for her vision to clear. She lay on the sofa by the piano, and stared up at the underside of the mezzanine. The King knelt next to her. His eyebrows were furrowed.

Another face, equally concerned, solemn, and gentle stood over her. It had cinnamon-bread eyes.

"Oh," Azalea moaned, reliving her last memory. "I didn't faint?"

"You did," said the King.

Azalea groaned.

"Mr. Pudding is fetching a bit of bread. You've been skipping too many meals of late; it's very out of order, young lady." The King pulled a blanket close to her chin, and the smell of fresh linen and pine encased her. She realized the blanket was actually Mr. Bradford's dark, thick-weaved coat.

Humiliation tangled in her stomach, and Azalea tried to sit up. The King pushed her back down with a firm hand.

"Don't get up, young lady."

"Mr. Bradford," said Azalea. "What are you doing here?"

"Captain Bradford wished to try his hand at the riddle," said the King. "I told him no, of course. It is the holiday, after all."

"Some other time, naturally," Mr. Bradford said.

Hearing his mellow voice sent ripples through Azalea's chest. Mr. Bradford's face was etched with worry.

"You fell just before I came in," he said. "I'll leave straightaway, as soon as you have a little more color."

Azalea pressed her cheek into the brocade of the sofa arm and wanted to curl into a ball. Betrayal, delight, and despair all passed in turn at seeing Mr. Bradford's warm, solemn eyes. She didn't know why he even wanted to see her, but she did know he hadn't close family to spend Christmas with. Sympathy took over.

"Why not?" she said to the King, as he adjusted the coat at her feet. "Why can't he stay? He lent me his coat —and—his watch—and . . . please. He hasn't any family to stay with for Christmas."

Possibly the King thought she was rambling. He folded up the collar of the coat so it covered her chin.

"Well, Captain," he said finally. "It seems Princess Azalea should have you as our Christmas guest. Are you still willing?"

Mr. Bradford bowed.

"Hmm," said the King. "You are lucky we are both in a generous humor today."

Azalea slept through dinner on the hard library sofa, and awoke to eleven eager sisters flocking about her, pushing and poking her awake. They pulled her up to the room while shoving pieces of dinner roll at her mouth. Azalea felt groggy, but better. Slippers were tied, hair brushed and pinned in preparation for dancing that night. In spite of Azalea staring listlessly at her slippers, the girls were a chatter of excitement.

"You'll never guess who's here, Az," said Bramble as Clover brushed through Azalea's auburn tresses.

"Mr. Bradford."

Bramble dropped the pins she held.

"He's come to try the riddle," said Azalea, getting it over with. "I asked the King to let him; he hasn't any family to go to for Christmas. I couldn't turn him out."

"You invited him to stay?" Bramble's eyes narrowed, and her grin became terribly devious, like a fox among chickens. "For Christmas? Well, well, we-ee-elll!"

Azalea braced herself for the Merciless Teasing.

"Mmm," said Delphinium as the girls took poufs around Azalea. "Sturdy and tall. Such a long nose. But those eyes—*pow*!"

"Aye, you'll have childlets with brown eyes. The brown usually wins out, you know."

"Oh, honestly!" said Azalea.

A soft knock sounded on the door, interrupting them. It wasn't the pointed knock of Mrs. Graybe or the King's firm, hard knock. Azalea couldn't place it. Goldenrod, nearest the door, opened it a crack and peered out.

"No one's there," she said. She pulled the door open wide, letting in gust of air, to show the girls.

Tiny shivers crawled up Azalea's arms.

"I feel so odd," said Jessamine. Her glass-spun voice resonated with all of them. Azalea stood.

"Let's get this over with," she said.

The unsettling feeling followed them through the magic passage and into the silver forest. They huddled together, jittery. Azalea clutched at the lamp. It shook as she led them through the silver, and shook harder when Keeper bowed them in. His eyes met Azalea's before he backed away into the mist, and Azalea had to set the lamp down before she dropped it.

Even though they had missed the last two days, no one felt much like dancing. Azalea held Jessamine, who was still frightened, on her lap. Bramble pushed a smile or two, but remained on one of the pavilion sofas, pensive. Delphinium didn't want to bother teaching the younger girls, and Eve wasn't bossy enough to do it, either. The twins didn't know enough to teach. Clover was left to teach Hollyhock, Ivy, and Kale while everyone looked on.

"Try it again," she said in her honey-sweet voice as they gave awkward curtsys. "Mother—Mother used to say, it takes a thousand steps to make the perfect curtsy."

Kale's tiny eyebrows knit.

"Mother?" she said.

"Oh, come now, Kabbage," said Bramble, a length away. "You remember Mother."

Kale's dark blue eyes remained blank.

"She's dead," Jessamine whispered.

Azalea adjusted Jessamine on her lap so she could see her tiny white face. Funny, how four-year-old Jessamine could seem so old sometimes. Did she remember Mother, who had drawn her fingers through Jessamine's black curls and let her feel the baby kick? How could one forget something like that?

Clover pushed a strand of dark blond hair from Kale's eyes.

"She's just in heaven," she said, in a honey voice.

"Just in heafen!" Kale squeaked.

Azalea suddenly felt stifled, as though she had been overlaced in a stuffy room. She nudged the girls to go.

Keeper's dark form appeared through the mist of the entrance, and instinctively, Azalea stood, upsetting Jessamine on her lap. She ran to the front of the girls, putting herself between them and Keeper, who strode in silky strides to the middle of the dance floor.

"Is everything all right?" he said in his chocolate voice. "Only you seem in poor spirits tonight."

The girls, smiling shyly, assured him that everything was all right. Azalea said nothing. Her eyes locked with his in an intense glare. So intense the room pulsed with her heartbeat. Keeper broke it first.

"I thought to give you all a treat," he said, nodding to the girls. A roguish strand hung in his eyes. "A waltz. None of you have seen a closed dance for nearly a year. Miss Azalea?"

He held his outstretched gloved hand to her. Azalea stared at it. It seemed to grow bigger in her vision. His words from the dark pavilion reverberated in her mind. *Never to refuse me another dance again . . .*

After a lengthy pause, Azalea took his hand.

"Oh, goodies," said Delphinium, perking up along with the younger girls. Clover and Bramble, on the other hand, had confusion on their faces.

"But we haven't been properly introduced," said Clover, on her feet. "Mr. Keeper—"

"No," said Azalea, putting a halt to it. "It's all right.

You've got to see the gentleman's part sometime."

Keeper brought Azalea into dance position in the middle of the floor. He closed his eyes and inhaled, and his long fingers traced up and down the edge of her shoulder blade, just above her corset. Azalea held as still as she possibly could, trying not to breathe.

"You have such excellent form," he whispered. "If only you would stop shaking."

The music began; an Ungolian waltz. Keeper guided her smoothly in a traveling circle around the dance floor, into a hesitation step, an under-arm turn, and gently brought her back into dance position. Everything he did was exaggeratedly gentle. Somehow this made it worse. They brushed past the seated girls, Azalea's skirts sweeping over their faces. They giggled.

"Ah, you follow like an angel." Keeper's voice was a murmur. "You are the best I have ever danced with, and I have danced with many. I knew you would be the best. From the first time I saw you, gliding across the marble—"

Azalea misstepped. Keeper tenderly brought her into the rhythm again.

"You glide," he murmured. "Just as your mother."

Azalea stumbled, and this time it took several beats to ease into the flow of the music again. Azalea's hand shook in Keeper's flawless grip.

"Please, Keeper," said Azalea as the silvers whirled around her. "Please. I need more time."

"You have had a disgustingly *plentiful* amount of time, my lady," he said. He swept her about the girls again, and Azalea caught a flash of black—their dresses—as she spun.

"More time was not a part of the agreement. I suggest you look harder."

"Please—Mr. Keeper. The King is extending mourning. If I had more time—"

"You are a flurry of clever words, my lady," said Keeper. "Too many words, I think. Your mother sports that same malady. Or, she did."

Azalea tried to kick Keeper, but her knees couldn't support her. Keeper caught her with lightning rapidity. With a snap of his long-gloved fingers, the music stopped.

"Enough," he said, once again obnoxiously gentle. "I am sure your sisters want you back now. Do get some rest. I should very much like the next dance I have with you to be flawless."

CHAPTER 23

*A*zalea slept poorly that night, awaking from dozes with nightmarish jolts. Even so, she had the presence of mind that morning to dress well, mending a torn bit of her favorite dress, pinning her hair to perfection, and smoothing herself in front of the mirror. Mr. Bradford had seen her at her worst; she wouldn't let that happen again.

She arrived at the nook late, the girls halfway through their porridge, and everyone looked up as she quietly folded the doors behind her.

"*Well*," said Bramble. "Don't *you* look nice!"

A chorus of giggles rippled down the table. Delphinium whispered something to Eve, who in turn whispered it to the twins. The twins whispered something back. They scrunched their noses, grinning at Azalea. Mr. Bradford, on the other hand, just stared at her in a stunned sort of way, his spoonful of porridge halfway to his mouth.

"Good morning," said Azalea.

Mr. Bradford started.

"Good morning," he said, and he stood quickly, something he hadn't done when she arrived. Now late, the gesture made Delphinium and Eve giggle even harder. Azalea flushed.

"Oh, *do* sit by me," said Delphinium. The chair next to her was the empty seat by Mr. Bradford.

Azalea cast Delphinium a withering look and declined, sitting next to a porridge-covered Lily. Delphinium, Eve, the twins, and Hollyhock burst into another round of giggles.

"That will do." The King, at the head of the table, looked up from a letter stamped with a green seal. His eyebrows knit when he saw her. "Azalea, you should be in bed."

"I'm doing better," said Azalea. "Really."

The girls broke into another chorus of giggles.

"Much, much, *much* better," said Bramble.

Azalea closed her eyes, wishing for death.

"Now, Lord Bradford," said Flora, bringing her bowl to sit next to him. Goldenrod, on the other side, brought out a folded piece of paper. "We've made up a whole schedule for you—"

"There's no lessons today, you know—"

"It's Christmas Eve eve!"

"Holiday!"

"Let's see—nine o'clock, we'll show you the tree, and you can help us put the ornaments on the top branches. We need someone tall for that."

"And then at ten, we'll play a bit of spillikins—"

"And then we'll show you the great pine in the gardens—"

"If it stops snowing, of course."

Azalea stared at her porridge, nudging the mushy grains with her spoon before she decided she wasn't hungry. She pushed her bowl to Ivy's spot and slipped out the folding doors, the last scene meeting her eyes being all the girls, flanking Mr. Bradford, chattering and waving spoons, Kale tugging on his suitcoat and trying to get a spoonful of porridge in his mouth, Ivy sneaking a bit of porridge from his bowl, Lily climbing on him and grabbing his nose, and the King staring at the green-seal letter, deep in thought.

The gallery was breath-puffingly cold, but Azalea did not stir up a fire. She ignored the mourning rules and pulled open the drapes of one window, letting in bright snow light. Flakes fluttered past the glass in swirls. The shadows of the flakes danced over Azalea and the sword on the pedestal.

Azalea stared at it for a long time.

348

It was already on its last leg. Cracked and nicked and dented. It would snap in half without much trouble. Did she possibly dare destroy it?

It would free Keeper. Azalea's mind twisted at the possibilities of that. Keeper magicking the palace all over again. Trying to take over the kingdom, and there would be another reign of terror. And . . . the blood oath. Azalea's feet curled in her boots, along with her stomach. He would go after the King, surely.

Azalea stepped away from the pedestal. She refused to put more of her family in harm's way.

Although . . . if she *did* free Keeper, the King would finally know about everything. He could get rid of Keeper before he did anything, couldn't he?

Except . . . the blood oath. Keeper couldn't die until . . .

Azalea pulled sharply away, leaning up against the frosted window, curling her fingers. She still felt Mother's cold hands on hers. She felt awake in a nightmare.

At the end of the hall, the doors burst open in a melee of delighted voices. The girls shaded their eyes against the light and flocked to the window, pressing their hands and noses on the cold pane to watch the blizzard.

"I thought you were going to play spillikins?" said Azalea, backing away so the window had more room.

"Changed our minds," said Bramble. "We're taking

Mr. Bradford on a tour of the palace."

"An' we're not even charging him a penny!" squeaked Hollyhock.

Mr. Bradford, who had Ivy tugging on one hand and Kale tugging on the other, managed a bow.

"My ladies are most generous," he said.

His brown eyes caught Azalea's, and they had a mischievous sparkle in them. Though he was solemn faced, Azalea knew he was grinning inside. The girls sat in the rectangle of light beneath the window, smoothing their skirts and scrutinizing him.

"You once said you had studied at the university," said Eve shyly. "What did you study, please?"

Azalea blushed. It was all right for the girls to interrogate normal gentlemen, but this was one she wanted to keep.

"Ah," said Mr. Bradford, coloring as well. "Politics, actually. Some philosophy, and sciences. But . . . mostly politics, I'm afraid."

"How very appropriate," said Bramble. Her face was completely blank.

Flora raised her forefinger. "Please, sir," she said. "Did you study dancing?"

Mr. Bradford smiled and inclined his head to Flora.

"One cannot enter a dance floor in Delchastire," he said, "save one has a dance master."

The girls let out a unanimous gasp of delight, and the air buzzed with excitement. Ivy actually clapped her hands.

"We learned," said Mr. Bradford, now smiling his crooked smile in full, "how to escort a lady, how to turn her in an under-arm turn without clipping the flowers in her hair. How to bow to a lady at the end of the dance." Mr. Bradford bowed with one arm at his waist, the other behind his back. "And how to hold a lady's hand." He took Goldenrod's hand and folded his two gloved hands around it. "As gentle as a dove's wing."

As Flora's shadow, Goldenrod never harbored much attention, and she blushed pink to her ears. She beamed. The girls begged Mr. Bradford to teach them the fashionable Delchastrian dances. He wavered, glancing at the draped windows.

"I'm not very good," he said.

"That's all right!" squeaked the younger girls. "Oh, *please*!"

"You can dance with Azalea." Clover smiled a honey-sweet smile. Mr. Bradford's face lit.

"May I?" he said. He bowed to Azalea, his eyes twinkling part hope, part nervousness, and part mischievousness. "If my lady isn't engaged?"

"Take his hand!" cried Hollyhock.

Azalea took it. It dwarfed and encased her own hand,

and she felt the large knobbliness of knuckles under his gloves. She resisted the impulse to stroke them with her thumb.

Her stomach fluttered as he led her to the middle of the hall, away from the glass displays and red velvet ropes. Leaning on his steady arm, she felt a touch dizzy. She caught the faint scent of fresh linen, and her heart began to beat in an Esperaldo jig stomp.

Azalea's skirts swished as he brought her into dance position. He was tall; she straightened into the best form she could, her eyes level to his chin. The girls leaned forward, memorizing each movement as Mr. Bradford placed his hand on her back, just beneath her shoulder, and lifted her other hand, gently. He had excellent form.

"It will probably end up with Azalea leading," said Delphinium, across the hall. "She's so bossy."

Azalea closed her eyes. Sisters! She could *strangle* them!

"A *trois-temps* waltz," said Mr. Bradford, smiling crookedly. With his rumpled hair and uneven cravat, it seemed to make him symmetrical. "If that is agreeable."

Beneath his steady form, Azalea thought she felt his fingers trembling, just a touch.

"I love the waltz," said Azalea. She dimpled.

The girls, at the edge of the hall, held their breath as Azalea and Mr. Bradford began.

Mr. Bradford was not a perfect dancer. His steps were a bit flat, and he stumbled through the transition steps, but . . .

He was shockingly easy to follow. The pressure of his hand, the step of his foot, the angle of his frame . . . it was like reading his *mind*. When he leaned right, they turned in perfect unison. He swept her across the gallery in a quick three, a dizzying pace. Gilded frames and glass cases and the window blurred in her vision, and Azalea spun out, her skirts pulling and poofing around her, before he caught her and brought her back into dance position. She could almost *hear* music playing, swelling inside of her.

Mother had once told her about this perfect twining into one. She called it interweave, and said it was hard to do, for it took the perfect matching of the partners' strengths to overshadow each other's weaknesses, meshing into one glorious dance. Azalea felt the giddiness of being locked in not a pairing, but a dance. So starkly different than dancing with Keeper. Never that horrid feeling that she owed him something; no holding her breath, wishing for the dance to end. Now, spinning from Mr. Bradford's hand, her eyes closed, spinning back and feeling him catch her, she felt the thrill of the dance, of being matched, flow through her.

"Heavens, you're good!" said Azalea, breathless.

"*You're* stupendous," said Mr. Bradford, just as breathless. "It's like dancing with a top!"

Azalea stumbled through the transition step.

"A top?" she said.

"Ah, a very graceful, delicate spinning top," he said, coloring.

Azalea laughed. He brought her into a hesitation step, and time hiccupped to a stop. Azalea was so close she could smell the starch on his cravat.

"I didn't think I would have a moment alone with you," he said, his voice richer now it was quiet. He hesitated and touched a strand of auburn hair, brushing it away from her cheek. "Princess Azalea."

Everything flashed to the moment she had stood at the cab door, wrapped in a lady's old coat and shivering in the morning air, and her words, starkly painting the frosted silence with the dark, jagged letters, *I'm Princess Azalea.* . . .

The internal music faded.

"Mr. Bradford, why are you here?" said Azalea. "I mean here. At the palace."

The spark in Mr. Bradford's eyes faded, a touch. He opened his mouth, then closed it. And kept it closed. Azalea pulled away.

"I think you ought to dance with Bramble, not me," she said.

His dark eyebrows did not move a fraction.

"That was *it*?" called Bramble from the other side of the hall. In the rectangle of window light, the girls pouted and folded the arms. "That was just a waltz! And not a fancy one, either! We feel cheated."

Mr. Bradford's crooked smile returned to his face, and he pulled Azalea into a sudden dance position with a rustling of skirts.

"Let us show them *my* favorite dance!" he said. "The polka!"

Azalea had only danced the polka twice in her life, and now she relearned it at neck-breaking speed as he danced her across the floor in a galloping flourish. She hadn't expected Mr. Bradford to be a polka sort of gentleman. Lord Teddie, yes, but Mr. Bradford? He was quite good! Azalea's skirts billowed and bounced. The energy caught, and all the girls leaped to their feet, dancing, clapping, and singing a bright tune. When Azalea spun away, dizzy and breathless, Mr. Bradford swept up Kale and threw her into the air. She shrieked with delight. Everyone whirled, black skirts blossoming around them over the long red rug. The snow outside twirled with them.

Hollyhock jumped about with such fervor that she paid little attention to where her leaps took her, and laughing, she *whumpfed*, hard, against the sword's case.

Everything happened slowly, as though underwater.

The entire case fell in an arc and smashed against the floor.

Glass exploded. Someone cried out. The sword skittered across the floor and came to a rest beneath one of the forbidden sofas. A sick, panicked feeling erupted throughout Azalea. Her mind shrieked. She fled to the sofa, knelt, and grasped for the sword.

Though dented, pockmarked, and mottled as always, it was unharmed. Azalea nearly fainted with relief. She placed it gently—ever so gently—on the sofa. After making certain Hollyhock wasn't cut or bruised, she sent Flora and Goldenrod for the broom, and made the youngest girls sit on the sofas before they cut themselves. Mr. Bradford was beside himself, apologizing profusely while picking up the larger pieces. Flora and Goldenrod arrived minutes later, to everyone's chagrin, with the King.

"He followed us," said Flora in a tiny voice.

"It fell by itself," squeaked Hollyhock. "It really did."

The King sucked in his cheeks at the display of smashed glass, overturned pedestal, and frightened girls. Azalea didn't give him time to lecture but scooped up the sword from the chair.

"Sir," she said, taking it to him. "It could have broken. Will you take it to the silversmith? Right now? It *must* be mended. Please."

The King frowned at her pleading face.

"It is a blizzard out, Miss Azalea."

"Tomorrow then. As soon as possible. Please."

Perhaps softened by her concern, or her pale, pinched face, the King agreed, at Azalea's insistence, to take it first thing in the morning. He helped them clean up the broken glass, lecturing all the while to the younger ones about how they would have to mend their own stockings to pay for such an expensive repair, and at the same time taking care that none of them stepped near the glass. Azalea swept up the pieces, deep in her own broken, troubled thoughts.

The knock sounded again that night.

Azalea was leaning against the mantel, feeling ill, while Ivy and Kale pestered her to tie their slippers, when the tentative, polite knock came. Goldenrod opened the door and, once again, showed the girls. No one was there. Azalea's eyes narrowed as the trembly feeling of something awry flickered underneath her skin.

"I don't like this," said Hollyhock. "It gives me the shivershakes."

Azalea went out into the hall, looking up and down an empty corridor. The odd sensation stayed with her. She swallowed a panicky feeling. Was Keeper growing stronger? Could he conjure magic outside of the pavilion now? Was it from the sword's fall earlier?

"I think you should all stay here tonight," said Azalea. "This feels too odd. Let's stay here. We already danced today, anyway."

Everyone protested loudly at this. Gritting her teeth, Azalea clenched the lamp in her hand as they descended into the silver forest. Each silver-encrusted step she took made the feeling increase, and dread filled her at the thought of seeing Keeper again. It did not help that the girls were jumpy. Jessamine clung to Azalea's skirts and whispered in a crystalline voice, "Someone's here. I think someone is here!"

"Jess, will you shut up!" Bramble seethed, clutching Lily with shaking hands.

Hollyhock, at the end of the line, gave a shrill yelp.

"Someone stepped on my shawl!" she cried.

She dove into the center of girls, leaving the shawl strewn across the silver path. It was Clover's and much too large for Hollyhock, who had been dragging it, leaving a trail of silver sparkles. Azalea pushed her way to the back.

"Nonsense," she said, holding up a trembling lamp. The silver leaves glittered. "I'll bet you just caught it on something. These branches, see?"

Azalea knelt on the path and brushed pine needles from the knit shawl. Shaking it and sending a puff of silver dust from it, she folded it, stood quickly—

And hit her head against something hard and solid.

"Ow!" she stammered.

"Oh, forgi—"

The man's voice cut abruptly. Azalea blanched at the empty mist. *No one was there!* Behind her, the girls' eyes grew as wide as tea saucers.

"It's a ghost!" squeaked Flora.

The girls screamed. They clutched their skirts in both hands and kick footed it to the bridge.

Azalea was faster. She rounded them off at the arc of the bridge, grasping the handrail and blocking them.

"Go back," she said. "Don't you see? Keeper's trying to scare us. I've had enough. We need to go back. *Now.*"

The girls stared at her, both frightened and sad. Jessamine's bright blue eyes, Hollyhock's muddy green, Eve's dark blue, all of them blinking.

"But," said Ivy, "we only have tomorrow left."

"We never should have come here in the first place. It was stupid."

"Calm down, Az," said Bramble, shifting Lily in her arms. "We don't like Keeper either, but why stop dancing? You don't have to be a bully about it."

Azalea's fingers gripped the cold, sleek railings.

"Is there a problem?"

Keeper's smooth voice sounded behind her. He leaned against the arched doorway, arms crossed, cloak dripping over his shoulders. He looked roguishly amused.

"'Zalea says we have to go home," said Hollyhock.

"And she's absolutely right," said Keeper, straightening, cutting a fine, hard figure against the silver-white dance floor. "I hardly have enough time as it is, getting everything ready for the ball tomorrow night."

The girls' mouths formed perfect Os.

"A . . . real ball?" said Hollyhock.

"We're not of age," said Ivy.

"Ah! But you are invited to this ball. As princesses, it is your right. And I, your host."

Keeper clapped his hands together, unfolded them, and blew. Like when they had first seen him, months ago, glittering brilliant snow whorled from his hands and swirled around them. They sparkled in pieces, bright flashes against the mist. For a moment Azalea was almost taken by it, feeling it brush past her face in a magical swirling breeze. She could see it, dancing in the pavilion with this magic snow as their partner, whirling about them in a flurried, glittering spin, the dessert table piled with caramels and chocolates, the ceiling dripping with arcs of white holly boughs and gleaming ornaments.

Flora gave a cry of delight and pulled a card from her black apron pocket. In simultaneous excitement, the rest of the girls produced cards, magically created in their pockets. They bounced with eagerness as they shared the stationery, silver embossed with their names, an invitation for the next evening. Azalea flicked her own into the lake. It floated for a moment and disappeared beneath the misty surface.

"So as you can see," Keeper said, his voice lulling as the glimmering snow flurried into the lake around them, "you really should go back. I have quite a bit to do."

"Naturally," said Bramble in a half smile of awe. "That is—take all the time you need. Az hasn't felt well anyway. We'll nurse her up for tomorrow." Bramble gave Azalea a wry smile of encouragement and prodded the girls to the willow branches.

"A moment," said Keeper. "Miss Azalea."

Azalea's heart dropped. She turned against her will, and glared at Keeper's dead eyes with all the strength she could muster.

"I ask a dance of you," said Keeper. "I should very much like to dance the Entwine. We never finished the last."

The girls nudged Azalea, smiling, their eyes alight. The Entwine was their favorite dance, too. Even Bramble perked up a touch. Clover, on the contrary, took Azalea's hand.

"No . . . Mr. Keeper," said Clover. "She's ill, can't you see?"

Keeper snapped out the crimson sash, burning color against the whites. Azalea cringed, thinking of the thread.

"No—no, it's all right," said Azalea, touching Clover on the shoulder and slipping her hand away. "I'll dance."

The girls watched from the bridge, biting their lips in anticipation, and Azalea found herself on Keeper's hard arm as he half escorted, half dragged her to the middle of the gleaming dance floor. Azalea took the end of the long red sash with only one thought in mind: to get the dance over with and get out of there.

"Good luck, Mr. Keeper," said Bramble as the girls sought for better views between each other. "Azalea's never been caught. You can try, though."

His dead eyes on her, Keeper produced Mr. Bradford's watch from his silk waistcoat, clicked it open, and tossed it to the floor. Azalea cringed at the clatter.

"Three minutes," he said. He snapped his long gloved fingers, and the music began.

The tempo was breakneck—faster than Azalea had ever gone before, and she was caught off her guard from the very first step. She whirled in and out and underneath the sash, dodging its tight snaps before it wrapped around her wrists with blinding speed. Keeper did not say a word. His mouth pressed tight, razor thin, and his eyes narrowed.

Azalea kept up with the furious pace of the music, but each breath burned, and sweat trickled down the front of her corset. Three minutes had to be up by now. Angry, Azalea ducked out of capture again, and kicked Keeper in the knee.

Keeper yanked on the sash, so hard it brought her in sharply. She stumbled out of the rhythm. Using one hand, Keeper spun her hard, pulled her arms up with the sash, and wound it around her wrists, like a spider wrapping up a moth.

Smooth. Tight. So quick, Azalea didn't realize she had been caught until her wrists throbbed with the tightness, and she was pressed, hard, against Keeper's chest. Her fingers pulsed red.

Keeper wound one arm around her waist, the other gripping the twisted sash at her wrists.

"She's been *caught*!" The girls' cry of disappointment echoed from the bridge.

Azalea tried to writhe free. Keeper held her firmly. The sash burned.

"Now, now," he said, breathless. He turned his hands a touch, and the crimson sash dug into Azalea's skin. "Excellent dance, my lady. You *are* the best I have ever danced with. You should take pride in that."

"Let me go."

"You have very pretty lips," he said, keeping his hand at the pinching sash. "I've often wondered if you kiss as well as you dance. . . ."

His fingers tightened about the sash, sending shoots of pain up her arms and making her knees weak. He brought his hand from her waist and entwined his long fingers into her hair, cradling and twisting at the same time.

And then, he leaned in to her neck, breathing against it. The hairs on the back of Azalea's neck rose. Choking, she couldn't cry out as his fingers gripped her hair, and his lips traced, just touching her skin, to hers—

In a jolt, Keeper jerked back, his head yanked at a full square angle. He made a strangled, inhuman noise.

Azalea caught a glimpse of an Adam's apple a-bob, and shook free of the sash. Blood rushed to her fingers. She gathered her skirts and ran out the entrance, down the silver stairs, choking back something that was like sobs but not quite.

"Az!" Bramble caught Azalea before she collapsed onto the bridge. "Are you all right? You're dead pale. Why wouldn't he let you go? His back was to us. What happened?"

Azalea shook her head. "Nothing—nothing."

"What—what happened to him? At the end?"

Azalea looked at Clover, uncertain.

"He . . . lost his balance," said Clover. "Or . . . something."

"It looked like his ponytail had revolted against him," said Bramble.

"Look," whispered Goldenrod.

They looked. In the pavilion, Keeper swept about, his cloak billowing behind him. He was *prowling*. His eyes glinted as he searched over each piece of the dance floor.

"Let's get out of here," said Azalea. "We're not coming back."

CHAPTER 24

zalea's wrists throbbed as she helped the girls undress and unpin, tugging slippers from their feet and tucking them in. She built up the fire and turned down the lamps. Then, with a candle, she slipped down the two flights of stairs to the ballroom. To her relief, it was unlocked. She slumped in front of the nearest pier glass, shaking. After a moment to breathe in the calming, familiar nutmeg-and-fabric smell of the ballroom, she pushed up her sleeves to examine her pulsing wrists.

They were swollen and red, a welt ringing each like a mottled bracelet. Azalea touched them and winced. Her eyes stung.

Keeper had guessed she had given up. She had. She felt as though a needle and thread was sewing her throat shut, piercing and winding. She buried her face in her hands, throat too tight, and quaking too hard, to even cry.

"Princess."

Azalea jolted away from the mirror, nearly overturning the candle.

"I'm sorry. . . . It's . . . only me."

In the dim light, by the ballroom doors, stood Mr. Bradford, rumpled as always, but face sober with a deadly solemnity. He walked to her and knelt. Over his arm was slung an old, ragged piece of fabric. Azalea recognized the cloak that hung in his shop's closet.

"Are you all right?" said Azalea. "Why are you—?"

"Miss Azalea, I followed you."

Azalea's brows knit together as he brought out his handkerchief. He unfolded it in his hand, and revealed an old gold pocket watch, with swirls about the cover, black inside the creases. He took Azalea's hand and pressed the watch to it.

Azalea frowned at it, taking in the worn gold swirls. Realization dawned.

Giving a cry, Azalea reeled backward, and the pocket watch clattered to the marble.

"Your watch!" she said.

Mr. Bradford took her trembling hands in his large ones. His fingers brushed her sore wrists, and Azalea gave a shuddering gasp. In a moment, his suitcoat was about her shoulders, and he had lit a fire in the grate.

"Yes," he said, still trying to calm her. "Yes, I *followed you*, followed you. Through the passage. And the silver forest. Everything."

Azalea felt as though she was bumbling through an unfamiliar dance step, her feet late on the rhythm and catching underneath the gentleman's.

"H-how?" she managed to stammer.

Mr. Bradford fumbled with the threadbare, moth-eaten cloak over his arm.

"It is a family secret, of sorts. See here."

He stood, strode several paces from her, and with an awkward flourish, brought it over his shoulders.

He faded into the darkness.

Azalea leaped to her feet, searching over the red velvet curtains, turning hard to see where he had faded to. *Disappeared* to. It frightened her—it was too much like Keeper!

In an instant, Mr. Bradford reappeared, solid and visible again, the cloak now off his shoulders and rippling in his hands.

"A wraith cloak!" said Azalea as he pulled her to the fireplace. Azalea's legs shook, and relieved, she dipped to the floor, dress pooling around her.

"The same." Mr. Bradford clumsily folded it, and knelt in front of her again. "It has been passed down in our family. Your ancestor, Harold the First, gave it to us, but, ah, as uneventful as Eathesbury is, we've never used it. When I saw you at the graveyard, looking so white, I knew something was wrong. I *knew* it."

Azalea stared at him, the fire flickering highlights in his eyes.

"So . . . I thought I should do something," he finished lamely.

"You saw everything?"

Mr. Bradford gave half of a crooked smile. "I did knock."

"You didn't see Mr. . . . . Mr.—"

"Mr. Keeper?" Mr. Bradford spat the name. "Oh, yes, I saw *Mr. Keeper*. Rather hard not to. I saw him try to kiss you. Or what he *said* was a kiss. I want to snap his head off!"

Azalea had her hand over her mouth, shocked that someone as solemn and dignified as Mr. Bradford could have such venom. He took her hands, gently, and pushed up her sleeves, revealing her swollen wrists. His fingers traced the bruises.

"You stopped him," said Azalea. She bowed her head, shy. "You kept him from—from—"

"Ah, yes, my lady!" Mr. Bradford smiled his crooked smile in full. "His ponytail was simply *begging* to be yanked."

Azalea gave a surprised laugh. Mr. Bradford grinned.

"Tell me everything," he said, sitting down beside her. "Everything you can."

The story fell from Azalea in gushes, as though it had been dammed up. She told him of the discovery, of Mr. Keeper, the slippers, dancing every night, the oath, and the watch. With difficulty, she told him about the haunted ball, and Mother, and realizing who Keeper was.

She tingled as she told him everything, but it wasn't breath-stealing or overwhelming. The oath magic could somehow see that Mr. Bradford knew the secret.

When she had finished, the fire had dimmed. She sat next to him, studying his knobbly gentlemanish knuckles, wishing to rub her cheek against his shoulder. Mr. Bradford brought his knees to his chest, deep in thought.

"My father told me about the High King," he said to his steepled fingers. "I never believed that he could actually capture souls. I always thought it just rumor. Souls. That's the deep sort of magic. It really was your mother?"

Azalea could still feel Mother's lips pressing against her fingers. The thread's weave. She turned her head.

"It was . . . ghastly," she said.

In the warm hearthlight, Mr. Bradford took her hands and gave her a weak, crooked smile. "Princess," he said, "I haven't taken the oath. We've got to tell someone."

"The King!" said Azalea.

"Just so!" Mr. Bradford squeezed her hands. "This devil Keeper has got to be freed sometime. I doubt very much your father will care to have the High King D'Eathe living underfoot! We can organize the cavalry and bring him to a court of law. If he must be freed, then we do it on *our* terms. *Not* his."

The blood rushed to Azalea's cheeks in a warm wave, but quelled at a new thought.

"I'm not sure Keeper *can* be killed," she said. "The blood oath—"

"Flummery," said Mr. Bradford, bringing a smile to Azalea's lips. "The King surely would know what to do. He knows magic better than any of us."

Us. That word, and Mr. Bradford's firm, steady hand about hers, sent courage to Azalea's heart. It wasn't just her anymore. Azalea wanted to cry and dance and sing all at once. She leaped to her feet, the weak dizzy-headedness of missed meals tripping up her steps.

"Oh, Mr. Bradford!" she said. "You're *wonderful*— oh—I could *kiss* you!"

Azalea immediately pulled back, the hot flush prickling to the very roots of her hair.

"Oh," said Mr. Bradford, who was pink, even in the dim light. "Well."

"I—I suppose I should go . . . wake the King, then," Azalea stammered.

"Oh—yes. Oh—no. Don't. It's nearly morning, and you're dead on your feet. First thing tomorrow? We'll find the King."

"Oh—yes. Naturally—first thing. Of course."

"Naturally."

"Of course."

"Wait . . . here."

Mr. Bradford produced a small package from his suitcoat pocket and, going to her, unfolded a napkin from a crumbled muffin. They had eaten cardamom-egg muffins for tea, a great holiday treat. Azalea couldn't bring herself to eat hers, so she had given it to Ivy. Ivy, in turn, had given it to Mr. Bradford, which meant that she was awfully fond of him. She never gave up food willingly. Mr. Bradford now offered it to Azalea in his large, cupped hands.

Azalea took it, blinking away almost-tears. She looked at him, his soft brown eyes and tall form, and contemplated raising herself on her toes and kissing his ear, or his cheek. In a great blush, she *almost* did—then pulled back, remembering that morning just a few days ago.

Instead, impulsively before leaving, she reached up and smoothed his mussed hair.

Mr. Bradford beamed.

Azalea awoke the next morning, late and to an empty room, but giddy and glorious, fully embued with Christmas spirit. She sang when she dressed, sang when she pinned up her hair, and daintily danced her way through the corridor and down the stairs. Every time she turned a corner, she added an extra spin, her skirts brushing the wallpaper.

After a quick, late breakfast of cinnamon bread and cream (holiday breakfast—Christmas Eve), Azalea learned from Mrs. Graybe that the girls were out giving Mr. Bradford a tour of the gardens before it snowed again. Azalea grinned, thinking of what sort of tour that would be. They would make him pull them across the frozen pond, and probably balance on the bridge railing, just to see if he could do it.

The King was out in the gardens, too, said Mrs. Graybe, discussing R.B. with a gentleman. Terribly impatient to find him and Mr. Bradford and get the whole business done with, Azalea donned a cloak and began to comb the bright, sunny-snow gardens.

It was nearly tea, the wind blowing in gusts and ushering in a storm, when Azalea found the King in the straw-smelling stable, saddling Dickens. Over Dickens's back, in its rapier sheath, was the sword. Azalea remembered that the King had promised to have it mended today.

Next to Dickens stood an unfamiliar chestnut horse.

Azalea recognized the owner. It was the rain cloud fellow—
Mr. Gasperson. Azalea wondered what his business was,
to be with the King on Christmas Eve. They spoke in low
voices, and Azalea glimpsed a silver wax seal on a folded
letter. The royal imprint.

". . . as soon as Miss Bramble is willing, of course,"
said the man in dark, rumbling tones. He mounted
his horse.

"As you say." The King looked up from Dickens's
side, seeing Azalea at the stable door. "Miss Azalea,"
he said.

"I've been looking for you," said Azalea. "I need to
talk to you. I'm not interrupting?"

"No, it is quite all right."

Intrigued, Azalea waited until the gentleman had
ridden away, giving her a polite nod as he passed, before
she pulled the creaking door closed. The King remained
at Dickens's side, buckling and harnessing and adjusting
straps.

"Bramble?" said Azalea. "Willing? What did you
give him?"

The King cinched the saddle. "It is going to snow," he
said. "You should head in."

"Mrs. Graybe says you've been talking to him all
morning," said Azalea, stubbornly curious. She did not
like how the King deflected her question.

"Azalea, did you have something to talk to me about?" said the King.

"Oh, yes," said Azalea. She hesitated. "Tell me about Bramble first. Please. I'm supposed to watch out for the girls."

An odd expression crossed the King's bearded face. He considered Azalea, sizing her up. He paused.

"Well," he said.

"Well?" said Azalea encouragingly.

The King gave a nod. From his suitcoat he produced a green broken-sealed letter. He handed it to Azalea.

"He has inundated me with letters this past week," said the King. "Three a day at least. He's even bought a town house on High Street. This is his most recent letter. Tell me what you make of it."

Azalea eagerly unfolded the much-creased letter and read the hurried, loopy handwriting.

> *Your Most Exalted Majesty, Your Grace, etc., etc.:*
>
> *I don't know what ruddy else I can offer. You won't have a fig to do with my lands or my money or anything, I suppose, of value to anyone else. I suppose that makes you a good father but it certainly makes things rum for me. I haven't anything else to*

offer, but a sincere heart, one that aches for Bramble, her sweet, plucky spirit, her smart whippish mouth, her heart, and her dear hand.

"Her *hand*?" said Azalea.

I'm in agony now, hoping that my steward will convince you. If not I think I'll break all the windows in the house and drown myself in a bucket.

A most sincere heart—

Lord Edward Albert Hemly Haftenravenscher, Esq.

Azalea stared at the letter.

"Marriage!" she said. "Lord Teddie wants to marry her! Marry Bramble!"

The King smiled. "Just so," he said. He slipped the letter from Azalea's hands. "He thinks her a run-a-hoop in a croquet game, raspberry jam on toast, cadmium red in a paint set. That is what he has written."

"He's around the twist," said Azalea. "Breaking all the windows? He's mad."

"Ah, no," said the King. "It's only madness if you actually do it. If you *want* to break all the windows in the house and drown yourself in a bucket but don't actually do it, well, that's love."

Azalea was consternated. "You told him of course not, didn't you?"

The King paused. In a long, heavy moment, everything turned upside down, and Azalea thought, Oh, no . . .

"Ah, Azalea." The King put a hand on her shoulder. "I told him he could."

"What!"

"I just sent the marriage contract with his steward," said the King. "I certainly told him *no* often enough. But—ah." The King placed both his hands on her shoulders. "He loves her. He doesn't give a fig for her dowry; he loves her for who she *is*."

Azalea mouthed wordlessly at the King until words finally pushed themselves to her mouth.

"But—but—that's not the way it's done," she stammered. "You can't just arrange Bramble's marriage without even asking her! That's not how it is done nowadays!"

"I am perfectly aware of how it is done nowadays," said the King crisply. "I am not *that* old. You yourself said that if Lord Teddie proved himself in earnest—"

"Not like *this*!" said Azalea.

"And furthermore," said the King, his tone rising in volume and crispness, "since when are any of my wishes not met with outright rebellion from you all? Do you honestly think if things were not arranged as such, Bramble would even *consider* it?"

We watch out for each other, Azalea had promised Bramble. *The King would never arrange your marriage— and I would never let him—*

Azalea's nails dug into her palms, clenching so hard they broke the skin. She paced up and down the aisle between the stalls, scattering straw with each step. Her skirts snapped as she turned. Her cheeks blazed, hot and feverish. Dickens grew skittish at Azalea's sudden movements.

"How *dare* you!" said Azalea, fists shaking. "My sisters *will* have a choice! Sir, you've got to get that contract back!"

"I will not—"

"Mother *never* would have allowed you to do such a thing!"

"*Don't* tell me what your mother would do or would not do!" The King yanked Dickens to the mounting block. "I am already aware I am not her. You shall have to accept me and my decisions, painful as that is!"

The rage snapped.

In quick, sharp movements, Azalea yanked the reins from the King with her own stinging hands. With a sleek, almost dancelike leap, Azalea maneuvered past the King and jumped from the block onto Dickens. Her black skirts settled over his sides and tail.

"I'll take the sword to the silversmith," she said. "I broke it, didn't I?"

"Come now, Azalea, don't use that tone," said the King, holding out his hand.

Azalea kicked it away with the flat of her boot, and dug her heels into Dickens's flank, just as a gentleman would. Dickens leaped forward. The jolt nearly threw her off. In a moment she was galloping off through the stable door.

"You haven't a coat!" the King yelled. "You are going to fall off!"

The King would saddle Thackeray and be after her in a heartbeat, but Azalea pushed Dickens hard through the cobblestone streets of snow and ice. Holiday market people clogged the roads, with rattling carriages, everyone bustling about before the storm came. Azalea searched fervently for the chestnut the steward had ridden away on. She would find him and make him see reason.

The crowds thinned as the cold wind began to bite, and in a moment of luck, Azalea spotted the chestnut and the steward's emerald green overcoat. She kicked Dickens into a gallop, gripping tightly to his mane to keep from jostling off.

Snow began to whisk in the wind, and it seemed all

at once the streets were deserted. By the time she reached the Courtroad bridge, snow had formed over the carriage ruts, making everything icy and slick. Dickens shied.

"Dickens, *please*," said Azalea. "Just through the bridge!"

Dickens shied again. Her fingers burning, Azalea dug her boots hard into his flank. He leaped forward with a jolt.

In a heart-stopping moment, the scrabbling of hooves on ice, and a hard clang, Azalea was falling.

Her stomach realized it before she did. Dickens had lost his footing, and together—Azalea's hand tangled in the reins, so tightly it numbed—they slid down the rock-crabbed, muddy embankment. Her hand slipped free, and she tumbled off, skirts and crinolines twisting in the air.

She slapped into the water. It enveloped her, frigid. Breaking to the surface, she wheezed for air and had to fight the current as she crawled to the bank. Her clothes clung to her skin like a heavy sheet of ice.

Dickens, dripping, had righted himself. Mud matted his fine coat. Coughing and sputtering, Azalea used the reins to pull herself up.

What was she *doing*? The cold water had slapped the heat from her temper. Had she run mad? Galloping off in the middle of a blizzard? She had nearly killed both of them!

Home. Azalea had to get back, or she would freeze to death. The storm whipped through her frozen wet clothes. She had to change and get to a fire. Shivering hard, Azalea tried to grasp Dickens's saddle. She missed, her hands frozen blocks; they knocked against the leather casing of the sword.

The sword! Azalea fumbled at the top metal ring and felt as though she had fallen into the icy water again. Except this time, it drenched her inside, coating her stomach.

The sword was gone.

CHAPTER 25

$\mathcal{S}$hivering violently, Azalea sludged through the icy water for any glint of silver or flash of light. She searched through the blizzard, up and down the bank, the wind so cold she couldn't feel it.

The sword was gone. She knew it. She had known it the moment she heard the hard clang of it against the rocks when they fell, and had had the same choking, empty feeling she felt when the King had unmagicked the sugar teeth. Except this was a thousand times worse. Azalea fell against Dickens. She had to find the King.

Azalea didn't know how she managed to mount, or how Dickens picked his way up the rocks and muddy embankment and through the thick foggy snow to the palace. She let him steer his own way back. When he trotted into the stable, Azalea hadn't the strength to hang on anymore, and she fell.

She was awkwardly caught just before she hit the dirt floor.

"There now, Miss! You're frozen up!"

"Mr. P-P-Pudding," she chattered. She had to blink several times to see him and a partly saddled Milton clearly.

"Where have you been, then, Miss? The household is in a right state of worry for you, and the King has been out and about for you, Miss! You're soaked through— come along, we'll get you warm then, I'll send for Sir John. You're burning up and up!"

"The K-k-king—"

Mr. Pudding spoke in his gruff, soothing way, but it filtered into Azalea's mind as vague *wuh-wuhs*, and the words needled through her ears. She was only vaguely aware of being carried to her room, Mrs. Graybe and the girls fussing over her, changing her dress, and putting her to bed with masses of blankets. They brought hot bricks from the hearth, wrapped in cloth, and tucked them between Azalea's sheets. Sir John came, and Azalea was too weak to even acknowledge his poking and prodding.

"Look at this" came Eve's voice, and Azalea felt the red scars, the burn of the reins, the cut skin of her palms being inspected, before blackness faded in on her.

Pain awoke Azalea. Her head pounded with her heartbeat, and one of her ears stabbed into her throat. Her fingers burned. So did her eyes. She felt the aura of a fever burning from her skin. She heaved the blankets from her, dots filling her vision, and stumbled to the round table, where the lamp and a cold pot of tea sat. A note lay next to the stack of teacups. Azalea blinked away the blotches, and read.

Az

Well, YOU have caused quite the scandal. Where the devil were you? The King's been out all day, and because he wasn't here Mrs. Graybe made us eat soup for dinner instead of the Christmas Eve pudding. Thank you very much for that.

At any rate, we're going without you. Don't be cross, it's our last night, and we've never officially been invited to a ball before. Sir John said you oughtn't be gotten up for the next few days, but if you wake up, come down. (Did you know Clover had a silver watch? Where did she get that kind of lolly?!)

If not, we miss you, but not enough to stay up here.

Toodle pip.

B

Azalea *fled* to the fireplace.

She sprang through the passage in such a hurry she scattered hot coals through the billowing curtain, trailing soot as she raced down the staircase. She slammed into the floor at a run, the abruptness making her fall to her knees.

The staircase ended sooner than it had before. Azalea's head pounded as she grasped her bearings, her eyes adjusting.

The room she stood in was large, the same size and layout of their own bedroom, with brick for the walls instead of wood paneling. It felt sharp, real, and smelled of must. Next to her along the walls, organized in trunks and boxes, lay ribbons and tin and glass ornaments. The Yuletide ornaments! Azalea stumbled to her feet and took one from a hatbox, a tiny gazebo with a ballerina figurine that spun in the middle. It glimmered on its string. The musical movement inside pinged.

"Our storage room," said Azalea, the ornament trembling in her fingers.

The magic was gone.

A rustle of fabric sounded behind her. Azalea turned.

Soft blue light filtered down from a tiny window near the ceiling, falling over a limp figure. Unpinned hair lay in curls over the wood floor, and a mended dress. Azalea dropped the ornament.

"Mother?" she whispered.

The figure lay unmoving.

Hardly daring to believe herself, Azalea ran to her side and turned her over, feeling Mother's form, solid and real, beneath her hands. The blue light fell in a ghostly way on Mother's face; edges blurred as though she were made of mist, or something from a rough pencil sketch. Azalea swallowed a cry. Mother's lips were still sewn.

"Mother," she whispered. "Mother, is it really you? Wake up." Azalea fumbled for the scissors in her pocket, only to realize they were in her other dress. Even so, when Mother's eyelids flickered, hope surged through Azalea.

"It's all right, we'll get them," said Azalea, touching Mother's lips, as gently as she could. They were icy. All her skin seemed translucent, swirling beneath Azalea's touch. "It's all right. Don't try to smile or anything. We'll get you somewhere warm."

Mother felt lighter than Azalea expected, far lighter than a normal person, but still so *substantial*. Azalea ascended the creaking staircase, her arm around Mother's waist, helping her glide up the stairs, her feet moving as though not sensing each step. It frightened Azalea, and she gripped Mother's cold hand harder, afraid she would simply fade away.

Throbbing, she pulled Mother to the top step, laid her

gently as she could against the wood and brick. Mother settled, and her skirts settled after her slowly, floating to the ground. Azalea rubbed her own handkerchief against the D'Eathe mark until it burned. The silver glowed and burst, leaving the glimmering curtain of sheen.

Azalea turned to Mother, and though Mother's eyes hadn't opened, she saw tear streaks down her cheeks and into the stitches.

"It's all right," said Azalea, trying to not cry herself. "Don't cry—" She brought her handkerchief to Mother's cheek to dry it.

With the touch of the fabric to Mother's skin, the translucent swirls of her skin singed and burned and started to melt. Her skin dripped like a wax candle. Azalea yelped and pulled the handkerchief back sharply, her ears pounding as Mother's skin faded back into place.

"It's all right," said Azalea. "I'm sorry. . . . This magic—it's—"

Impulsively she turned to the hot coals she had scattered onto the landing not minutes before. One still glowed red. Quickly, she laid the handkerchief on it.

It lit, melted, and folded in on itself with an acrid burning smell. The empty feeling of an object unmagicked filled the air as it curled. The fire faded, leaving only ashes with a touch of glimmer to them. Azalea choked down air as she stared at the pile, then rushed to tend to Mother,

her eyes still closed, and helped her to her feet. She was light as paper.

"We don't need it anymore," said Azalea. "I didn't realize the magic would—here—" Azalea took Mother's cold hand. "Let's go, before it closes."

Mother's eyes snapped open. Azalea started, and gaped as the thread around Mother's lips faded into nothing, leaving smooth, unscarred skin.

"Mind your step," said Mother.

She shoved Azalea.

Azalea fell down the stairs, skirts and feet twisting over each other. The sound of ice creaked and cracked through the air. Azalea hit the wooden floor and caught her breath in time to see the ornaments rising from the boxes at the sides of the room. They clinked against one another and glinted as they flew into the air, rising above her like white petals in a windstorm.

They stopped abruptly and remained floating in the air, a frozen hailstorm of baubles. Azalea, shaking, peered up the rickety stairs at Mother.

She stood at the top landing. The blurred, unearthly translucence to her skin and form was gone, replaced with a sharp, dead pallor. Bloodred lips. She rested her elbow against her side, and an ornament dangled from the tip of her forefinger.

"Mother?" said Azalea.

Mother flicked the ornament into the air, snapped her fingers, and the ornament stopped at the peak of its arc. A tiny gesture of her hands, and the suspended ornaments swayed, then began to swirl around the room, with Azalea in the middle. A shimmering clinking filled the air.

Mother made a sharp movement, and the ornaments smashed to the ground—

And rose up again like spirits, their silver swirls blossoming into skirts, glass shards forming into fitted suitcoats, silver-toned ladies and gentlemen with powdered faces, white as frosted glass. They had gaping holes for eyes. Azalea shrank as they towered over her.

Mother descended the stairs daintily, her blue dress wafting behind her. She smiled at Azalea, and her eyes blazed black. The same dead black eyes flashed through Azalea's memory, and she remembered how they glinted when Keeper had leaned in to kiss her—

"*Keeper!*" Azalea spat. She leaped forward, but the skull-like dancers flocked to her, caught her wrists and waist and shoulders, pulling her back, holding her tight.

Keeper laughed a cheery laugh that bubbled.

"Oh, there now," he said in Mother's voice. "You didn't honestly think I was her? Were you so desperate to believe that a person had a soul, you were willing to believe in anything? Stupid, *stupid*. Many thanks with the handkerchief. It was the only bit of magic left holding me back. Well *done*."

"Where are they?" said Azalea. "What did you do to the girls?"

Keeper pulled away. The dimples and twinkling eyes smothered Azalea. He touched the brooch at his mended blue collar.

"They're not dead," he said, his voice light. "Yet."

Azalea struggled against the hands. They grasped her arms and waist tightly, fingers hard and thin like ornament hooks.

"You know, this would make an absolutely marvelous fairy tale," said Keeper, dimpling. "Just like the ones your mother used to tell you. You can even pretend I *am* your mother, if you would like. Let us see . . . how do they begin? Ah, yes . . . 'In a certain country . . .'"

Mother's voice was sweet as honey, with the added smooth sleekness of Keeper's chocolate timbre. He touched Mother's hand to Azalea's face, tracing it with a cold finger.

"There were twelve dancing princesses," he whispered. "And their little hearts were broken. But one day, they found a magical land of silver and music, where they could dance and forget all their troubles.

"But, alas! All things do not last forever. There was a debt to be paid; and when the accounts were balanced, the dear little princesses were found wanting. And so, when the young princesses arrived on Christmas Eve, they were magicked into the palace mirrors—"

Azalea screamed, cut short when the wiry hands slapped over her mouth, stifling her. Her heart screamed instead of beating.

"—and they died in but a few hours, huddled for warmth. The mirrors do that, you know. Something about moving matter mixing with static matter. Magic is quite scientific, really. And the eldest princess; she became trapped in this very room, only to be found weeks later, curled up in a dry little ball next to the passage door. Which was a pity; she was such a good dancer."

Keeper leaned in closely, so closely Azalea could see her own frightened reflection in the brooch, and the ghostly thin hands that grasped at her and held her back. He touched Azalea's neck with his lips. They were cold.

Azalea lashed out. The hands did not catch her in time, and she clawed at Keeper's throat, the fingers snagging at the brooch and ripping it from the collar of Mother's blue dress. The hands snatched Azalea back, clutching her wrists. Azalea yelped.

The brooch fell in an arc and clattered against the wooden floor. In an instant, like the snuffing of a candle, Mother had dissolved into the dark, handsome form of

Keeper. He did not move but remained smiling at her with his dashing laziness.

"Ah," he said. "And now you know why I *keep* things. The same reason your father keeps your mother's things locked away from sight, and keeps you in mourning. Every object a person owns, no matter how poor, has a piece of them in it."

"The King will never stand for it!" Azalea snarled. "You'll never be able to take over the country! The regiments will—"

Keeper pressed his hand over her mouth, his fingers splayed, stifling her and gripping her cheeks.

"Hush," he said gently. "Do you really think I care about your powerless, impoverished kingship? No, princess. There is only *one* thing I am after."

He pressed his hand harder over her lips, smothering her voice.

"Ah," he said. "I never finished my story. How do these things end? Ah, yes. And the palace was magicked again to its rightful owner, who in turn *finally* murdered the Captain General, and all was well. The end. Ever after happy."

Keeper leaned in, so close now that his lips nearly touched his hand smothering her face.

"And now," he whispered. "I have a blood oath to fulfill. Good-bye, my lady."

He pushed her into the mass of hands.

Everything swam in whites and grays and silvers around her. Azalea was shoved into a dance formation. A ghostly silence muffled everything; no music, no footfalls, no ruffling of dresses as they danced her into a silent schottische.

Azalea thrashed through the formations, trying to writhe free. She kicked and elbowed her way from the grasping hands, and in a moment of luck, broke free and leaped up the rickety stairs.

Her heart fell as she discovered an empty landing. The brick passage had closed up. She clawed the mark. She had no silver to get out.

Bony hands gripped her ankles and yanked her down the stairs. Azalea half stumbled and was half carried through the formations. Dancers crossed, changed partners, and pushed her into the right positions. If she fainted, they would probably keep puppeting her form about.

Of course it had been a trick. The whole business with souls—fake. And now Keeper, unhampered by any silver magic, was free to magick the palace. And the girls—

Trapped in mirrors . . .

And the King!

Azalea fought for the stairs with all the energy she

could muster. The eyeless, shimmering dancers surged after her. She made it to the third step before their bony hands dragged her back again. She tore against dresses and wigs, squirming and kicking against their grips. They shoved her back, hard, and she fell—

Fell—

Whu—

The rest of the sound never came; darkness cut it off.

When Azalea awoke, she wore her ballgown. She was also standing.

For a moment she just stared down at her dress. She rubbed her fingers on the gauzy folds of the skirt, feeling the weave against her skin. Her head didn't throb. She looked around.

Mother's room. Azalea stood in the middle of it, between Mother's chair and the dresser. Warm, drenched in the scent of white cake, roses, baby ointment, overwhelmingly so. Mend-up cards lined across the top of the dresser, everything lit with the cheery hearth.

The dream! This time, though, every smell, action, heartbeat, focused into a sharp, vivid picture. She could even see the bits of dust that floated in the window light.

In the flowered armchair, a hand on her with-child stomach, sat Mother. She smiled at Azalea, her cheeks dimpling. Somehow, instead of comforting Azalea, it made things *worse*. It was just a stupid dream, and tears stung Azalea's eyes.

"It's not real," she said. "None of this. You know, you always talked about that warm, flickery bit inside. But now I know it isn't true. It never has been. I'll wake up empty."

"Azalea?" said Mother. "Goosey, what are you on about? Are you all right?"

Azalea leaned against the dresser, clutching the knob of the drawers behind her.

"No, Mother," said Azalea. "No. I'm not all right. Nothing is all right. It never will be all right again."

Mother beckoned to Azalea, the twinkle in her eyes shining. She took Azalea's hand, having her kneel. Azalea's green, gauzy skirts poofed out around her. Mother kept Azalea's fingers clasped in her warm hand, and she turned Azalea's hand over, inspecting her palm.

In addition to the tiny crescent scars where her nails had dug into her skin so often, new red marks had broken into her flesh when Azalea had lost her temper earlier. They stung, with the additional welt of the reins when she had fallen. Mother considered, touching the palm gently.

"You used to do this," she said. "When you were younger. You would get so *angry*." Mother smiled. "I had hoped you had outgrown it."

Azalea pulled her hand back.

"Some things are worth getting upset over," she said.

Mother tilted her head, reached out, and brushed an errant strand of hair from Azalea's face, and wiped a tear streak away with her thumb. Azalea blinked and turned her head, a little surprised she hadn't woken up yet. The dream never lasted this long.

"You've done very well, Azalea," said Mother. "You've always taken care of your sisters. I'm so pleased with you."

"Right," said Azalea. "I've done a bang-up job, haven't I." She thought of her sisters, curled up in mirrors, and she cringed.

"But," said Mother. "Your father. You haven't done very well with him."

Azalea turned quickly. Her eyebrows knitted, searching Mother's face. Mother had the twinkle in her eye, the touch of a smile on her face, as she always did, but she searched Azalea's face with equal intensity.

"Sorry?" said Azalea.

Mother brought Azalea's hands into her own and, with a flash of silver, folded them around her handkerchief. Her hands were soft and warm, so warm they calmed Azalea's trembling fingers, the warmth spreading down her arms to her chest. Something twisted in Azalea's heart. She bit her lip.

"We're going to try this again," said Mother. She smiled, and the room seemed to brighten. "You'll take care of your sisters, *and* your father? Your whole family? Will you promise, Azalea?"

Azalea's throat tightened, and her eyes stung. Her palms throbbed at points, pressed together against the fabric.

"He . . . doesn't need anyone," she mumbled. "He said—he said he couldn't abide—"

"That was when he needed you more than ever," said Mother. "And he needs you *now*. He needs all of you. Please, Azalea. Please promise me."

Azalea looked into Mother's eyes, which shone with tears. Something pricked in Azalea's heart. She remembered all the times she had lashed out at the King with scathing words. How she had taken the oath with burning anger in her chest, and how she had danced out of sheer stubbornness. And now it was her fault that Keeper would—

Azalea pressed her hands tightly around the handkerchief and clenched her jaw. Her eyes blazed, but not with temper.

"Yes," she said. "I will. My whole family. I'll set things right. I promise."

A wash of tingles flowed through her body, beginning with her very center and enveloping the rest of her, flooding to her fingertips. The feeling overwhelmed, much stronger than it had been a year ago. It overcame her, filling her with breath. Azalea blinked and felt the droplets of tears on her lashes.

Mother smiled, and it wasn't tight with pain. Her eyes shone. She leaned down and kissed Azalea's hands. Her lips were warm.

And this time, Azalea didn't need to look at Mother to know her lips were the pretty rose red they hadn't been a year ago. Instead she closed her eyes and pressed her fingers against the weave of the handkerchief, and inhaled the scent of white cake and ointment, and felt Mother's warmth spreading through her. She let it fill her soul.

And then, she awoke.

—*unk!*

Her head smacked against the wood, bursting into throbbing pain.

Azalea lay sprawled on the floor. Her eyes and cheeks were wet. Everything—Keeper, sisters, the blood oath—flooded to her. She leaped to her feet.

No thin, hard fingers pushed her into a dance. About her, the dancers backed away from her in a ring, their eyeholes gaping.

And . . .

She clutched something in her fist that hadn't been

there before. Azalea opened her hand and squinted at it in the dim light.

It flashed silver.

Mother's handkerchief.

The embroidered initials; the bit of silver lace along the sides. Azalea swore she smelled white cake on it. The King's words, from several days ago, echoed in her mind:

This magic has caused many strange things to happen. . . .

"No kidding!" said Azalea. She held it up.

The dancers backed away. They became oddly translucent, like glass, flickered, and the moment before disappearing, their faces filled out with eyes and powderless complexions, before they fell to the floor as bits of ornament shards, a rainstorm of glass.

The black aura about the walls faded back into brick. The storage room was empty again, glass scattered across the floor.

A brilliant feeling overcame Azalea. It drowned out the throbbing and the pain in her ears. She sprang up the stairs, racing with a newfound energy. She had to save her family.

CHAPTER 26

*T*he palace wasn't the palace anymore.

Azalea emerged from the fireplace to find their beds of patched bedsheets and lumpy pillows and the round table gone, replaced with curling, crystalline baroque furniture. A chandelier dripped from the domed ceiling of painted cupids, and the darkness felt almost tangible swirling about her. The windows—no longer draped— now were thickly covered with a mess of thorny branches, pressing against the panes and strangling out the light.

"Just like in the history books," said Azalea. "With the palace surrounded by thorns—"

FFFFFput!

A tiny arrow, just the length of her hand with a little metal heart for the tip, had imbedded itself in the wall next to Azalea. Azalea pried it from the wall and looked up. Painted cupids swam about on the ceiling.

"Oh, *that's* not in the history books!" Azalea threw the arrow at them. The cupids scattered. She dove for the door.

FFFFputputputput!

A dozen tiny arrows hit the door as Azalea slammed it behind her. She wondered how much of the palace had been magicked, and looked at her handkerchief. If it was anything near as strong as the sword—and Azalea knew it was much stronger than it had been before—then perhaps Keeper wouldn't be able to magic anymore. It might even mean he would remain trapped inside the palace, like he had been trapped in the passage. This gave Azalea hope. First—her sisters and the King. Then she would find Keeper.

Azalea ran in a maze of gaudy, unfamiliar halls, searching in vain for stairs or anything that would lead her to the library or the ballroom, which was the only room in the household that had more than one mirror. The portraits had been magicked, and old parliament members and great-aunts leered down at her with bloodred eyes. Voices murmured and whispered, beyond her conscious mind.

In a swirling golden hall, which may at one time have been the portrait gallery, Azalea caught a flicker of light coming closer.

"Oh!" she called, taking a step back. "Who is that?"

A small *clickety click click* sounded as the candle drew nearer, far too low to be held by anyone. It moved on its own. The little brass dish had been split and the ends curved to points beneath it, giving it legs. It looked like a toddler, its candle to the nub, and it stumbled around in lost little circles.

"Oh . . . there now," said Azalea, leaning just in front of it. It reminded her of the sugar teeth. "Do you know how to get to the ballroom?"

The candle went *foof*.

"Ack!" said Azalea. She smothered the fire in the folds of her skirt, leaving the odor of smoked fabric. The candle skittered away on its ungainly brass legs. Azalea made to chase after it for a good kick, but stopped. A much larger *clickety click click* sounded at the end of the hall. In fact, it was more of a *clankety clank clank clank*.

The tiny candle fled behind a sofa leg. Light flared up at the end of the hall, and a giant mass of tangled iron clanked into view. Candles dripped from it. Azalea recognized the old chandelier from the north attic.

Azalea jumped to the fireplace in a billow of skirts as the chandelier sprang at her. She overturned the poker stand and snatched up a hearth brush. The chandelier dove at her, flame first. Heart screaming, head throbbing, Azalea jumped aside and smashed the hearth brush against it. Two candles went out, then sprang to life again.

The chandelier reared up. Azalea ran, leaping in bounds.

It smashed after her, onto the long, thick crimson rug—

Snap!

The rug encased the fixture in a smooth, snapdragon movement and curled in on itself, smothering the light and crushing the chandelier with a sickening *crunch*. Azalea panted as the last glowing light in the rug died.

"Right," said Azalea, relieved she had jumped over the rug instead of on it. "Let's not touch that."

The tiny candle *clickety clicked* to her, timid. Its flame was low, as though apologizing.

"Have you seen the King? Or the girls?" said Azalea. "The ballroom?"

The flame sprung to life and took off, little legs skittering like mad. Azalea, hope blossoming through her, ran after it.

Minutes later, through twisted golden halls of gaudy ornamentation and staircases with whispering pictures, Azalea skidded through the entrance hall and into the ballroom. This portion of the palace, she was relieved to see, had not been magicked at all; they remained the boring paneled wainscot white-ceilinged rooms they had been before.

She ran to the first ballroom mirror and nearly screamed.

Delphinium stared back at her. Tears streaked her cheeks, and she hugged herself, shivering. Her eyelashes were frosted. On her pretty, peaked face, next to her ear, slashed three jagged scratch marks. They bled.

Keeper! thought Azalea. She pressed her hand against the glass, and Delphinium's quavering hand met it.

"Delphi," said Azalea. "Bear up. I'll get you out of here. Where are the others?"

Delphinium spoke, but no sound came. She shook her head and pointed to the next pier glass.

Eve quavered from the inside of the next glass. She held her spectacles, which had frosted over, but her eyes lit with hope when she saw Azalea. Azalea managed some soothing words, then ran to the next mirror, which held Ivy. She huddled on the reflection's floor, her cheeks tear stained, chewing on a strand of her hair. Azalea pressed her hand against the glass, trying to comfort her.

In the next curled Hollyhock, rolled up in a little ball, her hands tucked up her sleeves. Then Flora and Goldenrod, hugging each other to keep from quaking. Clover, Kale, and Lily pressed close in the mirror next. Clover had wrapped both the girls up in her shawl and had her arms about them to keep them warm. When she saw Azalea, like the other girls, her eyes lit.

Jessamine worried Azalea the most. She huddled alone in a ball, unmoving, not even shivering. When Azalea spoke to her, she did not stir. Only when Azalea knocked on the glass, hard, did Jessamine's eyelids flicker. She was so tiny—only four. She couldn't keep warm for long.

A knocking sound came from the eighth and last mirror, and Azalea found Bramble, hands pressed against the glass and long red hair coming unpinned in strands. Her thin lips were purple, but she looked determined. She gestured feverishly at Azalea, her lips pursing even thinner all the while. She held her hand out flat and pretended to scribble across it.

"Write . . . a letter?" said Azalea.

Bramble nodded. She pretended to shove her hands in pockets she did not have, and bounced up and down on the balls of her feet, before breaking into silent chatters.

"To Lord Teddie?" said Azalea.

Bramble, trembling, nodded.

"Yes?" said Azalea. "To say what?"

Bramble swallowed and opened her mouth, then closed it, then swallowed again. She shivered, keeping her yellow-green eyes on her feet.

She mouthed the words "I'm sorry," and shrugged. There was a tear streak down her cheek.

Instinctively, Azalea brought up the handkerchief to wipe Bramble's face. It seemed to put a light into the mirror, and Bramble's eyes lifted. She warmed her hands near it, as though it were a flame.

"Magic?" she mouthed.

Azalea, hopeful, rubbed furiously against the glass. Perhaps she could somehow rub her sisters out of the mirrors—

But it did nothing. Bramble shuddered and shook her head.

"Not enough," she mouthed.

Even so, Azalea ran to Jessamine's mirror and pressed the handkerchief against it. After several moments, Jessamine stirred, and her eyes opened a touch. Behind her figure, in the mirror, the tiny spider candle skittered away, leaving a streak of gold. A dark, handsome figure crossed the floor behind them, and Azalea turned quickly, keeping the handkerchief pinned to the mirror behind her. *Keeper!*

He did not go to her, but instead went down a length to Clover's mirror, and placed his fist hard against it. All three girls cowered under it.

"Release it, Miss Azalea."

Azalea hesitated. Keeper smashed his fist against the

mirror, a hard *cranch*, and it cracked. Kale gave a silent cry.

"Release it!"

Hating herself, Azalea threw the handkerchief to the floor. In an instant, her head thwacked against the marble and Keeper's long, pointed fingers wrapped around her neck.

"Where is your father?" he snarled.

He hadn't found the King yet! Azalea tried to blink the blotches from her vision.

"Well?" said Keeper, his fingers tightening.

"I don't know," said Azalea.

Keeper shoved her against the marble again, and colors burst before her eyes.

Graveyard.

The word came to her mind, fully formed.

"Graveyard," Azalea said in a choked voice. "He's in the graveyard."

Keeper's black eyes narrowed at her.

"Mother—" Azalea's throat seemed to squeeze to her ears. "She died a year ago today."

Keeper's eyes remained thin slits, but he lightened his grip, a touch. Azalea inhaled fresh, sweet air.

"The *graveyard*," he said. "Naturally."

In a moment he stood before Jessamine's mirror, giving the handkerchief a wide berth. Jessamine was curled up and shivering, her dark curls askew. When she saw Keeper looming above her, she began to cry in tiny, noiseless wails.

He stretched out his fingers and, with some effort, stroked the mirror like a beloved pet. He placed his palm flat against the glass and closed his eyes.

His face became gaunter, almost translucent, and the mirror changed as well. Like light against a dark window, Azalea saw her own heaving reflection, transparent on the glass. Slowly it grew stronger and more opaque until Azalea was fully reflected. Jessamine's reflection let out a cry—

—and Azalea saw it was the real Jessamine, curled on the ballroom floor.

Head pulsing, Azalea rushed to her side, hoping to warm her quivering body. Keeper shoved her away and snatched Jessamine up, striding out of the ballroom. Azalea staggered after him, realization pouring hope into her chest. She'd been *right* about the handkerchief! Keeper couldn't leave the palace!

"You know where the graveyard is, Miss Jessamine?" he said, carrying her under his arm like a sheep. He pulled the entrance hall door open. Tangled ropes of black branches twisted over it like snakes, masking the doorway.

Keeper closed his eyes and placed his hand on the

tangled mess of branches, and his face grew ashen—just as when he had raised the water, those many months ago. His breathing labored. The tangled movements of the branches sped, and they parted in pieces, letting a stream of sunlight through.

"You can't come back in until you find the King," said Keeper, heaving for air. "The bushes won't let you in unless you have him with you. Understand? Don't be gone long, my dear."

Azalea grabbed a shawl from the coatstand and wrapped it tightly around Jessamine.

"Don't come back," she whispered. "Find the King. But *don't let him in*. Don't come back!"

Jessamine blinked her bright blue eyes at Azalea. Keeper grasped Jessamine's arm and threw her through the opening in the branches. She stumbled out and nearly tripped down the long, gray stone stairs.

"Yes, find the King," he said. "Tell him I am killing the eldest princess—*slowly*." He slammed the door.

Azalea dashed for the handkerchief, but Keeper caught her first, boxing her into the ballroom, and threw her into the curtains of one of the windows. The rope tassels twisted and wound of their own accord, wrapping themselves around her already-sore wrists. She bit back a cry as they tightened, sending shoots of pain up her arms.

"Let's savor this," he said.

With the utmost delicacy of his long fingers, Keeper tugged the pins from her hair and flicked them behind him; they clinked against the floor. Azalea struggled, squirming to keep her head away from Keeper's fingers, but the cords kept her bound. Tendrils of auburn hair cascaded to her waist. The girls in the mirrors watched on with wide eyes. Azalea writhed with humiliation.

"There now," Keeper whispered, when the last pin had clinked to the floor. "Don't you look pretty."

He leaned in to her. Azalea could smell the musty, empty-teapot metallic smell he carried with him. She couldn't believe how she once had actually wanted to kiss him.

"Tell me," he said in a low voice. "How *did* you get the handkerchief back? I should like very much to know—"

He stopped short at a tiny sniffling noise behind him. Turning, he stepped back to reveal Jessamine, standing at the ballroom doors, small and shivering beneath the shawl. Her black hair hung over her shoulders, stringy and dripping from the melted snow. She was alone. Keeper's eyes narrowed.

"How in the world," said Keeper, snapping his cloak behind him as he swept to her, "did you get back in here? Alone? Mmm?"

Jessamine's eyes shone bright with fear, but she did not back away. A touch of defiance sparked in them.

"My father says," she whispered, raising her chin. "My f-father says . . . he says . . . if you hurt us . . . he will *box your ears.*"

Keeper stared down at her trembling figure. A smile grew on his face.

"Oh, *did* he?" he said. "I am shaking in my boots, I assure you."

He knelt in front of Jessamine and took her tiny hand in his.

"Let's play a game," he said. "I've heard some children do it with crickets, but it is so much more fun with people. I was so dearly hoping to do it to your father, but, alas." Keeper sighed. "He is not here. Shall we begin with your thumbs?"

He grasped her thumb with a black gloved hand and—

Was soundly thwacked across the face.

The punch came from nowhere, and it echoed across the ballroom. Keeper fell back, colliding with the marble. There was a very satisfying crack of his head smacking against it.

He had been boxed in the face!

CHAPTER 27

Immediately Keeper sprang to his feet, massaging his cheek. His eyes narrowed to slits, searching.

"It seems we have a guest." Keeper gave a half smile, showing one long dimple, but his eyes glinted hard. "Welc—"

Thwap.

Keeper smashed to the floor again.

"Oh, we shall see about *this*!" he growled. With catlike dexterity, he jerked about and lunged at nothing. His hands caught on something invisible, clawing it to the ground, wrestling. A twist, and the invisible something had slammed Keeper to the floor again.

The wraith cloak!

Mr. Bradford! Azalea's heart jumped.

But no—the invisible figure's movements were . . . stiffer. Firmer. Harder.

"Sir!" cried Azalea.

Keeper clawed at the air, tearing it, revealing a floating head with blood smeared across the cheek. Another hard yank, and Keeper tore away the rest of the old, tattered cloak, revealing the King.

The King managed one more resounding punch to Keeper's face before Keeper, with great effort, thrust the King into the drapes, two windows away from Azalea. In a moment, the golden rope cords bit into his suitcoat, restraining him tightly. It must have hurt, but the King made no sound. Instead, bound to the drapes, he glared at Keeper with such a look in his eyes as Azalea had never seen before.

"Well, well, *well*," said Keeper, breathing heavily. "What a marvelous surprise, Your Grace. And a wraith cloak! I welcome you both heartily." Keeper gave a mock bow and paced around the King, scrutinizing him. He smiled. His teeth gleamed. "So pleased to meet you at last. We've been having a marvelous time, these past months, your daughters and I. You know, you really shouldn't have raised them to be so trusting."

Keeper leaned in to the King, just inches from his face, breathing quiet words on his skin. "I've waited hundreds of years for this moment, thinking of all the ways I could possibly hurt you most. This will be amusing."

413

The King did not reply. His face was so taut Azalea could see veins and muscles.

Keeper strode to Azalea, untangling her from the cords, and dragged her in front of the King. He grasped her hard around the waist, her hands in back, the pain keeping her from writhing out of his grip. She managed a good kick to his leg.

"Eldest to youngest," said Keeper. "If the ones in the mirror don't die first. That is the unfortunate side effect of the mirror charm. You leave them in too long, and they die. Pity, pity. And now, I remember a very pretty curtsy Miss Azalea once did. What was it called? Ah, yes . . . the Soul's Curtsy . . ."

He snapped Azalea about to face him, and the world spun in her vision. She swallowed a yelp. Her trembling hands were grasped tightly in Keeper's long fingers, her hair tangled over her face. He twisted her fingers and bent them back, pain coursing to her shoulders, and her knees gave way. She fell hard to the floor. She gave a choked cry.

"What fun—"

Crack—snap—CRASH!

Keeper released Azalea as the drapes and rod ripped from the wall, gilded iron, thick bolts, heavy velvet and all crashing to the floor. Azalea collapsed to the ground as the King tackled Keeper and threw him against the marble.

Crack.

A pistol's shot, from beyond the twisting bushes, ripped the air.

The world exploded.

The sharp sound of smashing glass burst through the air. From all sides, the velvet draperies billowed. Hooves clacked against the marble, crunching over the smashed glass, and the curtains struggled in the form of velvet-horses and riders, fighting against the inky branches that snagged and cords that tangled.

Far on the right, a horseman broke free, revealing none other than Minister Fairweller on LadyFair. At the same time, through the window nearest the ballroom doors, Mr. Pudding had ripped a rod from the wall and contended with the snaring, scratching branches at Thackeray's feet.

Sir John fought through, and next to him, branches gouged a gentleman, untangling them from his mount's neck. Mr. Gasperson, Lord Teddie's steward! Azalea only just had time to recognize him, when Lord Teddie on horseback bashed through the window next to her, face scratched, trailing tangled branches after him. Determination was written across his face. He kicked the branches away, and they broke to pieces, splintering across the floor like glass.

And then, at the window over her, Dickens's hooves

smashed through, mounted by Mr. Bradford. Azalea caught a glimpse of hard stoniness in his face, a pistol flashing in his hand, snow whirling around him. The dappled light of the falling glass reflected in fragments across the wall. The ballroom blasted in bright, shouting, chaotic pieces, glass grinding under horses' hooves, gentlemen and horses alike scratched and bleeding.

Azalea managed to push herself upright, dodging the discord of horse and glass. A hand grasped her wrist, and though the grip was not hard, it still hurt. Azalea swallowed the cry when she saw it was the King. His face had jagged claw marks across it, bleeding.

"Do you still have it?" he said.

Azalea knew precisely what he meant. She dove for the handkerchief across the ballroom floor, pain rippling through her, and rushed to the mirrors.

Delphinium shivered in the first pier glass. Her lips were purple. The King grabbed a fire poker from the stand by the hearth and wrapped the handkerchief at the tip. Azalea took it by the end, and the King's sturdy hands wrapped around hers. Pulling back, she let the King's force guide her hands to bash the mirror to pieces.

Shards crashed, revealing a tarnished backing. Terror seized Azalea. But as the mirrored pieces of Delphinium fell to the marble, each one left a bit of her behind, forming a real Delphinium, as though she had been huddled in front of the mirror the entire time.

Immediately the King's suitcoat was around Delphinium's shoulders, and he pulled Azalea to Eve. Eve drew back as they swung, hammering the mirror with the poker. The pieces smashed to the floor.

It felt a blur after that. Eve's teeth chattered as she searched among the shards for her spectacles. Mr. Pudding wrapped his own ragged suitcoat around her and brought her to the ballroom fireplace, where a fire had been stirred to life. The next mirror crashed to the floor, and Lord Teddie wrapped Ivy in his suitcoat and carried her to the fire, for she was too cold to walk. Hollyhock was carried as well. The twins cried when they were released, sobbing in fits and starts. Clover next, with Kale and Lily, who seemed to fare the best of all of them.

By the time Azalea and the King reached the last mirror, their strength flagged. It took five hits to smash it, pieces of Bramble gliding together as shards fell. Bramble bent over, coughing, white as death. She had enough Bramble in her, though, to say, "Az, you look awful."

All the girls huddled by the fireplace, crying and trembling. Azalea fell against the wall, feeling the sharp, snowy wind blow over her from the broken windows.

The King's hand dripped blood, and his face colored

a sallow green. Still, in his formal, measured way, he plucked the handkerchief from the end of the fire poker, his eyes combing the ballroom.

"Con*found* it!" he seethed.

A visual sweep of the ballroom confirmed what the King was *confound*ing. Keeper was gone. And, after another sweeping glance of the bright gray-white ballroom through the pawing horses and broken glass, Azalea realized the cloak was gone, too.

"He can't leave the palace," said Azalea as the makeshift cavalry gathered about the King. "The handkerchief won't let him. He hasn't much magic to do anything."

The King nodded.

"We will make a search of the palace, then. Sir John—" The King pushed away the doctor, who tended to the King's hand. "The ladies first. They've got to be taken somewhere warm."

A harried discussion ensued. They wanted to take the girls out, to Lord Teddie's town house or to the Silver Compass Coffeehouse, but the King, his eyes passing over the shivering and blue-lipped girls, refused.

"It's too cold," he said. "We haven't enough horses. And I will not let them from my sight. Lord Haftenravenscher, Mr. Gasperson—scout for an unmagicked room."

Lord Teddie gave a gangly salute and bounded out

the door in an instant. Mr. Gasperson followed after.

Exhaustion fell over Azalea as she started to feel the heat of the fireplace. Her body felt one all-encompassing throb. She leaned against the wall, but not even that could support her, and her legs gave way.

Mr. Bradford caught her.

"Are you all right?" he said.

Azalea nodded, too tired for words, but she smiled. She allowed a portion of her fear and pain to ebb as she leaned on his steady arm. A warm sort of glow replaced it. He helped her to a velvet chair next to the fireplace, made certain she was well enough, then tended to his pistol. She watched him as he reloaded it. He did so in a businesslike way, though he was only in sleeves and a waistcoat—blood streaked and disheveled at that—his face taut. It was easy to see him as a regiment captain here.

Azalea pieced the events together in her mind. She imagined Mr. Bradford helping the King search for her, telling the King about Keeper, then forming whatever cavalry they could when they saw the thorny branches about the palace. Azalea curled her toes in her boots (even that hurt) and smiled at Mr. Bradford. He caught it, and gave a crooked one back.

Lord Teddie came lolloping back into the ballroom with shockingly long strides. Mr. Gasperson clumped after him.

"The library, sir!" he said, breathless. "Just across the hall! It hasn't been touched, and there's an ember going!"

The King gave a short nod and, though bleeding, scooped up both Kale and Lily with one arm. The other gentlemen began to help the girls up. Lord Teddie thrust his hands out to Bramble. His linen shirt was stained rusty red with his blood, but still he beamed.

"What are you doing here?" said Bramble, cringing at his bleeding hands.

"Helping you up," he said.

"Shove off," said Bramble. She looked near tears. "If you'd stayed in your stupid country you wouldn't be . . . all cut up right now—"

She tried to stand, but shook so badly she couldn't. Lord Teddie jumped in and helped her.

"*Eep!*"

The simultaneous scream sounded from the twins. Both clasped their hands over their mouths, their eyes wide with horror. Azalea followed their gaze.

There, in patches of light, a scratched-up Fairweller held a weeping Clover in his arms, cradling her head against his shoulder. He murmured into her ear.

Delphinium screamed.

"Oh, Clover, how could you?" said Eve.

"Is he a good kisser?" said Hollyhock.

The King had no words as he strode to them. In an

instant he had torn Fairweller away from Clover, wound up, and *boxed* Fairweller straight in the face.

Fairweller stumbled backward and fell to the floor, glass crunching beneath him.

"You may fill out your resignation paperwork tomorrow," said the King. "*Ex*-Prime Minister Fairweller!"

The group of limping, ragged girls and gentlemen stumbled and were carried to the library. Azalea trailed at the end, wishing for everything to be over so she could fall into a deep, deep sleep, snuggled in pillows and downy blankets. She rubbed her lip, which stung, and her hand brought back blood. Instictively she fumbled for her handkerchief, and in a panic, realized she didn't have it.

She ran back through the entrance hall to the ballroom, her gait uneven, trying to recall if the King had unknotted it from the end of the fire poker. She scuffed the shards of glass, searching among the fallen drapery.

Just as she spotted the fire poker, by the last mirror's mounting and decidedly without the handkerchief— Azalea now remembered the King plucking it from the end—a hand slapped across her mouth and yanked her backward.

At least, it felt like a hand. She couldn't see it. Another invisible arm wrapped around her waist and pulled her off her feet. Azalea kicked and struggled against the invisible force. Keeper!

"Yes, cry out," said a chocolate voice in her ear. "He will come looking for you. Compassion or some tripe like that. And when he does—"

His hand shook over her mouth, and Azalea took courage. He hadn't strength at all—surely he had very little magic left! She spun on one foot, snagged at the invisible force with all her might, feeling the coarsely woven fabric in her grip. She leaped and rolled, clutching the end of the cloak, biting her lip to keep silent.

Keeper appeared headfirst, and clawed the end of the cloak before the rest of him appeared. He yanked. Azalea held tight, sliding across the marble. She twisted the cloak around her wrists for a better hold, sending reams of pain up her arms.

"Ah!" said Keeper. "You want to dance the Entwine? This is a rather untraditional dance position."

He pulled Azalea to her feet, and Azalea leaned back. Keeper let the cloak go slack. Azalea, with wavering balance, spun and ducked as he slashed at her, across the ballroom floors, to the windows.

"You know," he said, panting, "I really *did* invent the dance. No lady ever won. As hard as they tried. You came closest, I think."

Keeper pulled the cloak to him and boxed Azalea

weakly across the face. It didn't blast colors in her vision as it had before, but her grip wavered as the world around her spun. She leaned back, nearly out of one of the broken windows, dizzy. The breeze and snow swept through her unpinned hair. Keeper yanked—

—and slipped.

Hairpins clinked across the ballroom floor. Keeper's feet swept out in a great arc from under him, and he fell back onto the marble. Azalea toppled through the window with the cloak, falling into the spiky broken branches.

It took a moment for the blotches to clear. Azalea had to steady her breathing and calm her pain. Every part of her ached and stung. With shaking hands, she slowly untangled herself from the bushes. The horses, which had been shooed out the windows and into the front court, watched Azalea's valiant fight with the thornbushes with lazy horsey indifference. LadyFair even came to the bushes and nosed Azalea's hair, sniffing with great nostrils.

Azalea pushed LadyFair's nose out of the way with the same vigor she shoved the prickly, scratching branches aside. Her hand was smeared with blood. She managed to push herself back through the window, remembering the wraith cloak just in time, before Keeper could leap at her.

She threw the torn, ragged fabric over her shoulders.

A flickering shudder ran through her body, and her skirts disappeared. The world blurred in a glass weave.

She braced herself for Keeper's assault, but it did not come. Azalea looked about her.

The ballroom was empty.

The oath. He was going to use his last bit of strength on the King, and he already knew they had gone to the library. Gripping the cloak at her neck, Azalea gathered her skirts and *ran*.

CHAPTER 28

$\mathcal{I}$nvisible, Azalea brushed past a forlorn-looking Fairweller at the library door. The warmth of the library engulfed her, burning her nose and cheeks. She took in the scene by the draped piano and walls of books. Sofas had been moved in front of the fire and were crowded with girls, their black dresses limp. They wore gentlemen's coats and suitcoats about their shoulders. They were still shaking with cold but their color had greatly improved.

And the King! Azalea exhaled slowly. He was all right. He stood by the desk, talking to the rest of the gentlemen with a low voice. Blood was smeared across his face, but he was all right. Keeper wasn't here.

Azalea breathed a sigh of relief. She made to fling off the cloak, until she saw Mother.

She stood among the girls at the stiff striped and

flowered sofas, her voice clipped and low. Mr. Bradford stood next to her, looking distracted and speaking to her in an equally low voice. Azalea slipped closer, and her heart yelped as she realized that the square jaw and the touseled, unpinned auburn hair wasn't Mother's—

It's me! Azalea's mind screamed.

Keeper!

Azalea dove at herself—then pulled up so sharply her skirts engulfed the back of her legs. The slight gust of wind ruffled the girls' hair. Her copy image held a flash of steel in her hand. Mr. Bradford's pistol!

Gritting her teeth, she proceeded with caution. Her vision still blurred from the hood of the cloak, she neared Keeper carefully. It was odd, to walk without seeing her skirts in front of her. She pussyfooted to just by Mr. Bradford, next to the twins' sofa. They watched with wide eyes, whispering among themselves.

". . . don't think I can?" Keeper clutched the pistol and held it to her—or rather, *his*, Azalea-like chest, keeping it from Mr. Bradford's outstretched hand. Azalea wondered if that really was her own, ghastly pale face—and if it was, she certainly didn't look a picture, all scratched up and bruised, trembling all over.

"No, nothing of the sort," said Mr. Bradford. "I just didn't think you knew *how* to shoot."

"She doesn't," said Bramble, from the sofa behind him.

Azalea-Keeper flicked the pistol around her finger, spinning it so quickly it flashed in the lamplight, a circular blur of metal. She threw it into the air at a spin, snatched it with the other hand, spun it, and stopped it barrel up with a *smack*.

The girls' jaws dropped. Mr. Bradford blinked, looking Keeper over from skirt to tangled hair, with a slightly bewildered—then suspicious—expression.

"Only one shot?" said Keeper, fiddling with the pistol in shaking hands. His voice sounded strikingly like Mother's. "They haven't invented pistols with, say, thirteen shots yet? Ha! Joking! One is grand!"

"I think you're ill," said Mr. Bradford, advancing on Keeper. He made to take the pistol. "Miss Azalea, the regiments will be here in hardly twenty minutes—you don't *need* it—"

"Yes, I *do*!" Keeper snarled, backing away toward the draped piano, green eyes looking wildly around the library. He raised the pistol away from Mr. Bradford's outstretched hand, above his own head.

A firm, stiff hand grasped Keeper's wrist from behind. Keeper blanched, which made the scratches on his—Azalea's—face stand out even more. Azalea could see how he tried to struggle against the King's grip, but he was either too weak or the King too firm. Possibly both.

Even so, Keeper did not drop the pistol. His dainty fingers wrapped around it so tightly the knuckles glowed white. The King sighed and made to pluck the pistol from Keeper's hand. When Keeper would not release it, the King's brows furrowed.

"Miss Azalea," he said, in a clipped, impatient voice. "We are all frightened, but now is hardly the time. Give me the pistol."

"No."

"Azalea, let go of the pistol."

"No."

"Azalea—"

"I *won't*!" said Keeper, writhing against the King's steel grip. He kicked back against the King's legs, driving the boots' heels into him, but the King showed no signs of feeling it. He was the most solid gentleman Azalea knew. Azalea slipped closer.

From the sofas, the girls watched, both fascinated and ducking behind them, eyes peeking above the backs of the chairs. If the pistol went off now, it would hit the ceiling.

"Miss Azalea," said the King. "Let go. If your mother were here—"

"*Don't* tell me what Mother would or would not do!" Keeper snarled. "She's *dead*!"

Azalea winced. For a moment, the King's hand

gripping Keeper's faltered. Then it was back to a steel clamp.

"Azalea—"

"She's *dead*!" said Keeper, the green in his eyes blazing, intense. "Dead, *dead*—"

Azalea gripped the cloak at her neck. It was like she was being slapped.

On the sofas by the fireplace, Kale and Jessamine curled up into little balls and began to cry. Jessamine in her delicate, crystalline wails, and Kale in her piercing sobs. Lily, in Clover's arms, sensed discord and began to cry, too.

"Lea, stop," said Clover.

"Miss Azalea," said the King, who kept his hand firmly around Azalea's wrist. "I think we are all aware of that. For now we will have to bear up—"

"What the devil for?" said Keeper. Her voice rang through the room. "It won't be the same. Not with *you*."

The King's hand at Azalea's wrist shook. There was an odd, awkward moment, a hiccup of time, as though the air were being turned inside out. The King's face seemed far more lined, and as Azalea drew close to him, she saw how old he suddenly looked. Azalea was reminded of the uncomfortable moment, last summer, when his internal thread twisted so; and now it seemed twisted so much, it made all his features taut and strained.

"We must do what we can, Miss Azalea," he managed to say. "In this family we—"

"You are *not*," Keeper spat, "a part of this family."

The King released Keeper's hand, sharply, and Azalea realized, with a flash of memory like a slap across her face, those had been *her* words.

"How *dare* you!" Azalea screamed. She threw herself at herself, the wraith cloak fluttering to the ground behind her, and pummeled Keeper to the ground, before he even had a chance to raise the pistol. It clattered across the floor. "How *dare* you! *I'll tear your eyes out!*"

"Oh—oh—" Keeper cried. "Oh—ow!"

Azalea had punched him across his dainty scratched face.

Instantly the gentlemen pried them apart, gripping their arms behind their backs, looking both horrified and slightly fascinated. Both Azalea and Keeper didn't need much binding—they shook from both weakness and anger.

The King, whose features still were twisted with tightness, took charge.

"What *is* all this?" he said.

Both Azaleas broke into yelling, Azalea furious and Azalea-Keeper defensive, and both of them wincing at the gentlemen's grips over their sore wrists. The girls behind them broke into cries. The King held up his hand for silence.

"Miss Azalea," he said.

Both Azaleas broke into cries again.

"Sir, can't you see, I'm the real Azalea—that's Keeper! He's using magic!"

"You rotter!" said Azalea. "You ghastly— He's trying to kill you!"

"You sound *nothing* like me!"

"Enough!" said the King.

"Oh, sir!" Lord Teddie bounced on his feet. "Sir, I read about this sort of thing once, sir! The only way to solve it is to kill both of them. It was in the Bible!"

The silence rung. Lord Teddie cowered at the King's look.

"Ah, never mind," he said.

"Sir, here is evidence," said Keeper, writhing weakly against Mr. Bradford's hold. "Keeper took the wraith cloak, and he has it *now*!"

"Sir, here is evidence," said Azalea. She raked her mind for the object of hers that Keeper had taken and was using now. But then, another thought arrived, and Azalea lifted her chin.

"The handkerchief," she said. "You *know* about the magic."

The King turned to her, as though seeing her for the first time. His eyebrows rose.

"Yes," said the King. "Yes."

And from his waistcoat pocket, he pulled out the wadded silver handkerchief. Azalea remembered now, seeing him pluck it from the end of the fire poker. In the stained-glass lamplight of the library, the silver shone. Keeper's green eyes flashed at it.

"Fold this for me, will you?" said the King, crisply, to Keeper.

Azalea found it oddly delightful to watch the color drain completely from his already drawn face. His eyes flitted from the door to the pistol on the ground in front of him, then back to the handkerchief.

"Him first," he said in Azalea's voice, jutting his chin at Azalea.

The King, without taking his eyes from Keeper, gave the handkerchief to Azalea. She folded it smartly, pressing the seams at each fold, and raised it for the King to see. The King's voice was hard.

"Captain Bradford," he said.

Keeper writhed against Mr. Bradford's hold and shoved back. In a hard glissade, Keeper broke free, hitting the piano before crumpling to the ground. Before Mr. Bradford could help Azalea-Keeper up, she stumbled to her feet and raised her chin.

"Of all the silly—" she said. She thrust out her hand to Azalea. "Give me the handkerchief."

Her hand quavered. In the other, hidden by the

folds of her skirt, Azalea caught a glimpse of steel.

The pistol!

Azalea did not even think. She lunged at Keeper before he had a chance to raise it. They fell on the rug together, and the pistol skittered out of reach underneath the piano. Azalea grasped at Azalea-Keeper's black skirts, pulling her back.

Keeper twisted around and lashed at Azalea's arm. Drops of blood smattered across her cheek, and she lost her grip. He stumbled to his feet and leaped for the door.

"After him!" the King commanded. He swept the pistol from the ground and lunged after Keeper through the sliding door. "No—the *gentlemen*! Ladies stay here!"

"The devil we're staying!" Bramble cried.

As they took off in a mass of skirts, Azalea ran after them, clutching her arm. By all rights, her feet shouldn't have carried her up the stairs in sleek, dancelike steps. But her temper seared, the heat in her veins overpowering the ache. She passed the girls, the gentlemen, and even the King, taking a great lead and leaving them behind. She ran through the unfamiliar palace of white gilded walls and haunted portraits.

At the end of the hall, she paused, breathless. A timid light clicked out from underneath a white silk sofa. It pointed a stubby leg toward the stairs. "Many thanks!" said Azalea, leaping up. Keeper was headed for the tower.

Several minutes later, a fizz in her blood, Azalea leaped onto the creaking tower platform, heaving for air. Everything felt stifled, as though the tower held its breath. The gray-blue of the snowstorm through the clockface cast shadows of numbers across the floor. Smaller shadows whorled past them in pinpricks.

A sharp clang sounded, along with a wretched *eeEeeErrEEEuh*. The clock, a waking giant, creaked to life. Azalea had a moment to realize that Mr. Bradford's clock stopping had been undone before skirts rustled behind her; Azalea ducked. The hearth shovel brushed past her head and smashed against the clockface.

The glass showered Azalea in prickles, tinkling against the wood. The blizzard billowed onto the platform. Azalea pulled away as Keeper yanked the shovel from the broken clockface and slammed it where her form used to be. She ran, leaping up the spindly stairs of the bells platform at the side, retreating into carriage-wheel-sized gears. Keeper sprang after her in graceful bounds, shovel raised.

Grasping her skirts to keep them from getting tangled, Azalea picked her way among the gears and dangling counterweights, squeezing between the dusty, metallic-smelling bells. A click sounded, and Azalea sensed the impending strike of the clock's quarter-to peal. She threw herself to the gritty floor, pressing her skirts down as the bells creaked and swung above her in a rain of dust. The *dong* was so loud it seemed to pierce through her mind.

Scrambling to her feet, streaked with dust, Azalea had a moment to twist out of the way of Keeper's swing, stumbling backward into the grinding mass of gears.

The clock creaked to a halt. Azalea tried to get to her feet, but they slipped from under her. She craned her neck at the gears behind her, and saw her skirts wedged in the teeth, a mess of crinolines and hoops. Azalea clawed at the caught fabric, twisting for a better grip. Keeper appeared above her, smiling a sweet Azalea-smile. His teeth glinted in the dim light. He raised the shovel.

"Azalea—"

Both Azaleas whipped their attention to the lower platform, visible in pieces through the gears. The King!

Keeper's emerald eyes flashed. He dropped the hearth shovel with a clang and squeezed through the tangle of machinery.

"Sir!" Azalea cried. "Look out!"

The King whipped about, holding the pistol. His eyes caught Keeper, rushing to him, skirts snapping behind.

"Sir!" he said, breathless and panting. "Shoot him! Shoot him! Hurry!"

He pointed a delicate, shaking hand at Azalea. The

King peered through the mechanisms to see Azalea, caught on her knees. Their eyes met. The King's face lined.

Azalea held up the handkerchief.

Whap.

The King threw Azalea-Keeper against the floor and held him down, pistol pointed at his pretty head. His auburn hair tendriled over the dusty wood. Snow swirled over them through the broken clockface.

"Up here!" the King yelled, not moving a muscle. "Up here!"

Keeper struggled weakly beneath the King's grip and let out a strangled noise. He began to cry.

"Please," he said. "Please don't hurt me."

The King wavered.

Keeper writhed, and for a moment even Azalea felt pity for him, a mewling kitten, tangled auburn hair and scratched face, pretty cheeks wet.

"Please," he said in Azalea's voice. A sob choked his throat. "Please, *Papa*—"

The King dropped the pistol. It clattered against the wood. He pulled back.

"No," he said. "Azalea—"

"It's not *me*!" Azalea cried.

Keeper's eyes glinted.

"God save the King," he said, and he raised the pistol to the King's chest.

Crack.

As slow as a nightmare—so slow the snowflakes hung in the air—the King fell forward.

Keeper caught him in the chest by the flat of his boot, and kicked him back, hard. He hit the floor. The limp *thumph* echoed through the tower.

No—*no*—

"No!" Azalea screamed. She wrenched her skirts with her full weight. They ripped free with a stark tearing sound.

The clock groaned to life. Gears whirred and ticked. Azalea clawed her way through the pulleys, stinging all over, and hardly feeling it.

Keeper, gaunt, slipped back into his own form with the ease of a breath. He threw the pistol to the side with a clatter, tried to get to his feet, and fell on his hands and knees, coughing, hacking. Horrified, Azalea pulled back, watching as Keeper began to change.

His hair turned silver white, then tangled into stringy clumps, falling to pieces in the storm's wind. His skin clung to his skeleton face. Azalea choked as she recognized the ancient Keeper—identical to the portrait hidden in the attic.

The blood oath. Azalea reeled, watching years of being kept alive pour over Keeper. He writhed, pockmarked, the skin melting from him like a candle. In the dim light, his black, sagging eyes flicked to the King's limp figure, then to Azalea. They danced with triumph. His voice was like the pages of an old crinkled book.

"I win," he said.

Azalea dove at him, but not before the wind eroded him, blowing him into streams of dust, his arms and head, blowing away into nothing. Azalea, stunned, pulled back. A final gust of wind snatched the handkerchief from her hand, out the clockface, and into the blizzard.

It flashed silver in the wind, and disappeared.

Dong. The tower chimed.

Azalea swallowed, backed away from the ledge, and scrambled to the King's side.

"Sir," said Azalea. "Sir!"

She touched his cheek. It was clammy. The King did not move.

Mr. Bradford arrived at the top of the stairs, out of breath.

"Fetch Sir John!" said Azalea. "Hurry!"

Mr. Bradford disappeared down the steps in an instant. Azalea tried to think. Hold a mirror to his face, it would fog—no, she didn't have a mirror—staunch the blood—she hadn't a handkerchief, and there was too much—far too much. She felt for the pulse on his wrist, but her hands shook too hard to feel anything.

Azalea's sisters arrived at the tower platform, and

their eyes widened when they saw the King.

They didn't make a sound. Not a gasp, not a scream, not a cry. Snow streamed and whirled around them as they stood, frozen. Flora held her hands over her mouth. Kale and Lily clung to Clover's skirts. Clover shook. Bramble was so white, the snow looked gray.

From a memory deep inside her, so faint it only held sounds and slips of color, a tiny, three-year-old Azalea wailed, *"Papa."*

"Papa," said Azalea to the lifeless form of the King. The word was so foreign, it choked her throat. "Papa . . . you can't leave us, Papa . . . It would be very . . . out of order—"

Bramble knelt opposite her, grasping the King's bandaged hand.

"She's—she's right, Papa," Bramble stuttered. "We have . . . rules. . . ."

Clover fell to her knees and pressed her handkerchief to his chest. Blood soaked through.

"Papa," she whispered.

The girls knelt around the King, their skirts spread out like forlorn blossoms, swallowing, and whispering one word.

"Papa."

"Papa."

"Papa."

It whispered among the gusts of wind stronger than the whistling gales of snow or the creaking, ticking of the clock, which felt strange and distant. Azalea gripped the King's lifeless hand.

"*Papa,*" she said.

Through the broken clockface, the wind gusted stronger, and became—

Warm.

The snow, which had been sticking to Azalea's skin, cold and icy, *burned*. The storm burst, bright, and Azalea realized it wasn't the storm—it was her.

Inside her chest, a warm, billowing *something* swept through her, to the tips of her fingers, the bottoms of her feet, shining like a brilliant beam of light. It wasn't the hot, boiling feeling of her temper, nor was it the cold wash of tingles that Swearing on Silver brought. It was deeper. It didn't just pour through her body, but penetrated her soul.

Azalea gasped.

The feeling faded until it was just a flicker of warmth inside her chest, lighting her heart like a candle. The wind howled, cold again now, and snow flurried around her, landing cold on her cheek—but the warmth was still there.

Breathless, Azalea looked at her sisters.

Clover had one hand pressed over her heart, breathing tiny gasping breaths. Bramble's thin eyebrows arched so high they reached her hair. The twins grasped each other's hands, and Hollyhock rubbed her face with her skirts. Even the little ones, Kale, Jessamine, and Lily, didn't cry anymore, but blinked wide-eyed at one another. Delphinium was so pale that if she fainted, no one would believe it fake. They all looked as stunned as Azalea felt.

"Great waistcoats," Bramble managed to choke. "What *was* that?"

Between Azalea's hands, which grasped the King's hand so tightly she wrung his fingers, something twitched.

Azalea clasped a hand to her mouth.

His hand was warm. So warm, in fact, that it matched the flicker within her chest.

The King's weak voice matched his limp attempt to push himself up. "Ow—"

"Sir!" cried Azalea. She threw her arms around him. "Oh—Sir! Pa*pa*!"

"Ow—"

"Pa*pa*!" cried all the girls.

They tumbled and threw their arms around the King. Azalea tried to keep them back but was too overcome. Their shouting voices and cries of happiness echoed up the tower, and the snow fell around them, white and clean and fresh.

CHAPTER 29

Azalea awoke to a strange thing: sunlight.

She also awoke among masses of fat, fluffy pillows. She would have thought it a dream, if she were not aching everywhere. She was not in her room, or even in the palace, but in a fashionable manor room with striped wallpaper and Delchastrian casement windows.

Azalea could recall euphoric happiness, the gentlemen arriving at the top of the stairs, the snow, and then—black. Ah, she had fainted. Again.

Flora and Goldenrod, who had been at the foot of the bed, leaped in delight when Azalea stirred, each grabbing her hands, tugging over her like a beloved rag doll, and chattering like mad.

"You're awake!"

"You've slept for nearly *two* days!"

"Sir John says you'll be all right, just that you needed rest."

"Oh!" Flora slapped a hand to her mouth. "They made us promise to get them when you awoke!"

The twins ran out of the room. Several minutes later, it was filled to bursting with Azalea's sisters. Still dressed in black, a bit shabby and pale, they were in high spirits. Even Delphinium, whose pretty face had jagged lines across it, smiled. They were all pleased as pink punch to see her awake. Azalea was thrilled to see them, too.

"Welcome to Fairweller's manor," said Bramble, grinning and pushing a cup of minty tea to Azalea's mouth. "Very fancy, very *neat*. We've already stained the dining room rug, to the delight of the servants."

"Mr. Fairweller is staying at his town house, at present." Clover handed her a dainty biscuit with a flower imprinted at the top.

"It's just until the King finds the sword and can unmagic the palace," said Bramble. "Or until the King murders Fairweller."

"Until *Papa* murders Fairweller," squeaked Hollyhock.

"Yes. Papa. Him." Bramble grinned. "Papa, Papa. We've got to get used to that."

Azalea smiled around a mouthful of biscuit. The King was all right, then.

The girls had the servants draw a bath for her,

chattering as they helped Azalea out of her clothes. Azalea had never seen a bath like this one—there was an actual room meant for bathing, and the bathwater steamed. Up to her neck in bubbles, she slowly removed the bandages from her arms and hands, washing away the dried blood. The younger girls played with the bubbles while the older ones told her what had happened.

"We should have listened to you," said Eve. Her spectacles had fogged up from the heat. "About not going to the pavilion. You were right."

Azalea waved it away. "What happened when you went through the passage?"

All the girls' faces became clouded.

"The pavilion . . . wasn't the same," was all Bramble said.

Azalea remembered the dark pavilion, its mesh of half-beast, half-human dancers, and the bony hands grasping her ankles. She imagined what it must have been like for them, to arrive to that, and then to be magicked away into mirrors. She shuddered.

"Never mind," she said. "Let's not think of it."

The girls, however, pressed Azalea into telling her story, and she started it from the beginning—from the haunted ball, and Mother, and finding out about Keeper, to the wraith cloak and brooch charm. By the time the story had ended, Azalea's bathwater had cooled to only mildly warm, and the girls hugged their knees to their chests, eyes wide.

"What a story," said Bramble. "Wouldn't the *Herald* die to hear that!"

Servants arrived with more steaming water, and with them, Delphinium, her arms full of fabrics of silks and velvet. Azalea, so used to black, stared at the brilliant pinks and purples and blues hungrily. As the servants left, everyone rushed to Delphinium's side, tugged at the fabrics, and shook them out, revealing dresses of all sizes.

A flurry of fluffing and exchanging blouses brought the right outfits to the right hands. Delphinium, flushed with excitement, laid out a skirt with ruffly blouse over a bathing-room chair for Azalea. With a flourish, she added a matching collar bow.

"The dressmaker says she already had them ready, and she *hopes* they all fit! Oh, Eve, that positively makes your eyes pop! Lavender is just right for the twins, don't you think?"

"But where did they come from?" said Azalea.

"The King!" said Flora. "He gave them to us."

"P-Papa," Goldenrod corrected, unbuttoning Flora's black dress.

"Yes, Papa. He said it would be his Christmas present to us!"

"He did?" Azalea's brows knit. The King had wanted to stay in mourning. Hadn't he?

"We won't look like Fairweller's spawn anymore." Bramble grinned. It faded, however, when she saw Azalea's expression. "I mean—you're excited, right?"

Azalea cupped bubbles in her hands, then dipped them into the water, thoughtful.

"Yes," she said. "It's just . . . he told me not long ago he didn't feel ready to lift mourning."

"But now he is," said Delphinium, beaming. Her smile disappeared when she saw Azalea's face, and she clutched her pink dress to her chest.

"He never remembered our birthdays," she said.

"Do you remember his?"

Delphinium flared pink. "Well . . . that's different."

Azalea rubbed the cool porcelain beneath her chin. "Only I was thinking," she said. "He's always gotten us gifts for Christmas, but . . . we've never given *him* anything."

Bramble shrugged. "He's never asked for anything."

"He has. Just in a different way. He's our papa, isn't he?" Azalea raised her eyebrows at her sisters, a trace of a smile on her lips. "Well, now we're going to act like it."

Azalea was proud of them. She couldn't help but be proud. All of them, even Delphinium, had agreed to dress again in black. None of them knew how long the King would want mourning to last, yet not one complained. They rollicked through Fairweller's austere peppermint-smelling manor of waxed floors, doilies, and boxes of chocolates, and pulled the curtains closed. Even the servants helped, after Clover explained things to them.

"Good-bye, sunlight." Delphinium sighed as she closed the drapery in Fairweller's gallery. It dropped shadows over portraits of Fairwellian ancestry, all dressed in black. "Good-bye, daytime."

"Sunlight, daytime," said Bramble. "Hullabaloos!" She pushed the curtains of the next window closed with a flourish.

"Bramble," said Azalea suddenly. "Have you written Lord Teddie yet?"

"Who?"

"Lord Teddie," said Azalea. "You wanted me to write him. Don't you remember?"

"What are you on about?" said Bramble, smiling at her with knit brows.

Azalea glanced at Bramble's hands, clutching the curtain fabric. Her knuckles were white.

"What is all this?"

Azalea nearly leaped for joy at hearing that voice, though every piece of her ached. The King stood at the end of the gallery, leaning heavily on a walking stick, his military satchel over his shoulder.

"Papa!" said Azalea, as they flocked to him like sparrows to bread. "Oh—sit down. You're going to fall over."

"I am not falling over," said the King as the girls pushed him to the nearest chair. He eased himself onto the brocaded velvet, wincing. He was winded, bandaged, pale, and worn, but—his beard was well trimmed. A good sign. If he could shave, he was certain to feel all right.

"You are up at last, Miss Azalea," said the King, inspecting her as she fussed over him. "You are looking better."

"*You* are looking better, for being shot!" said Azalea, as the girls sat down around him, on the polished wood floor.

"The ball hit his waistcoat button," said Eve. "That's what Sir John said."

"And . . . it pierced his skin." Bramble looked entirely unconvinced.

"I beg your pardon?" said Azalea. "His *waistcoat button*? Didn't you see all the blood?"

"Azalea," said the King.

"You all saw it! It was all over the floor! *Pints* of it!"

"Azalea," said the King again, and something in his

tone made her stop. She met his eyes. An odd light shone in them, and she remembered snow that burned.

"You're all right?" she said.

"Well enough." The King gave her a trace of a smile.

"Your satchel is so heavy," squeaked Hollyhock, who fiddled with the clasps. "What's in there? Open it up."

The King smiled, shrugged the satchel off his shoulder, and pulled out a wrapped bundle. He unrolled the fabric, and a long, heavy piece of silver fell onto the floor, clanking against the fine wood. He gave the fabric another shake, and a hilt clattered on the ground.

"We dragged the river for it," said the King.

"The sword!" Azalea scooped up the pieces. "I've ruined it!"

"Ah, well. Yes and no," said the King. "It would have broken sooner than later. Of course, the circumstances *could* have been better, but—" The King smiled, and Azalea saw a touch of wryness to it, almost like Bramble's. "It can be mended. Now, what is all this? Draping the windows? What of your dresses? Hadn't you new ones?"

The girls clasped their hands in their laps, turning their eyes shyly to the ground. Azalea spoke.

"It's our gift," she said. "To you. We know mourning means a lot to you. And . . . we don't really mind it. We can go without dancing and things a little longer."

"Especially since our Great Slipper Scandal quickened the undead and nearly destroyed the palace," said Bramble. "It put us off dancing for at *least* an hour. Anyway. Merry Christmas . . . P-Papa."

"Merry Christmas," peeped Hollyhock.

"Merry Christmas," all the girls chimed.

An unreadable expression fell over the King's face. He opened his mouth, then closed it. He placed his hand over Lily's dark curls. Lily had pulled herself up to his trouser leg and gnawed on it, leaving a wet spot. He lifted her to his knee.

"We never thought about how you felt," said Azalea, closing her hands in fists so she didn't have to see the red marks across her palms. "We'll be better. *I'll* be better."

The King placed his firm, solid hand on Azalea's shoulder. She looked up into his eyes, and saw they had a light in them not so different from Mother's.

"And I," he said. "You will be a fine queen, Azalea."

Azalea flushed from this unexpected praise, but beamed as the girls giggled and nudged her. The King stood, Lily wrapping her arms about his neck.

"Mourning is over," he said. "I am in earnest. Draw the curtains. Your mother would not have wanted it to last as such."

The girls cheered and danced, tugging on the King's suitcoat as he helped them to open the drapes.

The sword was mended and sworn on in parliament. In spite of the King's limps and bandages, he set to work on the palace with the help of Mr. Pudding and the regiments. What couldn't be unmagicked with the sword's weakened force was burned or replaced. Regiments with axes cleared away the thorny bushes that choked the palace and gardens. Spider lamps were destroyed, and the mirrors and windows replaced. The ceiling was repainted white, too, the cupids cowering at the corners until they were painted over. It was surprising, the King said, how much Keeper had magicked within the short time he had been able.

Every day the King would return long after the sun had set, arriving at Fairweller's manor, leaning heavily on his walking stick. The girls, waiting for him, flocked to his side and brought him to the dining room for hot pheasant and other Fairweller-esque food, and they would eat as a family.

"All this work and replacements," said Azalea as they ate dinner one evening, roast quail and artichokes. "How can we afford it?"

"Parliament has granted us a sum," said the King. "And we will accept it graciously. The palace has needed renovation for quite some time."

"May we come with you tomorrow?" piped Flora. "Oh, please?"

"No," said the King.

"Oh, but we miss it so much!" said Goldenrod.

"Please, let us go!"

"Pwease, oh, *pwease*!"

The girls leaped from their chairs and swarmed to the King, tugging on his suitcoat.

"Please, Papa! Papa!" they cried. "Oh, Papa, *please*!"

They went.

The palace felt different. It wasn't the hustle and come-and-go of cranes and workers and glass smithies who mended the facades and tower and windows, bowing when the girls peeked at them working. Nor was it the eager *Herald* reporter who perched about the gate of the palace, inkwell at the ready, begging to be invited in, and only getting a slammed gate in reply from the King. And it wasn't the way the sunlight shone through the palace in patches, like it used to.

For the past year, there had been a tension about it, weighing like the darkness. But like the drapery, it had gone. The palace hadn't felt this bright since before Mother had taken ill.

"Most of the palace has been unmagicked," said the King, leading them into the east wing, to the gallery. "But you all have keen eyes. If you see anything I missed, raise the cry. Don't step on the rug. It's a bit . . . peckish."

Azalea searched the familiar gallery, taking care to

stay away from the rug, wanting to hug the spindly, stain-prone furniture and kiss the portraits. None of them had red eyes now. They looked lifelessly ahead, to Azalea's relief. A second glance revealed a somewhat changed portrait of Great-Aunt Chrysanthemum. Her eyes were crossed.

"Ah," said the King, following Azalea's gaze. "I unmagicked that one at the wrong time, unfortunately."

"Papa?" said Flora as the younger girls gathered around a new portrait leaning against the wainscot. It was a fine portrait, one thick with strong brushstrokes and rich colors. Azalea gaped at the figure; tousled auburn hair, sweet smile, and a light in her eyes that sparkled nearly off the canvas.

"Great scott," said Azalea, wanting to embrace the painting. "It looks just like her!"

"I know," said the King. He looked pained.

"How could we possibly afford it?" said Bramble, her fingertips twitching as though to touch it. "This was done in a Delchastrian conservatory, for certain."

"Miss Bramble!"

The words rang through the gallery. Everyone turned quickly. Bramble blanched.

There, in the doorway at the end of the hall, stood Lord Teddie. He loped across the gallery floor, over the magicked rug, and halted several paces from Bramble.

She clutched the sides of her skirts so tightly her hands shook.

"Lord Haftenravenscher," she said, unsmiling.

Lord Teddie shrank. He shoved his hands in his pockets, took them out, shoved them in again. He nodded at the portrait.

"I—just brought it," he said. "I—hoped you would be here. Do you like it? I remembered your mum from ages ago, and when I found out she . . . you know . . . she—anyway, I thought, wouldn't it be chuffing if I collected all the pictures I could find of her and had Carrivegh—that's our family painter, Carrivegh—paint her. And it could be a surprise for you all. Because, well. You hadn't a mum now."

Bramble's lips were tight. Her fists still shook.

"Take it back," she said. She gazed at the floor, but the words whipped. "We don't want the picture. We don't want your *charity*. Take it back!"

Teddie drew himself up to his full, towering taffy height.

"N—dash it—O!" he said. "It's not *charity* and I won't take it back! It's a gift! A *gift*, dash it all! Because I liked your mum! And I like your sisters! And *you*, Bramble! I *love* you!"

The words echoed. Everyone's hands clasped over their mouths, and they stared at Lord Teddie, who panted but kept a tight chin up. Bramble's lips were still pursed. They were white.

"Young man," said the King gently. "Your ship leaves soon?"

Azalea guessed that, with the fiasco of everything, the King had annulled any arrangements between Bramble and Lord Teddie. Lord Teddie's entire taffylike form slumped. He turned to go, all bounciness dissolved.

"Do you mean it?"

Lord Teddie turned quickly. Bramble's lips remained tight, but her gaze was up, blazing yellow.

"Gad, *yes*," said Lord Teddie. "I love you so much, my fingers hurt!"

"Oh!" Bramble slapped her hands over her mouth, and doubled over. "Oh—oh-oh-*oh*!" She shook. It was hard to tell if she was crying, or coughing, or ill. *"Oh!"*

In a billow of skirts, Bramble leaped. It was a grand jeté worthy of the Delchastrian prima ballerina. She landed right on Lord Teddie, who had no choice but to catch her, and threw her arms around his neck. Then, to everyone's shock, she pressed her lips full on his.

"Oh . . . my," said Clover.

No one seemed more surprised than Lord Teddie, who stumbled back under Bramble's assault. He staggered onto the magicked rug. In a blur of red, the rug clapped over them like a red snapdragon.

The entire package overbalanced and fell to the ground with a *whumpf.*

No one moved inside the rug. Everyone stared.

"Sorry," said Eve. "What just happened?"

From the rug came a muffled *Mmm mmm mmfph.*

"We'd better take them out," said Azalea. "Before they start to digest."

With Clover's help, she peeled the carpet back to reveal Bramble, snuggled in Lord Teddie's arms, her nose buried in his bright green bow tie, and nearly crying.

"—the ballroom windows and when I saw you I thought I would *cry,* you were so brave—"

"I say," said Lord Teddie. "I say!"

The King grasped Bramble around the middle and pulled her from Lord Teddie's arms. The carpet end slipped from Azalea's hands and snapped again over Lord Teddie.

"Bramble, really!" said the King.

Bramble's face had the largest grin Azalea had ever seen on it.

The King looked at a loss. He ran his fingers through his hair, distracted. Azalea, knowing Mother would have been able to manage this, stepped forward.

"Lord Teddie?" she said. "Will you stay for tea?"

"*Rather!*" said the carpet.

Before Lord Teddie's ship left, he was allowed one hour in the gardens with Bramble, chaperoned by Mr. Pudding. All the girls stared out the windows, watching Lord Teddie and Bramble chatter up a storm, then run off, leaving Mr. Pudding lost in the snowy gardens. The girls made a great search for them, and finally, after an hour's hunting, they found them in the butterfly forest, Bramble sitting on an overturned bucket and giggling while Lord Teddie kissed her fingers. Both Mr. Gasperson *and* the King dragged him away, late for the ship. Bramble leaned on the newel post, looking dizzy, and beaming.

Bramble's constant gushing chatter of Lord Teddie did not improve things with Clover. As much as Azalea disliked Fairweller, she couldn't bear hearing Clover weep late into the night. Clover had lost her appetite, too, only picking at her food and giving most of it to Ivy. Azalea worried.

"I honestly don't know *how* in the *world* you could even *like* him, Clover," said Delphinium, one morning as January drew to a close. They had moved back into the palace, now that the windows were all set, and were delighted to be back in their own boring, unmagicked room. Sunlight poured through the windows as they dressed, casting gold over everything.

Clover remained sitting on the edge of her bed, clutching the ends of her shawl and saying nothing.

"Let's face it," said Bramble, tying a green ribbon around her collar. "We haven't heard a word from him since Christmas. That was ages ago! He's abandoned you. Surprise!"

Clover's hands tightened over the ends of her shawl.

"Oh, wait," squeaked Ivy, who looked out one of the west windows to the front court below. "He hasn't—Fairweller's here!"

Clover leaped to the window. The other girls flocked around her. Below them, gentlemen walked across the gravel, LadyFair tethered to the balustrade.

"His steward is here, too."

"Oh, look, the King's gone out to greet him."

"With a *gun*," said Bramble.

Everyone leaned forward.

"Pistols!" cried Clover. She fled the room.

"Clover—duels aren't—oh, hang," said Bramble. "She's going to do something rash. Well, at least we can see it from here."

Two seconds later, Clover streaked out the entrance hall doors, down the marble stairs, her skirts flying behind her. The gentlemen had a split moment to look up before Clover threw herself onto the King in a scatter of gravel, sobbing as she hung about his neck.

The window muffled their voices. Everyone leaned even farther forward.

Clover fell to her knees and kissed the hem of the King's coat.

"Oh, now, let's not go overboard," Bramble muttered.

Fairweller removed his coat and set it over Clover's shoulders; the King threw it off and put his own coat over her shoulders. Then he gestured Fairweller to follow him inside.

The girls paced outside the library, waiting for Fairweller, Clover, and the King to finish. The King's voice carried through the door at intervals—usually angry. Clover's honey tones came through, strong and unstuttering. No one could make out the words, however.

After some length of time, the door slid open, and Fairweller emerged, looking like a man who had been rescued by a choir of angels. Dazed, hair mussed, he looked around him with glazed eyes. Clover beamed.

"Not a day before—" snarled the King.

"Yes, naturally," said Fairweller. "As you say, Your Grace."

"And you will leave—"

"Yes—straightaway. As you say."

He bowed deeply to the King. And to Azalea's surprise, swept a bow to her and all the girls. Then he delicately cupped Clover's hands in his, and kissed them with a brush of his lips. He left, almost walking on air.

"Oh, *Papa*!" Clover cried when the door had closed. She threw her arms around the King. *"Thank you!"*

"Don't—don't—don't!" said the King. "I am very cross with you, young lady! Azalea!"

He leaned in to Azalea as Clover released his neck and danced across the entrance hall rug, twirling the younger ones with her in a reel.

"You will have to introduce Clover to a lot of gentlemen at balls and soirees and such," he said in a low voice. "Before she turns seventeen. You *must* get her acquainted with other gentlemen. Preferably those of our own party!"

"Of course," said Azalea, watching the laughing, hopping girls about Clover. The light that filtered down from the half-moon window above the door cast bright golden highlights in Clover's hair and, smiling, she looked the prettiest Azalea had ever seen her. "Only . . . well. He certainly seems to love her."

"Traitor," said the King.

CHAPTER 30

"*W*hat's kissing like?" said Delphinium, one morning in early February. The King had gone out to tend to R.B., and the girls crowded in the nook over bowls of steaming mush, their eyes hungry, but not for porridge.

For the past few days, Bramble and Clover had been positively nauseating. They wrote lengthy letters to their gentlemen, Bramble chattering on about how *ripping* Lord Teddie was, and Clover speaking of how kind and sober Fairweller was. Sober. That was the word she used.

"Mmm—like dancing, actually." Bramble pushed her porridge to Ivy and grinned. "You know, the part after a spin, when the room turns around you. What do you think, Clover?"

Clover shook her golden head.

"I think it more . . . when the gentleman catches you in his arms, that warm feeling that makes your toes sort of curl."

Bramble's face twisted. "No . . . that's not right. Well, dash it, if we knew more dances—"

"Azalea knowf *lotf* of danfef!" piped Ivy through a mouthful of mush.

"Oh, yes!" said Flora. And then, catching Azalea's expression, her face fell. "Oh—no, I suppose not," she said.

Azalea stood so sharply her chair knocked against the rosebush ledge.

"No, definitely not!" she said. She threw her wadded napkin at Bramble—who at least had the decency to look contrite—and stormed out of the nook.

When she reached their room, she did not cry. She was too angry for it. Instead she cleaned, punching pillows in place, wadding up strewn dresses and throwing them into the basket, mending stockings with a vengeance. It was unbearable, to hear Clover and Bramble go on, when she hadn't heard a word from Mr. Bradford. She worried, in an overwhelming twisting-stomach pain, that he did love her, but not enough.

Azalea was at the point of unpicking the stockings and re-darning them when the King arrived.

"The girls said you would be here," he said, from

the doorway. He watched Azalea stab at the linens with a needle.

"Azalea," he said.

"Yes, I've been up here," said Azalea, in a brittle, happy voice. "Of course I would be, mending and things need to be done, Clover and Bramble haven't been tending to it, so I will. I've got the time, haven't I?"

Her eyes stung. The King tapped his fingers against the door frame.

"Follow me," he said. "I have something I want to give you."

The King produced a worn silver harold from his pocket and walked to the fireplace.

"Oh, no—no, no," said Azalea, pulling back. "I'm not going down there again."

"Come now. Bear up," said the King, taking her hand. He gently pulled her through the silver curtain and allowed her to grip his arm with a shaking hand as he helped her down the musty wooden stairs. Azalea looked about her, swallowing the unpleasant memories of it.

The storage room was bright, a window at the top casting light across them. Broken Yuletide ornaments had been swept into a pile at the corner of the room. The King went to a box, tucked in the corner, and produced a small piece of jewelry.

It was the brooch. The King walked back to her and placed it in her hands.

"What? No!" said Azalea, fumbling with it. "I can't—this is Mother's!"

"It is yours, and your sisters', now," said the King. He placed his hand over hers. "It is only glass, you know. Nothing fine or grand. Your Mother knew it, when she accepted it with my hand. And she knew I danced as well as a tree. She knew about the politics and duties and responsibilities of marrying into royalty. She knew all those . . . unfortunate things. Things some people might even call *ghastly*."

Azalea looked up quickly. A smile tugged on the corner of the King's lips.

"But—ah! Wouldn't it be sad if she had not?"

Tears pricked Azalea's eyes. Her fingers curled around the brooch. She imagined her father, a young king, and wondered if he had had finely dressed ladies flocked about him, flattering with false, pretty words . . . not because they cared for him, but only because they wanted to be queen. For the first time it occurred to her that even though the King couldn't dance, he understood her completely.

Azalea threw her arms around him.

He was stiff and solid. She loved that about him.

"Well," said the King, looking both awkward and

pleased as Azalea pulled away. "Haste away, young lady. A young Captain Bradford is waiting for you in the ballroom. He's spent many hours filling out parliamentary paperwork, as well as a lengthy wait for parliamentary approval, before I would allow him to see you."

The full meaning of this sank into Azalea's mind, and she fairly leaped up the stairs, giddy to her center. She paced impatiently with a toe-touch side turn as the King followed after, retrieving the silver coin. A glimmer caught the corner of her eye. She turned.

Next to her foot lay a small pile of ashes.

Azalea forgot her rush, bent down, and touched it. The ash stuck to her finger, and sparkled as she turned her hand in the dim light.

"Sir," said Azalea. "Papa?"

"Mmm?"

Azalea's voice caught in her throat.

"Never mind," she said. She brushed the soot from her finger, leaving streaks of gray-silver on her skirts, remembering the light that seemed to wash over her, how warm the King's hand had been—and the flicker of warmth she still felt inside of her. And she thought she understood. She knew now why that sort of magic— the deepest magic—hadn't been named. Some things couldn't be.

Azalea helped the King down the staircase to the ballroom, becoming more and more nervous. The King, for some reason, seemed to feel the same, fidgeting with his pocket watch and slowing as they reached the ballroom doors.

"Er . . . Azalea," he said.

"Yes?" Azalea raised herself to her toes, down again, anxious.

"I forgot to mention something."

Uh-oh, said a voice in her head.

"There's, ah, going to be a proposal, you know," said the King.

Azalea nearly leaped out of her boots with delight. She spun around the King, her feet lithe as springs.

"I . . . rather suspected," she said, laughing and hopping at the same time. "Well . . . hoped, really. I mean, now that he's running for parliament and everything and . . . Bramble and Clover are already engaged, and—"

She stopped mid-spin at the King's expression.

"Ah, Azalea," said the King. "He's not going to be the one proposing."

The springs in Azalea's feet went *poioioing.*

"Sorry?" she said.

"You *outrank* him, you know." The King shifted, uncomfortable. "It would be highly inappropriate for *him* to propose to *you.* The Delchastrian queen had to propose—"

"I will do no such thing!" said Azalea.

"Azalea," said the King in a firmer tone. "Come now, follow the rules. Besides, it is your chance to have the final say, is it not?"

"I always have the final say!" said Azalea. "How horrifically unromantic!"

"Well, do you want me to send him away?"

"No! Don't do that!"

"Go to it," said the King, pushing her through the ballroom doors. He nearly closed them on her skirts, in his rush to shut them. Azalea turned about in a whip of crinolines and *kicked* the door.

"Thanks a lot!" she said.

A polite cough-laugh sounded behind her. Azalea turned to the marble dance floor, seeing the highlights of sun against the new gilded mirrors and the crisp light cast over Mr. Bradford. Wearing a fine suit, he looked the most uniform Azalea had ever seen him—his collar lay flat and his cravat was pinned straight. His blond-brown hair, however, remained incorrigibly mussed. He clutched his hat, kneading the rim, and beamed at her.

"Princess," he said.

"Captain!" said Azalea, hugging the door behind her. She beamed at him, giddiness tickling her. It was all she could do to keep from giggling.

"You look pretty, as always," he said.

Azalea grinned, deciding not to remind him that the last times he had seen her, she had been soaked, frozen, unconscious, and a torn mess of the undead.

"You're running for parliament?" said Azalea.

"Yes—I should have done ages ago. I was a coward, I think."

"Balderdash. You don't smash through a ballroom window if you're a coward."

Remembering the task at hand, Azalea's smile flickered, and she swallowed. She remained hugging the ballroom doors, the latches pressing against her back.

"Mr. Bradford," she said. "I'm not going to propose to you."

The twinkle in Mr. Bradford's eyes faded. So did his smile. He managed to keep it on his face. It looked painful.

"Oh," he said.

"Mr. Bradford?"

"Yes?"

"Would you mind it so very much if . . . you know . . . you proposed to me?"

The light in Mr. Bradford's eyes jumped to life. He beamed so largely it almost wasn't crooked.

"If you want," he said.

He walked to Azalea, put her hand on his arm, and escorted her to the middle of the ballroom. Azalea's boots *click clicked* across the marble.

"Before anything," he said as he brought her around to face him, "I want to give you this."

Fumbling in his suitcoat, he produced a small package wrapped in brown paper and string, and gave it to Azalea. Curious, she tugged at the strings of the light package until they unknotted. The paper fell away.

It was a silver handkerchief. Supple and soft, just as Mother's had been. In the corner were the embroidered initials A.K.W.

Azalea laughed and cried at once. She threw her arms around Mr. Bradford's neck, wanting to embrace him so deeply she could feel his soul.

"Yes," she said. "*Yes!* Yes, yes, *yes!*"

"Well—I—never even said anything," he said.

Even so, he pulled her closer, wrapping his arms around her. Azalea pressed her cheek into his collar, rumpling it, and breathing into his cravat. It smelled of fresh linen. She felt Mr. Bradford's cheek pressing the top of her head. His lips touched her hair.

A muffled voice startled them both.

"When are you going to *kiss* her?"

They pulled away. In the ballroom windows, noses and hands pressed against the glass, were the girls. They stood among the prickly rosebushes, beaming wicked little grins. Delphinium and Eve whispered and giggled to each other; Bramble wore a magnificent grin on her face and a spark of light in her yellow-green eyes.

Another figure stood among them. This one had his arms folded across his chest, stiff and firm and formal. . . .

. . . Yet he did not look displeased.

"Those rotten little spies!" said Azalea.

Mr. Bradford laughed and threw his hat across the ballroom floor. He pulled Azalea into an under-arm turn, her skirts flaring out and brushing against his trousers. His hand led her so easily, with just a turn and twitch of his fingers, that Azalea felt dizzy; happily so. He brought her in again, and spun her out.

This time, Azalea didn't spin back into his arms. Instead, she dipped into a curtsy. She gave this curtsy her all; every muscle and fiber of her focused on melting into a deep, flawless dip. Legs twisting, she disappeared into the poof of skirts pooling around her. She buried her nose in them, nearly kissing the floor, her right arm extended to Mr. Bradford, her left tucked behind her. A finer Soul's Curtsy, Azalea was sure, not even Mother could do.

She dared a peek at Mr. Bradford, whose mouth hung slightly agape. When she giggled, he laughed, too, and fell to his knees in front of her. He nudged her. The thin, crystal string of balance snapped. Azalea fell over, and into his arms. She blinked up at his face.

He smiled, but more intent and solemn, and Azalea instinctively closed her eyes as his large hand gently touched her face, bringing it to his in a kiss.

It *was* like dancing—both dizzy and giddy, but with the soft warmness of a gentle touch. It thrilled her soul and made it leap.

The ballroom doors burst open with a gust of cold air and a chatter of voices. Mr. Bradford pulled Azalea to her feet as the cheering girls ran to them, tugging on Azalea's skirts and Mr. Bradford's suitcoat.

Azalea, breathless and laughing, made them all take hands for a reel. A welcome-to-the-family reel, like the one they had given Lily over a year ago. There would be one for Lord Teddie, and for Fairweller, too, Azalea knew.

"Well done, Ivy," said Azalea. "Perfect form! Jess—hold hands. We'll go slow so Lily can manage, now that she's walking. Marvelous, Delphi. All set? Wonderful! Wait—"

Their circle was incomplete.

Azalea turned to the King, who stood several paces outside the circle, his arms folded and a bemused smile on his face. Azalea offered her hand to him.

"Dance with us?" she said.

A frown tugged at the corners of the King's mouth.

"Certainly not," he said. "You know how well I dance."

Azalea did not care. She, and the girls running after, took his hands tightly in theirs. They pulled him into the circle with them and danced slowly, so he could follow their steps. Even so, Azalea felt a warmth flicker within her. It was the best dance they had ever done.

The End

Acknowledgments

Special thanks to:

Martha Mihalick
Edward Necarsulmer IV
Christa Heschke
Dean Hughes
Ann Dee Ellis
BYU Animation & English departments
Helen Dixon
The Mellings
Room 5446
Dipped in Bronze
The fam